Carol Marinelli recently filled in a form asking for her job title. Thrilled to be able to put down her answer, she put 'writer'. Then it asked what Carol did for relaxation and she put down the truth—'writing'. The third question asked for her hobbies. Well, not wanting to look obsessed, she crossed her fingers and answered 'swimming'—but, given that the chlorine in the pool does terrible things to her highlights, I'm sure you can guess the real answer!

Sue MacKay lives with her husband in New Zealand's beautiful Marlborough Sounds, with the water on her doorstep and the birds and the trees at her back door. It is the perfect setting to indulge her passions of entertaining friends by cooking them sumptuous meals, drinking fabulous wine, going for hill walks or kayaking around the bay—and, of course, writing stories.

Discover more at millsandboon.co.uk.

THE MIDWIFE'S
ONE-NIGHT FLING

CAROL MARINELLI

BABY MIRACLE
IN THE ER

SUE MacKAY

MILLS & BOON

First Published in Great Britain 2018
by Mills & Boon, an imprint of HarperCollins*Publishers*
1 London Bridge Street, London, SE1 9GF

The Midwife's One-Night Fling © 2018 by Carol Marinelli

Baby Miracle in the ER © 2018 by Sue MacKay

ISBN: 978-0-263-93354-3

MIX
Paper from
responsible sources
FSC™ C007454

This book is produced from independently certified FSC™ paper
to ensure responsible forest management.
For more information visit www.harpercollins.co.uk/green.

Printed and bound in Spain
by CPI, Barcelona

THE MIDWIFE'S
ONE-NIGHT FLING

CAROL MARINELLI

MILLS & BOON

Dear Lucinda
Love you more xxxx

PROLOGUE

'You must be getting excited about the big move to London?'

It was a question Freya Ross had heard many times in recent weeks, and although the knot in her stomach tightened at the thought of what lay ahead she smiled.

'I'm very much looking forward to it.'

As a midwife at the birthing centre attached to Cromayr Bay Hospital, Freya was examining Mrs Roberts while her three little boys ran amok in the rather small cubicle. Most patients preferred to be called by their first name, but not Mrs Roberts.

'Jamie!' Mrs Roberts scolded as her boisterous three-year-old climbed on a chair.

Freya was more than used to working with toddlers underfoot, and she was also very used to holding in her thoughts.

She had told no one of her misgivings about moving to London. Not her parents, nor her best friend, nor her colleagues. Certainly she would not burden a patient with her worries.

No one could possibly guess that now her leaving date was almost here Freya was dreading making the move from the small Scottish town of Cromayr Bay to London.

The news of her leaving had come as a complete surprise to everyone. No one had known she'd gone to London for an interview. This was no mean feat in Cromayr Bay! Even swapping her off-duty days had been complicated—Freya hadn't been able to lie and say that she was visiting the dentist, given that the dentist was the husband of Betty, her senior midwife. And, had she called in sick—well someone would either have mentioned that her car had been seen at Cromayr Bay station, or they'd have dropped in to check that she was okay.

In the end Freya had said that she was catching up with a friend with whom she had trained.

'Oh? Who?' Betty had asked...

Feeling as if her nose must surely be an inch longer after such a complex lie, Freya had taken the train to Edinburgh's Waverley Station and from there had travelled down to London to the Primary, a large, modern hospital.

Freya's general nursing training had taken place in Cowdenbeath, and she had done some placements in Edinburgh during her midwifery training, so she wasn't unfamiliar with busy hospitals. The Primary was incredibly large, though, and the interview had been very thorough.

Her training had been excellent, and Freya had kept her skills up to date with regular shifts in the main Cromayr Bay hospital, which the birthing centre was attached to.

She had been offered a six-month contract by the London hospital, commencing in the middle of July, and Freya was starting to get nervous.

Not that she showed it.

Instead of revealing her feelings now, she made small talk with Mrs Roberts as she palpated the baby. 'We've got my leaving do tonight, over at the Tavern,' Freya said. 'You're actually the last patient that I'll see before I go.'

'I'm sorry that you shan't be here for the birth.'

'I am too, Mrs Roberts,' Freya agreed. 'Although I know you are going to do just fine.'

'I expect Alison is feeling the same as I do about your leaving?'

Freya's hands paused mid-examination. Alison had made it clear that she didn't want the news about her pregnancy getting out just yet.

'We're best friends.' Freya decided to give a non-committal answer, just in case she had misinterpreted the question. 'So, yes, she was a bit upset when I told her that I was moving—but I'll be coming home regularly.'

'I meant about the baby,' Mrs Roberts said. 'It's okay, I'm not asking you to break any confidences. I just heard the other day that she's expecting again. It's lovely news.'

'It is,' Freya agreed, though inwardly she sighed for her friend at the fact that the news had got out. Very few people knew. And, even though Alison was past her first trimester, she had wanted to keep it to herself for a while yet.

But nothing stayed a secret for very long here.

'I just hope...' Mrs Roberts voice trailed off. 'Well,' she said. 'I hope that things go better for her this time.'

Freya gave a small nod, but refused to be drawn into a discussion about the loss of Andrew.

Last year had been a hard one.

Following an uneventful pregnancy, Alison had arrived at the birthing centre in active labour. But while checking the foetal heart-rate Freya had realised something was terribly wrong.

Alison had been transferred to the attached hospital and a crash Caesarean had been performed. The little boy had been resuscitated and then transferred to Edinburgh, where there had been a NICU cot available.

He'd been beautiful and utterly perfect. A chunky baby, with long, dark lashes, big cheeks and pudgy hands. But the lack of oxygen from cord compression and subsequent meconium aspiration had left him severely brain damaged.

Despite best efforts Andrew had died two days later, leaving Alison, her husband Callum and their families shattered.

Freya had been his godmother and proxy aunt, and she still woke regularly from nightmares, with the ominous sound of the CTG bleeping seeming to fill her bedroom. It felt as if her chest was being crushed whenever she recalled the devastation on Alison's face when it had become clear that things were going terribly wrong.

'Freya?' Alison had pleaded.

The fear in Alison's voice was something that Freya would never be able to erase from her memory.

Alison had never blamed Freya. In fact she had drawn on her friend, and Freya had stayed strong for Alison even through a serious relationship break-up.

And now, not by a flicker did she reveal her own heartache as she focussed on her patient and the little life beneath her hands.

'Everything's looking grand,' Freya said as she felt the baby's position. 'The head is down and baby is a good size.'

'Aye.'

For Freya, the real beauty of working at Cromayr Bay was the chance to really get to know her patients and their families, and now, after being more than willing to chat about Alison's pregnancy, Mrs Roberts's short response when discussing her own, concerned Freya.

It wasn't just that, though. Over the months Freya had been trying to gauge Mrs Roberts's feelings.

This pregnancy had come close after the birth of twins, but Mrs Roberts insisted it was all part of the plan as she wanted her children to be near each other in age.

Freya was quite certain that Mrs Roberts was struggling, but she was a very proud and private woman. Earlier, though, she'd seemed more talkative, and Freya wondered if she actually wanted to speak to her.

Jamie, the eldest, was getting restless, and the twins were going through their mother's handbag. Freya was in no doubt that Mrs Roberts would want to dash off as soon as her appointment was done.

As she went to the desk to write up her findings Mrs Roberts dressed and then came over and took a seat.

'Jamie!' She scolded her son, who had pulled over a jar of cotton balls. 'I'm so sorry, Freya.'

'It's not a problem. I shouldn't have left them at a three-year-old's level.' As Mrs Roberts went to retrieve them Freya stopped her. 'He might as well play with them,' she said—not just because the cotton balls would now have to be discarded, but also because it might keep Jamie amused for a few minutes.

'He's into everything,' Mrs Roberts explained. 'I need eyes in the back of my head.'

'You're certainly going to be busy when the new baby comes,' Freya agreed. 'Is there anyone who might be able to help once the baby is here?'

'Och, I'll not be bothering others. I just have to get on with things.' Mrs Roberts straightened herself in the chair.

Freya felt for her. She too was very private.

With two younger brothers, Freya had always been 'the sensible one'. Her mother, Jean, had relied on her to look out for the boys and soothe their hurts rather than her own.

As Freya wrote up her notes she thought how she came across to her patient. Her long dark curls were pulled back into a ponytail and she knew that her green eyes could sometimes come across as guarded rather than shy. She was a quiet person, and that generally suited her patients just fine.

However, like Mrs Roberts, Freya could appear a touch

aloof at times—abrupt, even—although not, she hoped, with her patients. And, while she tended not to chat too much about herself, that wasn't an issue in Cromayr Bay, where everyone knew everyone else's business anyway.

But Freya wanted to reach her patient and to be sure that she was coping, so she decided to open up a little to Mrs Roberts in the hope that the woman would reciprocate.

'Actually,' Freya said, 'although I'm telling everyone that I'm excited about moving to London, I'm really quite nervous. It's a big hospital and I shan't know anyone.'

'You'll be fine…' Mrs Roberts started, and then paused as Freya gently spoke on.

'I expect everyone is asking if you're excited now that the baby will soon be here?'

Mrs Roberts nodded. *'"Not long now!"'* She mimicked the regular phrases being thrown daily her way. *'"You'll be hoping for a girl after three boys."'*

'Are you?' Freya asked. She knew the sex of the baby.

'Of course not. I didn't get pregnant to try for a girl. In fact, I didn't…' It was the closest Mrs Roberts had come to admitting the pregnancy had been an accident, but she quickly rallied. 'Healthy will suit me just fine.'

'Of course,' Freya agreed, and Mrs Roberts changed the subject.

'So you're nervous about leaving?'

'Terrified,' Freya now admitted. 'And I'm wondering how I'm going to fit in.'

'You'll fit in just fine.'

'I hope so,' Freya replied. 'But I'm starting to think I've made a mistake.'

'Well, I know *that* feeling.'

Freya watched as Mrs Roberts closed her eyes and finally admitted the truth. 'It's not that I don't want it—well, I'm sure I will once the baby's here. I just honestly don't know how I'm going to cope. The twins are into everything and Jamie runs wild. Davey's no help. Och, he tries—but he's out the door for work at seven, then not back until six and wanting his supper. I'm trying to freeze a few meals for when the baby comes…'

'That's good.'

'It'll take more than a few frozen dinners to see us through, though.'

Freya saw the flash of tears in Mrs Roberts's eyes and then watched as she buried her face in her hands and started to weep.

'Mam!' Jamie toddled over and pulled at her skirt. 'Mam!'

'Mummy's just a little tired,' Freya said as she gave Mrs Roberts some tissues.

When his inquisitive eyes fell on her stethoscope, Freya took it from her neck and played with it on him, to give Mrs Roberts time to cry by herself.

'Do you want to have a play with it now?'

Delighted with his new toy, Jamie wandered off.

'I'm sorry, Freya.' Mrs Roberts sniffed into the tissue that Freya had pressed into her hand. 'How on earth am I going to manage with another one? I don't get a moment to myself as it is.'

'Have you thought about asking your sister to come and stay with you for a wee while once the baby arrives?' Freya knew that the two women were close.

'I have,' Mrs Roberts nodded, 'but it's a huge imposition.'

'Did she say that?'

'No, no—she offered to come. But I think it's asking too much from her.'

'You'll need help at the start, Mrs Roberts. It's better to take it than to do too much and find yourself overwhelmed and exhausted. If you talk about it with her now she can start to make plans.'

And making plans was what Freya and Mrs Roberts did next.

Her sister Norma would come, and also there was a small crèche that Mrs Roberts occasionally used.

'I might see if they can go there—just one afternoon a week, maybe two—so I can have some time with the new baby.'

'I think that's a wonderful idea,' Freya said. 'Did you know, once I've moved, I've got Mrs Hunt coming in to service my cottage between tenants?'

'I dinnae need a cleaner.'

'Well, I'm only mentioning it in case you might. She's very thorough and her prices are reasonable.'

The appointment went well over time, but it was worth every minute because Mrs Roberts was actually smiling as she retrieved the contents of her bag from the floor.

'You wee monkeys,' she said to the twins. 'Jamie, give Freya back her stethoscope.'

Before the cubicle door was opened Freya had a final word. 'If you're ever feeling overwhelmed when the baby is here—'

Mrs Roberts broke in. 'Then I'll speak to Betty. I honestly will. I feel so much better for talking with you.'

Mrs Roberts rounded up her three sons and Freya saw them to the desk. There she pulled up the appointments on the computer screen and made one for the next Thursday.

'Thanks so much, Freya.'

'You're welcome, Mrs Roberts.'

'Leah, please.'

Freya smiled, for it was high praise indeed to be invited to call Mrs Roberts by her first name.

'I wish you all the very best in London.'

'Thank you.'

Once Mrs Roberts had left Betty came over, and Freya explained a little of what had happened.

'It would have taken a lot for her to admit she's struggling,' Betty agreed. 'Well done, Freya. And don't worry—I'll be keeping a very close eye on her.'

Freya took in Betty's knowing eyes and kind face and knew Mrs Roberts was in the very best of hands. Betty had been a midwife here for nearly forty years. She had, in fact, delivered Freya herself. Right now, though, she was just trying to get the clinic closed somewhat on time.

'I'll shut down the computers and you go and tidy up the cubicles,' Betty said. 'You're going to be late for your own leaving party.'

Goodness, Freya thought when she saw the chaos of the cubicle. It looked as if it had been snowing!

Yet not for a second did she regret that the check-up had spilled more than an hour over time.

Freya tidied up and as she came out saw the waiting room was in semi-darkness.

'Everything's done,' Betty said. 'I'll lock up.'

And then it was finally here—the end of her time at the Cromayr Bay birthing centre.

Freya looked around the waiting room and beyond the desk, thinking of the two birthing suites behind. Then she walked out through the familiar room and into the office to collect her coat before a dash home to get changed for her leaving do.

She hoped her ex wouldn't show up.

Alison would be there. She had cried when Freya had told her that she was moving to London,

'I'll be back all the time,' Freya had reassured her.

'It won't be the same.'

No, it wouldn't be. But then, things hadn't been the same between them since Andrew had died.

Freya had always been private. The only person she really opened up to was Alison—but of course the loss was Alison's, so Freya had tried to remain stoic and strong for her friend, not burdening her with her own grief.

She said goodbye to Betty, who promised she would join them all at the Tavern shortly, and then drove the short distance home in her little purple car.

It was July. The holidaymakers were back and the town was busy.

She parked outside her tiny fisherman's cottage which, although a bit of a renovator's nightmare, was certainly a home.

Each of the houses along the foreshore was a different colour, and Freya's little cottage was a duck-egg-blue with a dark wooden door. Opening it, she stepped into the surprisingly large lounge with its open fireplace, seeing on the mantelpiece her favourite pictures and little mementoes.

Freya headed into the tiny alcove kitchen. It needed a complete overhaul, but everything worked—and anyway, Freya wasn't much of a cook. In pride of place was a coffee machine that Freya was having to leave behind in the move, as there really wasn't that much room in her father's car.

It would be nice for the tenants, Freya thought as she made a very quick coffee.

Freya had the house rented out over the summer, but in October it was going on the market to be sold.

In the cellar she had boxed up some of her belongings. The tiny spare bedroom looked a little bare, but it was ready for its new occupant with a pretty wrought-iron bed and a small chest of drawers.

Freya headed into the main bedroom to change out of

her uniform and get ready for her leaving do, but for a moment she paused.

The unobstructed view of The Firth had sold the place to her on sight. Often at night she simply lay there in bed, looking out, and she had watched the new Queensferry crossing being built. It was a spectacular cable-stayed bridge, and Freya had watched the huge structure unfold from either side until finally the two sides had met.

It was her favourite view on earth, and as she gazed out to it Freya asked herself again what the hell she was doing leaving. Here, she had a job she loved and friends she had grown up with as well as her family, to whom she was very close.

Yet, the very things she loved about Cromayr Bay, were the very reasons she felt she had to leave.

The loss of Alison's baby had hit everyone.

After it had happened Freya had often walked into a shop or a café, and on too many occasions the conversation would suddenly stop.

Everyone knew everyone's business—which wasn't always a good thing. Take tonight—there was a fair chance that her ex, Malcolm, would be at the Tavern. Not that she really thought of him much, but it was always awkward to run into him and see the hurt, angry expression in his eyes before he turned his back on her.

It wasn't just about Malcolm, though. Freya wanted more experience and a fresh start.

She would be thirty soon, she reasoned. If she didn't make the move now then she never would.

Deep down, though, she knew she was running away.

It was going to be hard to leave, but for Freya it was simply too hard to stay.

CHAPTER ONE

'Is anyone…?'

Freya looked up and quickly realised that the woman in theatre scrubs wasn't asking if she might join Freya at her table in the hospital canteen. Instead all she wanted was one of the spare chairs at Freya's table.

People, Freya thought, didn't even bother to speak in full sentences down here.

'Help yourself.' Freya nodded.

And so the lady did.

It was orientation day at the Primary Hospital, and apart from being asked her name and shown where to go Freya really hadn't spoken to anyone. She had tried during the coffee break, but Rita, the woman she had sat next to during the lectures, had gone off to call her husband.

The schedule had been a full one. First there had been an introduction to the Primary—a large general hospital with a major trauma centre. The volume of patients seen in Casualty per annum was, to Freya, staggering, as was the number of deliveries in Maternity, which had reached seven thousand last year.

There was no such thing as orientation day at Cromayr Bay—a new staff member would be shown around and introduced and made welcome. Here, though, Freya sat with approximately fifty fellow nurses, admin staff and ancillary workers who were commencing, or had just commenced work at the Primary this month alone.

Freya felt like a very small fish in a very large and rather cold sea.

On Friday she had been in to collect her uniforms and her lanyard and had got rather lost on her way out of the huge building. Today, though, sitting in the lecture theatre, she had found out that the red strip painted on the corridor wall led to Casualty and the main exit. So that was good to know. The yellow strip, she had then been told, led to Maternity and the blue to Outpatients.

'It helps not just the staff and the patients,' the admin manager had said, 'but it is also far easier to give directions to visitors. We shall soon be adding a green strip for the Imaging Department. Any more than that and the walls will start to look like rainbows!'

After a morning of lectures and films they had been told to head off for lunch and to be back at one.

There was no coloured strip that led to the canteen, but by following the overhead signs Freya had found it quite easily

The place had been packed, and Freya had rather wished she had thought to bring her own lunch, as most of her fellow orientation candidates seemed to have done. Perhaps that was why she sat alone.

She hadn't brought any change for the vending machines, so she'd queued up and selected a salad wrap, a packet of cheese and biscuits and a coffee, and then scanned the busy canteen for a table.

They'd all been rather full, but there had been a couple of seats that had seemed free on a table for four.

'Do you mind if I join you?' Freya had asked.

'We're just leaving,' the man there had said.

They had also left their plates, glasses and cups.

She had to stop comparing things to Cromayr Bay, but all this was just so unlike anything she was used to.

Since her father had left her at her one-bedroom flat, four days ago, Freya hadn't really spoken to anyone. Well, apart from a couple of shop assistants and a worker on the Underground who had helped Freya to buy a travel pass.

She had rung her mother and assured her that everything was fantastic.

'Your dad said the flat's a bit grim.'

It *was* rather grim, but Freya had reassured her mum that it was nothing a few rugs and pictures wouldn't pretty up, and reminded her that it was a brilliant location—just a ten-minute walk to the Underground.

'Is anyone…?'

Freya looked up as another unfinished question was asked by an elderly man in a porter's uniform.

'No,' Freya said, and gestured to an empty seat. 'Help yourself.'

He said nothing in response, just took a seat at the table and opened up some sandwiches, then pulled out a newspaper and started to read.

There was no conversation.

Having finished her wrap, Freya peeled open the foil on her cheese and crackers. But she really wasn't hungry so she put them down and pushed away her plate.

Glancing at her phone, she saw that there were still another fifteen minutes left until she was due back.

'Is this seat…?' asked a snooty, deep, but far from unpleasant male voice.

Freya was suddenly sick to the back teeth of unfinished questions.

'Is this seat *what*?' she asked, but as she looked up her indignation took a rapid back seat as she was momentarily sideswiped by six feet plus of good looks dressed in blue theatre scrubs.

He had straight brown hair that was messy, and was so crumpled-looking that, despite the hour, he appeared to have just got out of bed. A stethoscope hung around his neck, and in his hands was a very laden tray.

Freya regretted her brusque response, but consoled herself that he probably hadn't understood a word she had said.

Oh, but he had!

'Is this seat *taken*?' he enquired, more politely, though the smile he wore had a tart edge.

'Please,' Freya said. 'Help yourself.'

He put down the tray, and Freya assumed when he looked around and then wandered off that he must be locating a spare chair for his companion. On his tray there were two mugs of tea, a carton of milk and six little boxes of cereal—the type that her mother had used to get when the family had gone camping, or in the holidays as a treat, when she and her brothers would fight over who got what.

But instead of a chair and a companion he returned with a spoon.

'Len,' he said to the porter by way of greeting. He got a 'humph' in return, but the good-looking stranger didn't seem in the least bothered by the less than friendly response.

As Freya drank her coffee she tried not to look at him, and pretended not to notice when he opened each box of cereal in turn and poured them into the one bowl with all the flavours combined. It was a heap of cornflakes and chocolate puffs and coloured circles, and then he added to his concoction the small carton of milk.

No, there was no companion about to arrive, for next

he added sugar to both cups of tea and made light work of the first.

And still Freya tried not to notice.

A domestic came round with a trolley and started to pick up the collection of cereal boxes, as well as the mess that the previous occupants had left in their wake.

'Done?' she asked Freya as she reached for her plate.

'Yes, thank you,' she said, and then blinked as the porter—Len—actually spoke.

'Do you mind?'

'Sorry?' Freya asked as he pointed to her plate.

'You're not going to eat those?' he asked, pointing to the open cheese and crackers that Freya hadn't touched.

'No.'

'Do you mind if I have them?'

'Go ahead,' Freya agreed—because, really, what else could she do?

'Ta very much,' Len said, and took out a piece of kitchen paper from his pocket and wrapped the cheese and biscuits in them.

The domestic didn't seem in the least perturbed by this odd exchange, and cleared up the boxes and plates. Then as she wheeled her trolley off, The Man Who Liked His Breakfast Cereal, spoke.

'Here you go, Len.' He pushed a granola bar across the table to him.

'Cheers!' Len pocketed his bounty as he stood up and then walked out of the canteen.

Goodness, Freya thought, people here were *so* odd. She simply couldn't imagine asking a complete stranger for the leftover food on their plate.

But then that deep, snooty voice spoke again and attempted to clarify things a little.

'He only talks to the animals.'

'I'm not with you.'

'Len,' he explained. 'He's miserable around people, but he visits an animal shelter in his free time and he's always after treats for them.'

'Oh!' Freya let out a little laugh.

'You're new,' he said, glancing at her lanyard.

He had realised she was staff, but was quite certain he would have noticed her before if she wasn't new.

She wore a dark shift dress that accentuated her pale bare arms, and her black curly hair was loose and down to her shoulders. From the little he had heard, he guessed she was far from home.

'I'm here for my orientation day,' Freya said.

He grimaced. 'I've done a few of those in my time. The fire lecture, the union rep...'

'We haven't had a fire lecture yet,' Freya said. 'That's this afternoon. I think it's a film, followed by a demonstration.'

'Fun,' he drawled as he rolled his eyes. 'Mind you, I did have a patient who tried to set fire to the ward once...'

She waited for more, but he'd gone back to his cereal

'Breakfast?' Freya asked.

'And lunch.' He moved on to his second mug of tea. 'Are you new to London as well as the hospital?'

Freya nodded. 'I got here last week.'

'I worked in Glasgow for a while.'

'For how long?'

'A year. I couldn't understand a word anybody said. "Pardon" became my most-used word.'

'I'm having the same problem—although in reverse,' Freya admitted. 'I have to keep repeating myself.'

'I can understand you.'

'Then you're the first.'

'You're not from Glasgow, though?'

She was far too soft spoken for that, he thought. But not soft. He had liked the edge to her tone when he'd asked if the seat was taken. Richard *loved* the challenge of a sullen woman.

'No, I'm from Cromayr Bay.'

'Never heard of it.'

'Fife,' Freya said. 'Overlooking the Firth.'

'Never heard of it,' he said again.

But this time he smiled just a smidge and she couldn't tell if he was teasing.

'How are you finding London?'

'It's early days.' Freya gave a small shrug.

'Ah, after a few late nights you'll come to love it.'

It was then that she noticed his eyes—or rather, it was then that she *properly* noticed them.

In his good-looking face there were several standouts. If she'd been describing him to Alison, his sculpted cheekbones and attractive full mouth were two features she might easily have named, and that his hazel eyes were just so much *more* than hazel. They were the colour of burnt amber, with a smatter of golden flecks, and they made Freya feel as if she were gazing upon an open fire.

Or was that more from the way he absolutely held her gaze as she replayed his words in her mind?

'Ah, but after a few late nights you'll come to love it.'

Those words had sounded like an invitation.

As Freya held their eye contact steady, she wasn't quite sure how, but he made her his sole focus.

And he was hers.

Gone was the canteen, and gone too was the noise.

But then he spoke, and Freya found herself blinking at the intrusion of words.

'So, where will you be working?

'Maternity. I'm a midwife. The name's Freya,' she

added, and she was not just being polite. His stethoscope was hanging over his lanyard and she wanted to know his name and just who this delectable stranger was.

She would have to wait to find out, though. His pager was trilling. As he looked at it he scooped the last of his cereal into his mouth and then gulped down the remaining tea as he stood.

'I expect you to be fully versed in the operating of a fire extinguisher the next time we meet.'

'I'll do my best,' Freya said, but he had already gone, his large frame moving swiftly through the tables as people made way to let him past.

She watched.

And not idly.

The overhead chimes started then, and Freya heard that the Cardiac Arrest Team was needed in Casualty.

Through the glass windows of the canteen Freya watched as he ran down the corridor, and then she turned her head and surveyed his empty cereal bowl and the two empty cups of tea.

Freya didn't know his name, just that he was gorgeous. Effortlessly so. And way more gorgeous than *she* could handle.

She hadn't been born yesterday. In fact, Freya's thirtieth birthday was fast approaching. And there was something about him that told her he had learnt to flirt from the cradle. There had certainly been a tease and a flirt in his eyes when they spoke—especially with that little quip about late nights.

Well, there would be no late nights spent with *him*! She was far too guarded and sensible for that.

With her lunch break over, Freya headed back to the lecture theatre for the afternoon session of her orientation day. Sure enough it was the fire lecture. She watched the film and tried not to smile when they were given a demonstration on how to use the various fire extinguishers.

And even as she watched and listened Freya wanted to know more about the time her lunch companion's patient had tried to set fire to the ward.

And she wanted to know his name.

Fully versed in the fire policy at the Primary, as well as in the various codes used for emergencies of different natures, and how to report safety hazards, Freya found that it was time for coffee—and, she guessed, another fifteen minutes of standing alone.

'There's a lot to take in, isn't there?' said Rita, the woman who had earlier been sitting next to her.

'There is,' Freya agreed. 'Where will you be working?'

'I used to be a domestic on Maternity. I'm hoping they'll send me back there, but I haven't been told where I'm going yet. You?'

'I'm a midwife, so I'm *certainly* hoping that they'll be sending me there!' Freya joked.

'Pardon?'

'Maternity,' Freya said instead.

'Well, I hope to see you there.'

They headed back for their final lectures about the pay office and superannuation. Rita took furtive notes and Freya did her level best not to tune out completely.

Finally orientation day was concluded, and the fifty or so new Primary Hospital workers all headed for home.

Freya followed the red line, and sure enough was soon approaching Casualty.

And there he was.

The man who had understood her when she spoke.

He must be hungry again, Freya thought, watching him feed coins into a vending machine.

Gosh, he really was good-looking—and just so tall and

broad. Even side-on there was a presence to him. She wondered if she could come up with a witty line about fire extinguishers in the few seconds she'd have before their paths crossed again.

Except she didn't come up with any witty lines, and neither was one needed—because he collected a bottle of water and a bar of chocolate and headed back into Casualty without noticing her at all.

Freya headed towards the Underground, as did seemingly fifty million other people, and stood squashed between them for the four stops to her flat. And surely those same fifty million people were getting off at the same stop, for they all seemed to be herding towards the escalator with her.

She thought of her little purple car at home. The one that would never have survived the motorway—which was the reason her father had driven her here. And she thought of the short drive from the hospital to her home and the gorgeous view that awaited her there.

'Cheer up love!' called out a man working at a flower stall. 'It might never happen.'

Freya jolted as she realised he was calling out to her.

She walked into her dingy flat and let out a sigh.

The place looked no better for her efforts over the past four days. She had washed down the walls, but really they needed several coats of paint. The curtains she had washed had shrunk, Freya had realised when she'd put them back, and now they didn't properly close, falling a foot short of the floor. And there was an awful picture of a horse and cart that had to come down!

Tomorrow, Freya decided. When she would also get a rug to cover the mustard-coloured carpet, she thought as she headed into the kitchen.

It was even worse than her kitchen at Cromayr Bay.

But it wasn't just the flat that was upsetting her. Apart from that gorgeous guy at lunchtime she had barely spoken to a soul since she'd arrived here.

It would be better soon, Freya told herself. Once she got to the maternity unit she would start to make friends.

Wouldn't she?

She was starting to think the flower seller had picked up on her mood correctly. 'It' had indeed happened.

Moving here, Freya was sure, had been a mistake.

CHAPTER TWO

'FIONA, CAN YOU go to Labour and Delivery? I mean Freya.'

Freya nodded. She was getting rather used to being called the wrong name by Stella, the associate unit manager.

'Sure.'

'And can you buddy with Kelly?'

Freya had been working there for a fortnight now, and today she was to go to the labour and delivery unit. 'Buddying' meant that she and Kelly would check each other's CTG readings to ensure that two sets of skilled eyes overlooked the tracings. Even after two weeks it was no less daunting than it had been on her first day.

She had spent the first week in the antenatal clinic and the past few days on the maternity ward, and now she was on her second day in L&D.

There were *so* many staff, and each day there seemed to be new faces. Freya had really clicked with one midwife yesterday, but as it had turned out she'd just been doing an agency shift, so Freya had no idea if she would see her again.

Everyone was so busy, and though they were all professional and nice, there just wasn't the same vibe from her colleagues that Freya was used to.

As she walked to L&D Freya rolled over the top of her

trousers as they were way too loose. Her uniform consisted of dark blue trousers and a pale blue top and it was less than flattering. She couldn't care less, but the sizing must be off because it hung off her. Although she *had* lost a bit of weight since she'd arrived, due to the constant busy pace and the lack of time to do a proper shop.

As she pressed the green button and the doors to L&D parted she saw a woman pushing an IV, walking the corridor with her support person. Freya gave them a smile.

She checked the board and saw that Dr Mina was the obstetrician in charge today. In the short while she had been at the Primary, Freya had worked with her several times, and found her incredibly efficient as well as a calming presence to the patients.

The hand-over was in depth, so that everyone was well-versed on all the patients—both those present now and those expected to arrive over the course of the shift.

'Freya, can you take over from Angela in D5?' asked Pat, the midwife in charge of L&D today. 'She's awaiting an epidural, but finding an anaesthetist this morning is proving a rather hard ask.'

'Has the second-on been paged?' Freya asked, and that earnt her a wry smile from her colleague.

'*Everyone's* been paged, but there's been a five-car pile-up on the M25 and there was already a dissecting triple A being rushed to Theatre, along with a collapse on the paediatric ward. Then we had to call the Crash Caesarean Team out half an hour ago. Right now Anaesthetics are snowed under, and it's a case of if a patient's screaming then at least they're breathing.'

Freya took a breath of her own. That patient-load sounded like a full week's work in Cromayr Bay at the height of summer, but it was just another morning at the Primary.

Or not. Because then Pat explained that it had been an exceptionally busy night in Casualty too.

'Just remind Kathy in D5 that she hasn't been forgotten. Her husband, Ben, is getting upset.'

Freya checked her patient's details and then went into the delivery suite. The lights were low and the suite was dim, and Kathy was kneeling up and holding on to the head of the delivery bed as Angela pressed a hot pack into her back.

'Hi, there,' Freya said as she approached. 'I'm Freya. I'm—'

'Are you an anaesthetist?' Kathy's husband snapped.

'No, I'm a midwife,'

'Not good enough! My wife has been waiting for two hours for an epidural.'

'Please, Ben,' Kathy implored, but then her face screwed up and she leant on her forearm as a contraction came.

Angela helped her through it as Freya checked all the equipment. Angela brought her up to speed with Kathy's progress, but then gestured with her head to the door. Freya followed her out.

'The husband is getting really tense and it's upsetting Kathy,' Angela said.

'I can see that.' Freya nodded.

'He's a great guy—he's just terrified. But Kathy has still got a good way to go. I've called down to Casualty but two of their patients are currently being transferred to ICU, so they're very tied up. The anaesthetist in our theatre is aware, though he's probably half an hour or so away.'

'Okay…'

'You could try calling Switch and asking—'

'No need.'

A voice she recognised, though she hadn't heard it since her orientation day, caused Freya to turn around.

'Oh, Richard!' Angela sighed in relief. 'Am I pleased to see you.'

'Not as pleased as your patients will be. What room?'

'D5 is first,' Angela said. 'It's all set up for you.'

'Thanks, Angela,' he said. 'Freya.'

She gave him a smile. 'Richard.'

Finally she knew his name.

And, more than that, he was still *stunning*.

He had been wearing scrubs when they'd met, but this morning he wore a dark suit and a crisp white shirt with a silver-grey tie. His straight hair was damp, and rather more in need of a cut than the last time she'd seen him, and he was unshaven.

In seconds she took in every delicious detail, and the last few didn't quite fit. He was so well turned out that the unshaven jaw stood out for Freya.

Instead of heading to the suite, he took the patient's notes and walked over to the desk. The sharp, fresh scent of his cologne lingered. Freya saw him removing his jacket as she followed Angela back into D5.

'Good news,' Angela said. 'The anaesthetist is here.'

'Well, where is he, then?' Ben demanded.

'Dr Lewis is just reading up on the notes.' Angela gave Kathy a lovely smile. 'I shall leave you in Freya's hands. You've been amazing, Kathy.'

Kathy nodded and tried to say goodbye, but was overwhelmed by another contraction. Freya took over, rubbing Kathy's back and trying to establish a rapid bond with the woman, and also with her husband.

'Would you like to come and rub her back?' Freya suggested, but Ben stood against the wall and gave a tense shake of his head.

Yes, it was all terribly different from anything she was

used to. Usually Freya would have seen her patients at antenatal clinic, and often their partners too.

'Well done, Kathy,' Freya said as the contraction faded. Knowing that the anaesthetist was here, Freya suggested that Kathy empty her bladder and walked with her, pushing the IV pole, to the en suite bathroom attached to the delivery room.

'He's nervous,' Kathy said, explaining Ben's behaviour.

'Of course he is,' Freya said. 'It's hard work for the women but it's hell on the men.'

That made Kathy laugh a little.

Freya waited outside, and when Kathy came out after washing her hands, she asked Freya a question. 'Do you have children?'

'No.' Freya said. 'I've got nieces and nephews, and my best friend's expecting, but I'd definitely like my own someday.'

She was actually enjoying getting to know the women here, and opening up to people who didn't know her at all, Freya realised. At home, had she said that it would have been all around town that she and Malcolm were trying for a baby.

'We tried for ages...' Kathy sighed. 'I thought it would never happen.'

'Well, it clearly is.'

'Thanks, Freya,' Kathy said as Freya pushed the IV pole. But as they got to the door she paused. 'Please...' she said. 'Don't mind Ben. His bark is far worse than his bite.'

'I know that. You'll be feeling a lot more comfortable soon, and I'm sure he will too.'

She was just helping Kathy back onto the delivery bed when the door opened and she saw the beautiful man she now knew was called Richard come in.

'Where the *hell* have you been?' Ben said by way of greeting.

'I'm Dr Lewis,' he responded. 'Consultant anaesthetist.' Then he smiled at his patient. 'Hello, Mrs Hudson.'

But Ben wasn't finished yet. 'She was booked to have an epidural hours ago, but she's been left screaming in pain.'

'I'm aware of that, Mr Hudson, and I agree that it's unfortunate, but I'm here now.'

'It's more than unfortunate, it's not good enough,' he retorted.

'Ben, please…' Kathy pleaded, but her husband still wasn't done.

'Where were you?'

'Actually,' Richard said as he rolled up his sleeves, 'I was in bed when I was called to see if I could come in. I'm not supposed to be here until eight.'

It was only just after seven. And Freya understood now why he hadn't shaved.

'Now…' He looked over to his patient as he tied on a plastic apron. 'Would you prefer me to call you Mrs Hudson or Kathy?'

'Kathy.'

'Well, Kathy, we'll have you feeling a lot more comfortable soon.'

He was very meticulous. As Freya helped Kathy to sit on the edge of the bed for the procedure Richard Lewis went through all that had been set up. He made no small talk as he checked and rechecked everything.

'Right,' he said, as if to himself, and then he addressed Kathy. 'You're going to feel a sting from the local anaesthetic and then a bit of pressure. I'll need you to stay as still as you can—do you understand that?'

'I do—but what if I get a contraction.'

'It's fine. I'm used to them. I'll work around it.'

He went through everything that she could expect to feel, and as the next contraction came he put on gloves, waiting for the pain to diminish before the procedure commenced.

'I'm sorry,' Ben said suddenly.

'It's fine,' Richard responded. 'It's awful to see someone you love in pain. However, by all accounts your partner has been doing marvellously. Let's try and make this last bit a whole lot easier for her, shall we?'

Whoa! Freya thought as she held on to Kathy. He had somehow accepted the apology while reminding the husband just who this day was about.

'Why don't you come this side?' Freya suggested to Ben. She knew he was really just terribly anxious. 'You can hold Kathy's hand.'

This time he didn't shake his head and came and took his wife's hand.

Richard worked quietly and soon the epidural was in. Kathy lay back on the delivery bed.

'You'll need to stay in bed now,' Richard reminded her as he disposed of his sharps and then removed his gloves. 'Thank you, Freya. Can I leave my mess to you? I believe I'm wanted in D3.'

'Sure.'

Freya checked Kathy's obs, and those of the baby, and by the time she had tidied up Kathy was indeed starting to feel the benefits of the epidural.

'You should try and get a little rest now,' Freya suggested. 'I'll be in and out, and there's the call bell if you have any concerns at all.'

'Freya!'

Her name was called the second she stepped out of the room. 'Can you go and take the baby in D7?'

Freya nodded and headed to delivery suite number

seven. 'Taking' a baby was wonderful indeed. It combined all the joy with barely a hint of the pain.

Stepping in to the delivery suite, she found the atmosphere was lovely and peaceful. Kelly, one of the other midwives was there, along with the soon-to-be father, who had his arms wrapped around his wife's shoulders.

In fact Kelly was so calm that even when she told Freya that Dr Mina and the anaesthetist had been paged she did it in such an open way that there was no jolt of alarm from the mother.

'The baby is small for the dates and the head is smaller than expected,' she said, and Freya checked all the equipment was ready.

Despite the unexpectedly small head, everything seemed to be under control.

'Try not to push, Sita,' Kelly said. 'Just pant.'

'Okay,' Sita said, and fought against the urge.

'Good girl,' said Kelly. Her focus was totally on the delivery, and she didn't look over when the door opened.

'Hello, there,' Richard said quietly, and Kelly calmly told him the reason for him being paged.

'Thirty-seven weeks and small for dates,' Kelly explained.

The room was getting crowded. Stella had come in after Richard, followed by Dr Mina just as the head was delivered. And now there was Guy Masters, the paediatrician on call, whom Freya had already met.

'Well done, Sita,' Dr Mina said. 'Just breathe and do as Kelly says. Dr Masters is a paediatrician and he's here to check your baby.'

The head really was tiny, and Freya found she was holding her breath as the body slithered out. But even as she accepted him he started to cry. His huge eyes were blinking at the light and his little face was wrinkled.

He was utterly gorgeous, Freya thought as she held this tiny piece of the future in her hands. Tiny, but perfect. And as she rubbed him down Guy was already examining him.

'One that is better out than in,' Guy said.

The baby had clearly not been getting sufficient nutrition in-utero, but he was angry and defiant and utterly perfect.

'I don't think we need you, Richard,' he said as loud cries pierced the room and the baby pinked up beautifully.

'Not with those lungs,' Richard agreed. And it was just as well he wasn't needed because his pager was going off.

He left unnoticed by all, Freya thought. All except her.

'I think he's ready to meet his mum,' Guy said, and Freya popped a little hat on the baby to keep him warm, wrapped him, then carried him over to his waiting parents.

She smiled as she watched a family being born. Freya loved delivering babies, but *taking* them was special too. They always tried to deliver them straight to the mother, but sometimes, as with this unexpected small size, the baby needed a proper examination. Apart from his size this one was doing just fine. Another perfect new life.

The day seemed to be running away from her. Busy, a bit crazy, and after her hectic morning she could only take a coffee break on the run at the desk.

There, Dr Mina was speaking with Richard and Kelly was chatting with Stella about a film they were going to see at the weekend.

'It's supposed to be really good,' Freya commented, subtly fishing to be asked to go with them, but Kelly just nodded her head.

Freya took her lunch in the staff room, and just as she returned she was told that Kathy was ready to push.

When she got to the delivery room Ben was white with fear and Freya gave him a smile.

'I thought you'd gone home,' Ben said.

'And miss out on this?' Freya asked.

Ben proved to be a champion when it came to coaxing Kathy to push. It was clearly an excellent epidural, because she could feel the sensation and some pressure but had no pain.

'Another big push,' Freya encouraged. 'Come on—a really big one, right down into your bottom.'

This time it was Kelly who arrived to take the baby and soon Freya delivered a chunky baby boy. He was gorgeous, and there were tears from both Ben and Kathy as he lay on her stomach, blinking at the world.

'Are you going to cut the cord, Dad?' Kelly asked, and Ben came over with tears in his eyes to have that special moment with his son.

Baby Hudson didn't have a name yet, but by the time Freya was ready for home he'd had his first feed and Kathy had had a well-earned cup of tea.

It hadn't been a particularly busy day, or so Freya had been told, and yet she was exhausted.

The high of Baby Hudson's birth lasted right through the Tube journey, but faded as she began the walk for home.

Freya had never been surrounded by more people, and yet she had never felt more alone.

There was a social club at the hospital, but she was hardly going to walk in on her own, and making friends was proving a lot more difficult than she had anticipated.

However, later, rather than sit alone with her noodles, Freya reminded herself that she did indeed have friends and called Alison.

'How are things?' Alison asked.

'Busy,' Freya said. 'Well, work is—the social life, not so much.'

'But you're in *London*!' Alison said.

'I know...' Freya sighed, because Alison's observation just made it worse. 'I *am* trying,' she admitted. 'I sort of hinted to a couple of girls at work that there was a film I'd like to see, but I felt like a bent coin in a vending machine.'

'Rejected?' Alison laughed.

'Exactly.'

'Keep at it. Just say yes to anything you're invited to.'

'I'll have to be invited somewhere first.'

'You *will* be.'

'How are *you*?' Freya asked. She felt her throat clamp tight, but she swallowed and pushed through, trying to keep her voice casual and light. 'How's the baby.'

'All good. I'm fifteen weeks now, and I swear I've got a bump, although Callum says it's too early.'

Freya hesitated, because women sometimes showed more quickly with a second pregnancy, but she couldn't gauge whether or not that was the right thing to say to Alison now.

Freya dealt with pregnant woman every working day, and she dealt with loss too. And, what was more, she prided herself on dealing with it well. Yet when it came to her friend she felt like an absolute novice, and simply didn't know how to be around the subject of Alison's pregnancy.

Freya was terrified she might break down, and Alison didn't need that. Of course they had both cried together in the days following Andrew's birth, and then his death, but right now Freya was sure it was time to be strong.

'When's your ultrasound?' Freya asked.

'In two weeks' time. I'll believe it's really happening once I've heard its little heart.'

Alison's voice broke then, and Freya closed her eyes when she heard it. 'It will be okay,' she offered.

'You don't *know* that, Freya,' Alison snapped.

'I know, but...' Her voice trailed off.

'Sorry,' Alison said.

'Don't be.'

And then Freya turned on her midwife voice and said all the right things, just as she would to a patient.

But Alison was her best friend. It was awkward and it was difficult and things were different between them.

There was no escaping that.

CHAPTER THREE

RICHARD LEWIS REALLY was stunning.

Even asleep he managed to bring a little skip to Freya's heart when she walked in and saw him, lying across several chairs in the staff room.

Pat and Kelly were deep in conversation there, and didn't seem bothered in the least by the sight of Richard sprawled out.

It bothered Freya—or rather it bothered her senses. She tried not to peek as she stirred her soup, but she didn't try very hard because her eyes kept wandering over.

He hadn't shaved again, and Freya knew he must have been working all night. It was now late morning.

She had been at the Primary for a month now, and he was no less intriguing and no less gorgeous.

During the course of her working week Freya saw him regularly. He had a new registrar, who wasn't yet able to do epidurals unsupervised, so Richard was in L&D quite often to oversee his work. And he was always called if there was a difficulty with a delivery or a Caesarean.

There was rarely time for conversation, though.

Freya considered the Maternity Unit here extremely busy, but *his* workload was incredible. He rushed to emergencies all over the hospital—and that was aside from Theatre and patients in the ICU.

Of course there were many anaesthetists in such a busy hospital, but Freya, despite her warnings to herself, was only interested in one!

Her instincts had been right. He was a heartbreaker, indeed. She had found that out from the other midwives. Not that they'd actually confided in her! No—she was still struggling to fit in. But she had overheard a couple of conversations, and apparently he'd just ended a brief fling with a nurse in Casualty. And Von, one of the other midwives, was *still* hoping that she and Richard might get back together.

She looked over at him. He needed a shave and a haircut. Or rather *he* might think that if he looked in the mirror, but to Freya he looked just fine.

Better than fine!

He was like a bear, Freya thought. Not a fat bear, more like a bear just out of hibernation, all slender and restless and hungry.

And then she smiled at her mad thoughts.

Pat was chatting to Kelly about the film that Freya *still* hadn't seen. 'I was thinking I might go this weekend,' Pat said.

'You *have* to,' said Kelly. 'It's amazing.'

Freya again tried to be brave. 'I'm dying to see it,' she admitted.

'You should.' Kelly looked over and nodded, and then she stood. 'Come on, Pat. We'd better get back.'

Once they'd gone Freya let out a sigh. Over and over she'd been mentioning that she'd love to go and see the film, but there had been no takers. How much more of a hint was she supposed to give?

She sat staring at the television and took a sip of her revolting packet soup. And then a voice—one she had really come to like—chimed deep and low.

'I'll take you to the bloody film.'

She looked over.

'I can take a hint.'

'Sorry?'

'You keep suggesting it every time I'm near. All you have to do ask.'

'I wasn't hinting for *you* to take me!' Freya said, and actually found herself going red. 'I was waiting for one of *them* to ask me along.'

'You're too subtle,' he said, and lay there smiling at her. 'Poor Freya-no-Friends.'

'Don't!' she said, but she was smiling.

'You have to invite yourself—or just go along with them.'

'What? Just turn up? Like a stalker?'

'Well, maybe not.'

'I've *always* had friends,' Freya said, for she had been giving it some considerable thought. 'But I've realised that's because we all grew up together. I've never actually had to *make* any.'

'Rubbish,' he scoffed. 'You're saying that because you grew up in a village you all get along?'

'It's not a village.'

'Well, town or whatever,' he said. 'But I'm sure there are people you don't like there. You're not automatically friends with everyone you grew up with. God, I loathed Derek next door, and we had to play together all the time.'

'Why?'

'That's for another time.'

He stretched and yawned and sat up, more bear-like than ever as he gave himself a sort of shake.

'I'm starving,' he said.

'I've got some soup.'

'No, thanks.' Richard pulled a face. 'I'm going to head down to the canteen. What time do you finish?'

She'd thought he must have been joking about going out. 'Not until nine.'

'Well, I'm covering for Simon until eight, so I doubt I'll get away much before then. I'll meet you at the entrance to Casualty.'

'I don't even know if the film's on,' Freya said. 'Or the session time.'

'Times,' he corrected. 'It's on everywhere. You're not in Cromayr Bay now, where they have to come and change the reels...'

He was teasing, yet it made her laugh. 'It's not *that* bad.'

'Give me your number and if I can I'll text you if I'm not going to make it. But if I'm not there by a quarter past, just head for home. It'll mean I'm stuck somewhere—nothing else. I won't be avoiding you!'

He even turned the subject of her being a little lonely into a smile.

'I'll look forward to it,' Freya said, and recited her number. 'And, no, I won't be upset if...' she started, but her voice trailed off as Stella came in.

'Freya, I know you're not due back yet, but we've got a bit of a rush on.'

'Of course,' Freya said, and she stood and finished the last of her soup, a little surprised when Richard spoke again.

'I'll see you around nine, then?'

Freya felt her cheeks were a little warm as she walked back round to the unit—because he had made it clear in front of Stella that they were meeting up tonight.

It meant nothing, she told herself. It was just two colleagues going out. If it had been Kelly or Pat or anyone else she wouldn't be giving it too much thought and Stella was surely the same.

'See Rose?' Stella said, and pointed over to Rita, the domestic who had done her orientation with Freya on her first day.

'Rita,' Freya corrected as they walked.

'Rita, then.' Stella nodded. 'See how it looks like she's emptying the rubbish…?'

'Er…yes,' Freya answered.

'Well, she's not—she's actually collecting all the discarded hearts…'

Freya pressed her lips together as she realised what Stella meant, and even managed a wry smile as Stella spoke on.

'Oh, look, she's going under the bed. Must have found another one. You know how he dashes from one emergency to another?' She didn't await Freya's response. 'Well, he's the same with women.'

'Stella.' Freya stopped walking and gave her senior a wide smile—because she knew his reputation and because Stella had made her smile. 'We're going to the cinema. No more, no less.'

'Don't say I didn't warn you.'

It was a slow evening by Primary Hospital standards, which would have meant a chaotic one back home! But by nine Freya was in the changing room. She took her phone from her locker, as she chose not to have it on her at work, and found herself letting out a breath of relief that there was no text from Richard to say he couldn't make it.

And then she swallowed, because relief possibly wasn't the right word.

Freya was nervous about tonight.

She so wanted to make friends.

Only this didn't feel like any friendship Freya had ever known!

She pulled off her horrible uniform, changed into the grey linen dress and ballet pumps she had worn into work and let her hair down, pulling her curls out with her fingers.

In the end it was actually Freya who was a little late, and when she arrived at the entrance to Casualty he was checking his phone.

He was out of scrubs and in a suit, although minus a tie, and beside him Freya felt rather drab.

She looked far from drab, though. In fact, Richard thought as she walked towards him, she was wearing the same dress she had been on the day they had met.

And that was concerning, because usually he couldn't recall what any woman had worn the previous night, let alone in previous weeks. He'd even joked to a friend that he'd be hell at reporting a missing person because he'd be unable to tell the police what the missing person was wearing.

He didn't really notice such things, other than thinking, *Oh, she looks nice.*

With Freya though he'd be able to describe in detail to any police officer that the dress was grey linen, and it was a touch looser than it had been on the day they had met.

Yes, Officer, she had on black pumps and no stockings, just pale slender legs. And her hair was worn down. It didn't actually sit on her shoulders since it's too curly for that, it just holds its wild shape there. And she has green eyes, Officer, and soft full lips.

Anything else? the officer would ask.

Well, she's been a bit lonely since she arrived here, he would say. *I didn't give it too much thought at the time...*

But he was giving it some serious thought now.

Not that he showed his concern. Richard, thanks to his job, was incredibly good at that.

'Right,' he said as they headed out onto the street. 'The film is on at ten, so if we skip all the trailers we'll have time to go and get something decent to eat. I am sick of eating on the run.'

'That sounds brilliant.'

'Are you on in the morning?' he asked.

Freya nodded.

'And me.'

And then Freya was delivered another thinly veiled warning as Stella dashed past them to a car in which presumably her husband had come to meet her. 'Enjoy *the film*, Freya!'

'I will,' Freya called back.

'Has she been telling tales about me?' Richard asked as they walked out onto the street.

'No!'

The street was busy enough that it could have been a Saturday during the day back home, and she was glad it was dark enough that he'd hopefully missed her blush as she lied.

'Of course she has,' Richard said. 'And they're all true.'

'Then it's a good job we're just heading out to see a film,' Freya said.

'Indeed.'

But first they would eat...

'Is Italian okay?' he checked, and she nodded as he led them to a very lovely casual-looking restaurant, tucked away from the main street.

Freya only realised just how hungry she was as the gorgeous scents inside hit her, and they were guided to a table looking out onto the street.

'Can I get you some drinks to start?' the waiter offered.

'Freya?' Richard asked.

'Just water.'

'And me,' Richard said. 'Sparkling?'

'Lovely,' Freya agreed.

The menu was delectable, and she decided on a creamy carbonara, while Richard settled for *osso bucco*.

'So,' he said when their order was in, 'how are you finding it at the Primary?'

'It's fine,' Freya said, and she saw his eyes narrow. 'Well, it's a bit overwhelming. I expected it to be busy, of course, but I didn't realise it would be quite so full-on.'

'What was it like where you worked before?'

'I was in a birthing centre attached to a hospital. We saw the mothers for all their antenatal care, then right up to the postnatal check.'

'How many deliveries at the centre?' Richard asked.

'About a hundred a year. So it's been a big change for me to come somewhere that averages more than that in a week. Still, I wanted the experience.'

'You could have got that more locally,' Richard said, tearing open a bread roll. 'The Women's Hospital in Edinburgh surely delivers a similar amount?'

'Yes,' Freya agreed. 'I did a stint there during my training. But I wanted something completely different, and it was sort of now or never.'

'Are your parents back home?'

'And my brothers.' Freya nodded.

'Do you all get on?' he asked, because despite himself he wanted to know more. Surely there must be more of a reason she had left—not just in her work, but her home, friends and family too?

'Oh, yes. I've got my own place, but I see plenty of them. The older brother, though they're both younger than me, has got two children. I delivered the younger one.'

'I can't imagine having a sister-in-law, let alone being that close to her.'

'Don't you have siblings?' Freya asked.

'No, there's just me.'

'And are you from London?'

'Kent.'

'Do you get back there much?'

'Now and then,' Richard said, and then he hesitated.

He rarely spoke about his family, but he felt no sense of her probing beyond what he was comfortable with, and actually he found it was nice to sit and chat.

'I see my father sometimes, and my mother's here in London. She's just got engaged.' He rolled his eyes, just as their meals were delivered. *'Again.'*

Then came the pepper grinder, and the parmesan cheese, and he thought certainly they would speak about the food now, or the film they were about to see—or even, as Richard usually would, get on with flirting. And yet he was still curious to hear more about her.

'Do you miss your old job?'

'Yes and no,' Freya said. 'I was often delivering the babies of people I'd been to school with, or their wives. And I know a lot of people around town. And while it's nice knowing your patients…'

He nodded. 'My father's a GP. I know only too well the downside. He was never off duty—even going out for a meal like this he'd be interrupted. The only time I remember him getting away from work was if we went on holiday, and even then patients would call him for advice.'

'I don't mind that so much,' Freya admitted.

Her dismissal of the intrusion aspect of things surprised him.

'It's more the fact of everyone knowing everyone else's

business,' she explained. 'And of course when a pregnancy goes wrong it's much harder.'

'It's just part of the job,' Richard said.

'Yes, but it's more difficult when you know the patient.'

'Perhaps...'

To Freya, he didn't sound as if he necessarily agreed. 'There's no *perhaps* about it.'

He opened his mouth to say something, but then changed his mind. It had been a very long day, and they were here to relax after all.

Still, there was something he really would like to know. 'Was there a break-up involved?' he asked.

'Sorry?'

'Is that the reason you left—is there an ex-Mr Freya back home...'

'No!' She laughed. 'I've never been married, but I did break up with someone earlier in the year. It really didn't have anything to do with my decision to leave, though.'

'Are you sure?' Richard frowned through disbelieving eyes.

She was very guarded and, although they were chatting easily, he sensed she was being prudent in her responses.

For once he wanted to dig for the truth from a woman.

'Well, it might have had *some* influence on it,' she admitted reluctantly. 'There's nothing much worse than going into a pub or a restaurant and knowing there's a pretty good chance that your ex will be there. It was a bit messy, I guess.'

'Who ended it?'

'Me,' Freya said. 'We'd been together for ages and I just...' She didn't want to talk about Alison's baby and the pregnancy that had gone wrong. But it had been that which had heralded the end for her and Malcolm. 'I was going through a bit of a tough time and he didn't help matters...'

She gave a thin smile. 'And so, before even the very curl of his hair started to irk me, I ended it. I guess he wasn't the love of my life.'

'There's no such thing,' Richard declared. 'Work is the only love of my life and I intend to remain faithful to that.'

'How do you do it?' Freya asked. 'I know how wrung out *I* feel after an emergency, and yet you deal with them each day.'

'It's my oxygen,' Richard said. 'There's nothing I'd rather be doing. Although,' he admitted, 'I don't want to end up like my father. There has to be a balance. I go away a lot on my days off —try to get well away from the hospital.' He gave a tight smile. 'I have some choices that need to be made.'

'Such as…?'

He gave a small shake of his head that told her not to go there. And when she didn't push for more information Richard could have reached over and kissed her there and then.

He didn't, of course, but the thought was there as their eyes looked.

Freya felt the heat spread over her cheeks as their eyes held, and yet she did not tear her gaze away.

God, he was good, Freya thought, for he turned her on without so much as a touch.

And despite her insistence that tonight was about nothing more than seeing a film, she was now heeding Stella's warnings.

It had been lust at first sight, she knew.

And she would not be acting on it.

Freya wasn't like that. One boyfriend at the end of school and throughout her nursing training. A gap of two years and then Malcolm.

A fling with a sexy anaesthetist was so *not* something

Freya would do. And it *would* be a fling, for he'd warned her—was warning her right now—that everything she'd heard about him was true.

So she reached for her water and tried to think of something to say as she peeled her mind away from sex.

Because that was all it would be.

Sex.

Ah, but it would be sex with *him*.

'So your mother's engaged?' Freya asked. 'Again?'

He knew she was changing the subject.

Although they were speaking about his family, their minds had just been on sex. He wanted to feel her hair… he wanted to delve into those mixed message eyes.

She almost scalded him with a look, and behind the walls she'd put up there lurked desire.

And he liked her odd sullen moments, interspersed by the brightness of her smile.

But, no, this was not what she needed.

He might have a well-deserved reputation, but he wasn't an utter bastard.

Freya was by her own admission a little lonely, a touch overwhelmed, and he would not be meddling with that pretty head.

So, back to her question. He had to think for a moment what it was. Ah, yes, the many loves of his mother's life.

'My mother is about to enter into her fourth marriage. My father isn't quite so bad. He's only been married and divorced twice. I doubt he'll be taking that step again.' He gave a tight smile. 'Thank God! It really is hard coming up with a new speech each time.'

'Her *fourth*!'

He nodded. 'She left us when I was fifteen, and I'm now thirty-three, so it's not quite as bad as it sounds.' He saw her wide eyes. 'Well, maybe it is. My mother is high-end drama and she just wasn't cut out to be the wife of a country GP. She loathed it. And since she broke up with my father—'

He went quiet, for the first time since they had met. And then…

'Freya?' he said.

'Yes?'

'We've missed the film.'

'Oh!'

She looked around the restaurant and noticed the other diners were thinning out, and then she glanced at her phone. It was coming up for eleven.

'Do you want dessert or coffee?' he offered.

'No, no…' She shook her head.

He walked her to the Underground station and there, she assumed, they would go their separate ways.

'I'll see you home,' he said, when she told him where it was.

'It's only four stops,' Freya protested—but not too much. She still wasn't quite used to the Tube, and she did feel a bit nervous at night. It would be nice to have company.

Or rather it would be nice to have *his* company.

'We're here,' Freya said as they arrived at her flat.

'Well, I'm sorry you didn't get to see your film.'

Freya wasn't sorry.

'It's fine,' she said, toying with whether or not to ask him in and deciding that it would be foolish at best. There was a kiss in the air—she could feel it—and as she looked up at him she wondered how that gorgeous unshaven jaw would feel pressed hard against hers.

'Well, another time, then,' Richard said, resisting the urge to kiss her against the wall.

She wanted a friend, he reminded himself. No more than that.

'Thanks for a nice night. It was good to…' She gave a shrug. 'Well, it was nice not to be talking about babies.'

'All work and no play?' Richard said.

'Something like that.'

She took out her key and he watched as she put it into the lock. That was the difference with Freya—she didn't stand there awaiting his kiss. She didn't seem to want the complication of *them* either.

And yet there was want.

It was a sultry summer night that deserved to end in bed, but Richard was behaving himself.

'Night, Freya.'

'Night, Richard.'

She walked inside, closed the door behind her and leant against it, taking a long breath in.

Had there been a double-lock she would have turned it. Instead she made do with the security chain.

But only to keep herself in.

There was a kiss waiting on the other side of that door—she was sure of it.

And not just a kiss.

Who was she kidding?

It hadn't been a kiss in the air out there—it had been *sex*.

But a fling with Richard Lewis would be foolish at best. Freya didn't do that type of thing. And it *would* be a fling—she knew that. He'd as good as told her so himself.

She told herself that she could never regret a sensible decision. That in the morning she would wake up and be delighted that she'd avoided the awkwardness that would have surely followed.

Except in the morning Freya didn't feel delighted.

She only felt regret.

CHAPTER FOUR

'HOW WAS THE FILM?' Stella asked as Freya walked with her from the changing room.

'Great,' Freya answered. 'It's well worth seeing.'

She was saved from further questioning as the overhead chimes went off, summoning the Trauma Team to Casualty.

She certainly wasn't about to tell Stella that they'd never actually made it to the cinema, as she knew Stella would just read more into it than there had been.

It was unusually quiet, so Freya took the lull in proceedings as a chance to check stock. She had just pulled out the suction catheters and was ticking the order form when the overhead chimes went off again.

They were a common occurrence in a busy hospital such as this, but the summons that came was one that Freya hadn't yet heard.

'Obstetrics Squad to Casualty.'

Freya wasn't a part of the Obstetrics Squad. She had been told about it during her interview, though. Each Maternity shift, a senior midwife carried a pager and would attend to any obstetric emergency elsewhere in the hospital, along with an obstetrician and anaesthetist.

New staff had to attend at least three off-unit emergencies as an observer, and then Dr Mina had to approve them before they were made a part of that team. But just because she wasn't part of the team it didn't mean that there was nothing for Freya to do.

She ran down to the equipment room and opened up the door, and was pulling out the emergency trolley as Stella and Kelly came running from opposite directions.

'Dr Mina's already down there,' Stella informed Kelly, who held the pager for the Obstetrics Squad today. 'Freya, go and observe.'

Freya nodded. She was nervous about this role, yet keen for the experience.

The chimes were pinging again.

'Here…'

It was Len the porter, who had caught up and took over the other side of the trolley, allowing Kelly to run on ahead.

There was everything that might be required, including a neonatal cot, even though there would be one in Emergency. The trolley was set up for any eventuality.

As she swept into Casualty, Freya acknowledged that she was nervous but consoled herself that she was just there to observe. Even if she never made the team it would be good experience for when she went back to Cromayr Bay.

When.

There was no time to dwell on that word, though it jolted her.

Richard was at the head of one of the resuscitation beds and only briefly glanced up when she came in.

'Next bed,' he said, clearly knowing that she wouldn't have been down there before. He gestured with his head to a curtained area beside him, from behind which came the sound of equipment and people, and above all that the screams of a woman.

They were terrified screams and the woman sounded in pain.

'Thanks.' Freya stepped in and saw there was organised chaos taking place.

Dominic, his registrar, was at the head of the bed and
the trauma team were around the woman. So too was Dr
Mina, tiny in green scrubs and yet authoritative all the
same.

She had a Doppler on the woman's stomach and there
was the sound of a rapid heartbeat.

'Stay back and observe,' Kelly said. 'You'll be doing
this yourself soon.'

There wasn't actually room for her to do anything *but*
observe.

An older woman dressed in scrubs was talking to the
patient. 'You're okay, Louise,' she said in an Irish brogue.
'We're taking care of you now...'

Louise had on a hard collar, and from what Freya could
make out she had been involved in a high-impact motor
vehicle accident. There was blunt trauma to her chest and
abdomen as well as a head injury.

And she was twenty-six weeks pregnant.

'Louise.' Kelly moved near the head of the bed. 'Your
baby has a strong heartbeat...'

But nothing would calm the woman. Louise Eames was
absolutely terrified and perhaps, after her head injury, confused too.

There were also concerns that she had abdominal bleeding.

'I'm May, the Unit Manager in this madhouse.' The
Irish woman stepped back and spoke to Freya as Kelly
took over reassuring the patient. 'I'm a midwife myself.
All looks well but, as you know, pregnant women can mask
symptoms. I'm worried that she's worse than her observations are showing.'

It was nice to be talked through it all. Most of it Freya

knew, but she hadn't actually seen the Obstetrics Squad in action.

'I've told NICU to hold a cot, in case she has to be delivered.' May said. 'Here's Richard now.'

Richard spoke for a moment with Dominic, and then Dominic stepped out—Freya guessed to take over the patient in the next bed.

'Hello, Louise.'

He spoke as if they had already met, Freya thought. There was just something so reassuring about his voice.

'I'm Dr Lewis, Consultant Anaesthetist.'

Louise screamed again.

'No,' he said. 'No screaming. Save that oxygen for your baby. Now, I want to have another listen to your chest.'

'That's a good girl,' Kelly said to Louise, who was quietening down—though that wasn't necessarily a good sign.

'We're going to get her round for a CT,' Dr Mina said. She and Richard discussed sedation, but Louise seemed a lot calmer now.

The CT was swift, and showed a small tear on Louise's spleen, but everything looked fine with the baby.

'Louise.' Dr Mina spoke to her. 'The hard collar can come off now and you'll be more comfortable. The baby is doing well, but we're going to move you now to the Intensive Care Unit, so that we can keep a close eye on both of you.'

'Will my baby be okay?' It was all Louise wanted to know.

'Everything is looking fine for now,' Dr Mina said. 'But, Louise, if we need to deliver you, then we will.'

ICU was all ready and waiting, and absolutely the right place for Louise to be.

Freya listened as May gave a detailed hand-over to the Critical Care Nurse. It was scary for Louise to be there, no doubt, but after the noise of Emergency it was certainly a lot calmer here.

'Thank you,' Dr Mina said to the midwifery staff as they gathered up their equipment to leave.

Richard didn't look up as he was already with another patient and completely focussed.

God, what a job he had, Freya thought as they headed out.

'Poor thing,' Kelly said, as they made their way back, but then she moved straight on to business. 'We'll have to check the trolley as soon as we get back,' she told Freya. 'Just in case we're called again.'

'I hope we're not,' Freya said.

But hope didn't work.

Just after three the chimes went off again. Freya was taking a baby for Pat when she heard them, and they didn't even share a glance—instead they focussed on the little life coming into the world.

Working at The Primary was, Freya thought as she came out of the delivery suite, just all so *intense.*

'Were the chimes for Louise?' Freya asked Stella, who was writing up the board against a background of screams from a woman in the bathroom.

'Yes.' Stella nodded. 'Maternal compromise.'

And then there was paperwork—so much paperwork—only today Freya used it as an excuse and a reason for lingering at the nursing station until well after four, when Kelly came back.

She was wearing a pink theatre cap and still somehow brimming with energy as she and Stella commenced restocking the emergency trolley.

'Mum dropped her blood pressure. Thankfully they were straight onto her. The baby's out.'

He was doing well for dates, but it was Louise that was

the main concern. The small tear on her spleen had extended and, as Dr Mina had explained, the signs of hypovolemia were more subtle in pregnancy.

Freya was utterly exhausted as she made her way home.

'Cheer up, love, it might never happen,' said the flower seller, and Freya managed not to shoot him a look.

She stepped into her flat and just flopped onto the couch—lay there staring at the peeling paint on the ceiling, feeling utterly wrung out. Every second at work she felt as if she were on a roller coaster that didn't allow time for catching her breath, or time to reflect.

Poor Louise... She'd been incredibly well taken care of—Freya knew that—but it was all so different from everything she was used to.

Which was what she had wanted, of course. And she was certainly getting experience. But it was draining her.

Stella had told her there would be a case follow-up for Louise, in which Dr Mina would go into greater detail, and Freya was truly grateful that she'd been sent down to Casualty to observe. She really was gaining experience, and if ever a mother came into Cromayr Bay with blunt force trauma...

Freya halted herself there, but it was too late. She knew in that moment that she was imagining herself back at home, just as she had this morning.

But she wasn't *just* here to gain experience. If she'd wanted that, as Richard had pointed out, she could have gained it rather more locally.

No, she had *moved* to London.

Freya hauled herself to the shower and then, having pulled on a robe, surveyed the contents of her fridge.

There wasn't much. She had meant to stop and pick up a few things on her way home. Now she had neither the energy nor the enthusiasm to go out again.

A knock on the door had her padding down the hall—she guessed it would be her neighbour, as their post got muddled on occasion.

Instead it was an unexpected sight for sore eyes.

Richard.

He'd had a haircut and was clean-shaven. And he was wearing a suit, but no tie, and he looked incredibly tired but still breathtakingly handsome.

'What are you doing here?' Freya asked.

He tried not to notice that she wore only a robe and that her hair was wet as he answered. 'We have a film to see.'

CHAPTER FIVE

'STELLA ASKED ME earlier if I'd enjoyed it...' said Richard.

'She asked me too.' Freya smiled. 'What did you say?'

'I said it was very good, and then I had the awful feeling I was going to be questioned further, but thankfully she had to rush off...'

'Yes, it's been one helluva day,' Freya said. 'How's Louise?'

'Critical.'

'I'm not a reporter, Richard. You can tell me how she really is.'

'She's very unstable. She's had a splenectomy and a Caesarean and has been given a lot of blood. It's going to be a very long night for her.'

'Poor thing.' She was about to let him in, but then she shook her head. 'To be honest, I'm not really in the mood to go out.'

'Fair enough.' Few women refused him, but he found it was rather refreshing. Richard liked her ways.

'We'll do the film another time, maybe?'

'Sure.'

Freya looked at him. He was a man she could never keep, but that didn't matter now. For in her heart Freya knew she would be leaving London soon.

'You can come in,' Freya said. 'If you want to.'

And Richard did want to.

He came through the door and Freya could feel his eyes on her bottom as she led him down the hallway.

His eyes *were* on her bottom—for a moment—but then he looked at the trail of moisture her hair had left on her robe, and then he looked down to her long, bare legs.

He didn't notice the mustard carpet, nor the curtains hanging too short, he simply noticed *her*. As he had from the very first day they had met.

They faced each other, and the want that had been there for a long time, certainly on the doorstep last night, seemed to have followed them into her flat.

'I'll go and get dressed.'

Please don't, Richard thought, but didn't say.

As if she could hear him Freya looked up into his eyes.

'If you disappear on me, at least I'll know what to tell the police,' he said.

'Sorry?'

'She was wearing a pale robe…'

'Oh.'

Freya didn't really understand, but there was a smoky edge to his voice, and as he further explained their eyes locked.

'I don't usually notice what women wear—well, not to the extent that I do with you.'

This morning Freya had regretted her sensible decision last night not to invite him in. Now she wanted to be reckless.

Richard felt as if he could see the barriers between them tumbling down before his eyes. And, yes, desire *did* reside behind her green gaze.

'What else was this woman in a pale robe wearing?' Freya asked. 'Slippers?'

'No,' Richard said, his eyes never leaving hers. For he

had already seen her painted toes. 'Her feet were bare and her hair was damp…' His hand came up and he picked up a heavy coil of black hair, as he had ached to do from day one. 'And,' he added, 'I'm quite sure she didn't have any underwear on…'

He watched her mouth part in a smile and lust punched like a fist as they teased and flirted and turned each other on.

'I wish you hadn't shaved,' she whispered as his mouth came to hers.

And then she changed her mind, because instead of rough kisses she got the tang of cologne and Richard's clean-shaven cheek against hers.

'Smooth can be good,' he told her as his hand slid behind her neck.

Her skin flared beneath his fingers and the feel of his cheek had her mouth searching for his.

But then he spoke. 'Freya…'

She frowned at the slight hesitation in his voice, for it was unfamiliar. He was always, *always* so confident and direct.

Freya pulled back her head and those gorgeous eyes of his awaited her.

Richard was not one to spoil the moment, but his conscience niggled and he wanted to make things absolutely clear to Freya. People could trust him with their lives, but not with their hearts, and he wanted to be sure she understood that before things went further.

'Don't rely on me.'

It was the oddest thing to say, perhaps, and yet the kindest.

'I get it, Richard.'

He wasn't going to be the cure for her loneliness. Richard Lewis wasn't going to be the love of her life.

Yesterday it might have mattered. But now she knew it didn't have to last for ever, or even for more than this night, because her time in London was finite. And she *wanted* this night with him.

It was Freya who moved to close the gap between their mouths. But it was definitely Richard who kissed her, softly at first, but warmly and thoroughly. Freya's mouth felt so exquisitely tender that even the gentlest of his kisses felt bruising.

The moan as his tongue slipped inside came from her. And then, for the first time since she'd arrived, London fell silent. Save for the sound of *them*.

His breathing was ragged and their mouths were frenzied. And surely he'd kissed the oxygen from her because he made her dizzy, and his tongue was so expert and thorough that it made her crave more of him.

His hands undid the belt of her robe. He freed one arm, then the other, and as it slid to the floor she felt cool air on the back of her body—a contrast to the warm rough fabric of his suit and the press of metal and buttons on her naked front.

Freya had never known such raw passion. Their tongues jostled and then she was pressing herself into him, her hands clutching his hair as his hands spanned her waist.

He guided them so that they moved to the wall as if as one. His kisses were certainly not smooth now—they were indecent and delicious and Freya was lost in them. Their chins bumped, their teeth clashed. She wanted to climb him and wrap her body around him.

Freya was tackling his belt, to free him, and then she felt his hard warmth leap towards her hand.

Richard reached into his jacket pocket for a condom, and it was an impatient pause for them both as he sheathed himself. She ached to have him inside her, and he ached to be there too.

And so he rectified things, thrusting in and taking her against the wall.

Freya had never been so thoroughly taken, and it felt sublime. He lifted her so that her legs could wrap around him and she knew she had never moved so seductively. He exposed a side to her that she did not recognise, because she had always been a touch reticent in bed.

Not now.

His fingers dug into her buttocks as she ground against him, and instead of feeling herself holding back, she was *more* herself with him.

She was so light that he could put one hand against the wall and hold her round her waist with the other. And then he changed the pace…

There was a scream building in her throat, which was clamped closed, so it waited there, trying to burst free. And then there came a breathless shout from him, followed by a rush of energy along her spine as he came deep within her. Finally her scream found its release, but it came out in staccato sobs as she throbbed to his beat.

His hands soothed now, rather than inflamed, and he seemed to know that this wasn't a Freya she knew.

And it wasn't.

Her head came to his shoulder and she felt the fabric of his jacket. He was completely dressed, and she was utterly naked. And now there was a smidgen of shame creeping in for Freya—just a curl of guilt as he lowered her down to the floor, yet still held her tightly.

He buried his head in her damp hair and then she felt his lips near her ear. 'I only wanted a cup of tea.'

Richard made her laugh. He just did.

Having sorted out his clothes, he picked up her robe

and helped her into it, then did up the very same belt she had so readily allowed him to open.

They were both still a touch breathless, still trying to find their balance again,—but, *God*, they felt better.

She went and sat on the sofa, where she'd been lying earlier. Richard looked utterly normal—not even particularly dishevelled. His hair fell into perfect shape, whereas Freya was quite sure hers was in knots.

But she didn't care.

He came and joined her on the sofa, and though they didn't speak it wasn't awkward. It was nice to lie down with her head on his lap, looking up at him as he played with her hair. It was relaxing *not* to speak.

He looked around at her flat and saw for the first time the mustard carpet and odd curtains. Even odder, though, was the fact that there was nothing that spoke of *her*.

Well, there were some books and magazines on a shelf, but there was a large picture on the wall of a horse and carriage, and he was certain it hadn't been wrapped in a blanket and lovingly moved down from Scotland.

'Do you like horses, Freya?' he asked.

'Not particularly. Why?'

'There's a picture of one on your wall.'

She looked over to where his gaze fell. 'I know. I can't get it down.'

Well, that wasn't quite true. Freya had a little step ladder, which she'd used when she'd re-hung the curtains, but she simply hadn't got around to taking the horse and cart picture down. It wasn't as if she had anything to replace it with. It would do for now.

And, anyway, there were far better things to look at. Gosh, it was nice to lie there, Freya thought, looking up at Richard.

And for Richard it was nice too—nice to feel her hair, because it had entranced him.

He looked down, but not into her eyes. Her robe was hanging open a little, and he could see the curve of her breast and the edge of a pink areola beckoning. He wanted to slip his hand in...

But sustenance first.

'I'm starving.'

He wasn't asking her to cook for him—a bowl of cereal was his usual choice when in a rush, and he *was* in a rush. To resume proceedings!

He hauled her off his lap and walked through to her tiny kitchen, where he opened up the cupboards while Freya lay there, liking it that he hadn't asked if he could do so.

Usually that would have made her tense. She recalled well how she had sucked in a breath when she had bought her little cottage and Malcolm had opened her fridge. But now she lay smiling as Richard opened and closed her cupboards.

'You have absolutely nothing to eat,' Richard said when he came back. 'Not even cereal.'

'I meant to stop at the shops on the way home from work. I think there's some soup...'

'That's not going to cut it. Come on,' he said. 'Get dressed.'

'We could always ring for pizza,' Freya suggested.

He was tempted. There was a huge appeal in the thought of having pizza delivered and then moving straight to bed. And he had seen from his search of the fridge that there was a bottle of wine there.

A perfect evening.

Except—rarely for him—the pleasure was laced with guilt.

Did she fully get that he didn't *do* the dating thing?

He wasn't that bad—it wasn't *all* bed. Just…mostly.

He had come here tonight fully intending to take Freya to that damned film—which was actually quite a concession for him. Richard couldn't remember the last time he had been to the cinema.

But now he had to be clear. Richard wanted to make sure that she didn't think this might lead to anything more than a few casual dates and a whole lot of bed.

While he hoped he had spelled things out yesterday—and although getting pizza and going straight to bed would be easier and far more pleasant—Richard knew that he needed to tell her that this night wouldn't change anything.

Yet clearly it was going to.

For they were soon back at the Italian restaurant—but as lovers this time.

CHAPTER SIX

TONIGHT IT WAS Richard who had the carbonara.

Freya chose spaghetti, and it came with a rich, meaty tomato sauce.

'You did it again,' Richard said.

'What?'

'When I saw your carbonara last night I regretted my choice...' And then he stopped, because he'd been about to say that next time they came here the spaghetti with the rich, meaty tomato sauce was what he'd want.

But he didn't.

Instead he remembered he was off work tomorrow and ordered a bottle of red.

'I don't like drinking if I'm working the next day,' he explained. 'But I've got a few days off now.'

'And me.' Freya smiled.

He wondered if she was waiting for him to suggest they do something together.

Ah yes, *The Talk*, Richard reminded himself.

Except Freya got there first.

'I'm going home for a couple of days before a stint on nights,' she said. 'I've got a new lot of tenants arriving at my cottage next week.'

'Holidaymakers?' Richard said.

'Yes, they're there for two weeks and then I've another

lot coming in. I've arranged for someone to come in and clean, and change the sheets and things, but I just need to sort a few things out.'

'Don't you hate having people staying at your house?'

'I've put a lot of stuff in the cellar,' Freya said. 'And that's locked. It doesn't bother me.'

'But isn't it a hassle?'

'Not really.' Freya shrugged. 'And even if it is at times, then it's worth it. It helps a lot with the mortgage, though in a couple of months it's going on the market...' Freya halted.

Or was it?

She recalled that just before Richard had arrived her plans had started to change. She needed to be alone to think about that, to decide what she was going to do, and so she asked about him instead.

'What about you? Do you have plans?'

'I have an interview.'

'Ah, that explains the haircut,' Freya said as she twirled spaghetti around her fork.

'Not really. I was well overdue for that. It's not an interview as such—more an informal lunch to suss things out...'

He let out a sigh and promptly forgot the reason he had brought her here. Instead he told her what tomorrow was about. No-one else knew.

'There's a role coming up.'

'I thought you loved what you do?'

'And I do, but it *is* consuming. I'm actually heading to the airport after the lunch. I'm going to Moscow tomorrow for a few nights, to get away completely.'

'Moscow?'

'It's a bit drastic, I know, but I love getting away. I don't put my phone on, so the hospital can't call me to come in—or if they do I don't hear it.'

'Well, you don't need to go all the way to Moscow for that. There are more than a few places in Scotland where you can't get a signal.'

'Please…' He grinned. 'I was teasing about changing the movie reels.'

'I know you were,' Freya agreed. 'But, trust me, there really are plenty of places you can't get a signal. I went away for Christmas with my family last year and we all had to keep going for walks just so we could make a call, or check emails and things. And in summer, depending on what provider they have, the tourists often can't get a good signal. We have a wee laugh, watching them walking around with their phones in the air.'

'Well, I'll bear that in mind,' Richard said.

'So, are you keen for this job?'

'I'm curious, certainly.'

He told her the name of a very exclusive private hospital which made her look up from her pasta.

'I've a friend, Marcus, who's director of anaesthetics there, and there's a position coming up—a very attractive one…' He didn't get to finish, for Freya had a question.

'But won't you miss the adrenaline?'

'Yes,' he said. 'But there are days when I think no, I won't miss it at all. It's a big decision—but you'd know all about that, given you've just made a big move yourself.'

Freya gave a shrug. 'I just knew that I wanted to get away.'

He looked at her through slightly narrowed, assessing eyes. 'Why?'

'Lots of reasons,' Freya said. 'I had a bit of a rough year. Well, not myself, exactly…' She didn't know why it was so hard simply to say it. 'My best friend lost a baby last year… Andrew.'

'Were you present at the birth?' Richard asked.

'Not at the actual birth, but I was there on admission.'
Freya said. 'Alison ended up having a crash Caesarean.
She came in a week before her due date, everything about
the pregnancy had been fine, and then I went to check the
foetal heart-rate…' She paused a moment as she recalled
it. 'At first I thought I had picked up Alison's…'

She didn't, of course, need to explain to him that the
mother's heart-rate was usually a lot slower than the baby's.

'But then I knew the heart-rate was the baby's…'

'Not good.'

'No.' She shook her head. 'My senior, Betty, was there,
and a doctor was there within a minute, and everything
was set in motion. We got her straight upstairs to Theatre.
I didn't go in. Betty knew I was too involved. He was born
flat and was resuscitated but died two days later. Cord
compression and meconium aspiration…' Freya screwed
her eyes closed for just a second but then opened them
and gave an uncomfortable shrug. 'Anyway, it was a difficult time.'

'Did she blame you?'

'Oh, no—nothing like that. It was more…' Freya didn't
know how to describe how she'd felt when she didn't really know herself.

'You blamed yourself?'

'A bit,' Freya said. 'Well, I questioned myself. It made
me realise that being so involved with my patients isn't
always ideal.'

'So you came to nice, anonymous London?'

'It wasn't just because of that,' Freya said, 'but it is nice
to be not so involved with the patients.'

'I'm sorry—you don't get to do a job like yours and
not get involved.'

'It's not that easy…'

'I never said anything about *easy*.'

That annoyed her. Richard was too brusque, too direct, and he had hit a nerve.

'You don't know me.'

'I'm trying to.'

It was a rare admission for him, because while he might be talking about getting involved professionally, he certainly did his best not to on the personal front.

'You cannot do this job, Freya, and not care. Or rather, you cannot do this job in the way you want to do it and not care.'

He signalled for the bill and then remembered that they still hadn't had *The Talk*.

It didn't seem so important now. Freya was off to Scotland tomorrow and he to Moscow. And she certainly wasn't jumping up and down demanding to know when they would see each other again as they headed to the Underground.

'You really don't have to see me home,' Freya said.

'I'm not,' Richard said. 'I believe in equality—it's your turn to see me to my door.'

CHAPTER SEVEN

UH-OH!

Freya woke to a very un-lumpy mattress—in fact, she felt as if she was wrapped in cotton wool. And then she heard Richard speaking into the phone.

Her one and only one-night stand was over.

And, instead of regretting it, she smiled as she lay there, recalling last night.

They had arrived back at his gorgeous apartment and he'd poured them a drink and headed off for a shower.

She'd ended up in there with him.

And then they'd taken their drinks to bed.

Oh, it had been bliss.

She lay there listening to his lovely deep voice.

'No, I'm away until Tuesday, so I can't,' he said. 'How is Mrs Eames?'

As soon as the call ended, his phone went again.

'No,' he said, very brusquely. 'You cannot come and stay.'

Freya wondered if it was an ex, trying to get her toes back past the bedroom door, but she blinked when he spoke again.

'Mother, I have a friend staying at the flat while I'm away.' Pause. 'I *do*. Currently she's living in a terrible rental and I've loaned her the place for a few days. So, no, you can't come and stay. If you need a break from your fiancé then I suggest that perhaps you actually speak to him about that fact, rather than go away.'

Another pause and Freya rolled over and looked at him, not even politely attempting to pretend she was asleep.

'What do you mean, you don't believe me?' he said. 'Freya, would you tell my mother that my place is yours for a few days?'

Gosh, what a way to meet the parents, Freya thought as he handed her his phone.

'Hello, Mrs…' Freya didn't know what to call her, given she had divorced Mr Lewis three husbands ago.

'Amanda,' the woman said for her. 'So you're staying at Richard's?'

'Just for a wee while,' Freya said. 'While my landlord's sorting…'

'Pardon?' his mother said.

Richard took back the phone.

'So you see there is no spare room at the inn. I'll talk to you when I'm back from Moscow.'

He ended the call and his phone rang yet again.

'Work,' he muttered, and Freya didn't blame him a bit when he turned it off.

'Thanks for that!' Freya said with an edge, more than a little annoyed to have been put in that position and at his jab about her home.

'I never said you were my lover,' he pointed out, 'just that my apartment wasn't free. Anyway, she can afford a hotel.'

'Fair enough.' Freya said, but she was still sulking a little.

'I am *so* tired of her dramas.'

Freya said nothing.

'Can you see why I've been put off relationships for life?'

'I think so.' Freya nodded. He was *almost* forgiven. 'How's Louise?' she asked.

'Mrs Eames?' he checked. 'She's made it through the night and is holding her own. She's a lot better than yesterday at least.' He looked over. 'Do you want some breakfast or are you still cross?'

'Still cross,' Freya said and told him why. 'My flat isn't terrible.'

'I just said that as an excuse to my mother. She's hardly going to drop in and see it.'

'I guess…'

She let it go, and she decided he was completely forgiven when he got out of bed and returned with coffee, and toast topped with grapefruit marmalade.

Or was it the fact that she simply had to know more about this man?

'Were she and your father ever happy?' Freya asked as they ate their breakfast and got crumbs in his gorgeous bed.

'I think so. But she wanted a livelier social life and he is rather wedded to his job. She gave him an ultimatum and it backfired, I fear, because he chose work.'

'Your father married again?'

'Yes—his housekeeper. Or rather the woman who had been *their* housekeeper, so you can imagine how well that went down. My mother was convinced there had been something going on all along…' He rolled his eyes and then, putting his plate down, moved to take her mug. 'Can we talk about *our* sex-life instead, please?'

'But your parents' sex-life is so much more interesting!'

'Then I must be losing my touch.'

They made each other laugh and then, to Freya's surprise, and seemingly to Richard's, instead of taking her mug he lay back on the pillows and told her some more.

'She walked out when I was fifteen—a couple of days after their twentieth wedding anniversary. My father wasn't giving her the attention she felt she deserved. He had a terminally ill patient and had had to cancel their anniversary trip. I felt terrible for my father after the break-up—he just moped around. Then, just when I was starting my "A" Levels, he announced he was marrying Vera.'

'The housekeeper?'

'Yes. And the following summer my mother married an old friend of my father's. A more glamorous version of him, really.'

'What happened to him?'

'She left him after five years, and after that I kind of tuned out. Now all I know is that she's engaged to Roger.'

'Have you met him?'

'Yes—a couple of dinners. He's a cosmetic dentist.' He pulled a face.

'What's wrong with being a cosmetic dentist?'

'Nothing. I just feel his eyes on my mouth every time we speak. I think he's trying to work out if I've got crowns. In *my* line of work we just ask!'

He looked over to Freya and gave her a very nice smile that showed stunningly even teeth.

'And *do* you have crowns?'

'Two—thanks to rugby.'

She looked right back at him, and as she did so she thought about him asking his patients about their dental work before he put them under. She looked into his eyes and Freya understood why patients so clearly trusted him.

Because *she* trusted him.

Of course she didn't know him very well yet, but that much she knew. And, Freya thought as they stared at each other, if she were terrified and scared for her life, or her baby's, his would be the eyes she would want to see.

No, she would never regret this. In the twelve hours since their lips had first met she had come alive to her body in a way she never had before.

She wanted to put down her mug and reach for his kiss. Or at the very least to ask him what day he'd get back from his trip, in the hope that she could see him. But then she recalled their rules, and peeled back the sheet rather than leaning in to his embrace.

'I'd better go. I have a train to catch.'

'What time?'

'Ten.'

'Then there's plenty of time.'

'No, I need to get back to mine to pack.'

'Fair enough,' Richard said.

He lay there with his hands behind his head as she dressed. He kept his mouth firmly closed.

It was deliberate, because a long weekend in Scotland with Freya sounded tempting rather than flying to Moscow by himself and cramming in some sightseeing.

'Have a great trip,' Freya said.

'I will.' He put out his hand and she came and sat down on the bed.

'And good luck with your lunch,' she added.

'Thanks.'

It wasn't awkward when she left. More, it felt...*unfinished*.

Freya thought about him more than she ought as her train slid its way northwards.

It was packed, and there were no seats in the quiet carriage, so Freya put in her earbuds and tried to listen to music—but every song sounded as if it had been written about *them*. So she gave up with the music and chatted to the woman in the seat beside her.

She was a fellow Scot, so neither had to say *sorry*, or *I beg your pardon* once, and Freya found out from her that on weekends and public holidays you could sometimes get a cheap upgrade to First Class.

'I'll remember that,' Freya said, and then gazed out of the window and watched the rolling countryside. The clouds gathered and right on cue, as they crossed the border at Berwick-upon-Tweed, she saw grey skies and rain,

It made her smile.

The train travelled the rugged Scottish coastline, eating up the miles until they reached Edinburgh Castle. It was dark and powerful and towering over them, and her first glimpse of it in what felt like a long time caused Freya's heart to swell.

The train pulled into Waverley Station and it felt very good to be home. The station was busy as she checked the board for the next train to Cromayr Bay and saw that she had half an hour to kill.

Freya decided to buy some flowers for her little cottage, to brighten things up. As she was paying she could hear her phone beeping, and assumed it was Alison, or her mother, checking on what time her train would get in.

She nearly dropped the phone when she saw that it was Richard.

Lunch went well. I'll have my phone off for a few days now, but just wanted to say that I hope you have a nice break.

No kisses or fun little emojis. No clues to anything, really—but even getting a text was more than she had expected.

Freya hadn't expected anything. She'd hoped that she

might see him again—of course she had—but this simple text... Well, it confused her. This didn't fit with how he had said it would be.

She honestly didn't know how to respond.

A part of her wanted to fire back smiley faces and pictures of tartan berets and Russian hats—just to keep it all light and breezy. Yet light and breezy wasn't how she felt when it came to Richard.

And so, when most women would be firing off a rapid response to a text from Richard Lewis, Freya—because she didn't know how to respond—instead sent the promised text to Alison, and then stuffed her phone back in her bag.

Freya had no intention of telling people about Richard. Certainly she wouldn't be telling her parents. While Freya adored them, her mother Jean loved 'a wee natter', and—as Freya well knew—nothing stayed a secret in Cromayr Bay for very long.

Alison was a different matter. And she was there waiting when Freya got out at Cromayr Bay.

The clouds had parted and the sky was high and blue, and Alison was smiling widely as she waved to her.

'Look at you!' Freya smiled, because in the weeks that Freya had been away Alison had changed and was now sporting a lovely little bump.

'I know!' Her friend smiled back. 'Betty said that you can sometimes show a lot more quickly the second time around.'

Betty had clearly said easily what Freya hadn't been able to. And still Freya did not know why.

She had been dwelling on it for months now, and had even discussed it with Richard, but still she had a huge block when it came to speaking about the loss with her friend.

'I booked us a table at the Tavern for tonight,' Alison said as she drove her home.

'In the *restaurant*?' Freya checked, because usually they went for a curry, or just to the Tavern's bar. The restaurant was pricey, and rather grand, but she had heard right.

'Yes, it's closing for renovations next week. They're going to put a function room in at the top, and they're refurbishing the restaurant.'

Freya didn't like the sound of that—she loved it as it was.

'The bar's staying open, as well as the hotel, but I thought you might want to see the restaurant as it is one more time.'

Oh, she really did.

They took the hilly street approach and, rarely for summer, there was a parking spot close to Freya's cottage. They pulled in behind her little purple car.

'Do you want to come in?' Freya offered, but Alison shook her head.

'I've got to go and do a shop—I'll meet you in the Tavern bar at seven.'

'I'll see you there, then.'

'It's good to have you home, Freya.'

It was good to be here, Freya thought as she pushed open the door.

The drapes had been closed by Mrs Hunt after the last tenants, and Freya went around opening them up and letting in the late-afternoon sun. Then she turned on the hot water and caught up on her mail while she waited for it to warm.

And she did all she could not to think too much of Richard and what had happened last night.

She wouldn't be telling Alison. At least she didn't know whether or not to tell her.

Alison and Callum had been childhood sweethearts. And Freya wasn't sure her friend would understand.

Freya herself didn't understand.

She liked it that there was no risk of getting overly involved with Richard.

The break-up with Malcolm had been tricky. He'd kept messaging and coming round, turning up wherever she went, wanting to talk, to see if they could give it another go.

Well, she wouldn't be having that problem with Richard!

It was rather freeing.

It was nice to dress up and go out. She hadn't brought much with her, but she had a nice copper-coloured dress, and with heels it was dressy enough. Her hair was still rather wild from going to bed with it damp last night, so Freya wore it up and then added a dash of lipstick.

She glanced at her phone as she put the lipstick back in her bag, and then decided she'd do well to leave the phone at home, to prevent herself from replying to Richard.

She had no idea what she would say anyway.

Freya headed to the Tavern bar, and she felt herself tense a little as she walked inside. It was Friday night in Cromayr Bay, and that meant there was a fair chance Malcolm would be there. But thankfully there was no sign of him, and a moment or two later Alison arrived.

The Tavern really was gorgeous—a boutique hotel just off the main street, it was set high on a hill and offered a stunning version of Freya's favourite view of the Firth.

They climbed the steps to the restaurant and were shown to their seats by a waitress. Then Gordon, the owner, came over.

'Are you two here for a last trip down memory lane?'

'Something like that.' Freya smiled.

'I remember you coming here when you passed your midwifery exams—och, and for your eighteenth too...'

'I'm going to miss the old place.' Alison sighed.

'Well, hopefully you'll love the new one just as much,' Gordon said, and then he talked them through the menu.

They made their choices—which was tough, because there was lobster brought in from the pots just that afternoon, and there was Dornoch lamb, as well as Freya's favourite, game pie. But she'd had that the last time she was here...

'I'm going to have the lamb, please,' Freya said.

'And I'll have the spelt and mushroom risotto,' Alison said.

Freya had wine, and Alison a mocktail, and they chatted about Freya's move to London.

'So, have you made any friends there yet?' Alison asked.

'Not really,' Freya admitted. 'They're very cliquey...' she started. Only that wasn't quite right. They were all very nice. 'I don't know what it is. I try, I just don't seem to fit in. Richard says I'm too subtle.'

'Richard?'

'A friend,' Freya said.

'So you *have* made one.'

'A temporary one.' Freya said. 'He's being interviewed for a plum new job in a private hospital.'

'In London?' Alison checked.

Freya nodded. 'And he'll get it—he's brilliant.'

'Well, if it's in London that doesn't have to stop you from being friends. So you *do* have one.'

'I guess...'

Alison smirked, because she knew Freya well, and from

the little flush on her cheeks it was clear to her he was more than just a friend.

'It's just a temporary thing,' said Freya.

'Why?'

'Because temporary is all he does.'

'But that's not like you.' Alison frowned.

'Well, maybe it is. Look, we've been out a couple of times, and both of us know that it won't be going any further, and that actually suits me just fine.'

'Why?' Alison asked again.

'It just does,' Freya said, and gave an uncomfortable shrug.

She wasn't ready to tell Alison she was thinking of coming home for good once her contract was up, but thankfully then their meals arrived.

The lamb was delectable and the conversation became easier. Alison chatted about her and Callum's tenth wedding anniversary, which was soon coming up.

'Can you believe it?'

'Not really.' Freya laughed. 'It feels like just a couple of years ago that I was your bridesmaid.'

'Are you coming home for your thirtieth?' Alison asked.

'I think so,' Freya said. 'Though I'm doing all I can not to think about that.'

They had a wonderful night catching up. Although not about the things that hurt.

As Freya walked down the hill for home the air was salty, and despite the late hour the sky was still dusky. It was so much lighter here than in London. But autumn would soon close in.

It was one of the reasons she'd come home.

Tomorrow she had to speak to the estate agent about house prices and things, as soon the families renting for summer breaks would fade away and her little slice of potential heaven would be going on the market.

It would be a relief, Freya told herself. The rentals covered the mortgage, but there was a lot of work to be done on her home.

A lot.

She let herself in and smiled at the pretty flowers she'd set by the window. Then she made herself a hot chocolate, frothing the milk in her coffee machine, and took herself to bed.

Freya rarely closed the curtains. There was nothing between her little cottage and the water, and the sight of the bridges always had her in awe. They were miles away, of course, but it looked as if fairy lights had been expertly strung in the sky, and the new Queensferry Crossing was magnificent.

Tomorrow she was catching up with a few friends, and then there was a huge Sunday dinner at her parents' house to look forward to.

And then she thought about Alison and what she'd said about 'temporary' not usually suiting her. Perhaps now it did.

She took out her phone and read again the text he had sent.

Freya liked Richard.

A lot.

From the moment she had first seen him he had captivated her.

Yet she wanted to keep things breezy and light.

Or rather, she *had* to.

And not just because Richard Lewis had told her that it was the only way they could be. It was also because this place was home. Not London.

Freya had made up her mind now—she would not be selling her home.

* * *

He'd noticed her lack of response to his text.

Of course he had.

Richard had been moving through Security at Heathrow when he'd fired it off, and had regretted the simple message the second after he'd hit 'send'.

He did not report in to *anyone*—certainly not about things like interviews—and, furthermore, he loathed the cascade of texts that all too often came when he was seeing someone.

When he'd collected his phone on the other side of Security he'd seen that she hadn't responded.

Good, he'd told himself. A mistake had been made, but a lesson had been learnt, he'd decided as he had boarded the plane.

'Phones to be turned off now, please,' the steward said, but Richard had checked his again before he did so.

Four hours later, as he stood at Moscow airport, even though the very reason for his trip was to get away from the constant buzz of pagers and phones, he found himself turning it on.

No, she had not replied.

Freya could not have known the effect on him.

It made him want her more.

And that did not sit well with Richard.

CHAPTER EIGHT

'How was Moscow?'

This time it was Freya who put her tray down at his table in the canteen. It was morning—just after seven—and he was eating cereal.

Unlike her, though, he was starting his day rather than at the tail-end of a shift.

They hadn't really spoken since she had got back. Freya was just finishing a two-week stint on nights and their rosters hadn't crossed.

'Beautiful,' Richard said. 'But far from relaxing. All the signs are in Russian.'

'I wonder why!'

'Still, it was nice to get away. How was Scotland?'

'I had a great time. It flew by, though.'

'Have you finished on nights?' He frowned, because it was odd to see her down here at this time of the morning.

'Officially I have.' Freya nodded. 'But there's a twin pregnancy to deliver soon.'

Freya was lacking in experience there, as the birthing centre at home didn't accept multiple pregnancies. So she was more than happy to stay back—especially as through the night she had got to know Jeanette and her partner.

'Stella just came on, and she suggested I go and get

something to eat. Then she and Dr Mina are going to hold my hand, so to speak.'

Neither mentioned catching up with each other again. Some things were best left, Richard had decided.

He liked her a lot—perhaps because he couldn't quite read her. She was private, and he liked that. And her eyes could be sullen at times, but then she punched out a smile...

All Richard knew was that he liked her a whole lot more than he was comfortable with.

'Your interview went well?' Freya checked, alluding to the text she hadn't responded to.

'It was just lunch.'

He offered no more, for he had already told her more than he should. Yet deep down he knew she wouldn't have told anyone his potential news. He'd never have shared it with her otherwise.

Richard hadn't expected to be as impressed as he was by the private hospital set-up. The hours were far fewer, though he could take on more if he chose, and he would have considerably more annual leave.

'It would be a step up—a big one.'

'A step back too,' Freya said. 'From the pace here.'

It wasn't a criticism. She looked at him and could see his exhaustion, and then she looked down at the pile of cereal with which he fuelled his day.

She looked up again, at the closed look on his face, and knew she should not have come over. It wasn't just their rosters that had kept them apart. He was politely avoiding her.

Thankfully, this time around it was her pager that interrupted them. 'Woohoo!' Freya said as she glanced down and read the message it was time for her to go back up to Maternity. 'Wish me luck.'

She didn't wait around to hear him do so. Instead, she

made her speedy way along the yellow line to Maternity and pushed the gorgeous Richard Lewis out of her mind.

Having washed her hands, she headed into D4.

'You've been busy,' Freya said to Jeanette as she tied on a plastic gown. 'Well done, you.'

The next hour was sheer hard work for Jeanette and she did it brilliantly. Freya made sure there was no trace of tiredness in her own reactions.

The room started to fill up. Guy Masters and his registrar came—one for each baby—as well as Stella and Kelly.

'Listen to Freya,' Dr Mina said as Jeanette started to panic.

'You're almost there,' Freya encouraged. 'A big one now...'

She had never delivered twins before, but with so much experience in the room she didn't feel at all scared. And as Twin One was delivered onto Jeanette's stomach there was a sense of elation.

Yet there was more work still to do.

'Is she okay?' Jeanette kept asking over her baby's cries.

'She's wonderful,' Kelly said. 'Dad, do you want to cut the cord?'

With Twin One in Kelly's extremely capable hands Freya prepared to deliver Twin Two. The baby was in a good position, and Freya looked up and saw that Jeanette was starting to push.

'Well done,' Freya said. 'Jeanette, you are doing *so* well...' Being a midwife was such a privilege, she thought. 'Okay, I need another big push.'

And then Twin Two was there, a little stunned and straight off to Stella, and soon there was the delicious sound of two babies crying.

'Well done,' Dr Mina said quietly to Freya.

'Thank you.'

There was still the single placenta to come, and when it did both Freya and Dr Mina carefully examined it and checked the membranes.

Soon the room was clear. The paediatric team were happy, and Stella and Kelly had dashed off. Everything was under control here.

They were utterly adorable, Freya thought as she helped Jeanette feed her twins one by one. Once Jeanette was on the ward and wasn't feeling so shaky she would be helped to feed them both at the same time, but for now they lay in their mother's arms one at a time.

'You were completely wonderful.' Freya smiled.

'So were you,' said Jeanette.

Freya was feeling a little shaky herself after her first twin birth. She wrote up her notes and filled in all the paperwork, but the words blurred a little on the page.

Because of tears.

She was tired, that was all, Freya told herself as she pressed her fingers into her eyes. She was tired and over-emotional. And now that the birth was over she could take her thoughts back to the canteen, and to the ending of her and Richard.

Oh, but she'd been warned. Not just by Stella but by the man himself.

'Home?' Stella gently asked.

'Yes.'

Freya stood and made her way to the changing rooms. And suddenly, coming down from the L&D theatre, there he was.

'How did it go?'

'It was brilliant.' She smiled deliberately.

'Have a well-earned sleep, now.'

'Thanks.'

And that was it, Freya thought as she closed the door.

They were back to niceties on passing in the corridor and no more.

She peeled off her baggy top as she started to change so she could finally go home. But then came a knock on the door.

'Freya...?'

She lifted her top to cover herself, and then didn't know why she needed to bother, given it was him.

He wanted to apologise—to tell her the problem was him, not her—but they didn't get there.

Richard never brought any personal awkwardness to work. He had his pickings, but he never allowed things to get awkward *here*.

Yet suddenly they were kissing.

Deep, frantic kisses.

She found out that his rough unshaven jaw was possibly her preference over the clean-shaven version. And then he was thumbing her nipples through her bra.

'Not here...' he said, even as he pressed into her.

He had moved from her mouth and was kissing her neck, and his hand was creeping into the back of her navy trousers.

The scent of him was potent and she found his mouth again and...

Oh, God, she was nearly coming.

'Not here,' he said again, and sort of shoved her off him.

It was probably just as well, or they'd have been on the floor of the changing room, where anybody could walk in.

They both breathed through it and waited for it pass, but it was a couple of minutes before Richard was ready to head back out there.

'I'll text you about tonight,' Richard said.

Freya noted that he didn't sound happy or flirty or teasing. He sounded frustrated. As if it was *her* fault for the situation they were in, when it had been Richard who had followed her in here.

'And answer my text this time, Freya.'

CHAPTER NINE

BOTH OF THEM kept waiting for the bubble to burst.

Yet it didn't.

They tended to end up at his place, but one morning two months into *them*, and three months after Freya had moved to London, Freya stirred on her lumpy bed with Richard spooned in behind her.

It should be over with by now, she knew. Freya was waiting for Richard to discard her with the practised ease he was known for.

And, oh, it would hurt.

It would hurt like hell.

London would be lonely without him. Friends had proved very hard to come by, and the pace of the work still completely floored her. She missed being more involved with the mothers, and found she craved the community that had felt too small.

Freya was homesick.

For home, for family and friends.

Apart from during her time with Richard—which was wonderful, of course—Freya ached for home.

She was starting to do what he'd told her not to.

She was starting to rely on him.

And while Freya waited to be summarily dumped, Richard waited, as Freya had once said, for the very curl of her hair to irk him.

For the gloss to fade.

For the joy to wear off.

But it hadn't. It didn't.

If anything, it had intensified.

He lifted her hair and in the darkness could see her pale skin. He pushed down the sheet.

It was a cold mid-October morning and she shivered, both from the chill of the air and also the heat as he ran a finger down her spine.

And then he brought his tongue to her neck.

He slipped a hand under her so he could play with her breast, and she groaned as he toyed with her nipple.

'Wake up,' he whispered.

'I don't want to,' Freya whispered back. 'I'm having a lovely dream.'

She could feel him hard against her thighs, so she parted them a little and he slipped between their warmth.

He really should reach for a condom. But this was so nice...

He probed between her thighs, teasing, rubbing, caressing the edges of her intimate space without pushing in.

Freya knew she should halt things. Yes, she was on the Pill, but that wasn't the point. They had made no promises to each other—just sex for as long as they both wanted it.

But then there were the dinners and the breakfasts. and the talking into the small hours at times.

Though there was little talking now...

But, ever the sensible playboy, he did not slip into her inviting warmth. He pulled away from between her thighs and Freya lay with her eyes screwed closed in frustration as he sheathed himself.

She was losing her head—Freya knew that. And she dared not check her heart.

He came back to his previous position and groaned, '*God*, Freya,' as he slipped in.

She was so ready and tight, and pre-dawn sex had never felt better. He filled her and stretched her, and his body wrapped around hers felt like a blissful vice. He toyed with her breast in the way she had come to adore.

They moved in delicious unison, their bodies tuned to each other, pressing together until they found their climax.

They lay on their backs on her lumpy mattress, both sated and breathless, but when the near-miss with the condom came to her mind Freya gave him a scolding.

'We have to be more careful.'

But he hadn't *wanted* to be careful, and, Richard knew, neither had she.

'We'll talk about it.'

'No,' Freya said, 'we already have.'

She was not sleeping with someone who had told her never to rely on him without a condom.

And yet Richard was starting to rely on her in a way he had never considered he might.

Life felt a whole lot better with Freya in it.

Yes, work was crazy, but there was a counter-balance to it now, and he needed far fewer trips overseas to get away from the pressure.

Instead, he looked forward to the end of a work-day and to nights spent with her.

He didn't like coming *here* so much, mind… He didn't like her poky flat. But last night he hadn't finished until midnight, and he had hardly been able to ask her to hop on the Tube and come to his place. Or give her a key and tell her to come to his at the end of her shift and let herself in.

Surely it was way too soon for that? And, anyway, he'd sworn never to get so involved.

Yet more and more he found he was.

It was Richard who broke the silence. 'Marcus is pushing me for an answer on the new job.'

'And have you decided what you want to do?'

'Not yet. It would mean starting in the New Year.'

'That's ages away.'

'It will be November in a couple of weeks,' he pointed out. 'And I'd have to give a month's notice—more if possible. So if I want some time off between jobs then I need to give him an answer soon.'

'Which way are you leaning?'

'I'm still not sure,' Richard admitted. 'The private work would be at a slower pace, and seriously more money...'

'But you *love* what you do.'

'I know that, but...' He ground down on his jaw.

He wanted her take on things, but whenever he broached it with Freya she asked only what *he* wanted to do. And, while he liked it that Freya never put any kind of pressure on him, he kind of needed her view on this.

Because it might affect her.

God, he thought. He was staring up at the ceiling and wanting someone else's input into his future because he was starting to think, to *hope*, that the 'someone else' might be involved in it.

He thought it better not to say anything just yet, though. He really needed to think this through, and he needed to get the hell out of here before he went and said something stupid.

He had always been incredibly focused where work was concerned, and independent in his choices too. This way of thinking was a huge shift for him, and lying in the warmth of her bed it would be all too easy to offer her his keys, to move her in, because he did not want her here in this horrible flat.

He wanted her at his home.

'I'm going to go,' Richard said.

'There's still an hour before you have to leave.'

'Yes, but I want to have a shower...'

'Have one here.' Freya frowned.

'I don't like your shower, Freya,' Richard said, and climbed from the bed.

Ooh, what was that all about? Freya pondered as Richard dressed. He was in an odd mood, and as he went to leave he gave her only a brief kiss on the cheek—more like a family member might at a gathering, rather than a lover who had just left her bed.

Freya could not let it go. 'Thanks, Uncle Richard.'

'What?' He frowned.

'That's the sort of kiss my uncle gives me,' she said, and looked at him with accusing eyes.

He smiled, because he couldn't help but smile when she was around, and because she was such a snarky thing that he was tempted to dress her, pack a case and haul her back to his place.

For good.

'We'll talk tonight,' Richard said. 'You're on a late?'

'Yes.'

'Well, I finish at six, but I'll stay back and then we can go to mine.'

He walked out of her flat and Freya heard the slam of the door. She lay there, not quite so brave now.

Richard wanted to talk.

To Freya that could only spell one thing.

They were done.

She had known the winds would change eventually, and that one day he'd tire and Rita the domestic would be reaching under a bed with a broom for her soon to be discarded heart.

She had been duly warned.

Freya had sworn to herself that when the time came she would be ready for it and fully prepared to deal with it. Except she hadn't factored in how deeply feelings could be etched. Never had she felt such kinship with someone. And as she got up and pulled back the curtains a world without Richard in it suddenly looked a lot less friendly than even a cold grey day in London.

She showered and told herself she was overreacting. Of *course* Richard wanted to go home to shower—because hers was horrible, with dark green tiles, and the water ran cold for ages before you could get in. And the shower curtain needed to be replaced.

She had meant to get another one, but she was always running out of time in between work and Richard. Still, after her shift today she had two days off. She would get on with sorting out the flat then.

God, imagine being here without him, Freya thought as she sat on the Underground and looked at the endless faces that refused to acknowledge her and the eyes that flicked away the second the mistake of eye contact was made.

It was another busy late shift, and close to the end of it she turned at the sound of her name.

'Freya. There's a phone call for you. Private.'

'Oh.'

Very deliberately, Freya had left her mobile in her locker. The only people she could think of who might call her at work were her parents.

Tentatively she picked up the phone. 'Freya Ross speaking...'

'Freya?'

If ever the sound of your own name could drench you in ice, it did then to Freya. There was a begging tone in the voice that sounded like a final grab for a rescue rope.

It wasn't her mother, it was Alison, and Freya knew only too well the inflection of her friend's voice when it was laced with fear.

'I didn't want you to find out from anyone else,' Alison said, 'but Aunt Shona's already put something on social media and I'd rather you heard it from me…'

'What's happening?'

'I've had a bleed,' Alison said. 'I'm having tests, and Dr Campbell says that I might I have an abrupt—' She stumbled over the word.

'An abruption.'

This might well be serious and Freya felt sick.

And angry.

And scared.

But she held in her fears as Alison spoke again.

'They're not sure where the bleeding is coming from, but apparently I have an irritable uterus and they're monitoring how the baby is faring.'

'Are they looking to deliver?' Freya asked, and knew her voice had that odd, distant note she saved for Alison these days.

'Not at this stage,' Alison said, 'but they're monitoring me, and might transfer me from Cromayr to Edinburgh, if needed. Freya, I'm so scared.'

'I know you are, but sometimes bleeds happen. It doesn't necessarily mean—'

'Freya!' Alison interrupted. 'Can you come?'

Her request was unexpected. Welcome, yet unexpected. They were best friends, and yet somehow Freya had felt Alison might want her to stay away this time.

'Of course I'll come,' Freya said. 'I've a couple of hours

to go on this shift and then I'm off for a couple of days. I'll turn my phone on now and you can call me if anything changes. If you're transferred, tell Callum to let me know and I'll come straight in to see you at Edinburgh. I'll be there in the morning.'

'Is everything okay, Freya?' Stella asked as she hung up the phone.

'No,' she admitted. 'My best friend's pregnant and she's had a bleed and has been admitted. She lost a baby last year, so I'm going to head home at the end of my shift. I'll take the train.'

'Do you need me to take a look at the off-duty?'

'I should be fine. I've got a couple of days off.'

'Well, the night staff will be arriving soon, and there's enough of us on if you want to go.'

As their conversation was ending Richard arrived at the desk. He dealt with some questions that Stella had for him, and then the first chance he could Richard spoke to Freya. 'I shouldn't be too much longer,' he said. 'If I run a little over can you wait in the staff room?'

Oh, right, Freya thought. Their talk. He wanted to speak to her, and Freya was quite sure that it was about the end of them.

'I can't come over tonight,' she told him. 'Alison's had a bleed and she's asked me to go and see her. Stella's letting me go early, so I'm just about to go home and pack and then I'm heading to Euston.'

'How bad is it?' Richard asked.

'It sounds as if it's under control,' Freya said. 'And if there are any further issues then she'll be transferred to Edinburgh. I think she's just terrified...'

'And needs a friend?'

'I guess... Or maybe she doesn't understand what's happening and wants me to translate what's been said.'

'I'm quite sure they've told her exactly what's happening,' Richard said. 'If you can give me half an hour to sort out some cover, I'll drive you.'

Freya shook a head. 'It's fine. I'll just go home and pack a few bits—the Tube's just as quick.'

'I meant that I'll drive you up to Scotland.'

She'd thought he'd meant he would drive her to Euston.

'Sorry?' She frowned, unsure if she was hearing things right. 'Don't be daft. You're back on in the morning, and you're first on call.' Freya knew his roster as well as her own. 'We wouldn't even get there until then.'

'It's not daft at all,' Richard said. 'I'll sort it out. Just give me some time to arrange cover.'

'You don't have to do that.'

'Freya, in the same way I'd do it for them, my colleagues will cover for me when it's urgent.'

He could not know how much those words meant to her.

'You're sure?' Freya checked.

'Of course I am.'

This was unlike anything Freya was used to. *She* was the fixer. The one who sorted things. Even as she had hung up the phone on Alison she had already been mentally working out the off-duty roster and the train times to Edinburgh.

And yet here was Richard, calling on colleagues and rearranging his schedule.

Stella was marvellous too and, unasked, swapped around her next set of days off, so that she had four days off in a row.

'Though if Kelly is swapping her weekend with you, then I'll need you back for an early on Monday.'

Freya nodded. 'That would be great,' she said. 'Thank you so much.'

She had a quick shower in the staff changing rooms, and by the time she came out Richard was ready.

'All done.'

Richard made it sound like a simple feat had been achieved. He didn't burden her with the drama of it, he simply sorted it, and within the half-hour they were driving towards her flat.

There wasn't a hope of him getting a parking spot, but he said he'd drive around while she packed.

'Wait on the pavement for me.' Richard said.

He drove around and in the end he did find a spot, beside a small café. He ordered two coffees and four pastries and then headed back to her street. She was waiting for him, dressed in jeans and a long baggy jumper with an overnight bag beside her.

Richard negotiated the car through the traffic and filled her in with what he'd achieved while she'd been in her flat.

'I booked myself a room at the Tavern.'

'Why?' Freya frowned.

'Well, given your cottage is being rented out, I didn't want you to have to go to the bother of explaining me to your parents.'

'No,' Freya said, 'the last tenants are gone.'

'Oh, that's right—it's on the market.'

Except it wasn't on the market. Because Freya had decided against it, given that she knew she was coming back once her London contract was finished.

But she couldn't deal with telling him that tonight, Freya thought. She would save it for when she was summarily dumped.

Yet it didn't *feel* like the end of them, Freya thought, still more than a touch stunned that Richard had changed his busy schedule just to make things easier on her.

'The satnav estimates that we'll be there at seven,' Richard told her. 'Maybe call when we get closer and check that she hasn't been transferred?'

'I will.' Freya nodded. 'I'll pop in and see her when I get there, if she's still in Cromayr Bay, though I might have to wait until visiting hours if she's been transferred to Edinburgh.'

'We'll know soon enough,' Richard said.

They chatted idly for the first couple of hours, but then she decided to be brave and address what he had said this morning. 'You said that you wanted to talk to me?'

'It's nothing that can't keep.'

'We have five hours to go,' Freya pointed out.

But Richard shook his head. 'It's nothing that can't keep,' he said again.

Perhaps he didn't want a hysterical crying female in the car as he drove, Freya pondered, although she was determined to at least *pretend* to take it well.

She looked over to him and her heart skipped, as it always did. Yes, she'd sworn to take it well—it was what they had agreed on after all. But she would miss him so.

Richard turned the conversation to his work, and she could not know, just how rare that was—because usually he didn't discuss such things in depth with someone he was seeing.

Generally it was just a case of replying, 'Busy day,' to any enquiries about work.

Not tonight, though.

'I just signed off on Dominic performing epidurals,' Richard said. 'That's going to make things a lot easier.'

'That's good.'

'He's brilliant,' Richard mused.

'Have you told *him* that?' Freya both smiled and yawned as she asked the question.

'Not yet.' He glanced over. 'Why don't you try and get

some sleep?' he suggested. 'I'll wake you when we stop for petrol.'

'Okay, then I can drive when you get tired.'

'I'll be fine.'

Freya rested her head against the window and very soon was drifting off.

Occasionally she stirred, but there was just the radio playing and the lulling sound of a car eating up the miles.

When she finally woke she glanced at her phone.

'Anything?'

'No.'

'Well, no news is good news,' Richard said. 'We're coming up for the border—we'll stop after that.'

And there it was, the blue and white flag of Scotland as they crossed the border, and it felt both odd and nice to be doing it with Richard. It was good to be home.

The motorway stop was efficient.

She went and bought them something to eat while he filled up the car. 'Why don't you get flowers here for your friend?' he suggested.

Freya bought a gorgeous orchid, and a bunch of flowers for herself, and soon they were back in the car for the last leg. They were just merging onto the motorway when he let out a curse.

'What?' Freya said, looking around, assuming a car had cut them up or was driving too closely behind them.

'I forgot to get condoms.'

Freya was shocked, because she'd been expecting to be dumped but then she smiled. 'We do have shops in Cromayr Bay.'

'I know. But I've never run out of supplies or not had any to hand…'

'Never?'

'God, no. I wouldn't leave it to someone else. There

would be little Richards everywhere...' He gave a shudder at the very thought.

'I'm the same,' Freya said.

She didn't leave that type of thing to anyone else either, and kept right on taking her Pill regardless.

The hills were dotted with wind turbines, but rather than soothe her as they drew closer to their destination Freya found she was nervous.

'I don't know what to say to her,' Freya admitted as they neared the stunning Queensferry Crossing. 'I was so hoping that what happened last time was just a one-off.'

He glanced over. 'She's had a bleed—it could just be a scare,' he pointed out. 'Did the same thing happen last time?'

'No...' Freya shook her head and then sighed. 'It's not just the baby I'm worried about. Things have been a bit strained between us. I don't know how to *be* with her.'

'Just be yourself.'

Freya let out a laugh that was so close to tears it was almost a sob. 'I don't think she needs my anxiety right now. I'll just keep things calm and point out that this type of thing...' She halted, because when she had tried to say that to Alison on the phone, Alison had suddenly cut in and asked her to come.

'Can you stop being a midwife?' Richard asked.

'I'm trying to. We're really close, but I just don't know how to be around her lately. I keep saying the wrong thing, or not saying what I know I should. It's ironic, really, when I've been taught, and I'm well-versed on how to deal with grieving mothers.'

'Well, you can be trained to the back teeth, but it's very different when it's a private grief. No one *always* knows what to say,' Richard said. 'You try, of course, and then you find out that it wasn't the right thing at the right time, or it was the right thing but at the wrong time.'

He was speaking about himself, Freya realised. 'Did you lose someone?'

Richard nodded. 'Marcus—the guy I'm considering working with—his son died a few years ago. He came in at nine in the evening with meningococcal and was dead by sunrise the next day.'

'Were you working at the time?'

'No.'

He looked over again and saw the slight dismissal in her eyes that told him he couldn't understand what she'd been through. Richard had stayed quiet on the subject before, because that was when he had still been determined to keep things light between them. When Freya had still just been his way of getting away from things for a while.

He wasn't trying to get away from things now, and so he spoke on. 'For a long time I wished to God that I *had* been working.'

She looked at him. 'You don't mean that.'

'But I do,' Richard said. 'For close to a year, nearly every day I wished that I'd been on call that night and been the one dealing with him.'

He thought back to that time, and to the hopelessness and anger he had felt.

'I convinced myself that had I been on then I'd have picked things up sooner. In my God-like moments—' he gave a black smile '—the moments when I'm able to control the world, I decided that had I been there I could have changed the outcome. But in the end I worked out that no matter how much I wanted things to have been different, there are some outcomes that can't be changed.'

'No...' She had never really thought of it like that.

'Just stop for a moment and imagine that you hadn't been on that night.'

'I can't,' Freya said. 'I still have nightmares about it.'

'I know you do,' Richard admitted.

He'd never mentioned it, but he had felt her panic sometimes as he'd held her through the night. She would sit up for a moment, and then eventually settle back to sleep. It had felt like a private thing—something she perhaps didn't want him to have seen—and so he had left it. Because they weren't supposed to have the kind of relationship where you noticed things like that.

But he wasn't leaving things unsaid now.

'Suppose you were a teacher, or you worked in a shop, or even on one of the other wards and you hadn't been there that night…'

'But I *was* there.'

'Just stop,' he said again. 'Just take yourself out of the picture. Suppose you hadn't been on duty that night—how would you have felt?'

'I can't take myself out of the picture, Richard. I was *there*.'

They stopped talking about it then, because some sights were just too beautiful not to pause and take them in.

The dark sky had turned to grey, with soft blushes of pink starting to emerge, but now, as they approached the crossing, they were bathed in gold and pink and it felt as if they were driving through fire.

'That's stunning,' Richard commented.

'I know,' Freya said. 'I never tire of it. I can see the bridges from my bedroom. It's a sight to behold.'

She rang and found out that Alison hadn't been transferred and they arrived in Cromayr Bay along with the morning. Freya directed him along an easier route than the satnav recommended, and soon they were pulling into the parking area near the ambulance bay.

'I'll try not to be too long,' she said.

'Take your time,' Richard said. 'I'll be asleep.'

It was nice not to be running up the corridor harried after two train journeys and weighed down with an overnight bag. Instead Freya had on lipstick and was carrying a huge orchid as she made her way up the corridor. And, no, she did not need a red arrow to find her way.

Laura, the Matron, greeted her warmly. 'Things are looking better,' she said as Freya approached, putting her at ease straight away. 'We were going to transfer her last night, in case the baby needed to be delivered. It's still an option, of course, but everything has settled down and Dr Campbell thinks for now she can stay here. Any further bleeding, though, and she'll be off to somewhere with a NICU.'

Freya let out a breath of relief as Laura took her through.

'She's going to be so pleased to see you.'

And Alison was.

Sitting up in bed, strapped to a CTG monitor, she was having a cup of tea. She put it straight down and then promptly burst into tears when she saw her friend.

'It's fine,' Freya said, and gave her a cuddle.

She could hear the rapid bleep of the baby's heart and it was just the sweetest sound in the world. Especially now, today, here with her friend.

'I am so sorry to drag you up here. Especially now that things seem fine. But when they mentioned delivering me I just panicked.'

'Of course you did.' Freya said. 'But it sounds like things have settled down?'

Alison nodded.

'These things happen,' Freya said. 'It doesn't mean it's related to what happened with Andrew and that it's going to happen again.'

'So everyone keeps telling me—and the sensible part of me knows that,'

'But you're not thinking with your head?'

'No.'

They spoke for a good hour, but still Freya felt more midwife than friend—though by the time she was heading off Alison seemed a lot calmer.

'How long are you staying?'

'For a few days,' Freya said. 'They let me swap my off-duty, but I need to leave on Sunday. I'll come back at visiting time.'

'Did you come by train?'

'No.' Freya shook her head. 'A friend drove me.'

'Which friend?' Alison asked, with a look in her eye that Freya couldn't ignore.

'A good one.' Freya answered. 'And that's all I'm saying on the subject. I'll be back this afternoon.'

And that 'good friend' hadn't slept the hour away.

Richard had tried to, but he had found himself watching the distinct lack of emergencies at the casualty department at Cromayr Bay Hospital.

Oh, there was *some* activity—there were staff arriving for their shifts and some leaving—but not a single ambulance had pulled up.

One patient had arrived—a car had come into the forecourt and an elderly gentleman had spoken to a porter, who seemed also to man the doors. The porter had gone off and returned a few moments later with a wheelchair.

Richard had watched as they'd both helped a woman out of the front seat of the car. She'd been holding her wrist in a familiar way.

'Colles' fracture,' Richard had diagnosed from a distance.

God, he'd go out of his mind with boredom here.

And it was cold. So much colder than mid-October in London that he'd sat with the heating on in the car.

And now he saw Freya, smiling and walking. She stopped and chatted to the same porter, who must also be on duty for wheelchairs and things.

She was happy here. Richard could see that.

'Hey.' He gave her a smile as she climbed into the warmth of the car. 'How is she?'

'Better than it sounded last night. If she has another bleed they'll transfer her, though things are calm for now. I'll go in and see her again later today.'

'Sounds good.'

'It does.' Freya nodded. 'I can't thank you enough for this. It all seems like a bit of a false alarm now.'

'Well, thank God it was.'

'Did you cancel the room at the Tavern?'

'No,' Richard said. 'I thought that so long as your friend's okay we might both go there for dinner tonight. It sounds amazing.'

'The restaurant's new,' Freya said as she directed him the short distance to her home. 'I really want to see it. I hope they still do their game pie. It's the best you'll ever have tasted.'

'It will be the *first* I've ever tasted,' Richard admitted, and then he gave her thigh a squeeze. 'And maybe we can slip upstairs to my room after.'

'I think I like the sound of that.' Freya smiled—and then brought them down to earth with a bump. 'I need milk.'

'I need sleep.'

They pulled in at a small store, but after a moment, rather than wait in the car, Richard, knowing the emptiness of her shelves in London, got out to make sure that she got things like bread and eggs too.

Yes, he was hungry.

And, no, he would not be buying condoms, Richard decided.

Another thing to add to the discussion list tonight.

Romantic dinners in Scotland, discussing his work and then sex minus a condom—he'd be asking her to move in next.

The oddest thing of all was that the thought didn't terrify him...

He held open the door for a woman who was wheeling a pram and saw that Freya was standing behind a large gentleman, waiting to pay for her milk.

'Did you get bread?' he asked patiently.

'No.'

'Do you have butter?'

'No.'

'Is there anything else you need?' Richard checked.

'I don't believe so.'

'Anything else *at all*?'

He meant for tonight, and they both knew it.

And when he looked at her like that, when he smiled, she forgot her fears. She forgot the temporary nature of *them*.

'Nothing I can think of.' Freya smiled.

As he headed off to get bread and butter, and nothing else, he heard someone call her name.

'Freya!'

She turned and gave a huge smile. 'Mrs Roberts!'

'It's Leah,' she reminded her, and Richard watched as Freya peered into the pram.

'Oh, she's beautiful!'

The baby really was. A gorgeous smiling baby, who was wide awake and looking up at her. There were certain babies that just had to be held.

'Do you mind?' Freya checked.

Leah laughed 'Go ahead.'

Richard was back, so she handed him the milk to hold as she unstrapped the baby.

'Oh, my...' Freya said. 'She is absolutely *gorgeous*.'

'She really is,' said Mrs Roberts, and then she glanced to Richard.

Freya remembered her manners. 'This is Richard Lewis—he's a friend of mine from London.'

'It's lovely to meet you, Richard. I'm Leah Roberts. I went through a bit of a time and...well, Freya really helped.'

'I'm glad to hear it,' Richard said. 'What have you called your daughter?'

'Freya,' Mrs Roberts said, and then looked to Freya. 'And, no, it wasn't just because I like the name—though of course I do. You really helped me. You were so kind through my pregnancy. I kept wanting to talk to you, though I didn't know how to.'

'You did it in the end,' Freya pointed out.

'Yes—Norma came down to help, and I had Mrs Hunt come in for the first few weeks...' She looked at her daughter. 'I got to actually *enjoy* her. And though of course I didn't care if it was a boy or a girl, she was a wonderful surprise.' As Freya handed her back, Leah gazed fondly upon her daughter. 'She's a true blessing.'

'Everything went well with the labour?' Freya checked.

'It did. Betty was wonderful, of course, but I did miss you so.'

He drove the last few minutes to her home, with Freya directing him.

'Mine's the blue one—though we'll have to park a bit further up. It can be hard when there are lots of visitors.'

Richard parked, and as he climbed out the scent of the sea reached him. The sun was glistening on the water and there was an angry seagull squawking above as they walked down to her cottage.

Richard had to stoop to get in.

Her home was cold from being empty, and Mrs Hunt had closed the curtains. And yet it was gorgeous, Richard thought as they stepped in and she pulled back the lounge curtains and let in some light.

'I'll put the heating on,' Freya said. 'It's a bit early to light a fire.'

Freya ran a vase under the tap and put the flowers on the table, in the hope of brightening it up.

'Do you want a coffee?' she called out.

'No, all I want right now is bed.'

He was beat. A long day at work and a very long drive up to Scotland meant all he wanted to do was stretch out.

'I'll just have a shower first.'

'You'll have to wait for the water to warm—it will take half an hour or so.'

After turning on the tank in the airing cupboard she showed him the tiny bathroom, and then took him through to her bedroom. The curtains were already drawn closed, and as he stepped into the soft darkness of her room and saw the large bed, the thought of waiting half an hour for hot water held no appeal. So Richard started to undress.

'Are you coming to bed?' he asked.

'Not yet,' Freya said, because unlike Richard she had slept in the car. 'I should maybe let my family know I'm here, and then I might go and...' Her voice trailed off.

Because that was what looking at him did to her at times. Freya needed no reminders as to his beauty. All she ever had to do was turn her head. But here in the dark bedroom, with the lights off, it was not that which swayed her—more the thought of Richard in *her* bed, and the waste of a morning spent on the phone, taking care of a hundred little jobs, when she could be with him.

'I might just join you.'

He was already in. 'God, your bed's comfortable.'

'I know,' Freya agreed. 'I found this mattress topper...'

She was speaking to a less than captivated audience. The bear was asleep. In her bed.

Bears could be many things. Intimidating, irresistible... She stood there, mulling it over, but couldn't think of another adjective. She just knew that she wanted to lie with him, her bear, in her bed.

Freya set the alarm on her phone, so that she'd be up for visiting time, and undressed. She had forgotten how cold her house could get. Or maybe the goosebumps could be labelled as a sign of tiredness.

Either way, she was cold as she slipped into bed, and then she was colder still from the chill of neglected sheets against her skin.

But then Richard rolled over and wrapped her in his arms and she no longer felt cold.

She slept warm in his embrace, and struggled to wake to the sound of an alarm that was pinging somewhere, reminding Freya of where she needed to be.

She rolled onto her back and her brain scrambled to orientate.

She was home...

Alison. Visiting hours. Get up. Get dressed. Be there.

Except she was here.

Feeling his hot mouth on her breast and the sensual slow suck that had made a place low in her stomach draw tight.

It was as if he knew, for his fingers traced slow circles there, and then crept down, down, all the way down...

And then he left her breast, and as his mouth found hers his fingers worked magic.

She moaned, and he liked it. She should really reach for him, but she was feeling too selfish to move.

The alarm went off again, but neither of them cared. She was locked in the bliss of a kiss that delivered ten thousand volts and a hand that did the same.

Her hand went to the back of his head and he swallowed her throaty gasps. Freya could hear the sound of her sex, slick and wet, as he brought her to the boil. He kissed her while she came, and when he rolled atop her it didn't feel disorientating, more like the right place to be on this earth.

As he slid, unsheathed, inside her, her whole body shivered with desire.

It had never been better for either of them. The tight and yet slippery grip of her...the absolute union of them.

He moved, but it was slowly, and he savoured the feel of each thrust and the slow draw-out followed by the faster pushing in.

She was digging her fingers into his back in an effort to hold on to her thoughts and reel them in. Because they were making love, Freya knew. They were *making love*.

They had done many things, but never this.

They were kissing and then pausing to look at each other. And she was in a heated frenzy of passion and emotion as he took her deeply, because a part of her wanted him to pause, while the other part wanted him never to stop.

He took her harder now, and she forgot to hold on. Her thoughts simply unravelled until there was nothing left in her mind but the shattering of *them*. As he shuddered he spilled himself deep inside her and she throbbed against him. The bliss of her clenching made Richard moan, and those last precious drops came to the fading twitches of her climax.

And as he lay there, spent and still inside her, Freya opened her eyes and stared at the ceiling as she found the word she had been missing before.

Irreplaceable.

There would never be another who came close to him.

Richard Lewis was irreplaceable in her heart.

And that shook her to her core.

This wasn't some fling. It might have started as such, but now it couldn't end without regrets.

Not any more.

Freya knew that when it ended he would be leaving with her heart, and she must not let that show.

And so she wriggled out from under him and then climbed from the bed. 'I have to go and visit Alison.'

She really did have to go, or she'd be late for visiting time. But she knew her voice was distant, cold, detached.

'I'll just have a quick shower,' Richard said, pulling back the sheet.

But Freya stopped him. 'You don't need to get up—my car's outside.'

That surprised him. Richard didn't really know why. He'd just assumed that the little purple car blocking his way belonged to a tourist—a visitor or a neighbour. It had never entered his head that it was hers.

'My dad drives it to work once a week,' Freya explained as she headed for the shower. 'To keep the battery from dying.'

Richard dozed as Freya showered, and then she came back in, wearing the same grey dress she'd had on the day they had met. Now, though, underneath it, she had on a long-sleeved black top, as well as thick black tights. Her hair was up, and he saw she'd added a little lipstick as she came and sat on the bed.

'I'll be a couple of hours.'

'Take your time.'

'There's everything you need in the kitchen. Well, there's coffee, and your bread and things, but I'll bring us back a fish supper. They do the best here.'

'And there was me thinking you were finally going to cook.'

They parted with a smile and he heard her footsteps leave and then the sound of the door closing behind her.

Her father needed to drive her car rather more frequently than he currently was, Richard thought as he lay there, because it was taking her a few goes to get the engine ticking over.

Richard was fully awake.

Automatically he checked his phone, and then checked and checked again. But, as Freya had once predicted, he had no signal.

The seagull which had been calling for the last half-hour had found a friend or two, and they were all being rather vocal, yet it wasn't that keeping him from going back to sleep.

'To keep the battery from dying.'

Louder than the seagulls, Richard replayed Freya's words, frowning as he mulled over them. They felt important, and yet he told himself it had just been a throwaway phrase.

He gave up on sleep and headed through the lounge and into her tiny kitchen, taking a moment to work out her rather fancy coffee machine.

As he got the milk out Richard read a note on the fridge, presumably for holidaymakers, reminding them to turn the water off at night and explaining a few nuances of the place.

He walked through to the lounge, and while, yes, it needed a helluva lot of work, it really was gorgeous.

There were books on the shelves, and little ornaments and shells dotted around. As well as that there were paintings on the wall that *she* had put there—not prints of some ugly old horse and cart. And there were throw rugs on the sofa.

'To keep the battery from dying.'

Now he understood why he had stalled on those words. *This* was Freya's home.

And she was keeping it going as it awaited her return.

Richard walked through to the bedroom and opened the drapes and let in the view.

It was stunning.

Afternoon had given way to dusk and the lights from the bridge had come on. Richard found himself wondering what it must look like deep in winter.

He made another coffee and lay there, looking out but not enjoying it as he had on first sight. For he really knew her some more now.

'Two fish suppers, please.' Freya smiled as she placed her order. 'And a large tub of the homemade tartar sauce.'

'It's good to see you back, Freya. Are you here to see Alison?'

Of course the world already knew.

'Aye, I've just been in to see her—she's looking well.'

It was just the kind of normal idle chatter that happened in this place all the time, Freya thought, and she realised she had missed it.

'Will you be wanting pickled onions?'

She was about to say no, even though she loved them,

but perhaps they would both be eating them, Freya thought with a smile. 'Two, please.'

As she drove up the hill to the cottage Freya felt her spirits buoyed. Their lovemaking had been blissful, and Alison had been looking brighter. And now she was simply enjoying the familiar rhythm of home.

Made all the better because Richard was here.

Yes, her mood was good.

It was a lot darker here than in London, and the clocks changing in a couple of weeks would make it darker still. But, unlike many, Freya loved winter and embraced its grey approach.

She'd said before that it was a bit early to be lighting a fire, Freya thought as she parked on her street, but there was a cold chill in the air as she got out. A fire would make the cottage so very cosy.

And, Freya thought as she turned the key in the door, it would be nice to sit by the fire with him.

The house was in darkness. She guessed that Richard must still be sleeping, so she put the supper down and got out plates, then found glasses for wine.

And to hell with it.

She lit a fire.

'Richard?' Freya pushed open her bedroom door. 'Supper's...'

Her voice trailed off as she saw that he was awake and sitting up in bed.

'Enjoying the view?' Freya asked as she looked out fondly to where his gaze fell.

'Not particularly.'

She frowned at the unexpected response and looked out to the bridges. Such had been his tone that she had almost expected them somehow to have changed. For a fire to have broken out on one of them. Or some drama to be unfolding with flashing lights.

But the change was in him, in the room.

'You never really moved to London, did you?'

She frowned at his question, and at the slightly hoarse note in his usually smooth voice.

'I don't know what you mean.'

'I mean,' he snapped, 'that you've never really left here.'

'Of course I have.'

'Is the house up for sale?'

'Not yet.'

'Freya, why didn't you bring your coffee machine down to London?'

It was the oddest question, and she frowned as she gave a simple answer. 'Because I couldn't fit it in my dad's car.'

'And you bought flowers without thinking about it for this place, to pretty it up, yet your flat in London barely gets a look.'

'Richard, I've been busy, and most of my time off is spent at yours.'

'Oh, come off it, Freya,' he snapped again.

Since the moment she'd left to visit Alison he'd been giving it some considerable thought. And all his thoughts pointed to the same conclusion.

'Is this why you've no real interest in whether I take the private job or carry on at the Primary?'

Freya swallowed.

And Richard saw her swallow and knew he was right.

God! He had been going to ask her to move in with him—to take things further! He had even gone to Freya for her take on his career in case it affected *them*.

Well, he decided, she never needed to know that.

'It's been your intention to come back here all along.'

'No,' Freya argued. '*No*. Richard, when I left I thought

it was for good. I truly did. I was so tired of this place, and everywhere I went there were…' She didn't know how to explain it. 'Reminders.'

'Of Malcolm?'

He hoped not. God, he seriously hoped not. But he *had* to rule that one out.

He saw her eyes screw up and the tiny, impatient, shake of her head as she completely discounted that. He believed that it had had nothing to do with the other man.

'The baby?' Richard checked, and her silence was his answer. 'You left because you were upset about your friend's baby?'

He didn't say it scornfully. She saved the scorn for herself.

'Not just the baby. Alison too. I know it shouldn't get to me the way it does. Even Alison seems so much better, and I guess I appear so too. I should have got over it—I know that…'

'Freya, you're grieving.'

'No.' That sounded too dramatic a word. 'Maybe at first, but it was Alison who lost—'

He spoke over her. 'There aren't numbered tickets given out for grieving. You don't get sent to the back of the queue just because the baby wasn't yours. You went through a bad time at work and the loss was a very personal one. Then you ended a long-term relationship.'

'I was right to.'

'Yes, but it might have been more than you could deal with at the time so you ran away.'

'No.'

But Richard wouldn't let her off that lightly. 'Did you know Alison was trying for another baby?'

'Yes.'

'You couldn't face it if anything went wrong and so you left, but you were always going to come home.'

Had she been?

Freya thought of her last days in Cromayr Bay and the ache in her heart as she had walked out of the delivery centre for the last time.

Not the last time *ever*.

A part of her had known that even then.

Even if she had brushed it from her mind.

'Yes.' She admitted it now. 'But I didn't know that when I applied to work at the Primary. I didn't even know it for certain when I started seeing you.'

'But you do now?'

Freya nodded.

And, for the first time in his life knew that the biter had been bitten.

'Richard, you and I...'

'We were a fling.' He let out a mirthless laugh.

She had meant them to be just that, Freya knew. It had never been going anywhere, or so she had thought, and so she had been able to close her heart and have fun for once. But it had been a grown-up game she'd been playing, which meant when it went wrong there was a greater risk of hurt.

He climbed out of bed—and it was odd the things you noticed, she thought, but he turned away from her to get dressed, when he had never come close to doing so before. A glimpse of that beautiful body was denied to her.

'Do you know what *really* annoys me?' Richard's voice was as brusque as the hands that tucked in his shirt.

'That I wasn't honest with you? I accept that, but I truly didn't know how I felt—'

'No,' Richard interrupted. 'The part that *really* annoys me is that you never gave London a chance.'

'I did.'

'No, you had it pegged from the start as cold and un-friendly.'

Given the circumstances, Richard figured he deserved a chance to be mean, and he used it well.

'I'll tell you why you've got no friends, Freya. It's be-cause—unlike me—people probably sensed that you were never really serious about being there.'

'I take my job very seriously.'

'I'm not questioning your midwifery skills. I'm say-ing that you never gave London a chance.' He shook his head. 'I'm going.'

'Where?'

'To the Tavern. I hear they do a nice game pie.'

'Don't go,' Freya implored. 'We can talk. Surely?'

'And say what? Is it your intention to come back and live here?'

There was no point dressing it up, so Freya told him the decision she had made. 'I'm going to see my contract out and then I'm moving back here. It doesn't mean we have to stop seeing each other. Lots of long-distance relation-ships work out...'

His laugh was almost a shout. Every word sounded foreign to him.

Long. Distance. Relationship.

A few months ago it might have been ideal. He had been growing tired of casual relationships. With Freya in Scotland he could still focus on work...

God, they were so bloody good together that if he stayed—if they ended this row in bed—he could actually see himself saying that he might consider moving here.

But his decision as to what to do was already compli-cated enough. He did not need another iron in the fire. He was not, *not*, going to consider living here.

Never.

'Enjoy the view, Freya.'

He didn't need to slam the door, for the bitter tone to his voice reverberated through her far more than the sound of wood on wood could.

Her one-night stand had proved to be more.

And yet he had gone without working through it.

Gone without hearing her side.

Gone.

CHAPTER TEN

FIRST CLASS.

It felt incongruent to Freya that she should lug her broken heart back to London in style, but she'd learnt a few tricks, having made the journey so often, and, given it was Sunday and there was a spare seat, she'd got a cheap upgrade.

Freya wasn't just lugging her heart home, though.

She had thought hard about what Richard had said about her never having given London a chance, and she had spoken about it to Alison too, when she'd visited.

'I'm torn,' Freya had admitted. 'If I stay it will only be because of him. And what happens when he decides it's not working out? He won't even talk to me about it. No.' She'd shaken her head. '*This* is home.'

'Well, why don't you try and make *London* home for a while?' Alison had suggested.

'That's where I'm headed tomorrow.' Freya had given her friend's stomach a tender caress. 'If this wee one behaves.'

Between visits to her friend Freya had braved the cellar of her home and filled up some cases.

The coffee machine would have to wait. It was simply too heavy. But she had packed some rugs and photos and ornaments, and now she sat on the train with her luggage stowed as a tall woman pushed the buffet cart to the side of her table.

An elderly lady stirred nearby and gave Freya a smile as she selected a Ploughman's sandwich and a bag of crisps and then promptly fell back to sleep.

Freya was grateful for the silent carriage, for there was only the lulling movement of the train and the stunning countryside to take the edge off the frequent barbs of her thoughts.

Richard's words had stung so much because they were true. Freya hadn't set out to hurt him, yet inadvertently she had.

And so she looked at her phone, which was on silent, and this time there was no thought of Russian emojis or tartan berets.

This time her text was from the heart.

I never thought I would feel the way I do about you.

While he sat in his gorgeous apartment, surrounded by tiny pieces of Freya—a silk scarf over his sofa, a pair of earrings on his table—knowing that there was some of her washing in the tumble dryer, he read her second text.

Does it have to be all or nothing?

Her question was both sensible and ridiculous.

Sensible because they'd been seeing each other for just a couple of months, and it was too early in the piece to be speaking of career and country moves. Ridiculous because they both knew how they felt.

Richard texted back.

Can you see yourself staying in London?

Freya answered.

I don't know.

Freya had answered, but sensed that now wasn't the time to lie.

She looked out of the window as the train slowed down and they arrived at Berwick-upon-Tweed. She recalled being in his car as they crossed the border. The feeling of being home.

And then, as they left Berwick-upon-Tweed behind, she felt torn from the land of her heart. No, she could not see herself permanently in London.

Not really.

And so she sent another text.

No.

Silence was his first response. But as the train pulled into Newcastle her phone pinged.

There's no point, then.

He was as brusque as ever.

Richard, we can't do this by text. I'm on the train now. Can I come over?

He read the message and gave a wry smile, for all too often a lover had pleaded with him via this very vehicle not to end things, and asked could they please just come over and talk.

This felt like a very different message from the familiar.

It would end in bed, rather than tears, Richard knew, and they would be no further along than they were now.

No, you can't come over. I'll meet you at Euston.

Richard wasn't on the platform, but as she came through the barrier and stepped out into brighter skies her heart sank. He looked amazing, in black jeans and a thin black jumper, but when she saw her own bag over his shoulder Freya knew that the things she'd left at his flat were inside.

'I'm sorry I wasn't honest with you,' Freya said. 'That first night we went out I'd only just started to figure out that I wasn't planning on staying after the end of my contract.'

'Pardon?'

She looked into his gorgeous eyes and managed a pale smile, because she knew he was teasing, as well as trying to ease the pain and make their parting of ways as good as it could be.

'I kept waiting for you to dump me,' Freya said, and poked at his lovely big chest. '*That's* what it said on the box. I went into this with eyes wide open, knowing we had a fast-approaching use-by date...'

'I know you did.' His sigh was a weary one, and it came from lack of sleep—though for once that had nothing to do with work, for he had been on days off.

'Nothing has to change...' Freya attempted, but even she could hear the futility behind her words, because so much already had.

He handed her the bag. 'I don't want us to see each other any more.'

'Richard, please,' Freya said, even when she had sworn she would never beg him not to leave. 'Don't rush off.'

He had to.

Lest he stayed.

'You don't have to make a decision now,' Freya reasoned as she ran after him.

'I've already made it,' Richard said.

'I can't believe you won't let us talk.'

Infuriatingly, he shrugged.

She spoke on. 'I've still got a couple of months to go here, and *some* long-distance relationships work…'

He didn't want to hear it. Richard did not want this dragged out. He did not want his precious days off spent on the motorway, and he did not want her the best part of a day away. So, rather than admit to the hurt he felt, instead he was blunt.

'I like sex a bit more regularly than once a fortnight.'

Her mouth clamped closed. She really didn't have an answer to that.

But Richard hadn't finished yet.

'You wanted a bastard you could readily leave behind, Freya,' he reminded her. 'Don't complain when I deliver.'

And, as she had been promised by all and sundry, as she had known would happen on the day she had accepted a night out in his company, Richard Lewis broke her heart.

'Don't!' Freya warned the flower seller at the Underground station, before he could tell her again to cheer up because it might never happen.

But then she relented.

It had already happened.

She had lost Richard.

And the worst thing about that was that in everything he'd said he'd been right.

So she bought a huge bunch flowers, even though she didn't really feel like it, and lugged her cases up to her flat.

As she opened the door Freya winced.

Really! Imagine her bringing Richard back *here*.

The carpet was vile, but she had ordered a huge rug on-line that would soon be here, and she had brought loads of things from home.

Loads.

Okay, she only had three more months left here, but she was *not* going to just sit it out.

So she threw some gorgeous quilts over the sofa and scattered cushions on top, and then she set to work putting out ornaments and pictures.

It was better that than focussing on a seriously broken heart.

At work, he ignored her.

Not in front of the patients, of course. And Richard was far too smooth to do something silly like call her 'Nurse'. He still called her Freya if he had to—just not quite in the same way he had said it before.

A couple of weeks into her heartache he came to the nurses' station, where Freya and Stella were sitting. He was wearing scrubs, and still had on a paper theatre hat.

Stella was sorting out the off-duty rota and Freya was feeding a very fussy Baby Glover, whose mother had been taken to Theatre post-delivery when complications had set in.

'How's Mrs Glover?' Stella asked.

'She's fine.' Richard nodded. 'And she should be back on the ward soon.'

He didn't look over or say hi to Freya. He just sat and caught up with the notes he'd been writing before he'd had to dash off. Mid-stroke of his pen, though, he peeled off his cap and tossed it into the bin.

The cap had left his hair messy, just as it had been on the day they had met.

Now Freya knew why.

'Felicity,' Stella said. 'I mean Freya—can you swap from an early to a late on Tuesday?'

'That's fine.'

Freya no longer took it personally when Stella got her staff's names muddled up, because when it came to babies and mother's names she never did.

Never. Not once.

And with twenty-eight mothers and babies on the maternity unit this morning alone, Stella had a lot on her mind.

'You don't have plans?' Stella checked.

'No,' Freya said. 'Well, actually I'm trying to make some curtains, but I'm sure they won't care if I don't get to them that night.'

'You should speak to Pat,' Stella said, but didn't elaborate, and then, having finished sorting out the off duty, she got up and walked off.

There wasn't silence.

That would be too much to ask mid-morning on a maternity ward.

But there was silence between *them.*

How she missed him.

'Richard?' Freya said, and looked up from the little infant she was feeding, 'Do you think—?'

'Is this about a patient?'

'No.'

'Work?'

'No.'

'Then you don't get to know my thoughts.' He stood. 'Dominic and my SHO are stuck in ICU, so I'm going down to Surgical to do the Pain Round. Tell Stella I'll be back to finish these notes when I get a chance.'

'Sure.'

He walked off.

Richard didn't *stalk* off—he didn't do anything other than put her neatly in her place.

He did the Pain Round and asked the patients over and over, 'On a scale of one to ten—ten being the highest—how would you rate your pain?'

'Ten,' some would say, while reaching for their cup of tea.

'Three,' some would say, just a few hours post-op, while wincing from the pull of stitches on their wound or the weight of a sheet.

And that night, when he went home to an apartment minus any little pieces of Freya, Richard dared not rate his own pain.

He had returned to London after their row to the sanity of a single life. It was now two weeks post-Freya and the pain should have improved considerably. In fact the old Richard would have been well onto the next woman by now. At the very least he should be out with a friend and mocking the fact that he had almost considered giving up all this for a career in Cromayr Bay.

Mocking it.

Laughing at the fact that in the days after they had ended things he had placed a call to the head of anaesthetics at Cromayr Bay and made tentative enquiries.

He had been invited for an informal visit in a couple of weeks, to be shown around. There were currently no vacancies, but he'd set the ball rolling. Richard knew he should halt it now.

He wasn't hungry enough to order take-away, so he ate cereal and then took off his suit and stepped into his pristine glass shower. But the trouble with that was he missed those awful green tiles at Freya's place, and the inevitable search for a towel.

Here he had his choice from eight white fluffy ones, all folded and waiting. Yet for all its luxurious bliss, his apartment felt as sterile as an operating theatre now that Freya wasn't there.

He lay in his non-lumpy bed and, though he might appear comfortable to some, he decided to rate his pain.

One to ten…with ten being the highest.

Seven? he attempted, because although it had hurt seeing her today he had been effective in cutting her off.

And yet he'd badly wanted to hear what she'd had to say.

Eight? Because he still hadn't cancelled his visit to Cromayr Bay, simply because he missed her so much.

Nine? Because he was a stubborn bastard and where his career was concerned he never backed down.

This damn thing called love hurt more than he'd considered it might.

Yes, love. And he missed her.

Ten.

Yes. Losing Freya was definitely a ten.

CHAPTER ELEVEN

As STELLA HAD SUGGESTED Freya had spoken to Pat—who, it turned out, was a fantastic seamstress.

'I'll do them for you,' Pat offered.

'I can't just bring you in a pile of fabric!'

'Don't be daft. I'll bring my sewing machine to you.'

It had been arranged for Sunday afternoon, and Kelly had come along, Stella too. As nervous as for a first date—in fact far more nervous than she had ever been on a date—Freya had bought cheese and nuts and crisps and worried.

But then they'd arrived, and it had been so much fun, Pat on the sewing machine, Stella on the ladder. And by the time they had left there had been deep crimson curtains.

They changed the entire room.

And he would never see them, Freya thought.

'Do you see him at all?' Alison asked one night when she called.

'A bit,' Freya said. 'Well, quite a lot. But it's not like before. His registrar, Dominic, can do most of the epidurals now, so I only really see him if there's an emergency.'

'Have you tried talking to him?'

'There's no point,' Freya said. 'He's made things completely clear. I don't see why I should have to give up coming home when he won't consider moving.'

There was silence. From both of them.

'I want you here,' Alison said finally. 'You know I do. But if Callum had to move for work—well, that's where I'd go.'

'Yes, but the fact is *you're* not working. You've finished work to have a baby,' Freya snapped, and then realised what she'd said. 'Sorry...'

'No!' Alison laughed. 'I'm delighted to hear the return of the real Freya. You've been...'

'What?'

'Too *nice*,' Alison said. 'Too *midwifey*.'

'I shall have to snap at you some more, then. Anyway, enough about me—how are *you* doing?'

Alison was doing well. The baby was due early in the New Year and Freya's contract was up in mid-January—which meant that Freya wouldn't be around for the birth.

Alison was having the baby in the main hospital, and if there were any further bleeds she would be transferred elsewhere, so there would have been no chance of Freya delivering her friend anyway.

Yet still she would have *been* there.

She thought back to the time when she had first put in her application to London. She and Malcolm had long since broken up, and Alison had just told her that she and Callum were expecting again.

They'd sat in the bar at the Tavern and Alison had said she wanted Freya to be with her in the delivery room.

'Callum's going to be so tense,' she'd explained.

'That might not be possible,' Freya had said, and had told her best friend that she was considering moving to London.

It had just tumbled from her lips, even before it had been a cohesive thought, and it had grown from there. Freya had applied for a job at the Primary the next week.

Richard had been right. She'd been running away.

There was no avoiding heartbreak, though. It just morphed into something else and found you wherever you were hiding.

Until you faced it.

CHAPTER TWELVE

RICHARD NO LONGER crashed out in the staff room, and they merely nodded if they met in the canteen.

Freya ached to know whether he had decided to stay with the NHS or go and work at the private hospital. Each week when the hospital newsletter came out Freya scanned it for information, but there was no mention of his leaving, nor of his replacement.

She'd find out on the intranet, perhaps. Or one day she would realise he was no longer here, Freya thought as she sat on the labour and delivery unit, where she'd been allocated today.

'It's so quiet,' Freya commented to Stella, for there was only the sound of a woman loudly humming her way through her contractions.

Pat was in there with her. And Kelly was in D5.

'Why don't you go and have your coffee break while it is?' said Stella.

'Freya,' Kelly called, because they were 'buddies' today. 'Can you check this CTG with me before you go?'

Freya did so. They both checked it carefully. There were a couple of anomalies—enough that they called over Stella, who then buzzed for Dr Mina to come and asses mother and baby.

'Go and have your coffee now,' Stella said.

Freya made a coffee and thought how odd it was that it would be a normal day in Cromayr Bay while she was here in London. They'd have the antenatal and postnatal clinics running through the day. And then there were care-in-the-home visits.

Freya loved those. Going into a home and seeing the new baby and its family. If there was a part of her job in Cromayr Bay that she missed the most, then it was that—following the entire journey.

Of course she followed up on certain cases here.

Louise Eames was doing incredibly well and had been discharged home. She was recovering from her trauma and visiting her tiny son.

But it didn't feel the same. Freya missed her old work, the longer preparation and anticipation of birth and the follow up too.

She was about to open a magazine when the overhead chimes went off.

Freya didn't rinse her mug. Instead she put it down on the coffee table and headed straight back to a department that was no longer quiet.

The light was flashing over D5, and Stella was running for the phone. Then she saw Freya.

'Let Theatre know we've got a crash Caesarean coming,' she told Freya, and then got back into D5.

Freya made the call and saw Richard running down the corridor and into the same suite.

'Freya?' Stella put her head out through the door. 'Can you check this?'

As Freya went over to check on the drugs she could hear a tense conversation taking place between the father of the baby and Richard.

'But I'm her husband—absolutely I'm going into Theatre with her.'

'He won't get in the way,' the patient pleaded.

She was lying on her side, with oxygen, and Freya could hear the sound of the baby's heart-rate. It was ominously low. Her waters were thick with meconium, which was usually the baby's first bowel movement after birth.

It felt like a replay of what had happened to Alison.

Andrew had died from meconium aspiration.

Of course it happened—Freya knew that—but she could hear the fear in this mother's voice and it sounded just like Alison's had...

'What's happening?' she asked.

Her calls did not go unanswered as Stella, Dr Mina and Kelly all took time to explain as they prepared her for urgent transfer.

'Baby doesn't like the contractions,' said Dr Mina. 'The slow heart-rate tells us that.'

Then Stella spoke. 'And the meconium shows us that baby's distressed...'

Guy Masters arrived then, and got the hand-over from Dr Mina.

'I want Abigail in theatre,' Dr Mina said, and looked over to Stella. 'Now, or we go ahead here.'

'They're preparing.' Richard said, a touch breathless.

No one would move from this room until a theatre was ready, even if it meant that the baby was delivered here.

'I want my husband with me,' Abigail said.

And then Freya found out what Richard Lewis could accomplish in seconds.

'I understand that you want your husband to be there for the birth, Abigail,' he said in his deep voice. 'But you're having general anaesthetic so it just isn't possible. We need to get your baby out quickly.'

'I *insist* on being there!' the husband cut in.

'Mr Dunstan,' Richard said. 'We don't have time to

debate. You *cannot* be there. From this point, I won't be leaving your wife's side.' He crouched down to be at eye level with Abigail. 'I will be with you the whole time until you are brought round.'

He didn't make false promises and say he'd be there after that, because he knew she would be handed over to the post-anaesthetic care unit, and at that point he might well be called to something else. He had just told the terrified parents how it would be, and had obviously reassured them at the same time, because Abigail nodded.

'Now,' he said as he stood, 'I've got another IV line in and I've gone through your history. I just need to ask if you have any dental crowns.'

'None.'

'Or any loose teeth that I should know about?'

'No.' Abigail shivered.

Everything was ready to go, and the emergency packs were ready for the short dash to Theatre, but until they were told it was ready they would not be leaving.

'Theatre's ready!' someone called.

And then they were off. Running down the corridor in a race to save the baby.

'Can you clear up?' Stella asked, when she saw Freya simply standing there in the middle of D5.

'Of course.'

She cleared all the discarded wrappings and equipment, and as she replaced the oxygen masks and tubing could see that her hands were shaking.

And then she stopped.

Just for a moment.

It felt as if she was shrouded in black lace.

Freya simply stood there and felt the fear and the absolute horror of that night with Alison. And then she did what Richard had suggested on the day that had ended them.

Her mind was in a time that had never been. Imagining a phone call and hearing that Alison had had the baby and it hadn't gone well. Or coming into work and hearing the news. Or Callum, Alison's husband, calling her.

'How would you have felt?' Richard had asked her.

Now Freya felt that moment without herself in the picture.

Devastated.

Only Richard wasn't there to know her answer.

Richard knew this patient would have upset Freya. It had been an incredibly close call.

Their aim was thirty minutes from alert to delivery, and in this instance it had been twenty-eight.

There could not be a more valuable two minutes saved, Richard thought now as he heard the cries of his patient's new baby and Abigail Dunstan was wheeled through to the post-anaesthetic unit. She had been extubated in Theatre and would soon come round.

Richard went over and spoke to Kelly. 'How is he?'

'Lucky,' Kelly said. 'He's well enough for a quick cuddle with Mum when she comes round, and then we're taking him up to NICU—but really just to be observed.'

'Good.' Richard said. 'Well done.'

'And you.'

It had been a good day. Or rather, a good hour. But at any given second that could all change.

Richard looked around at the efficient unit that he'd frequented so often and knew he was going to miss this place.

He was going to go private.

His decision was made.

Rather than hover, he headed straight from Theatre back to the Maternity Unit.

Yes, he should stay away from Freya, Richard knew that, but he was certain this case would have upset her.

He would check up on *any* staff member, Richard told himself. But he knew that he was lying, for every day involved drama after drama. If he checked in on everyone he'd never get anything done.

'Hey,' he said to Stella. 'Well done back there.'

'I heard he's doing well. What can I do for you, Richard?'

'I was actually looking for Freya.'

He didn't dress it up, or pretend he was here for another reason.

'She's gone home.'

'Oh.'

'A migraine, apparently.'

'I see…'

'She's back on tomorrow—on a late,' Stella said. 'And that reminds me… It's her birthday tomorrow. Can you sign the card?'

'I haven't got time for that. I need to get down to Surgical.'

'It will take two seconds!'

They did it for everyone. Just a cake and a card. It was nice that a staff birthday didn't escape unnoticed.

And so he took out his pen and scribbled a message.

Best wishes
Richard Lewis

Richard wrote what he always wrote—but he didn't feel like he always felt.

He needed time to think—but when did an anaesthetist in a busy hospital get that?

By the end of the day the good outcome with Baby Dunstan had been countered by the loss of a twenty-year-old, and as he drove home Richard changed his mind—no, he would *not* miss the place.

And the drama didn't end at work.

As the garage door beneath his apartment opened he was just pondering calling Freya, to check how she was faring, when he caught a flash of blonde hair. And as he got out of his car she rushed over to him and promptly burst into noisy tears.

Oh, God, Richard thought. *Not now. Please!*

CHAPTER THIRTEEN

THIRTY!

How the hell had *that* happened?

Freya awoke in a far less lumpy bed, thanks to the amazing mattress topper she had bought, and commenced her fourth decade on earth.

Whether she looked older or not, Freya thought as she came out of the bathroom and looked in the mirror, she didn't *feel* older—and she didn't feel wiser.

Freya just missed him so.

She was working a late shift, so she took her coffee back to bed and lay checking her messages. There were plenty, but Alison must have been waiting for her to switch on because her phone rang straight away.

'You're catching up to me,' Alison said.

'Ha-ha.'

'Thirty! It's awful, isn't it?'

'Not really. I feel the same as I did when I went to bed. It's just the numbers that have changed.'

'There's a parcel here for you,' Alison said. 'I'm not going to lie and pretend I've posted it. You're not coming home for your birthday?'

'No,' Freya said. 'I messed up my days off.'

'Any word on the man?'

'No. He's being very polite at work.'

'Well, that's good.'

'Not really.' Freya sighed. 'And I'd be mad to base staying on here just for a chance with him.' She was thinking out loud, really. 'He told me never to rely on him…'

Only that had been right at the start.

'And we were only together two months…'

'Freya,' Alison broke in. 'You're arguing with yourself.'

She had a lovely morning, spent mainly on the phone and opening the door to flower deliveries. There were some from her parents, from the staff at the Cromayr Bay birthing suite, and even a posy from Leah Roberts.

There was also a message in her inbox from Malcolm, saying that if she was coming home for her birthday perhaps it would be good to catch up and see where it might lead…

Hell, no!

Freya slammed her computer shut.

And then later she felt the utter joy that came with the job of delivering a little one who'd share the same birthday as her.

Sophie Reece started to arrive in the world one foot first, causing her midwife more than a moment of internal panic. But there was Stella, coming in through the door and being amazing, followed by Dr Mina, who was the most calming presence. And soon there was the body out, with just the head to come.

'Patience…' Dr Mina said.

Guy Masters came in, and Richard did too, just in case this little one needed some more help. But, no, she was fine. Better than fine.

'Happy Birthday!' Freya said to the tiny new girl, once she was settled with her very delighted mum.

She was ready for her coffee break—seriously so—as well as a sit-down, but that wasn't going to happen just yet.

'Happy Birthday!'

And there they all were. Stella, Kelly and Angela, and there was Rita, and Guy Masters, and even Richard, no doubt hauled back to come in while passing.

And there was a cake, with '30' written in glitter balls. Apparently Rita had made it.

But no candles.

'They set off the smoke detectors,' Stella explained.

Freya briefly met Richard's eye and tried, as she had that first day, to think of a quip about fire extinguishers.

But she didn't say anything—couldn't think of what to say that would fit the moment.

She read her card.

Best wishes
Richard Lewis

She looked up, about to ask him what the hell that was supposed to mean, but he was suddenly gone.

So she ate cake, and laughed with her friends, and when Len came sniffing round for leftover cake for his animals Freya had it ready and wrapped for him.

It really was a lovely birthday.

Almost brilliant, in fact.

Just minus him.

But deep into her shift, coming up for nine o'clock, Freya was holding little Sophie while her mother got some very much deserved sleep and he came to the desk.

'Hello, *Richard Lewis*,' Freya snarked.

'Hello, Freya Ross,' he said, and took a seat at the computer.

'Why are you still here, Richard?' Stella checked. 'I thought you finished at six?'

'Yes, well, I'm covering for Simon, but I'm just about done.'

By the time little Sophie was asleep and about to be put in her crib he'd turned off the screen.

'I'm out of here.' But he spoke too soon, for immediately there came the ring of his phone.

'Excuse me,' he said to Stella as he answered the call.

But then he stopped being polite.

'What?'

He was *very* curt.

'I don't know—and I told you not to call me at work. I'm heading to a long case in Theatre, so I can't speak.'

He clicked off his phone.

'You are *such* a bastard.' Stella smiled. 'You just told me you were going home!'

'God, no,' Richard said. 'I'm checking into a hotel tonight. That was my mother. She's broken off her latest engagement and is currently staying with me and she's driving me crazy.'

Stella laughed and headed off.

Freya didn't know where to look, so she turned her eyes down to gaze at Sophie.

'Freya?' he said.

'What?'

She was still smarting about him writing *Best wishes* in her card and the use of his surname.

'You know how you used me?'

'I didn't *use* you, Richard, any more than you used me.'

'Yes, you did—but it doesn't matter right now. I don't want to go to a hotel. Can you please use me again tonight?'

She laughed but did not answer him. And he watched

as she walked away and put down the baby, taking time to wrap her carefully.

'This is the best birthday ever,' Freya whispered to little Sophie, and then she took a key from her pocket and headed back over to Richard.

'No strings,' he warned. 'And no talk of long-distance relationships and other such unmentionables.'

'Just sex, then?' Freya checked.

'Just that,' Richard agreed. 'But with my *very* best wishes.'

She slid over her key and he took it.

Richard hadn't really given much thought to his reaction when he entered her home. But it *was* a home now.

The scent of flowers hit Richard even before he had turned on the light, and when he did click it on the room felt different. There were deep red curtains that fell to the floor, and as he walked around he felt a soft rug underfoot. There were photos of family and friends on the shelves, and he knew he would love to be among them

But they weren't friends.

They were lovers.

Only it felt a whole lot more than that.

And then he did something silly—which struck him as odd, because he never did things like that. He went to his car, where there was a mobile printer which he occasionally used for looking at cardiac tracings.

Today, though, he printed a photo of himself and tucked it behind one of the pictures on her shelf.

And then he headed to the kitchen. He saw there was still no coffee machine. But there were bananas on the bench and lots of lovely food in the fridge.

He went into the bathroom and saw there were new shelves there, and a shower curtain covered in pictures of shells that he recognised from her home in Cromayr Bay. When he turned on the taps the water ran hot within a minute, so Richard had a shower.

Then he put the door on the latch, so Freya could let herself in, and got into bed.

'Happy Birthday,' said Richard.

Freya sat on the bed. 'Everyone keeps asking me how it feels to be thirty.'

'How *does* it feel?'

'I delivered a baby for an eighteen-year-old today,' she said, and he smiled. 'I don't think I like it,' she admitted.

'You got a lot of flowers.'

'I did—and there are presents waiting for me at home.' Then she remembered the message from her ex and gave a little shake of her head.

'What?'

'Nothing,' Freya said, but then decided that if there was anyone she could tell it was Richard. 'My ex wanted to see if we might catch up.'

'And will you?' Richard asked. He found that he had to concentrate on keeping his voice even as a little snake of jealousy slithered up his chest.

'Of course not!' Freya laughed at the very thought.

And the little snake slithered away as she put her hands around his neck.

He was curious. 'Why did you break up?'

She gave a shrug. 'Just… Why does anyone break up? Why do *you* break things off with women?'

'Because I get bored.'

She looked into those hazel eyes that never seemed restless when they looked into hers.

'So why?' he persisted.

'We wanted different things,' Freya attempted. Only

that wasn't right, because she did want a family one day. 'When I moved into my cottage he seemed to think it was his. And then, when I had the worst day at work ever— possibly the worst day of my life—I came home and told him.'

'And…?'

'He told me he was sorry, and he told me that he believed me when I said I'd done nothing wrong…'

'And…?'

'And then he went to work.'

There was silence as they stared at each other.

He would never have left her that day. Richard knew that.

And so too did Freya, because on the day when a woman he had never met had happened to be bleeding, he had dropped everything, swapped shifts, got in the car and driven her to Scotland.

'Freya,' Richard said, trying to give the other guy a chance. 'You sometimes have to ask for help. You can shut the world out with one glare, and…'

He could see behind the guarded look in her eyes though. Freya didn't need to stand semaphoring her needs—he read them and he felt them. Pity the fool who left her on a dark, dark day.

And more fool *him* if he didn't follow his heart, Richard thought as Freya stood up, peeled off her top and then unclipped her bra.

She slid down her jeans, and then her knickers too, and then climbed onto the bed, sat on his thighs and began to play with him.

'Shouldn't I be taking care of *you* on your birthday?' he asked as he reached up to trace the curve of her breast.

'I'm using you—remember?'

'So you are…'

And she was—but in the nicest of ways, imprinting his beauty on her mind. His flat nipples and the swirl of his chest hair. His dark hair and the soft skin of his balls as she held them. The way he grew to her touch, and the way he put his hand over hers and showed her just how rough he wanted her to be.

'Get on,' he said.

And as she did so she closed her eyes—not just because of the bliss, but because of the threat of tears, for she had thought they would never be together again.

Then she opened them and they stared at each other as he moved her hips, and then they melded into a kiss. He cupped her buttocks, feeling the softness of them, and feeling the way her hair was so silky as it spilled onto his cheeks.

He loved it that she held on to her cries. That this private woman, even as she squeezed her thighs and gripped him tight, even as she groaned and he felt her tension, did not reveal her hurt.

He held her by the shoulders and pushed her up, so he could see the concentration in her face and the parting of her lips as she came. He lifted and drove into her, and shot deep and she took every precious drop.

He loved it that they did not speak of love.

Not yet.

And that there was no need for either of them to ask if there had been anyone else since the last time.

Freya collapsed onto him.

'Happy Birthday,' he breathed again.

'It is.'

Truly it was.

But then, every day was made better, even the sad ones, when it was shared with him.

CHAPTER FOURTEEN

HE LOOKED TIRED, Freya thought when she woke the next morning. Even asleep he looked tired.

And it wasn't down to last night—she knew that.

He'd looked tired on the day she had met him and every day in between.

And if ever there was a man who deserved breakfast in bed it was him…

Richard woke to the sight of Freya holding a tray.

There was toast and *loads* of mushrooms, and a poached egg too, as well as a glass of orange juice. There was even a flower on the tray from one of her many birthday bouquets.

'What's this for?'

'I don't know.' Freya smiled. 'It's a rarity.'

'Well, thank you,' he said as she climbed into bed. 'What are you up to today?'

'Not much,' Freya said. 'On Friday I'm doing the London Eye at sunset with Stella, Kelly and Pat. I told them I wanted to cram in more of London before I went home and so we're going for my birthday.'

She looked over to him and they stared at each other. It was such a relief to be honest now about her leaving London.

'You're making friends, then?'

She nodded, but nothing had really changed—home was still home. So she addressed it. 'Richard, you warned me never to rely on you…'

'I know I did,' he said.

'So I'm making the best decision for *me*. I don't know yet if I'll go back to the birthing unit, I'm actually considering the main hospital. I've got a lot more experience now. I can go up a level—maybe two.'

The lack of rental income from her cottage was starting to bite, plus there was her rent in London…

'I'm not moving to Siberia.'

'I know.'

'Have you made up your mind about the private job?'

But they were teetering on the edge of long-distance relationship speak now, and he could not stand the thought of that. So instead of answering he gave her a kiss.

'I'm going to go.'

'Why?'

'Because I don't want to say something I might regret.'

He sounded as if he was cross with her, but it went a whole lot deeper than that. He didn't want to tell Freya that he too was considering moving.

To Cromayr Bay.

He would only say it when he was sure.

Until he'd properly thought it through, Richard wouldn't be sharing it with a soul.

It didn't stop his mother from finding out about it, though…

'What the *hell*, Richard?' Amanda said by way of welcome as he stepped through the door.

She was holding a letter.

'Did you open my mail?' Richard snarled.

'I was looking for an envelope and it just fell on the

floor. Where the hell is Cromayr Bay and why on earth is the hospital there inviting you to come and have a look around?'

'It's none of your business.'

'Well, I'm making it my business. You would die of boredom. I know you, Richard. You're like me.'

'Don't terrify me, I beg you.'

'I mean it. You would seriously keel over from a lack of adrenaline. I should know. Have you *any* idea what it was like being married to your father and playing second bloody fiddle to his patients while looking at sheep all the time?'

Richard rolled his eyes.

'You've got an opportunity to go into the private sector.'

'I don't want to.'

'Oh, for God's sake stop lying to yourself.' Amanda was so appalled that she forgot to lie about her snooping. 'You've already signed the contract for the private hospital. You can't back out now.'

'You've seen that too?' Richard said, and he was so furious at this invasion of his privacy that he lashed out. 'I believe *you* signed a contract too…"till death us do part"… and then you went and did it another two times.'

'Don't!' Amanda roared. 'I only married in church once and I meant every word.'

'*Please…*'

'Richard, for our twentieth wedding anniversary I told your father to get a locum, and he did, but then some patient needed him…'

'Mrs Lockley was terminally ill,' Richard reminded her wearily, because he knew the story well.

'And so was our marriage! Yet she survived longer than *we* did! Two more months, in fact. Your *hero* father didn't want to leave her, and in staying with her he neglected me.

On the night of our wedding anniversary. When a locum could surely have dealt with things for once. But instead *he* had to be the one to go out to her.'

Richard just stood there, stunned, as his mother spun the mirror and for the first time ever he could see her side.

'Do you know,' Amanda raged, 'when he got back that night he asked me to make him some Horlicks and then complained that there were lumps in it? I told him he wanted a live-in nurse or a housekeeper—not a wife. I gave him an ultimatum…'

And then she started to cry.

Really cry.

Not the dramatic tears he had grown up with.

'I thought he'd change when I threatened to leave him, that he'd beg me to stay, but instead he let me go…'

She really hadn't meant to end it. Richard knew that now.

'And then what did he go and do?' Amanda sobbed. 'He married our *housekeeper*. I'm sure there was something going on before…'

'No,' Richard said. Of that he was sure. 'He was gutted after you'd gone. He just moped around. He's a stubborn old mule, he would never have begged you to come back, and I guess Vera felt like routine.'

'You're positive there was nothing going on between them while we were still married?'

'I'm as certain as I can be,' Richard countered, for though he'd always felt sure, he wasn't in the game of giving absolute guarantees. 'Anyway, they're divorced now, and I don't think it was a love match—though I bet she got all the lumps out of his Horlicks,' he said, and through her tears his mother laughed.

'I loved your father, Richard, very, *very* much. But he completely refused to compromise.'

'I can see that now.'

And now Richard wasn't only terrified of being like his mother, but like his father too. While he knew he'd shut Freya out, he wasn't merely being stubborn.

For this decision had to be his.

He had to be certain before he made it.

He would not offer her a life spent with even a shade of resentment. He'd grown up on that. So many ruined dinners because his father had been working.

He thought of Freya coming in with the breakfast tray, all smiling and being nice. Of course she'd understood that he'd had to dash off.

But what if it happened every morning?

Most nights?

'I don't think I was cut out to be a doctor's wife,' said his mother.

'I don't know about that,' Richard said. 'I don't think he knew what he had.'

Until it was gone.

Freya would soon be gone too.

But Richard would only make the move if he was absolutely sure he'd never begrudge the fact that he had.

He made his mother a cup of tea, and by the time he had done so Amanda had calmed down.

'Think again about going private, Richard. You wouldn't have signed the contract if it wasn't something you wanted.'

'I was just trying the idea on for size. It's signed—but it's not sealed, nor is it delivered.'

'What on earth are you doing, looking at Cromayr Bay?'

'I've met someone.'

'Freya,' his mother said.

'How do you know?'

'I spoke to her,' Amanda reminded him.

Richard remembered the first morning he had awoken with Freya in his bed, when he had handed her the phone.

'She's Scottish,' Amanda added. 'So I'm guessing it's no coincidence.'

'Freya was born there—she's got family and friends there. She's tied to the place in a way that I'm not tied anywhere. I don't get your argument,' he went on. 'You're saying my father put too much into his work and never gave you enough attention. This move might be my way to negate all that.'

'It was never about the hours he worked, Richard. It was about the way he spent the hours he had at home. He gave all he had to his patients and left nothing for me.'

Richard had, up to this point, been quietly on the side of his father. He'd tried to stay loyal to both parents—of course he had—but in truth he had thought his mother a little shallow.

He didn't feel that now.

'I'm sorry,' Richard said.

'For what?'

'All the eye-rolls over the years.'

She smiled.

'But you are *never* going through my mail again.'

'I won't—but don't rush into this, Richard,' she warned. 'Don't end up like me…resenting the person you love.'

CHAPTER FIFTEEN

'RICHARD'S LEAVING.'

It was said just like that—and not even specifically to Freya.

They were lining up to board the London Eye, Stella, Kelly and Pat, all present, and Freya's heart felt as if it had fallen through a trap door.

'How's Von taking it?' Kelly asked.

'She's hoping to get off with him again at his leaving do!' Stella laughed, and then grimaced. 'Sorry, Freya. You had a bit of a thing going on with him for a while, didn't you?'

Freya nodded, and then pushed out a smile. 'I can't say I wasn't warned.'

The view from the London Eye was incredible.

It was the beginning of December and the sky was white, the trees bare and silver in the evening sun. Freya's heart twisted at the sight of the majestic city. Buckingham Palace, the Houses of Parliament, and the grey of the River Thames.

It was beautiful, and in that moment, high above London, Freya wished they might never have to come down.

Afterwards they went for a curry.

Freya's diary was filling up now, because it was nearing Christmas and she'd been invited to a couple of parties.

He would be gone by then.

She let herself into her flat and it was a relief to close the door and be home.

Home.

Freya looked at the curtains. Though they didn't block out the noise from the street she found the sound of cars and buses quite soothing now. And then she looked at the cushions, and the flowers sitting on the coffee table, and thought, yes, this was starting to feel like home.

Yet soon there would be no Richard.

No chance of seeing him at work…no hope of him asking to be 'used'.

And no scold in his voice when he told her off for her empty cupboards.

Oh, why did he have to leave *now*? Just when her world was coming right?

She went over to the shelf and looked at a photo of her little house in Cromayr Bay. Then she picked up the picture of her and her friends taken when they'd passed their midwifery exams.

And then she saw it.

Freya wasn't really one for efficient dusting, and she'd never taken the photos down until now.

But there it was.

A black and white picture of *him*, cut out on paper. And she wished, how she wished it was colour—because one day soon she might not remember the details of his eyes. Or the way he said her name—the change in his voice—so subtle at times that no one else would notice—that made her his lover and was audible only to her.

This is what you've lost, Freya.

And then her phone rang and the world suddenly felt better.

'Hello, Aunty Freya.'

Freya could hear the rise of elation in her friend's voice. 'Alison?'

'It's a girl—a little girl—four weeks early, but everything's fine. She's not even an hour old yet...'

There was a waver in her voice and Freya closed her eyes as elation dimmed and Alison dipped into the valley of pain.

'She looks like her brother.'

And then, for the first time since that awful day, Freya knew what to say. If his sister looked like Andrew then it was certainly true. 'She must be perfect, then.'

For Andrew *had* been. Utterly, utterly perfect. From his soft brown hair down to his tiny toes.

And Freya had been so busy taking care of her friend, helping her through, that she'd somehow stuffed down her own grief.

It had been such a gut-wrenching loss. For Alison and Callum and their families, and for their friends and all who loved them too.

It was sometimes said that it took a village to raise a child.

Well, Cromayr Bay had mourned when Alison and Callum had lost theirs. He had been one of their own.

'When can you come and see her?'

'I'll see what I can do,' Freya said. 'I have to go in tomorrow, but I'll see if I can swap over the next couple of days. I'll call you in the morning. Go and enjoy...?'

'Eleanor,' Alison said.

It was hard to cry herself to sleep after such wonderful news, and Callum had been sending over pictures and, yes, Eleanor was utterly, utterly perfect.

But just after midnight Freya lay back on her pillow and sobbed.

* * *

Morning arrived and she woke with Richard's picture in the bed beside her. Before she headed for work she took a photo of it with her phone.

At work, she made a beeline for Stella.

'I hate to do this,' Freya said, 'but my friend just had her baby and Kelly has said that she'll swap with me. I'll work the weekend.'

'You haven't carried the Obstetric Squad pager yet, though,' Stella said, and then looked through the roster. 'It's okay—Pat's on, so she can do it. You need two more times observing and then Dr Mina needs to supervise you heading one.'

Freya nodded.

'What did she have?'

'A little girl—Eleanor.'

'Gorgeous,' Stella said.

Richard was coming out of ICU when Freya saw him. He was with Dominic.

'Hi.' Freya smiled.

'Freya,' he said as he passed. But a few steps on he excused himself and caught up with her. 'Are you free tomorrow?'

'I haven't got the energy to be used,' Freya admitted—because really she was terrible at flings.

When he was present she could forget for a while the hurt that awaited when he left. But when they were apart it was hell.

'I just wondered if you'd like to go to dinner.'

So you can tell me you're leaving?

She guessed it was for that.

A bastard he might be, to some, but she *liked* him—very much indeed—and perhaps he considered a hospital corridor with his registrar waiting not the ideal place for a goodbye.

'I can't,' Freya said. 'I'm away home after my shift. I'm getting the overnight train. Alison had her baby late last night.'

'You'll be wrecked. What time does your train get in?'

'Seven—though I'll hang around at Waverley for the shops to open and then I am buying up pink.'

'So a little girl?'

'Eleanor.' Freya nodded. 'Then later we'll all be over to the Tavern to wet the baby's head.'

'Well…enjoy.'

Of course there were no offers from Richard to drive her this time, and she had an awful feeling this might be the last time she would see him.

He gave her a nice smile and then, because he was Richard, no conversation lasted very long without the interruption of his phone or pager.

This time it was the phone. 'My mother,' he said and pocketed it. 'I'll call her back in a moment.'

'How is she?'

'Well, she's found an apartment that isn't mine, so that's good. I don't know,' he said. 'I think that I misjudged her…'

And he left it at that.

Yet she desperately wanted to know more.

There was just so much to talk about—so much of each other to explore and to know.

And she had blown it, Freya knew.

CHAPTER SIXTEEN

WHEN SHE GOT to Waverley Freya drank coffee and ate almond croissants until the shops opened, and then went on a little frenzy of buying pink.

Then she took the train to Cromayr Bay. And as she crossed the bridge she gazed out over her home.

Home?

Yet London was also home.

Freya had never felt more confused in her life.

Visiting Alison was brilliant—to see her holding the tiny bundle and to know that they were both healthy and thriving, even though she might be struggling more than most new mothers today, was wonderful.

Callum went for a walk, and to meet some aunties who were arriving, and Freya had her first hold.

Oh, the baby was so soft and pink, and she had beautiful little eyes and a pretty snub nose. And when Freya put her finger to Eleanor's hand little fingers closed around it.

'She's gorgeous—and she really does look like...' Freya hesitated and then made herself say his name. 'Andrew.'

Oh, grief was so hard when it was personal. At work she could do it, but here, sitting on the bed, it wasn't just Alison she was scared of hurting.

It was herself.

Richard, damn him, had been right again. *She* was grieving too. Because right about now she should be taking Andrew down to the café to give Alison and Callum a break.

And as she gazed down at Eleanor a tear splashed down Freya's cheek for a little toddler who wasn't there.

'Freya?' Alison asked. 'Talk to me.'

'I don't want to say anything that might upset you,' Freya admitted, and as she looked up she could see that Alison was crying too.

'You might,' Alison said, 'because I'm easily upset. Right now I'm both the happiest and the saddest I've ever been. Andrew should be here.'

'Yes,' Freya said, and her tears fell freely now. 'He should be.' And then she said something else too. 'I'm sorry if I haven't been here for you, Alison.'

'You have been '

Alison was honest. She had no reason not to be.

'You were there every step when he was born, and at the funeral too. And you were here when I had the bleed and you're here now. Freya, losing Andrew changed things. Not for better or worse, but his death changed things. The world felt out of order. In many ways it still does. But even if you'd still lived down the street it was still something that I had to get through alone.'

'You've got Callum.'

'Of course I do. And we've got through this together. But there are parts of this that you can only do on your own. Look…'

She gestured to the window and Freya looked out, and sure enough there was Callum, walking on the green. And as Freya watched he ran the back of his hand over his eyes before heading back in.

He was crying alone and trying to be strong.

'Is there anything I can do?' Freya asked, not really expecting there to be. After all, if there was she'd have done it already.

If love could have fixed this, then there would have been a big brother in the room.

'Could you take this to him for me?' Alison asked, and untied a little pink balloon from Eleanor's crib. 'Can you tell him he has a sister? And can you buy a blue one for him?'

'Of course.'

And they were friends again—well, they always had been, but they had both needed to find their own way to grieve.

The door opened and in came Callum, all smiles but with glassy eyes, and several aunts and uncles who had just arrived.

'Freya!' His voice was bright. 'We've waited for you to get here but we can wait no more. We're wetting the bairn's head over at the Tavern tonight.'

'I can't wait.' Freya smiled.

She headed down to the gift shop with the pink balloon in hand, and bought a blue one as Alison had asked. She bought flowers and a little windmill too.

Freya hadn't been to the cemetery since Andrew's funeral, yet she found his grave easily, for that sombre walk was etched in her heart.

She had been looking out for Alison then, worried that after surgery and all the exhausting emotion her friend might faint.

Alison almost had.

Freya walked down the path and there it was, his tiny grave. She looked at his name and the dates on the little cross. Two days he had lived, but he would never be forgotten.

'You have a wee sister,' Freya said, though the wind took her words, and it was so cold the heat of her tears stung her cheeks as she tied the balloons and then put the little windmill into one of the pots and watched it whirling for a while.

The wind was biting as she walked the short distance to her home, and once there Freya lay on the bed, a jumble of emotions pounding through her heart.

Was she considering staying in London for a chance with a man who had told her never to rely on him?

Only it wasn't just for Richard—she was coming to love the place too. The noise and the people and the flower seller who had, for no reason, given her a rose the other day. And grumpy old Len. Oh, and not forgetting cynical Stella.

Yet she loved it here too.

At six, Freya dressed for the celebrations.

She did her hair and her make-up, and put on a dark red wool dress, black stockings and boots.

She made every effort—because she was thrilled and happy and she wanted to celebrate Eleanor's arrival. And she was so pleased that they'd waited until she was there.

And then she put on a warm overcoat and headed for the Tavern.

The party was in full swing when she arrived, and Freya knew she had been wrong before. The hardest thing wasn't walking into a pub knowing your ex might be there.

It was knowing he couldn't possibly be.

She hung her coat up and then headed over to the bar, where a large whisky was thrust into her hand. It was as if the entire town was out, celebrating the marvellous news.

Betty and Dr Campbell were in good spirits and even Leah Roberts had found a babysitter and was there with her husband, Davey.

It was absolutely the best night.

Even with a piece of her heart missing.

A big piece.

Actually, now she thought about it, just a tiny part of her heart remained.

And then she saw him.

He was standing in the doorway, wearing a suit and looking around...

Not Malcolm.

Richard.

She thought she must be seeing things, surely, but then she met his eyes and gave him an uncertain smile as he walked over.

'What are you doing here?' Freya asked.

'I've got a booking in the restaurant,' Richard said. 'If you'd care to join me?'

The newly refurbished Tavern Restaurant was both stunning and familiar. The gorgeous traditional Scottish stone walls had been retained, but a deep moss-green carpet gave the momentary feeling that they were outside a rugged castle. The tables were dressed simply in white, and in the candlelight the silverware gleamed, while on each tablecloth stood a small vase holding thistles.

And she was here with Richard.

Over and over Freya had to keep telling herself that— not that she could forget it—in order to hold on to the dream, else he might disappear.

They ordered drinks and made small talk with Gordon and between themselves as they waited for them to arrive. But when Gordon started to go through the menu, she blinked at the slightly impatient note to Richard's voice.

'Could we have a moment, please?'

'Certainly...' Gordon nodded.

Freya looked over to Richard and could see his discomfort. And then she knew why he was here. They had been more than a fling—they both knew that—and now, Freya guessed, knowing she was in Scotland, Richard had decided that she deserved a little more than a hospital corridor goodbye.

'I'm not sure if you've heard,' Richard said, 'but I've given in my notice.'

'I heard.' Freya nodded and thought her voice was a little high, as if braced for pain.

'I've been doing a lot of thinking,' Richard said. 'I didn't want to rush into things. I don't like snap decisions.'

'But they're what you do best,' Freya pointed out. 'You think on the run.'

'At work, perhaps,' Richard agreed, 'but I've had fifteen years of training and supervision and amazing mentors. When it comes to matters of the heart I have no clue. I didn't exactly have exemplary role models in that department...' Then he paused, because that wasn't quite right. 'I never thought I'd be asking my mother for relationship advice, but I have been.'

'And what advice did she give?'

'To take the private hospital position and to hell with you—and, frankly, I agreed with her.'

And then he saw Freya's pain, and knew that his job, when at all possible, was to take away pain.

He took her hand. 'I agreed with her for about two weeks,' he said. 'I accepted the role with Marcus and gave notice at the Primary. But then I spoke to my father too.'

'And...?'

'I didn't ask him for advice,' Richard said. 'Instead I gave it. I told him that he could quit telling me he was lonely, because it was his own bloody fault. He lost the love of his life. I don't intend to do that.'

Freya looked up.

'My ties to London are through work and friends. I didn't go to school there. I don't have family there. I understand that this is your home—the place you love. Now, I'm not sure if Cromayr Bay Hospital is big enough for me, but I'll try it for size if it means being with you. I love you.'

She had it all in that moment.

The gift of his love was like a shiny parcel, momentarily blinding her, and this gift came with a velvet box. He opened it and there was a ring. She could see it, but not really see it, for it was blurred by the tears in her eyes.

They were not all happy tears.

She had everything she wanted, Freya thought. Yet all she truly wanted was him. Richard.

'That won't be necessary.' She looked up and saw his face bleach pale, realised he thought she was rejecting the ring. 'I mean the move—not the ring.'

'Freya…?'

'I went on the London Eye and it was an amazing view,' Freya said. 'Not better, nor more beautiful than here, just different. Richard…'

She tried to explain the jumble of her feelings with a heart that was pounding and a head that was slightly giddy.

'After we broke up I was scared that I was thinking of extending my contract in London just in the hope of getting back with you…'

There—she had said it.

'I'd been warned by several people—including yourself—not to count on a future with you. And so I made my decision based on what I knew. I'm falling in love with London and, as exhausting as it is, I love the work. And…' She could be honest now. 'I love *you*. I had to give us a chance.'

'You're staying in London?'

Freya nodded. 'Can you retrieve your notice?'

'God, yes,' Richard said.

He slipped the ring on her slender finger and they toasted their news with a single malt whisky that tasted amazing on his lips when they kissed.

'And now,' Richard said, 'I'm having that game pie.'

He'd been waiting for it for a very long time.

CHAPTER SEVENTEEN

A WEDDING IN Cromayr Bay would never pass unnoticed. That was the beauty of home, Freya thought as she dozed on the train on her way up to Waverley.

In the end it was the bride who had struggled to get time off from work. She'd had one more Obstetrics Squad Emergency to attend before she could be signed off, and Stella had wanted it done before she renewed her contract. As well as that, her trips to Scotland had meant she had very limited days off to indulge in planning a wedding.

A winter wedding.

Richard, though, didn't start his new contract until the end of February, so he had been up to Cromayr Bay a few times without Freya, and had finally sorted out his phone so that Freya could call him.

It was a silent coach, so instead of calling she texted him to say she'd arrived at Waverley and was taking the train to Cromayr Bay. She was secretly hoping that he would meet her.

I'll see you in the morning, then.

Freya was dying to see him, but there was just so much to fit in.

Has your mother arrived?

Not yet.

They were both worried about that, and pretending not to be. Richard's parents hadn't been in the same room without a judge present for seventeen years. But he refused to think of that now.

Richard loved Cromayr Bay. It had the bracing, salty, sharp air that his body required. It was a place he could retreat to and a place he could learn to relax in, for that was necessary indeed.

And then his parents arrived.

The day before the wedding.

The concierge at the Tavern, who doubled as the duty manager, called Richard down to meet Amanda, who stood in Reception bristling.

'My room's not ready.'

'It will be soon,' Richard said.

'You don't understand,' she hissed. 'Your *father's* here. He's over there at the bar.'

Great.

A fight between his parents on the eve of his wedding was the last thing he needed, and so after a few nips of whisky with Freya's brothers, along with many other new friends who had joined them, the bear retired to his cave.

And then a horrible thing happened.

From the room above his own he heard his mother laugh.

Not a bad thing on its own.

But then he heard the unmistakable rumbling sound of his father's laugh too...

By morning Richard had decided that, while the restaurant might have been refurbished, the squeaking beds at the Tavern still needed an overhaul.

He *had* to tell Freya—except it wasn't Freya who answered her phone. Instead it was Alison.

'No, you *can't* speak to her!'

Freya frowned when she heard Alison's firm tone.

She had seen that it was Richard calling, but, given that she was getting her make-up done, Alison had taken the call.

'Let me speak to him,' Freya said, holding out her hand for the phone.

'No!'

It would seem that Alison was taking her Matron of Honour duties very seriously.

'Is it a medical emergency?' she asked Richard.

It would seem not.

'Are you going to jilt the bride?'

Freya rolled her eyes and snapped her fingers, indicating that she wanted to be given the phone, but Alison had other ideas.

'Then there's nothing that can't wait. Anything urgent, have the best man call *me*—not the bride!'

The flowers in Freya's bouquet were the very same as the ones she had bought on the day she had decided to give London a go. The bunch of pale lilacs perhaps didn't appear a very opulent display, but they were now the flowers that made her 'cheer up, love'.

And Freya was both cheered up and nervous as she felt her father's arm beneath her hand and she walked towards the love of her life.

Richard did not stare ahead, instead he turned and watched her every step.

Yes, Officer, I will remember what she was wearing for ever.

Her dress was the colour of a pearl moon as it hung over the local bridges, and on her feet were silk ballet pumps. The flowers he couldn't name, but he knew that she bought them often.

As for her hair... Freya wore it down, and yet it sprang up in curls about her face. Wild and dark, it moved with her.

Make-up? That he would never recall. For as her father let go of her arm and Richard took her hands nothing else mattered.

'You made it,' he said.

'Just.'

They shared a smile and a couple of words in that moment before proceedings commenced.

The vicar spoke of the seriousness of the vows before them as he addressed the packed congregation. And Richard's voice was lovely and clear as he repeated the words which became his promise to her.

'To love and to cherish, till death do us part.'

Those words had always made her a little sad, talking of death at a wedding. And yet they were actually rather gorgeous to hear, she thought, when she was being held by Richard's eyes.

He was taking this as seriously as she, Freya knew. He had avoided and hidden from love, but—like heartache—love found you and chased you until you either denied it or faced it.

And they faced each other now, and smiled as they were pronounced man and wife.

Richard kissed his bride. Their smiling lips met, but he felt the tremble of hers beneath his as emotion caught up with her.

'It's okay,' he said, and briefly held her, 'we've got each other for life.'

They turned and walked down the aisle to see many smiling, friendly faces. Some were familiar to Freya but new to Richard, and some were the other way around.

Freya knew there were friends from the Primary, who had made the trip, but first she smiled to her parents and her brothers, and then to Richard's parents, who stood side by side.

Freya seriously hoped there would be no arguing between them tonight—though Richard had told her it was his parents' problem if they did.

And then there was Kelly, Stella, Pat, Rita and Angela and, it seemed, half the anaesthetics department, including Dominic, who was looking forward to having his old boss back.

They stood and smiled for the camera, and it actually wasn't too painful because Freya had insisted on only a few formal shots.

'It's too cold to stand outside,' she had said, and so, surprisingly quickly, they were back at the Tavern, in the gorgeous new function room at the very top of the hotel.

Freya hadn't seen it before. Only Richard, who had organised things, had been inside.

It was stunning.

Huge long tables were dressed with tall white candles, and there were large bunches of wild Scottish flowers.

It felt as if they were in a castle, Freya thought. And the arched windows looked out on the view she loved—though she really didn't notice the view as Richard made his speech.

He kept it short and sincerely thanked everyone, especially those who had travelled from afar—'Including me,' he quipped.

He got through the formalities, then admitted a truth.

'I never thought I'd be doing this,' Richard said, 'but

I am so honoured to be here. As some of you will know, Freya and I have two places we call home—one in London, another here in Cromayr Bay. I love them both. And, as I've found out, so too does my *wife*.'

He paused, not for effect, but more because it didn't even sound odd to be saying that. It felt right.

And it sounded just right to Freya, too, and she gave him a smile before he spoke on.

'It's not the house, or the location, or even the view. It's the *people* who make a place feel like home. But at the end of the day you close the door. Freya,' he said, 'I will always be happy to come home to you.'

It was the loveliest day of her life.

Freya found out via the best man about a few of Richard's more colourful escapades, and she shared a smile with Stella. She couldn't say that she hadn't been warned.

And then there was a toast to the bridesmaids and the formalities were done.

Almost.

'This is our first dance,' Richard said.

'As man and wife?'

'No,' Richard said. 'This is our very first dance.'

Indeed it was, Freya realised.

She and Richard hadn't yet made it to the cinema, let alone the dance floor. And so it was utter bliss to rest in his arms for a moment and savour their first dance. One she would remember for ever.

Perhaps they should be gazing into each other's eyes, Freya thought, but it was nice just to be held and to breathe in the scent of him and enjoy a quiet moment.

That was how he made her feel. Safe in his arms, whatever the adventure. And he made her feel something else too...

She looked up to him. 'I want to break out of my skin

and dance,' Freya admitted, and they both knew how rare this was, since she was not a dancing type of person.

'When we're alone,' Richard said in his most deadpan, sexiest voice, 'you can certainly break out of your skin and dance. I might even join you!'

He made her toes curl.

And he made her smile in a way no one else did.

But then she saw something.

His parents were dancing and it didn't look strained.

In fact, they were gazing into each other's eyes.

'Richard...' She raised her head, but he knew what she had seen.

'I know.' He spoke low into the shell of her ear. 'That's why I tried to call you. I think they might be getting back together.'

'No!'

'Yes,' he said, and then he lifted her chin, so that she looked deep into his eyes. 'We'll never be like them. I'm going to take care of the love we've found.'

'And me,' Freya told him.

They would both take the best of care of this very precious love.

EPILOGUE

'BUT WHY WOULDN'T you have him *here*?' Amanda asked.

They were discussing Richard and Freya's baby, which was due in three weeks.

'Firstly, it might be a she,' Richard pointed out to his mother. 'Secondly, it should be Freya's choice. We're going up at the weekend for a few days and we'll decide then.'

Except that they wouldn't.

Richard didn't know it yet, but Freya was already in labour.

She did *not* want a false alarm, nor to get to the hospital and find out that she wasn't very far along and so she had been keeping quiet.

But she was certain now.

The contractions were fifteen minutes apart and they were getting stronger. The decision as to where to have their baby had now, as of this afternoon, become a moot point.

They went home to Cromayr Bay a lot.

Richard's job remained as constant and as high pressure as ever, but now, instead of him flying away, they drove to there. And if they didn't feel like driving they took the train, because it really was the most wonderful train journey and so relaxing.

Apart from at Newcastle. Each time the train pulled

into there Freya and Richard would exchange a glance as they recalled that text exchange that had nearly put an end to them for ever.

Her cottage was slowly coming on, and Richard loved their time there so much that a role at Cromayr Bay Hospital still wasn't completely off the cards.

After a couple of days spent catching up with friends and loved ones, or simply unwinding alone together, they'd get back in the car, or board another train, and come home.

Freya had fallen in love with London.

Properly.

She had started to fall in love with it when she and Richard had broken up. It had been her friends there who had helped her through, even if they hadn't known just how broken-hearted she'd really been.

They had both been a bit undecided as to where they wanted the baby to born.

Amanda, though, had clearly made up her mind. 'I hope you have it here.'

'Why?' Richard asked. 'I thought you enjoyed your stay at the Tavern.'

'I did.'

'Good.'

There had been no reference to that night—no mention, no comment. If Richard hadn't been unlucky enough to land the room beneath them he might never have known.

'Richard,' Amanda said now, 'can I have a word?'

'Go ahead.' He would not be following her into the kitchen so they could speak quietly. 'I'll be telling Freya what you say anyway, so you might just as well say it here.'

'Very well. Now, I know after I called things off with Roger, that I said I was through with men but... Richard, please don't roll your eyes. Your father and I have been seeing each other since your wedding.'

Richard said nothing.

'We haven't rushed into anything. We've both done that before, and we didn't want to put you through another wedding, but we…we got married last week.'

Richard just stood there.

'It was a quiet wedding,' Amanda said. 'We didn't want a fuss—or rather I didn't want a fuss—and so we went to Gretna Green, and had a little honeymoon at the Tavern.'

'Why aren't you both here to tell me?' Richard asked. 'Is he too busy working?'

'No, we were both going to come, but then we decided that it might be a bit much for the two of us to turn up at your door saying everything's all right now. While it is for us—well, we know that it can't have been easy on you. That's why I came alone.'

He smiled and kissed his mother the perpetual bride. 'Congratulations. And I really do mean that.'

Freya kissed her too, and then Richard got out some champagne. As he did so, Freya excused herself and went into the bedroom.

The pains were getting strong now, that was for certain, but also there was a need to be alone as she thought of Richard and all he had been through with his parents.

For what?

Nearly two decades apart and a whole lot of heartache in between—because neither would back down or consider the other person's side.

Freya knew she had a lot to be grateful for.

Of course, when she came out Amanda showed them the wedding pictures, and Freya made herself scarce now and then, because she wanted to tell Richard that she was in labour alone.

At last Amanda looked at the time. 'I really do have to go or I'll miss my train…'

'Does my father want his dinner?' Richard asked, and his voice was wry.

'No, he's taking me out.'

'Good for you.'

They saw her out, and although Richard hadn't jumped up and down at the news, Freya could tell he was pleased.

'At least it will make things easier on the baby.' Richard commented once she had gone. 'Just plain old Grandma and Grandpa Lewis. We'll have to wait until he's old enough to fill him in on the last twenty years.'

He recalled what they had been discussing before his mother had shared her news. They *did* need to make their minds up.

'Freya, if you want to have the baby in Scotland then…'

'We're having it here, Richard.'

'You don't have to make your mind up now.'

'The baby already has. The contractions are ten minutes apart.'

'Is that why you kept ducking out of the room?'

'Yes.'

But she didn't duck out for the next one, and he felt her stomach turn to rock.

'They're getting worse,' Freya said.

'They're getting *stronger*,' Richard teased, because he heard a lot of midwife-speak every day at work.

But then he saw the chink of anxiety in those guarded green eyes that only he could read.

'Do you want to go to the hospital now?'

'Yes.'

It was a wise choice, Freya had decided. The Underground wasn't an option, and she knew the traffic was terrible on a Friday night, even though the Primary wasn't a particularly long drive from where they lived.

'Oh, God!' she shouted as they didn't even move an inch through one traffic-light-change.

'You're doing really well.'

'No, seriously, Richard! I can't have it in a car.'

'You're not going to. We'll be there soon.'

'How soon?'

'Soon-*ish*,' he said.

'I'm stuck in traffic with an anaesthetist and I'm going to be too far along for an epidural!'

Richard said nothing.

And then there was the hospital, and the ugly grey building had never looked more beautiful to Freya.

He held her hand as they walked the terribly long walk along the yellow line, and when they pushed open the doors to the maternity unit Freya had never been more relieved to be anywhere in her life.

'Freya—welcome!'

Stella had got her name right for once. But she was a patient now, Freya realised as she was helped into a gown and examined.

'You are doing an amazing job,' Stella told her. 'You're four…nearly five centimetres dilated.'

'Only four centimetres!'

'Nearly five— and that's a great time to call for an anaesthetist,' Stella said, because that was on Freya's birthing plan.

Richard said nothing, even though he'd guessed that Freya wasn't really about to have the baby. After all, he had given many, many epidurals.

He said nice things as he felt her disappointment that she wasn't further along. 'You're well into active labour. Sometimes having an epidural too early can slow down the contractions.'

And again he said nothing when Stella informed them

that Dominic would be getting to them very soon—well, just as soon as he could...

Richard knew that if Dominic was delayed when his boss's wife was here then it would be with good reason.

Yet after some more waiting Richard better understood just how awful it was to see someone you loved in pain and be unable to help them. Worse, to be able to help them but to have to step back.

But then the door to D5 was opened and a very nice sight for any labouring mother was there.

'Hi!'

Dominic was a bit breathless, but his smile was so nice he put Freya at ease immediately. And both Freya and Richard knew and trusted everyone in this room.

'I think I'm in love with Dominic,' Freya said when the pain had eased.

'I bet you say that to all the anaesthetists,' Stella teased.

It was a gentle evening.

Dr Mina came in and checked that all was well, and as always she made Freya feel calm, and then Freya dozed on and off and later was thrilled when the night staff came on and she saw that her midwife was Kelly.

Things really had moved along because now, just after ten, when Kelly examined her she told her it was time to start to push.

The lights stayed dimmed and with Kelly's encouragement she was soon pushing effectively. It was a good epidural that had been administered, because she could feel the pressure of the contractions but not the pain—though it was still exhausting first-baby work.

And then the room started to fill up.

Pat came in to take the baby.

And Dr Mina came back in too.

Freya assumed it was just because she was a member of staff.

Not so.

The room was still calm, but Richard could see that forceps were fast becoming an option.

He pulled back Freya's leg as Pat did the same on the other side, while Dr Mina tied on a plastic gown.

'Freya,' Kelly urged, 'I want you to give me a big push *now*.'

The last moments were here, and Freya went inside herself.

'Freya,' Kelly said again, and it felt as if her voice came from afar. 'I need you to *push*.'

'Good girl,' Dr Mina encouraged her.

Except Freya was both scared and spent. She was slight and slender, and Richard wasn't, and this baby was large.

'Freya?'

She opened her eyes to him and Richard stared deep into the darkest of greens. He loved this sullen woman and the fight it had taken to gain her trust. He loved how she did not jump to anyone's command nor readily hand over her guarded heart.

Yet with time she had handed it to *him*.

And now he watched as she rallied again, and then, deep in the early hours of morning, a promise for the future arrived.

A boy.

He lay on Freya's stomach, curled up and stunned for half a moment, but then he let out a husky cry.

'Richard?' Pat said, and held out scissors for him to cut the cord.

Unexpectedly, he declined.

For once neither Richard's head, hands nor heart were steady.

The boy was perfect.

Freya pulled him up into her arms and held him, taking in every finger and toe and tasting his breath as he cried.

'Do we know his name?' Kelly smiled as she wrote on the little birth tags.

'William,' Freya said, and looked down at little William, unable to believe he was really here.

And then everyone melted away and they were left alone to have time to get to know their baby.

Richard had a hold of his son. He held him to his chest in those lovely strong arms.

Freya had never felt so happy and so balanced with the world.

'There are going to be a lot of people thrilled to know you're here,' he said to his son, in that lovely low voice.

And there were.

Yes, soon the phone calls would start, and visitors would be welcomed in, but for now it was phones off and time alone.

For both knew the importance of time.

Time together, spent as a family.

* * * * *

BABY MIRACLE
IN THE ER

SUE MacKAY

MILLS & BOON

Writing is a lonely occupation,
and yet we as authors cannot do it alone.

Baby Miracle in the ER
is the twenty-fifth Mills & Boon book I have written
for the Medical Romance series, and it's dedicated
to the people who helped me along the way. Number
one—my husband. He has been unfailing in his
support through the good and bad times. More
dedications to my family, my dearest friends, the
Blenheim Writers Group and my writing friends.
Thank you all so much for being there for me.

CHAPTER ONE

'AHHH!' TEARS STREAMED DOWN the pregnant woman's face while fear glared out at paramedic Stephanie Roberts. 'It can't be a contraction!'

No, please not that.

Steph pushed her elbows into her sides to control a shudder. The baby was ten weeks too early, according to the garbled comments the woman's work colleague had uttered as she and Kath, her crew partner, had loaded their patient into the ambulance.

Steph's heart grew heavy as the woman's grip on her hand tightened unbearably. 'Melanie, I want you to breathe deeply and try to stay calm.'

'Stay *calm*? When I'm losing my babies again. Tell me how to *do* that.' Her voice rose on every word until she was practically screaming. 'It's not *fair*.'

I will do everything I possibly can to prevent that outcome.

Using her free hand to wipe her patient's forehead, Steph read the heart monitor. All surprisingly normal there.

'Babies? You're having twins?' That would explain the early contraction. Twins often didn't go the distance *in utero*, but this early was not good.

'Yes!' Melanie huffed. 'We had IVF.' Another huff. 'For the third time.'

That grip on Steph's hand would break something any second now.

It was nothing compared to the ache in Steph's heart, though. Having to undergo IVF in the first place came with a load of unbearable pain and stress. Losing the resultant baby or babies would be beyond description. She herself hadn't got that far, but it had been bad enough—and the consequences even worse. This woman was facing her third round of unbelievable heartbreak if these babies weren't saved.

Stephanie couldn't comprehend that—not even with her own experience of being unable to have children.

'If it's okay, I'm going to examine you. We need to know what's going on.'

Maybe there was some miracle floating around that would mean the pain was just a stomach ache. Not that Steph was into miracles. There hadn't been any going spare when *she'd* needed one, but Melanie might be luckier.

'My back's been aching all morning, my waters broke, and now I've had a contraction. I know what that means.'

The woman's teeth dug so deep into her lip Steph looked for blood. None. *Yet.*

'Except I want to deny it so that it isn't true.'

She doesn't want me confirming what she suspects. I totally get that. But I'm a paramedic, not a counsellor.

Tugging her hand free, Steph moved along the stretcher and gently lifted her patient's skirt and lowered her panties. Dilation had begun. She bit back a curse. They weren't carrying *one* incubator, let alone two.

Now what? These twins had to be saved. They just had to be. *Somehow.*

Tucking the clothing back in place, Steph stepped to

the front of the ambulance, where Kath was focusing on the road, and spoke quietly and urgently. 'We haven't got time to go to Auckland Women's. Those babies are intent on making an entrance and I doubt they're going to take their time about it. Head to Auckland Central Hospital as fast as you're allowed.'

Actually, faster than they were allowed—irresponsible or not. But of course Kath wouldn't do that. And nor would Steph if she were behind the wheel. Or perhaps she might, knowing what their patient was facing. The speed limit was there for a good reason, but sometimes rules were made to be broken.

'I'll let Central ED know the situation.' Kath reached for the radio handpiece while simultaneously pressing the accelerator a little harder. 'Sorry I handed you this one.'

Not half as sorry as I am.

'It's fine.' Steph's heart lurched as she returned to their patient. Life could be so horribly cruel. 'Has your husband been told what's happening?'

'Someone at work rang him. He's going to meet us at the hospital.'

'Then we need to let him know where we're taking you. Where's your phone?'

'You just said we're going to Auckland Central, but my specialist said I have to go to National Women's if anything goes wrong.'

Those terrified eyes widened, glittering with unshed tears, and Melanie's chest rose and fell, rose and fell.

'There isn't time. I get it.' The fear became agony. 'Why do we keep trying? Why are we putting ourselves through this when it never goes right for us? What have I ever done to deserve this? I only want a baby. People have them all the time—easy.'

Steph reached for her hand, let Melanie hold tight; too

bad if her metatarsals were fractured. Apart from taking obs and willing the ambulance to go faster there wasn't much else she could do. She certainly couldn't soften the truth; because she pretty much knew what her patient was going through.

'Please don't do this to yourself.'

As if the woman could stop.

If the outcome wasn't good, those questions would haunt Melanie for months, even years to come. But Steph would make sure that didn't happen. There was no room for things going wrong. Not this time—not today.

'Concentrate on breathing normally so you're not agitating your babies. I know it's hard, but we have to try.'

'You think *breathing* is going to save my babies?'

The eye-roll didn't quite come off but hurt still stabbed Steph under the ribs.

Because she couldn't save the babies if they persisted in coming out into the world before reaching the emergency department. That would take a team of gynaecologists and neonatal specialists and a room full of specialised equipment and—oh, look, none of those were on board right now.

And because... *Yeah, well.* Because some things were never forgotten. No matter how hard she tried, how much she turned her life upside down and all around, Steph understood some of this woman's anguish too well.

'Mark's going to be devastated.' Melanie gulped.

Concentrate.

'Your husband?' she asked softly around the lump of sadness building in her throat. Sadness for Melanie or herself? Both?

'Yes.'

'Want me to call him?'

Someone had to let him know their new destination and

that his wife was struggling at the moment. Not that Steph wanted to be the one to break his heart, but it seemed he was a stayer—had hung around after the first time this had happened. And the second. Chances were he'd do the same again. Melanie mightn't understand but there was *some* luck on her side.

'Would you?' Melanie tapped her screen and handed the phone over, her teeth nibbling at her lip.

Right, get this done. Tap the phone icon, listen to the ringing, ignore the thumping in your chest. Get it finished, then focus on making this ride as comfortable as possible.

Kind of impossible, given the circumstances, but she'd do all she could to—

'Ahhh!' Her patient's hands clenched and strain tightened her face.

'Don't push, whatever you do.'

Easy said...

Shoving the phone aside, Steph moved to re-examine the woman's cervix. And cursed under her breath. These babies had an agenda of their own and no one, especially their mother, was about to deflect them. What if the babies popped out before they arrived at the hospital? What could she do to keep their chances of survival alive?

Think, girl, think.

The CPAP for breathing. Blankets for warmth. She could only hope they'd get to ED before any of that was needed.

Another contraction was tightening Melanie's belly. 'I can't do this.'

'We're doing it together.' Steph reached for a chilled hand, squeezed gently before once again examining her patient—and not liking what she was seeing.

Straightening up, she reached for the nitrous oxide. 'Suck on that next time you have a contraction.'

'I'm such a failure.'

'Hey, don't beat yourself up. Right now we've got two babies to think about and how best to increase their chances. So, are you up to sucking on that gas when required?'

A sharp nod.

Steph didn't have time for any more chit-chat. The baby that had been crowning when she'd last looked was now about to slip out into the world.

Preparing for the birth by strategically placing the Continuous Positive Airway Pressure instrument nearby, and soft, light blankets ready to receive the precious bundle, she held her breath and watched and waited for the inevitable.

The blue of her gloves was a sharp contrast to the pale skin on Melanie's thighs. It seemed impersonal to be welcoming a newborn into the world with a pair of vinyl-covered hands, but it was safer, and this little tot would need all the protection from infections and bugs it was humanly possible to achieve. It had to survive, and survive well.

Melanie tensed. 'Here we go again,' she forced out through gritted teeth.

'You're doing fine.'

No point telling her otherwise. Baby was coming, ready or not. *OMG*. So tiny and vulnerable. And blue.

Steph worked fast but carefully, knew nothing but that she was trying to save the tiniest boy she'd ever laid eyes upon.

Why hadn't she trained as a paediatrician instead of a nurse?

A tap on her shoulder didn't stop her.

'We've got this.' A male command. 'Fill me in fast.'

A quick sideways glance showed a man in scrubs. A further look around and she gasped with relief. The ambulance had stopped, the doors were open and emergency staff were crowding in.

'First baby arrived…' she glanced at her watch '…three minutes ago. There's another coming. They're ten weeks early.'

She rattled off details and obs, handing over the baby to another scrubbed-up doctor, who immediately began working on the infant.

Suddenly she was redundant. That relief expanded. Those babies weren't relying on her and now had a fighting chance. Fingers crossed. She'd given her all, but was it enough?

Squeezing through to the front of the ambulance to avoid the crowd of medical staff at the rear, she hopped out through Kath's door and stood out of the way, watching as the experts delivered the second baby. At least this wee lad went straight into an incubator. The first baby had already disappeared amidst gowned, masked staff with one purpose in their minds—to save his life.

Steph's chest ached where her heart thumped. These babies *had* to make it. No other outcome was acceptable.

'Can you unload the stretcher for us?' someone asked.

Instantly Steph was at the back of the ambulance, unlocking the wheels as Kath took the weight to roll the stretcher out.

'Here we go,' she warned Melanie, who was looking all hollowed out, her face sunken, her eyes glittering with tears, hands limp on her less rotund stomach.

'Are they—?'

'Yes,' Kath said firmly.

Please, please live, Steph begged the babies. *Your mum needs you.*

Once Melanie had been transferred to a bed Steph

leaned close. 'I'll be thinking about you. Hang in there and all the best.'

Then she made herself scarce, not looking around the department where she'd worked until two years ago, not wanting those memories on top of what had gone down today.

Her knees were wobbly. Her head thumped. And, damn it, her eyes were tearing up. Quite the professional.

Around the corner, out of everyone's way and sight, Stephanie stopped to lean her forehead against the cold wall and clasped her hands together on top of her head, her eyes squeezed shut in an attempt to halt the threatening waterfall.

Her first day working as a paramedic in Auckland and history had slapped her around the head. Her one attempt at IVF five years ago had failed and her husband had refused to try again, saying it was a waste of time when the doctors couldn't find any reason for her infertility.

No problems in *his* department, apparently. And no relief for her empty arms that longed to hold her own baby. It had hit her hard today. Much harsher than it had in a while. She guessed that was what happened when she returned home to where it had all happened.

'Stephanie? Is that you?'

The deep, throaty voice spun her name into unwelcome heated memories and warmed her skin to knock sideways the chill that had taken over in the ambulance.

Michael. Don't move.

It might be that she'd imagined him. Anything was possible today.

'Hello,' he said. 'Welcome back. You've been missed around here.'

The air swirled around her, touching down on the exposed skin of her face, her neck, her hands. A shape lined up beside her. A peek to the right and there was no doubt about it. Her imagination had *not* been playing games. She wasn't sure if that was good. Or bad.

Dr Michael Laing's shoulders and back rested against the wall, those legs that went on for ever were crossed at the ankles and his hands—oh, yeah, she remembered those hands as much as his lips—were jammed into the pockets of his crumpled scrubs. Just as she remembered him—utterly gorgeous, with that never quite styled hair falling over his forehead in soft curls.

When he said, 'Still as quiet as ever,' she shivered.

She wasn't ready for this—not after those babies arriving in her unprepared hands. 'Hi.'

Now leave me to pull myself together.

Right then her nose ran and she had to sniff.

He dug into a back pocket, held a handkerchief out. 'Here, use this. I promise it's clean.'

Did he have to sound *exactly* the same? Couldn't he have grown a polyp in his throat? Or permanently lost his voice from too much shouting at the sidelines of a rugby game?

'Those babies got to you, didn't they? They would have got me too if I'd been there. Stephanie…' He paused, gentled his voice. 'They're in expert hands, and everyone in PICU will be working their butts off to save them.'

Pushing away from the wall, she eyeballed him. Nearly choked on a sudden inhalation of air. *Michael.* That open, friendly face, those intense azure eyes still with the thin layer of need he'd hate to be recognised, that tempting mouth…

'I know. Sorry for being a goof.'

'Hardly. You're human.'

His smile was warm. Tentative?

She blew her nose, gave herself breathing space. 'I'm fine. Really.'

I was until twenty seconds ago. Liar.

She hadn't been right since she realised her patient's IVF babies were coming far too early.

His gaze was caring. Oh, how she remembered that caring. It was his middle name.

'My thoughts exactly. Just having a bit of a kip against the wall. I get it. It's how I cope with a crisis too.'

Uh-uh. Not so. Her memory was excellent. This man dealt with harrowing issues by striding out for hours, those long legs chewing up kilometre after kilometre as he went over and over whatever was eating him up. Her leg muscles had ached for days after she'd stuck with him for nearly three hours, charging along the city waterfront, listening as he worked his way through grief and anger one particularly dark day.

'I haven't suffered a crisis.'

Not much.

So why were her knees feeling like over-oiled hinges?

His mouth quirked in a funny, heart-slowing way. 'You used to be embarrassingly honest.'

As in, *I feel something for you, Michael and would love to continue seeing you*, honest?

But unlike that day, when he'd intoned in a flat voice that he wasn't interested, now there was a friendly warmth in his voice that touched her deeply. Made her feel vulnerable as the longing to tell him everything cascaded through her.

Tightening her knees, lifting her chin, stuffing that need way down in a dark place, she went with a different truth. 'I'm gutted that I couldn't stop those babies coming.' Even though she was not a doctor. 'They're far too early.'

His elbow nudged her lightly. 'No one would've been

able to do that, Stephanie. Please stop beating yourself up. You don't deserve it.'

Seemed he cared that she got this right—which, if she wasn't prudent, could make falling into those eyes too easy, could make leaving today behind for a while effortless.

Some of the frost that had been enveloping her heart for so long melted. 'That doesn't stop me wishing I could've.'

His eyes lightened as he looked her over with that smile lingering at the corners of his mouth, offering her support when she most definitely hadn't asked for it. Not that she didn't want to ask, but laying her heart out for him to see when she was messed up over those babies would not be her greatest move.

Time to go back to base and hopefully a straightforward call-out to someone who thought they were having a heart attack but in reality had indigestion. Whoever it was would get all the care Steph was capable of before being handed over to the ED staff. And at least then she wouldn't feel as though the ground had been cut from under her.

'Kath's full of praise for you. Says you were awesome.' Michael held her gaze. 'Hold on to that thought. Stop punishing yourself. It's not your fault your patient was well on the way to going into full labour by the time you picked her up. There wasn't another thing you could've done.'

Ping. Her lips lifted of their own volition. 'Back at me, huh?'

Her words of wisdom from years ago weren't so easy to accept when they came from the opposite direction.

'Only because you were right.'

He hadn't thought so at the time—had said she didn't know what she was talking about, didn't understand his grief over losing that little boy.

'Being a paramedic seems harder because the buck stops with us until we get to an emergency department. I never felt alone when I was working in here, or so responsible for someone else.'

So gutted when the situation turned to custard. The odds on one, let alone both those babies surviving were long. A shudder rocked her and she wrapped her arms around herself.

'Yet even in here you fought tooth and nail for your patients, no matter who else was around.'

His words were a balm, a gentle caress of understanding, and she needed that.

Steph wrestled with the urge to lean in against that expansive chest, tightening her hands into fists, rocking on her toes, flattening her mouth, staying away.

This was Michael—the man she'd worked with, laughed and joked with, shared one intense night with while they'd walked and talked for hours about a wee boy who'd died under his care. A night that had ended in making love for hours and which had led to more nights of wonder until— *ping!*—it was over. Gone in a quiet conversation about responsibilities and life and not getting involved.

He was one of the reasons she'd scarpered out of town and away from the job she'd loved, leaving her family and friends, renting out her house, to head to Queenstown where she knew no one. *One* of the reasons. Another of those reasons had also raised its sorry head today. Obviously a day for reliving the past. Great—just when she was starting over. *Again.*

There'd been a lot of starting over during the last two years. Which might explain this sinking sadness pulling at her. As if she was being tested to see if this was what she really wanted.

Yes, she did. As she had every other move. And every time the excitement and certainty had run its course and left her confused and a little more lost. But this time she was back home where she belonged for good. This was where her family was, her best friend, her past: the good and the ugly. It *had* to work out or she had no idea what else to do with herself. She had to accept once and for all that she would never have her own baby.

'Ready to go, Steph?' Kath appeared in her line of sight.

'More than.' She almost choked on the words. The need to be busy doing something—anything—was beginning to suffocate her. 'Good to see you again, Michael.'

She acknowledged the man beside her, ignored the disappointment filling his eyes, and headed to the ambulance bay without a backward glance. The only safe way to go. She'd got that first meeting out of the way—now she could move forward, box ticked. But first she needed to pull herself together and look the part of a happy woman tearing through life like there was no tomorrow.

Michael stared after Stephanie, absorbing the protectiveness he'd felt for her the moment he'd laid eyes on her, wanting to banish whatever had caused all that hurting going on, knowing he couldn't unless he was prepared to let her close.

Stephanie Roberts really was back in town. Rumour had warned him—reality frightened him. He'd been prepared as much as possible to see her, had been ready to say *Hi, how's things?* and get on with his day. He hadn't been expecting the slam of recognition from his body at the sight of her, the intense longing for her to be at his side, with him throughout…*everything*.

What he wanted now was to wipe away that pain, bring on a smile full of warmth—not that tight *I-am-not-hiding-anything* grimace that actually hid nothing. Forget staying uninvolved. At least until she was smiling again.

What's wrong, Steph? What happened to throw you against that wall like you couldn't stand up by yourself?

He knew her as a strong woman who didn't buckle easily. Or so he'd believed. Something had undermined that strength today.

His jaw clenched. Tension rippled through his muscles. Did her mouth still tip up higher on the left side when she gave a genuine, big-hearted smile? He'd thought he'd conquered those sweet memories of how he wanted to sing and dance when she smiled. Of how her toffee eyes were easier to read than a toddler's book. Of how calm he felt around her.

She'd never asked anything of him—except to go to a football match with her which, when interpreted, had meant have a future together. That had scared the pants off him and had had him hauling on the brakes fast. Getting in too deep hadn't been an option. He hadn't been able to give her the certainty she deserved, the 'for ever' she wanted.

Yet five minutes standing beside her, worrying about what was wrong, and it was as though the mantra he lived by had vamoosed.

He shook his hands, flexed his fingers, worked the tension out of his gut. There hadn't been a lot of ease between him and Stephanie just now. Nor a lot of smiling. Stephanie's eyes, laden with sadness—or was that despair?—and the colour draining from her cheeks had been like a rugby tackle around his knees.

Had she made the wrong choice when she'd swapped scrubs for a paramedic's uniform and that was what was getting to her? No, there was depth to that sadness—close to deep pain. That didn't come from changing jobs...not even for dedicated Stephanie.

Why aren't you back here working with me, Stephanie? Us? When did you cut off all that long, thick blonde hair?

'How've you been? *Really?*' he asked her shadow as she turned the corner into the ambulance bay.

He'd missed her.

Not that he was admitting it. No way in hell.

A recollection of gremlins haunting her on bad days nagged at him. Shame he couldn't recall the story of what had gone down in her life before he'd joined the department. He had an aversion to rumours and liked facts. And today the key to all this was there, swinging just out of reach. To catch it he had to follow up on today and track her down for a catch-up.

Or he could wait, since they'd be bumping into each other regularly if she was operating out of the local St John base. So, no catch-up needed—which meant he could dodge a bullet.

They'd worked well together, had been friendly, and apart from those intoxicating two weeks had had little to do with each other outside of the ED. Best it was left like that. She'd handed in her notice a fortnight after they'd split and he'd felt uneasy ever since. As though he'd lost the one chance of real happiness he'd had because he hadn't been prepared to put the past behind him and take a stand.

'Shouldn't you be knocking off?' James, head of the next shift, nudged him. 'Unless you've got nothing better to do than hang around staring after Stephanie Roberts—which surprises me.'

Why? Any man with blood in his veins would be doing the same—which kind of said James had ink in his. Something to be grateful for.

'I'm on my way.'

Not that he had anything planned for the night. Doing his washing didn't count, and getting some groceries would take care of all of twenty minutes. Both his close mates were tied up with babies and wives and apparent domestic bliss. Lucky guys.

It's all yours for the taking if you want it.

He didn't. One divorce was one too many on his life CV. Besides, there were already more than enough complications going down outside of work that left no time for him to care about anyone else. *But...*

The word was drawn out. But sometimes he wished he was going home to someone special—someone to love and be loved by with no qualification. Instantly Stephanie came to mind.

Jerking his head up, he snapped at James, 'Have a busy night. Catch you tomorrow.'

Immediately he felt a heel. If this was what briefly seeing Stephanie did then he couldn't manage spending any more time with her. He'd be a wreck within hours.

Charging through the department to his locker as if he had the ball and was being chased by the opposition forward pack, he snatched up his jacket and the keys to his motorbike. A spin over the harbour bridge in the chill winter air might cool his brain and freeze Stephanie out. And if it didn't? Then he was in for a long night.

Once upon a time Monday nights meant drinks with the guys after rugby practice at the clubroom. Now it tended to be pizza delivery and catching up on emails and other scintillating stuff at home. Of course he got an earful of noise from his mates for being the only one still single. Jock and Max could never leave him to get on with his perfectly ordered life. They loved getting in his face about it too much.

The idea of pizza didn't excite him today. Truth? It had stopped being exciting after the fourth Monday in a row— about two years back. But he wasn't being picky if the alternative meant cooking something. Though the steak in his fridge *would* make a tasty change... *Nah.* Then there'd be dishes to do.

'I see Steph's become a paramedic.'

James was still with him, digging into his locker as well, apparently in the mood for talking.

'Wonder why she's gone to the other side?'

Michael hoped it wasn't because she couldn't work with him any more. But that was more likely his ego getting in the way of common sense. Whatever the reason, he should be glad she hadn't returned to this department as a nurse, despite his wishing she had.

Working together was not an option when she tipped him off his pedestal too easily.

'Crewing ambulances isn't too far removed from the emergency department. Still the same patients, the same urgency and caring.'

The same sadness when something went belly-up. Could it just be that she was insecure about her ability? He wasn't accepting that. Not from Stephanie Roberts.

'But she was *made* to be an ED nurse.' James looked puzzled. 'Then again, we haven't seen her in a while, so who knows what's gone down in her life recently?'

Nothing awful, he hoped.

'She's not the first to take a change in vocation. There are days I wish I'd stuck to my rugby career, though my body is eternally grateful I didn't.'

His half-sisters hadn't been so thrilled at the change either, when it had dawned on them that he had less time and money to sort their problems.

'You were good enough for a full-time career?'

The stunned look on James's face had Michael laughing—and swallowing an unexpected mouthful of nostalgia.

'You'd better believe it. I played franchise rugby for over two years. I was out on the wing until a heavy knock resulting in a second moderate concussion had me thinking that if I wanted to be a doctor after the rugby inevitably came to an end then I needed to look out for my brain. So I handed in my boots.'

He hadn't been able to afford the risk of not having all his faculties in working order when he'd had other responsibilities needing his undivided attention. His half-sisters were his priority—had been since the day his father had extracted his promise to be the man around the place and look after them and their mother when he was thirteen, and from the way things were going, always would be.

Chantelle, in particular, made big enough messes with her life. What she'd have done if anything had happened to him was anyone's guess. One that he no longer thought about. Instead he'd just accepted his role to be there for both of them continuously, to save them whenever things went wrong—as they did far too often with Chantelle. Thankfully Carly seemed settled in her new life in England. Strange how she'd managed to sort herself out once he hadn't been there to support her... Their mother had taken off overseas so there was no having her to sort out.

'No regrets?'

He didn't need this conversation, but he'd been short with James and wanted to negate anything bad.

'Some—but there'd have been a lot more if I'd suffered serious head injuries.' Playing such a physical sport always had its issues. 'Quitting was the right call.'

At first he'd missed the team camaraderie and the thrill of winning a hard-fought-for game, but he still had his two closest mates and it hadn't taken him long to get into his stride studying to become a doctor. He'd had plenty of practice helping his half-sisters out of the mischief and chaos they'd got into, so extending that help into a medical career where he dealt with vulnerable people daily—hourly—was natural. Which was why losing a patient despite giving everything he had in the tank always hurt.

Stephanie's earlier sadness had twisted his gut. She'd know those babies would now be tucked into incubators with monitors attached to their tiny bodies while specialists worked their butts off to save them. Yet he suspected she still needed a shoulder to cry on, or a friend to walk it out with, talk it through with—except, being her, there probably wouldn't be much talking.

What time did her shift finish?

Leave it alone. Stay uninvolved.

But he owed her. She'd been there for him when Jacob Brown had died in his hands. She'd listened without lecturing, she'd walked beside him as he dashed around the city for hours and had limped for days afterwards. She'd kissed him to the point when he didn't know where he began and ended. She'd fallen into his bed as eagerly as he'd taken her there.

Definitely stay away.

It had been two years. She wouldn't be the same woman. Must have another man in her life, in her bed by now

Anger flared.

Down, boy. You have no rights here. You sent her packing.

If there *was* someone special he should be pleased. She'd be able to talk out what was bothering her tonight.

The anger only increased, and he felt his hands clenched at his sides, his abs drawn tight.

Go—ride over the bridge, head north for an hour. Turn off the brain. Then order pizza.

Man or no man in her life, Stephanie had family and friends here. He knew that much from the past. She'd be fine. Better off if it wasn't *him* hanging around like a dog after a bone. He might make a mistake and touch her again. He still burned with the need to hug her that had floored

him the moment he'd first seen her pressed up against the
wall as though she could no longer hold herself together.

Hell. He had not given her what she needed. He'd let
her go without a word. Without a hug. Without an honest-
to-goodness *Glad to see you and I want to help you* smile.
Just like last time.

Wise move for him.

Unkind and unfair on her.

CHAPTER TWO

Steph slipped into her jacket with a grateful sigh. The ambulance was restocked for the night crew. Six o'clock had clicked over on her watch. Definitely time to be someplace else.

Only that meant picking up something from the supermarket to take back to the house to heat and eat while watching the second instalment of the thriller she'd recorded last weekend.

A night on her own wasn't appealing after the day she'd had. If only her brother and Jill weren't away on their extended honeymoon she'd go and hassle them and talk about random stuff that had nothing to do with babies or Michael.

For a moment her mood lightened. She still struggled to get her head around her brother marrying her best friend. Their relationship was grounded in history and love. A *lot* of love.

Stepping outside, she gasped as cold, damp air dumped on her. The Italian summer she'd enjoyed last month seemed for ever ago. The zip on her jacket pinched her chin when she tugged it high. When had this drizzle started? It had been dry on their last call-out—but then it *had* been dark and she hadn't been weather-watching.

'Hi, Stephanie.'

Only one person called her Stephanie. Usually she

didn't like it, thought it too formal, but in that particular deep, husky voice it was more than okay. Or was that only because she was feeling so out of whack?

'Michael.'

'You're done for the day?'

'Yes, thank goodness.'

The need to be busy had long disappeared, leaving her drained and despondent. Glancing around the car park she saw him standing at the open driver's door of a shiny hatchback—nothing like what she'd expected him to be driving. Too domestic. Did he still own a motorbike?

'It's been a long day.'

That was telling him too much. From deep inside, she dredged up a smile, denied the tightness those long legs and toned thighs filling his jeans created in her toes.

'Have you been loitering around the ambulance station?'

'Yep.' He grinned cheekily. 'I tried walking in but this place is like a fort.'

'We can't let in just *anyone*—especially doctors with nothing better to do with their time.'

What was Michael doing here? Surely he hadn't stopped by to say hello to *her*?

'Not sure if you know, but those babies are hanging in there, doing as well as can be expected. I phoned PICU as I was leaving for the day.'

He'd come to tell her that? Seriously? Mr Non-Involved had found out the most important news for her.

'No one would tell me a thing because I'm not related. I was desperate to know how they were doing.' *Careful.* 'That's fantastic.' Definitely better than the alternative.

'There are *some* advantages with my position.'

His grin was now a soft smile, winding around her like a cloud of kindness.

'Want some company for a bit? Talk some? Up to you.'

Amazement stopped her feet from moving forward, stalled her brain. He'd offered *that* to the woman he'd once told he didn't want anything more to do with outside of work? The man was still single. Or so she'd heard from one of the ED nurses. Not that she'd been asking…

Come on. He's hot, popular and fun. There's single, and then there's single with a woman on his arm.

There'd always been a queue of women waiting for his attention. Gorgeous young women who could have babies. Not a thirty-two-year-old with a chip on her shoulder bigger than the crater on Mount Ruapehu, who hadn't been able to conceive with her ex no matter how often they'd tried.

You promised to leave all this behind and start over when you returned home. One bad day doesn't give you reason to go back on that.

Yeah, yeah

'I'll take a rain-check.'

Wimp.

'I need to get out of my uniform, then eat something.' Now that her stomach had settled down to normal it was hinting that grub would be good.

'If food's what you're wanting it's pizza night.'

He wasn't begging, nor pushing too hard. He was saying she was welcome to share a meal if she wanted. And talk if she needed.

That was *not* happening.

'Pizza night? Because it's Monday?'

Michael nodded and gave a wry smile. 'Tuesday's Thai.'

Steph couldn't help it. She laughed. So much for keeping her distance. 'Cooking not your thing?'

'Always seems a bit pointless when it's only for me.'

'I can relate to that.' Definitely still single.

He locked his eyes on her. 'Well? Join me? You can

jump in and I'll call you a cab when you're ready to go home.'

She hesitated. It was so tempting.

Oh, get real. You came home to face up to Michael, work him out of your system once and for ever. So start now.

While one half of her brain was raving the other side thought spending some downtime with this man might not be the wisest thing to do. Especially tonight, when her emotions were already ragged.

'My car's right here.'

The sporty little number had been her big indulgence the day she'd arrived back in town. All part of the statement she'd made about settling down for good. Every time she climbed into the car it was a reminder of that. Some days it made her happy. Today she wasn't so sure she'd done the right thing.

'Then follow me.'

She hadn't forgotten where he lived. How could she with all those memories of what they'd got up to in his house?

Opening his car door, he paused. 'I'm not going to pressure you into talking about something you'd prefer not to, Stephanie. Chilling out after something that obviously upset you today could be cathartic. That's all.'

He was offering to do for her what she'd done for him when he'd been cut up over losing that little boy. Her chest squeezed painfully. Why not? He would do that for anyone, because he knew what they'd be feeling, thinking, wanting.

Anyone, Steph, not just you.

Which was why she answered with, 'I'll be right behind you.'

She could always take a wrong turn if she changed her mind in the next few minutes.

Except the pull of hot food that she didn't have to

prepare—meaning throw in the microwave—was hard to ignore. Her empty house would be cold. More than that, the idea of company for an hour or two was impossible to refuse. Especially Michael's company.

A car turned into the parking lot, its headlights swishing across Michael's car, showing what she'd been too busy focusing on him to notice. In the back was a child's car seat with a small child strapped in to it—which explained the family wagon.

Was that why Michael had aborted their fling back when she'd fallen for him? He'd already had a woman in his life? The mother of his child?

Her stomach clenched. But he'd said no commitment and claimed he was happy on his own. Interesting. Confusing. And the end to the idea of sharing pizza.

'Sorry—change of plan. I think you've already got enough people in your life without adding *me* to the mix.'

A frown appeared. Then he saw the direction her eyes had taken. 'You haven't met Aaron yet.'

'Very smart of you.'

It could be Michael Junior, for all she cared. She wasn't getting caught up in anything that involved another woman in his life—not even for some cathartic relaxation.

'Best I head away.'

His sigh carried across the wet concrete. 'Aaron's my nephew. I've just picked him up from daycare. We often hang out together in my house when I'm not at work. We'd love some company.' He stopped, his body more tense than it had been a moment ago. 'Okay, *I'd* like *your* company.'

He sure knew how to ramp up the pressure.

Or was it that she didn't know how to resist those friendly eyes filled with concern for her? Could it be that Michael was not quite as confident with women as he made himself out to be? Or was that just with her?

He hadn't often taken advantage of that queue of willing women, she recalled. Then again, it had been a while since she'd seen him and anything could have happened to change him.

Stop overthinking things.

What harm would a couple of hours' eating and chatting cause? It wasn't as though she was signing up for life. No, she was *getting over* him for life.

'Lead on.'

Her heart was safe, she assured herself. He'd already rejected her and they wouldn't be going back over old ground.

Her sigh was long and slow. Getting over him had seemed straightforward when she'd left Auckland. She wasn't falling for that trick this time. It was going to take time and patience and toughness—starting with spending time with him.

'Bugsy's gone!' Aaron hollered at the top of his lungs.

How could such a small body create so much noise?

'We're nearly home, buddy. I'll get him for you then.' Michael took a quick look in the rearview mirror at the following headlights. Stephanie?

A streetlight shone on the red paintwork of the racy little number that she drove. Surprise lifted his mood. Gave him a warm, fuzzy moment. As if he needed a woman's attention...

Stephanie isn't just any woman.

Therein lay his problem. He helped others—did not expect the same in return. When he'd promised his father to look out for his half-sisters he'd believed his dad would love him more. *Wrong.* His father loved each of them—but not enough to stay around.

Likewise his ex-wife. She'd told him he'd failed her,

hadn't lived up to the promises he'd made on their wedding day. He still didn't understand that—unless she'd meant he hadn't been supposed to change careers and move away from the fame and glamour of rugby to a set of ugly scrubs.

'I want Bugsy *now*!'

Ouch. His ears hurt. It used to be better when Aaron couldn't talk.

'Quieten down, buddy. I can't reach him while I'm driving so you'll have to wait.'

Reasoning with this lad was pointless, but he kept trying day in, day out, in the hope that eventually Aaron would start to understand that not everything would go his way all the time. Not that it helped when his half-sister immediately undid all his work by spoiling the kid rotten. It should be *his* role as uncle to spoil him, but someone had to be the sensible one in this family and it seemed the cap was made for him.

'Bugsy! Bugsy! Bugsy!'

It would have been funny if the stuffed monkey's name hadn't got louder with each utterance and tiny feet hadn't been pummelling the back of Michael's seat.

He chose to ignore the outburst. They usually didn't last long, and tonight he wasn't in the mood for an argument that would go nowhere. Tonight he wanted to indulge himself for a change. To allow some 'me' time with Stephanie. Not that he intended anything more than catching up on what she'd been up to since heading to Queenstown—and maybe learning why she was now a paramedic and not doing the job she'd loved so much.

Turning into his wide drive, he held his breath. Released it when her car pulled up beside his. She hadn't done a bunk. Which probably meant she was more upset than she realised.

He was under no illusions that she *wanted* to spend time

talking about those babies and how lucky they'd been so far. But why had she been so distressed? He'd seen her deal with losing patients, young and old. Once he'd had to pull her away from giving CPR when there had been no chance of bringing their patient back to life. Yet he'd never seen that level of despair and pain in her eyes.

'Bugsy!' A solid kick in the back of his seat.

'Aaron, that's enough. We're home now, and we've got a visitor. A nice lady you can say hello to.'

Lifting his nephew out of the seat, he had to hold tight as Aaron wriggled around to see who this stranger was. The lad loved people—knew no fear about approaching anyone. Only a good thing if the world was full of kind souls.

Stephanie flipped her key-lock and joined them, those slim legs and just right breasts filling her green and black uniform in ways the designers wouldn't have planned on. Her gaze trolled the front of his massive house.

'I'd forgotten how grand this place is. You did well getting your hands on it.'

Forget *hands*. It had taken a load of hard-earned money, and then some, but it had been worth every cent. Pride filled his chest. It was a very special house—one that had sucked him in the moment he'd seen it from this very spot. It was tucked neatly into a gentle slope, making the most of its location, while inside the floor-to-ceiling windows highlighted the view over Waitemata Harbour, and the deck was the best place in the world to sit and relax after an arduous day in the department.

'I bought it when I quit rugby and began studying full-time. Figured it would be a good investment and there'd be no temptation to fritter away my money over the years until I started earning again.'

'You played professionally—I remember. Why give up?'

Her gaze left the house to cruise his shoulders and chest, headed lower. To his thighs.

At least that was where he presumed her intense gaze was now fixed. Even if it was the concrete he stood on, his groin had tightened anyway. He cursed silently.

For the second time that day he explained. 'Rugby wasn't a career that'd take me into old age.'

The left side of her mouth lifted. His belly joined in on the tightening act.

'Can I carry anything?' she asked as he juggled Aaron and the bag of necessities that went everywhere his nephew did.

'I've got it.'

'You're a dab hand at this,' Steph quipped as he managed to unlock the front door and not drop child or bag. 'Had lots of practice?'

There was more to that question than the obvious. 'Only with this guy.'

That should stop any ideas she might be getting about him and any kids he might have.

The wind rustled the bushes and the drizzle got wetter. 'Come inside before it starts bucketing down.'

'I want Bugsy!' Aaron cried.

Oh, hell.

When he should have been retrieving the toy he'd been focused on watching Stephanie clamber out of her car, noting those legs he had X-rated memories of and that perfectly rounded butt.

'Bugsy!'

'Hang on, buddy. I'll get him in a minute.' First he had to unload onto the entrance table.

'Something I can do?'

'There's a stuffed monkey in the back of my car. Under my seat, I think.'

'I'll grab it.'

'Thanks.'

Car tyres squealed on his driveway. *Chantelle.* And in a foul mood, judging by the flat mouth and glittering eyes. Stephanie was about to learn more about his private life than she'd ever wanted to know.

'Michael, when are you going to stop interfering in my life?'

'Mummy!' Aaron wriggled out of his arms and trotted to Chantelle.

'Hey, baby.' Chantelle might be angry with him, but there was only love in her eyes when she swung her boy up into her arms. 'How's my darling?'

'Chantelle, I want you to meet—'

The love dipped as she yelled, 'I didn't ask you to pick him up. So I'll say it again. When are you going to stop interfering in my life?'

When you stop expecting me to... When you stand on your own two feet all the time.

'They phoned from the daycare centre to say you hadn't turned up and they couldn't get hold of you.'

He held on to his own temper, knowing from experience that losing it wouldn't help a thing—especially when Chantelle was in one of her rages. A quick glance across to Stephanie and his stomach curdled at her shocked expression.

'Chantelle, can we—?'

'That doesn't mean you can charge in and take over. I got there before they closed. That's all that matters,' Chantelle ranted.

No mystery about where Aaron got his lungs from.

Michael closed his eyes, dug deep for composure—because right about now he was going to lose it, and that couldn't happen. What sort of example would that set for

Aaron? Plus, he most definitely did *not* want Stephanie seeing him getting angry.

'Mike, you've got to stop taking charge all the time.'

The octave levels had dropped, and Chantelle was using 'Mike', meaning he was in for a lecture.

She began placing Aaron in the car seat in her own vehicle. 'I'm a good mum. You've said so yourself. I hadn't forgotten Aaron—I just got caught up with a tutor going over my last paper and time got away. It happens—and not just to me.' She stabbed the car's rooftop with a finger. 'I never forgot about him, and I knew I had to get to the centre before six-thirty.'

He lived with the dread that his beautiful sister would start the slippery slide back into hell and this time take his nephew with her. But she had a point. She was an excellent mother and she didn't neglect Aaron—she loved him to bits.

'I'm sorry.'

'Yeah, yeah.'

The door slammed, and then she was belting herself into her seat and revving the engine. At least she had the sense to back out slowly, and her speed down the drive was careful. Just as it should be with a three-year-old on board.

Stephanie stared after the car as the tail-lights disappeared out of sight. 'What just happened?'

'You haven't met my sister.'

Her eyes widened as she turned to look at him. 'That was your *sister*?' Disbelief echoed between them.

'We're not alike.' *At all.* Same father—nothing much else to show a connection. Though that wasn't true. They had the same colouring. The same wariness. Had learnt the hard way about sharing themselves with outsiders.

'You okay that you're not getting time with your nephew?'

'I'm good. I'd better order that pizza.'

He didn't move, suddenly exhausted. Watching out for his sister did that to him sometimes. He needed time out. Strange, but he knew Chantelle would be the first to tell him to go for it.

Stephanie was making him uncomfortable with her intense scrutiny. 'I'll take a rain-check. You look like you could do with some alone time.'

'Can't say I'm hungry any more. Sorry.'

Her hand gripped his arm. 'Michael, it's fine. Truly. We can catch up another time.'

'Thanks for understanding.'

'Who says I did?'

Her smile kicked him in the gut.

'See you tomorrow.'

Steph slid into her car, clicked the belt in place, watching Michael standing there, waiting patiently for her to leave. *Wanting* her to leave.

Would he phone his sister and have it out with her? Or did this happen often enough that he'd let it wash over him? He didn't look comfortable—had been tense from the moment that car had flown up the drive and Chantelle had leapt out. Talk about a human tornado...

Putting the gear in reverse, she started to back away. Hunger pangs hit her. The idea of something nuked made her wince. It wasn't the way to look after herself. Was there a restaurant on the way home that'd do a takeaway for her?

Something banged lightly on her window. She braked and Michael appeared at her door.

'Come inside. I invited you here and now I'm letting you go without feeding you.'

If she went inside with him his sister's accusations

would follow them, hold them back from relaxing over easy conversation.

'Not tonight.'

But they both needed to eat. An idea struck.

'Get in. We'll go for a beer and a meal at the pub round the corner.'

He'd say no. But the idea of sitting in a warm pub with lots of people to distract her was brilliant.

'I'm headed there.'

'I'm supposed to squeeze into this tiny thing you call a car?'

Turning her down was warring with interest in his eyes.

'See it as a challenge.'

He never dodged one of those.

The passenger door opened.

'My knees and ears are about to become best mates.'

She laughed. 'Do you want to tip the seat back so you can lie down?'

Finally the last of the ball of tension in her stomach unravelled and she played the piano on the steering wheel until Michael got belted in. Spending time with him was exactly what she needed—not her empty, lonely house.

At the pub, with drinks in hand and fish and chips ordered, they found somewhere to sit away from the noise of people talking too loudly. It was good to get a load off her feet and lean back against the leather-covered wall of the booth.

'Just what the doctor ordered.' She sipped her beer.

Michael mimicked her. 'Perfect.'

After glancing around the crowded room he came back to look at her.

'Tell me about Queenstown. There's so much to do outdoors—what did you try?'

Staying on safe subjects was good. 'I learned to ski—

or rather I started to. Falling off and twisting my ankle put me off *that* pursuit. Next I joined a tramping club and went on some amazing walks in the mountains—until a group of us had to sleep outside an overcrowded hut one night. Being woken by a huge possum crawling over my sleeping bag gave me the heebie-jeebies and I quit tramping.' She shuddered. 'Furry creepy beasts…coming right up to my head looking for food.'

'Then you took up crochet?'

Michael's smile sent her stomach into chaos. The fish and chips had better be a while away.

She choked on her laughter. 'Might've been wiser than salmon fishing.'

He groaned. 'What happened?'

'I never learnt when to stay still, always went one step too far—and I fell in, filled my waders with freezing water straight from the mountains every time.'

'Did you catch any salmon?'

She shook her head. 'They were totally safe when I was around.'

'I tried trout fishing in Taupo once. I'd rather be running around a rugby field.'

'You miss it?' It must've been hard for him to give up when he was still a rising star.

'Yes and no. The body's too old to take the knocks now. I like to win—don't take coming second very well.'

That was what had lifted his game from good to exceptional, or so his coaches had said in one article she'd read online.

He drank down half his glass of beer. 'It wasn't easy, giving up a lifelong dream, especially when it seemed half the world was watching me.'

'It was your choice?'

'Yes, it was—and I don't regret it.'

He must be strong to do that. At a young age the temptation to stay in the limelight would've been hard to ignore. She needed to follow his example as she got on with living back here. Days like today would occur occasionally, but she couldn't let them decimate her. Her reaction to the birth of those twins had to be a one-off—anguish to be dealt with and put away. She needed to be strong, too.

A big, warm hand covered one of her smaller, chilled ones. 'Tell me?'

He could see her thoughts? Probably not hard when her mouth wasn't lifted in a smile any more, her hands had grown cold and her body had sagged forward.

'I had IVF once.'

He didn't look shocked, only sad for her. 'You lost your baby?'

'I didn't get that far. Thank goodness. It was bad enough not conceiving with all the help available, but to get pregnant, feel your babies grow inside your belly and then lose them is beyond my comprehension.'

'That isn't a line I have to understanding things.'

Oh, God. This wasn't easy. Yet it felt good to tell Michael. She hadn't talked about this to anyone since Freddy had left her.

'I was probably way off the mark, but, yes, I hurt. For Melanie. For me. For those babies. Hers and the ones *I* can't have.'

Michael was up and around the table, sliding in beside her, his arm around her shoulder bringing her close to his warm body.

'You're resilient. You might've had a wee moment in ED, but then you straightened up and got on with your job—saving others.'

It hadn't been that easy, but she had found an inner strength. 'Thank you,' she whispered.

He pushed her glass towards her. 'Were you married or in a relationship?'

'Married for four years. Thought it was for ever. We both did. But the pressure of undergoing fertility treatment was hard…having it fail was much worse. We didn't survive.'

Gulping at the beer, she thought back to Freddy and his tears the day he'd told her he couldn't stay any longer, that he'd given all he had, his tank was empty.

'I don't blame Freddy for going. It was one of those mazes neither of us could find a way out of.'

Counselling might have worked, if Freddy had agreed to attend, but he'd refused. He was a man, and men didn't *do* spilling their hearts to strangers. Not him, anyway. Not even for her, no matter how much she'd pleaded. Over was over, and he didn't want to be with her any more.

'He should've stuck to you like glue.' Michael was tense against her, his voice fierce. 'Not walked away when the going got tough.'

She pulled away from Michael's arm, slid along the seat to put space between them. Staying curled against him was making her punch-drunk. His defence of her was wonderful, but it undermined her determination to go it alone in her quest to get her future sorted and never be rejected by anyone again. She'd promised herself she'd get over Michael when she returned home—not fall in love with him.

'Freddy did the right thing for him, and ultimately for us. At first I hated him for going, but I've accepted the inevitability of it. If we couldn't survive that, we weren't as strong a couple as I believe couples should be.'

Their fish and chips arrived at that moment, and Stephanie didn't miss the relief pouring through Michael. He didn't have an answer to what she'd just said. Hell, she hadn't even known that was what *she* thought until thirty seconds ago. It was all new to her, but it felt absolutely right.

Tapping her glass against his, she smiled. 'Thanks for listening. I feel a lot better than I have at any time since picking up Melanie.'

Now she'd eat, and enjoy the fact that Michael had come out with her, before heading home to catch up on much needed sleep. Oh, and to tick another box—she'd found she might have the courage to stay put for ever this time.

She'd also told Michael about her infertility. So what? That wasn't on her list, no, but at least there'd be no ugly surprises in the future if they did spend more time together. Which they weren't going to do. Getting over him once and for all was the goal. The ultimate box to be ticked off.

But there was no denying he'd made her feel soft and warm when he'd got so uptight about Freddy. She didn't need anyone guarding her back, but that didn't mean it wasn't kind of cool when Michael did it.

CHAPTER THREE

'CARDIAC ARREST!' STEPH YELLED through to the front. 'I'm going to counter-shock.'

Waiting for Kath to pull over and stop, she checked the defibrillator that had been attached to their patient since they'd arrived at the factory where he worked as an electrician. She set it to start the moment Kath gave her the go-ahead.

'Go!' Kath called as she clambered through to join them.

'Stand back.' Steph punched the button on the machine.

Gavin Broad's body jerked, then slumped.

Kath watched the flat line on the defib screen. 'Negative.'

'Stand back.'

Another electric current whacked the man.

'We have a heartbeat. Erratic, but it's there.'

Kath continued to read the printout while Steph took his respiratory rate.

'Thank goodness for small miracles.'

Their man had mistakenly cut a live wire with clippers that hadn't been insulated. His workmates had been quick to recognise that his heart had stopped and used the AED, but Gavin had arrested twice. A cardiologist was his best chance, and they weren't far from Auckland Central's ED.

Having to stop while applying the electric shock treatment was necessary for the patient's safety as well as Kath's and hers, but the delay sucked.

The ambulance lurched as Kath drove back out onto the road, sirens and lights going full blast. Steph focused on the heart monitor and on taking observations. This man was *not* going to die on her watch.

'Gavin, we're nearly at the hospital,' she told him. 'Then you'll be in expert hands.'

Michael's hands until the cardiologist arrived? He would pass up any case he was working on to take a stat one—unless another specialist was free already.

Her patient didn't react, just kept breathing shallowly. Not good, but at least he was alive. A third shock would be drastic, but she'd do it if she had to.

The ambulance swung in a wide circle, started backing up.

'We're here?'

'Yes, and we've got a reception committee waiting,' Kath answered.

She'd parked and had the back doors open as quickly as Steph had the defibrillator attached to the gurney and the Patient Report Form ready for handover.

'Who have we got?'

The question came from the man she'd been hoping to get a glimpse of.

'Gavin Broad, thirty-five, arrested twice.' Steph would've locked eyes with him, but he wasn't playing that game. However, he did take the PRF she held out. 'Initial failure due to a multiphase voltage event.'

With her at the head of the gurney and Kath at the other end they lowered it to the floor of the ambulance bay and rushed into the department. Urgency meant that the details would be gone through on the way.

'He's fortunate there was a defib on the premises.'

Michael strode beside the gurney. Even in ill-fitting scrubs there was no denying that magnificent body.

Not meant to be thinking like that.

Tell that to her hormones.

When he leaned towards their man to say, 'Hello, Gavin, I'm Dr Laing,' his broad shoulders filled her line of sight and stole the moisture from her mouth. They were wide, muscular, and she already knew how warm they could be.

Her hand tightened around the stretcher handle.

Don't forget he doesn't want a relationship with anybody.

Michael was talking to their patient as though Gavin was fully aware of everything. 'We're taking you into Resus, so we're prepared if another event happens. A cardiologist is on her way down to see you as I speak.'

Straightening up, those mouth-drying shoulders tight, he looked directly ahead as they rushed into Resus. No quick looks in her direction today.

Last night, after they'd got past her revelations and started on the fish and chips, they'd shared light-hearted banter. Aware that she wasn't getting over him in any way—more like getting more enamoured with him—she'd pulled the 'got to get some sleep' pin around eight-thirty and had ignored the slight widening of his eyes and tightening of his lips at the word 'sleep'.

Sleep...bed. There wouldn't be any sleep if they went to bed together. Not happening.

Today Michael was back to being the consummate professional, with no sideways glances in her direction, no acknowledging they'd had some down time together. *Grrr.* He was so good at that. What would rock him off balance?

Hello? How would that help with your need to get over him?

She had to try something, didn't she?

'Hear from Chantelle this morning?'

Michael looked down at the PRF in his hand. 'Nope, but nothing unusual in that.'

Unless Chantelle needed Michael to do something for Aaron.

Steph could read between the lines as well as anyone. She also knew when she was being ignored. There was a paramedic beside him—not the woman he'd shared an evening with. He was right. This wasn't the place for being disgruntled about his attitude. Except everyone around here usually took the time to be friendly, even if only with a sharp nod as they raced to save a patient.

In Resus, Steph took her place by Gavin and gripped the bedding, nodded to the other medical staff waiting. 'One, two, three.'

Gavin was instantly surrounded with ED staff and the cardiologist who'd walked in right behind them. Steph detached the ambulance defibrillator so the Resus unit could come into play.

Michael was talking to the cardiologist as a junior doctor listened to Gavin's heart through his stethoscope. Nurses were taking obs, attaching wires, monitors, and all the paraphernalia required to obtain the information to save Gavin if he went into arrest again.

She was no longer required. This wasn't her domain any more.

Walking away was easy. She might have loved working in here, been right at home with all the cases, the staff, the urgency, but she had all that and more now as a paramedic. Racing to a scene, lights flashing, sirens screaming, had her heart pounding and the adrenalin flowing. There were cases like Melanie's when she hated not having senior medical back-up, but those made her dig ever deeper to do all she could and more.

She began pushing the gurney out of Resus.

On Kath's belt the radio spewed a volley of words, their tone calm but urgent. 'Ambulance three, cyclist versus vehicle, intersection Grafton Road and Symonds Street.'

Kath answered. 'Roger, base. Grafton Road and Symonds Street. ETA five.'

As Steph picked up her pace she glanced over her shoulder. Michael was watching her, but immediately dropped his eyes when he knew she'd seen him.

Okay. Not sure what that meant, and don't have time to think about it. Shove the gurney in, click the wheel locks, slam the doors shut, buckle up and go.

Oh, yeah, this job rocked.

Kath spun the ambulance out of the dock, flicked on the warning gear. 'Head and shoulder injuries are cyclists' most likely damage. Then internal injuries.'

'Why do people get so passionate about bikes when they can get knocked off without trying?'

'Why do people cross roads on foot in peak traffic?' Kath braked as a car pulled out in front of them. 'Get out of the way, moron! What part of flashing lights and screeching siren don't you understand?'

With a glance in the rearview mirror and to the side, she jerked the heavy vehicle right into the oncoming lane which drivers had hurriedly vacated.

Steph laughed at this side of Kath, who was the picture of politeness when she was around patients. Needing to vent at people's total lack of concern for others in need of help was completely understandable.

'I could give them the finger,' she said. 'But I like my job too much.' Saying something out of anyone's hearing was one thing, making a public gesture would be going too far.

Kath chuckled, then sobered. 'Looks like that's our number—up ahead on the left-hand corner.'

As she parked Steph clambered through to the back to grab their equipment before dropping out through the back door and heading to the body sprawled on the road surrounded by people.

'Excuse me—stand back.'

One look and she knew this wasn't good.

On her knees, she said to the woman, 'Hi, I'm Steph—a paramedic.' She reached for a wrist, found an erratic pulse. 'What's your name?'

'Alison Knowles.'

Good response. 'Do you remember what happened?'

'Not really.' Her speech was bubbly and difficult to understand. but she continued talking. 'One minute I was cycling through the intersection...the next I was face-down on the road.'

Literally, if the swelling under her jaw and the missing front teeth were indicators. Alison had done quite the face-plant.

'I told the cops a van cut through a red light and collected her,' a man standing nearby informed them. 'Got her smack in the middle of his van and sent her flying through the air.'

'Better than going underneath the van,' someone else noted.

Kath had pads for the heart monitor attached to Alison's now exposed chest.

Steph stood up and looked around at the crowd. 'Thanks for helping this lady, folks, but can you now move back and give her some privacy while we attend to her?'

A uniformed cop pushed through. 'I'll take care of this.'

His shoulders were tight and his head high. He had a job to do. One he should've already been doing, but what had to be bum fluff on his jaw suggested he was hardly out of kindergarten, let alone the police academy.

Steph swallowed the impulse to grin. 'Thanks. The further back the better.'

Like the other side of the road.

Back on her knees, she asked her patient, 'Did you roll yourself over or did someone help you?'

'Two guys.' Her face was white and her eyes were glazing. 'I think…'

They should've left her as she was, in case there was damage to the neck and spinal cord.

'We're going to put a neck brace on. I need you to remain as still as possible while we do that, okay?'

Steph and Kath worked fast, asking questions, taking obs, checking Alison's head for trauma, then her shoulders, and finding the left clavicle was broken, and her right knee twisted, possibly dislocated.

Steph drew up some morphine. 'I'm going to give you some pain relief before we load you on the stretcher.' Not that it would negate all the pain, but any relief was better than none.

Alison didn't answer.

Kath shone a light in her eyes, got a small blink. 'Fading consciousness.'

Once the morphine had been administered they prepared to shift the woman onto the stretcher, with the help of two strong-looking bystanders. With Alison slipping in and out of consciousness time was important.

They were quickly loaded and the cop had the traffic stopped to let them out onto the road back towards Auckland Central.

'Impact injury to the right shoulder and hip,' Steph reported with surprise, seeing Michael when they arrived back at the emergency department.

Why did *he* have to be the one she handed over to every time today? Doctors didn't usually rush to meet them unless it was a Code One job. Was he on the lookout for her when he heard the ambulance bay bell ring? But he'd been ignoring her earlier. *Men.* Who could understand them? Not her, for sure.

'Trauma to the skull?' he asked as he scanned the PRF she'd handed him.

'Soft area at the front of her cranium, injury to the jaw and cheekbones.'

Further tests, including X-rays, would be needed.

As Steph began pushing the stretcher into the department Michael took the other side. *Huh?* Had he forgotten he was the doctor, not the nurse or paramedic? Had he forgotten he wasn't talking to her?

He glanced across at her and said quietly, so no one else would hear, 'Is this why you changed careers? You're an adrenalin junkie and speeding around with flashing lights turns you on?'

There was a level of censure in his voice that grated.

'Yes, that's *exactly* why I'm a paramedic. We get loads of attention, racing through the streets,' she snapped.

What was *this* about? They'd got on well last night, with Michael being so understanding about her infertility.

'That explains it.'

Now he was smiling that gut-clenching, heart-speeding smile, as if he was on a mission to upset her and winning.

Drawing a calming breath, moderating her tone when she wanted to yell at him, she said, 'I haven't really changed. I still care for people who are hurting one way or another.'

They'd reached a resus room, and as everyone moved

Alison across to the bed Steph gulped back unexpected tears. If he didn't want anything to do with her then he should just say so. He knew how to—had done it before.

Picking up the blanket, she turned to head back to the ambulance, leaving Kath to fill the medics in on their patient. She had a gurney to stow, equipment to tidy away, new blankets to place ready for their next call.

'Steph—wait.'

Michael appeared beside her.

'I'm all out of sorts today. Didn't get much sleep. But I shouldn't be taking it out on you when you're not the cause. I know how much you care about your patients. I really do.' His fingers shoved through his hair, displaced the errant curls on his forehead. 'Can we catch up tonight?'

'I don't think so.' Not very forgiving of her. *Okay.* 'Can I answer that later, when I know if I have to pick my parents up from the airport or not?'

'No problem.'

He headed back to Alison, who was now surrounded by doctors.

Kath joined her at the ambulance. 'You want to check how Melanie and her babies are doing? Here's your opportunity. The radio's quiet.'

Throughout the night she'd woken often with the sound of Melanie's pain ringing in her skull—only somehow in her dream it had become her own anguish. Familiar torment that had laid dormant for a few years but seemed all too happy to rise up and knock her for six now.

'I'll be quick.'

Fear and exhaustion greeted her through the PICU window. She didn't hang around, understanding that it wasn't her place, but was grateful to see the babies were still in their incubators, with mum and dad hovering over them.

There was a long way to go, but they'd made it this far. A positive start.

The next time she went into the ED with a patient Michael was nowhere to be seen. He'd probably knocked off a couple of hours ago. As she and Kath would when they got back to base.

Yet, futile as it was, she still scoped the department for a glimpse of scrubs-clad long legs and thick, unruly dark hair that her fingers itched to touch—and still came up disappointed when relief should have been loosening her tense muscles.

His comments about her being a paramedic still rankled, despite his genuine apology. Something must have caused him to say it in the first place. Was it *her* he was out of sorts with? Or was it himself he was having trouble with?

The way Chantelle had exploded onto the scene to snatch up her son had hurt him. She'd seen it in his tight mouth and sorry expression, in the need in his eyes. Need for what? A child of his own?

Her blood chilled. There was her escape route. There was nothing she could do if he wanted a family, so she had to get over him. And she wasn't going to do it by taking off for places unknown again. No more running away. Even if it felt as if her heart was breaking.

She continued her inner debate all the way back to base, and while she topped up the ambulance, went out to the car park and got into her cute red sports car. She sure loved this machine…

But what if family *wasn't* the cause of that need underneath all those other emotions that had skittered through Michael's eyes? Chantelle was family, and it seemed he looked out for her and Aaron big-time. More than necessary? More than Chantelle wanted?

Michael took responsibility seriously. She'd seen that in the department, even during those two weeks when she'd been having the time of her life he'd made sure she was comfortable about everything. She guessed she'd never really known him—and chances were she wasn't about to learn any more.

Which was good, wasn't it? Wasn't it her goal to get over him? But did all goals have to be met? Or could she change her mind? Go after him instead of trying to shove him back into a box labelled *Man Best Forgotten*?

A yawn sneaked up on her. There hadn't been a lot of sleep going on last night. Along with the rerun of negative pregnancy tests there'd been visions of Michael, lovingly holding his nephew. Pictures had rolled through her head on a circuit, waking her again and again.

Michael was committed to watching out for his sister and his nephew. He was committed to his work. He gave and gave—at home and in the department. Yet he said he didn't want commitment with anyone else. What did he do for himself? Did he have a secret hobby, like collecting stamps?

Steph laughed around another yawn. She could not picture that at all.

Waiting for the car's heater to do its thing before heading to the supermarket for something boring to eat, she felt an intense loneliness roll over and around her. It was like nothing she'd known before—not even when Freddy had left her in those bleak days when nothing had gone her way.

Now she was back in Auckland—seeing her parents regularly, getting to know her new work colleagues, and installed in her own home with all her possessions around her—she shouldn't feel despondent. This was what she wanted. *Wasn't it?*

How often had she said that? Starting out in Queenstown, then in London, in Italy… Her sigh was sour. To-night was different. She wanted this and more. There was so much love in her heart, still waiting to be shared. What was wrong with her that she couldn't find a man to love her for who she was? A man who wouldn't reject her when the going got tough?

A text landed in her phone.

Don't need picking up. Got back on earlier flight and took taxi. Going to bed early, exhausted. Love Mum.

So, home or Michael's? Home was safe. Michael's was fraught with emotions she didn't want to face tonight.

Undecided, she put the car into 'drive' and headed for the supermarket. Wherever she went she needed food. And maybe a bottle of wine.

Michael heard the low roar of a car in his driveway as he quietly closed Aaron's door. The kid had been fighting sleep for an hour but finally he'd succumbed. The last thing he needed was for him to wake again.

He knew who'd driven up. She hadn't phoned to tell him she'd be around, and yet he'd delayed phoning the Thai restaurant to put his order in.

Opening the front door, he leaned a shoulder against the frame. 'Your parents got home all right?'

Stephanie grinned up at him from the bottom step. 'All by themselves.'

He laughed. 'You wouldn't have taken that matchbox on wheels to collect them, would you?'

'Why not?' Her grin widened, then was stolen by a yawn. 'Sorry. Am I too late to add fried rice with pork to your order?'

She was standing in front of him now. He breathed her in. Honey and hot toast. Mouthwateringly delicious.

'Hello?' Stephanie waved a hand in front of him. 'Anyone home?'

'Don't know. I'll go find out.' He stood back to let her in, then remembered what she'd asked. 'I haven't ordered yet.'

'So you really *do* eat Thai on Tuesdays? Then this is perfect.' She handed him a bottle of Pinot Gris.

His heart slowed. 'You remembered.'

'Your favourite wine? Of course I did.'

There was no 'of course' about it. Two years was a long time to remember trivia.

Stephanie prefers Oomph-brewed coffee to Wake Up.

Okay, he got it.

She used to go crazy whenever I kissed a trail of kisses below her ear.

Michael slammed the door shut, wincing as he remembered the barely sleeping Aaron, and headed for the kitchen and some glasses. He needed a drink. Like right now. So much for trivia.

The kitchen was a mess, with plastic bowls and spoons and a fork littering the little table Aaron had used, with matching dollops of mashed pumpkin and potato on the floor.

'Tonight was an epic battle. But Aaron's finally, *finally* asleep. I hope.'

He shouldn't have said he was here. The questions were already lighting up in Stephanie's eyes.

'Chantelle was asked to work tonight. She fills shelves at the supermarket part-time.'

'Impressive.'

'She doesn't have to do it. I've offered to pay her university fees so she doesn't have to get a student loan or borrow for everyday expenses.' Stubborn didn't begin to describe his sister.

'She's got a child, is studying for a degree and works when you've given her an out? Even more impressive.' Stephanie twisted the cap off the bottle and took the glasses he'd lifted from the shelf.

'That's all very well, but she's constantly exhausted. And then there are the days I get Aaron because she's doing too much.'

'You don't *want* to look after him? I'm not believing that.'

He took the glass she offered. 'I adore my time with him. Watching him grow from a tiny baby to where he's at now, running and crashing, spitting out words in excitement over a moth crawling across the floor—I wouldn't miss that for anything.'

'So what's the problem? Seems to me Chantelle is doing a great job making a life for her son.'

He didn't like the way those lovely eyes were drilling into him, searching for answers to her questions. She wasn't getting them.

Snatching up the dishcloth, he bent to wipe up the mess. 'You're right,' he acknowledged, hoping that would shut her down.

'Want me to phone our order through?' she asked.

Relief loosened his tongue. 'The number's on speed dial on my phone. I'll have pork green curry—hot. Just tell them Dr Mike and they'll know where to come.'

'Dr Mike?'

'I was eating there one night when one of the cooks knocked a pan of boiling oil off the stove onto his leg. It was like a scene out of a horror movie, with oil everywhere, the guy screaming in agony, and blood from where his head hit the edge of the stove as he went down.'

'Is the cook all right now?'

'Good as new—if you don't count the scars.'

'Do they still charge you for meals?'

Her smile went straight to his heart. He cursed silently.

'They tried that one. Eat all I want as often as I want, for free.' He shook his head. 'I told them I'd go somewhere else if they didn't take payment, but now I get wontons or deep fried shrimps with every order.'

'Win-win. I like that.'

Her lips touched the rim of her glass and he watched as she took in a mouthful of wine.

That mouth, hot and slick on his skin, had been sensational, and it was another piece of trivia from two years ago. How had he found the strength to stop their affair? Must've needed his head read. Because right now he would not be able to stop if they were to start again.

'Here.' He thrust his phone at her. 'Order dinner.'

Her head tilted to one side. 'Yes, sir.' And she did as he'd demanded.

He'd been that close to reaching for her, removing the glass from her slim fingers and hauling her curvaceous body he'd been hankering after for two long days and nights up against him. He still was that close. Closer, because he'd taken a step nearer.

He needed to step back, because no way did he want to hurt Stephanie further down the track when he inevitably messed up.

But one kiss…?

'Bugsy's gone.'

Michael spun around to gape at his nephew, standing in the kitchen doorway rubbing his eyes. 'Hey, buddy, you're meant to be in bed.'

The little guy did have his uses. Stopping that potential hug, kiss, whatever might have followed, was mammoth.

'Bugsy. I want my monkey.'

'I'll find him.' Michael swept the little boy up into his arms, kissed his forehead. 'Bet he's hiding under the bed. That's his favourite place, isn't it?'

'Water!' Aaron cried.

'Of course.' Michael smiled.

Of course. And then it would be *I want a 'nana*.

'Stalling tactics?' Stephanie asked.

'You're on to it.' With one hand he filled a bottle with water from the fridge. 'There you go. Let's find Bugsy.'

'I want a 'nana.'

'You've had dinner.'

Aaron's mouth opened, the indignant cry already in his expression.

'All right—half a banana it is.'

'Softy,' Steph called from behind him.

'It's my middle name.'

Michael forked up rice and curry, chewed, swallowed. 'Tell me more about why you joined the ambulance service.'

Stephanie's fork banged onto her plate. 'We've already done this.'

'The flashing lights and screaming sirens bit, yes. But not the *real* reason that had you changing from a career you loved and were exceptional at.'

'Nothing like going from rugby to medicine?'

'Low blow.'

Tell her, it's no secret.

'My rugby career was stellar, yes, and at first I couldn't see past the hype and the excitement, the sheer thrill of playing in front of those large crowds. Two episodes of concussion wised me up, made me grow up. A third knock and doing anything as intense as becoming a doctor would've been in jeopardy. I'd always known rugby wasn't a lifelong career.'

'Not all players see it so clearly.'

'Unfortunately. But I do understand the attraction. It's exhilarating, being on the field with forty thousand people watching your team, cheering or booing—didn't matter, they were there because of us.'

Stephanie pushed her near empty plate across the counter to the sink. 'In Queenstown I did a couple of stints on a rescue helicopter when they were short-staffed.' She sipped her wine. 'I got a taste for the adventure—the thrill and the scary stuff. And then, while I was in London, an opportunity came up to do three months on the ambulances and I figured I might as well give it a go.'

When the silence spread out too long he coaxed her. 'There's more to it, Steph.'

Her eyes widened. 'Caught!' Her forefinger drew circles on the countertop. 'When I decided to return home I didn't want to slip back into the same groove I was in before I left. I didn't want to find that after a few months the two years I'd been away were smothered and that despite my experiences away from Auckland nothing had changed. *I* hadn't changed.'

That made sense. But what was behind it all? Infertility and a broken marriage would do it. And it had him on the back foot, afraid of hurting her again. Everyone he was close to he hurt eventually. Stephanie had had enough to contend with. It was time for her to have fun and laughter and love—things he couldn't trust himself to deliver.

During those two intense weeks they'd had together he'd have sworn she was well on the road to recovery. And yet that dreadful sadness knocking her off her toes yesterday showed she still ached over the past.

'So you're home for good?' He didn't know why, but he needed to know.

She nodded emphatically. 'Definitely. I loved travelling, and working in different places, but I'm a home body. This is where I know myself.'

His eyes drank in the sight of that body as she sat on a high stool opposite him, her elbows on the counter, her hands holding her glass. Curves, hand-sized breasts, that pert bottom... His groin tightened as her tongue licked her lips. It hadn't been getting much exercise for a long time.

Honey teased his senses again. Was it her shampoo? What else could it be?

Honey was one of his favourite things—liquid gold on hot toast and melted butter. His mother's treat when he was little.

His upper body leaned in so Stephanie was close enough for him to feel her heat. *Honey.* His mouth watered. Then dried as her tongue repeated that licking thing. Did she know she was doing that? How the hell was he supposed to turn away when his groin was thick with need?

His hand was on her upper arm, tugging her gently closer, so her body was lined up against his. His other hand raised her chin so he could dive into those enormous toffee-coloured eyes.

'Stephanie...' he whispered, and stood up, bringing her with him.

Her body tightened and she waited, holding her breath. Then, 'Michael...'

And she sank into him, her sweet mouth accepting his, opening for his exploring tongue. Giving him a kiss like those she'd given him two years ago. Hot, demanding, giving. All Steph.

'Stephanie.'

The air closed in around them, held them in a bubble.

The world had reduced to just them. How long they stood there, their bodies locked together, their kiss endless, he did not know. He could have stayed for ever—until kisses weren't enough.

His hand found hers, grasped it to pull her along to his bedroom. 'Come with me.'

He was all but begging. Would beg if he had to.

Her fingers laced through his. 'Michael…'

She stopped. Then doubt entered her eyes, slapped him upside his head.

'I've got to go.'

Really? When your body is as awakened as mine? When we want each other?

'Okay.'

That was all he said as he unclasped his hand with difficulty, not about to force himself on her. She either wanted to go to bed with him or she didn't, and he wasn't hanging around for her to change her mind.

'Okay.'

Sometime tomorrow, or next month, he might be glad she'd pulled the plug, but right at this moment he could almost be angry about it. *Almost.* Because she was probably the sane one around here at the moment.

CHAPTER FOUR

STEPH WOUND THE music up full blast in an attempt to drown out her brain and its ranting.

Stupid...crazy. Why kiss the man? Didn't she know how that would make her feel? How she'd keep wanting more?

She had the left side of her brain to thank for her not going to bed with him. If she'd listened to the right side instead she'd now be having an amazing time in bed with the sexiest man on the planet.

The left front wheel bumped on the kerb as she pulled into her drive. Braking hard, she snapped the ignition off. Why had she gone to Michael's in the first place? All very well thinking she had to get over him, but she'd only succeeded in making things worse.

She still wanted him. After years of having nothing to do with him her hormones craved his body, his smile, those kisses. She wanted him and cared about him more than ever.

Absence makes the heart grow fonder.

Yeah, right—and it also mucked up a girl's thinking.

Folding her arms on the steering wheel, she banged her useless head down on her forearms. Now what? Michael would have recognised her reaction for what it was—*need*. For *him*. Hopefully he hadn't seen her real feelings...

He started it.

Truly? The fact that she'd plastered herself to his body and willingly kissed him didn't make it seem as if she'd been fighting him off.

Where should she move to next? Wellington? Australia? Her heart sagged.

No, please no more moving around looking for the impossible.

The impossible was right here on her doorstep in the form of one sexy, beautiful, wonderful man. Returning home had always been full of difficulties, and this was just one of them.

Just? When her heart was still thumping and her core ached for him?

She should have taken what was on offer. If she couldn't assign Michael to the 'has been loved' bucket maybe she should make the most of any opportunity to have fun with the man.

Her phone interrupted that stupid thought.

Michael. He clearly hadn't ditched her number when he'd ditched her.

Don't answer.

'Hello?'

'You get home all right?'

'Yes.'

'Good. See you tomorrow.'

He wouldn't. She had two days off. 'Bye.'

Auckland sure was testing her. Making sure she really intended putting her feet on the ground permanently and not running away again. Well, she was going to pass these tests with flying colours, even if her heart got dented along the way. She had to. The alternative wasn't worth considering. She was done with being lonely. And if she got hurt on the path to finding happiness she'd deal with it. *Here.*

* * *

Eight-oh-five. A veritable sleep-in. Stumbling into the kitchen, Stephanie turned up the heat pump before filling the kettle. It took a cup of tea to wake up properly. Pouring muesli into a bowl, she found her thoughts straight away turning to Michael and how to act next time she saw him. Thankfully she wasn't on days again until Friday. He'd have forgotten he'd kissed her by then.

But if that kiss had affected him half as much as it had her it would hang between them like a tolling bell. *Bang, bang, bang.* Great kiss. Bad reaction. Could they do it again?

She only had herself to blame for her uptight state. She could have walked away before they got started. She hadn't. End of story. Get over it. People kissed all the time. Didn't mean the world had come to an end. Not even hers.

A low whine came from outside. A dog?

Pushing the curtains wide, she blinked at the sight of the black and tan dog shivering up against the sliding glass doors.

'Who are you, lovely?' Opening the slider, she gasped at the cold, wet air enveloping her. 'It's freezing out here.'

Rubbing her hand over soft, damp fur got her a gentle head-nudge before the most adorable pleading eyes focused on her.

'You're beautiful, aren't you?'

Thump, thump. Its tail whacked the wooden deck.

She glanced under its belly. 'Well, boy, I don't know what you're doing here, but this isn't your house.' There were tags on his collar. Council registration and a name. 'Zac.'

Thump, thump.

A wind gust drove rain under the overhang, straight at

her. And Zac. Straightening up, she stepped backwards through the door and the dog followed.

'Hey, I don't think you should come in. You don't belong here.'

But pushing him outside wasn't really an option when he was still shivering and now she'd seen how his ribs pushed at his skin and the concave shape of his belly.

'I don't have any dog food...'

There was plenty of meat in the freezer, put there by her dad for when the family dropped by for a barbecue—which hadn't happened yet, because someone always seemed to be out of town at the moment. When they finally all caught up at the same time for one of those family dos she might start feeling more at home in her house. At the moment it was empty and cold, as though the rooms were waiting for people, laughter, lots of talking. Things her family would provide in shovelfuls.

Setting the microwave on defrost, Steph placed a pack of steak inside and then dried Zac off with an old towel. Next she filled a bowl her mother had given her for a birthday with water, and sighed happily as the dog lapped the liquid up. Her visitor was cute and he gave her the warm fuzzies.

While Zac gulped the meat down she poured another mug of tea. 'I'm going out soon. The dentist's beckoning.' *Shudder*. 'You'll have to go home then.'

The dog dropped to the floor, laid his head on his paws and stared up at her with that pleading look back in his eyes.

'You can't stay here. Someone must be missing you.'

He was heart-meltingly beautiful. And her heart was responding to that plea. Too much. Someone out there must be frantic, wondering where he was.

Four hours later, when she returned from retail therapy,

trying to dissipate the discomfort produced by a heavy-handed dental technician cleaning her teeth, Zac was still there, leaning against the door she'd found him at earlier. He bounded up, his tail wagging as he nudged her butt with his head.

'You're a naughty boy. You were meant to go home. I'm not getting any more meat out of the freezer.'

She sighed. Or maybe she was.

'I'll ring the council dog pound and find out if anyone's been asking for you.'

What if they hadn't? Could she keep him? *Melt, melt*, went her heart. It wouldn't be fair. She worked twelve-hour shifts four days in a row. What would she do with him on those days? It didn't matter. Zac might look a little malnourished, but his coat gleamed now she'd dried it and he hadn't cowered from her once. He was well looked after. Someone out there was missing him.

'Zac belongs to a Mrs Anderson. She hasn't been in touch to report him missing so she might be away. We'll be investigating. She should've made arrangements for the dog if that's the case.'

The woman at the pound ranted on for interminable minutes when Steph rang the council. She also gave her over Mrs Anderson's address.

Should the woman be telling her those details?

'Will you phone and tell her I can drop Zac off?' Steph asked. She was more than happy to deliver her new friend home, since he came from a street only a couple of blocks away.

'The ranger will be round pick up the dog later this afternoon.' *Click.*

Fine. Thanks. Why give her the address, then? 'Someone's going to take you home.' She rubbed the silky head resting on her thigh. 'Isn't that great?'

There went any idea of keeping him.

There were a few text messages on her phone she hadn't heard coming in. One from Michael.

Kelli's dropping in to the department around two if you want to catch up.

Kelli and her fake engagement to Mac, which became real. A true love-match—even if it *had* taken some teasing to bring it out into the open.

The last time she'd seen those two had been at her farewell drinks in the bar over the road from Auckland Central Hospital, before she'd moved to Queenstown. All loved-up and happy beyond description.

Will do.

Having texted him back, she knew there was no avoiding Michael now. His message hadn't given her any clues as to what he was thinking about her, though if he'd wanted to avoid her he wouldn't have sent it in the first place. He could have denied still having her number. Why *did* he still have it?

Woof.

'You, my boy, are going outside again.'

She wouldn't be here when the ranger arrived to pick him up, but there was nothing she could do about that. Probably for the best anyway. It would take very little to tempt her into keeping him.

'Steph, look at you! You haven't changed a bit.'

Kelli's arms wrapped around her the moment they saw each other. Hugging her back, Steph laughed. 'Still exaggerating everything.'

'I wouldn't.' Kelli pulled back and glanced around before saying, 'Michael's as good-looking as ever—and still single, I hear.'

'Apparently so.' How did she stop heat pouring into her cheeks? 'What've you and Mac been up to since I last saw you?'

'You and I need to catch up for lunch one day when you're not working.' Kelli grinned. 'As for us—making babies.'

'You're pregnant again?'

For once the usual hollowed-out sensation didn't hit her with its full debilitating hardness, but her stomach still dropped to her knees and her heart landed in her throat. Babies—babies everywhere. Just not for her. It still sucked, big-time, but she wouldn't let that show—couldn't dull Kelli's happiness because of these selfish feelings.

Throwing her arms back around Kelli, the nurse she'd worked alongside when she was going through her own version of hell, she said, 'That's the best news I've heard in a long time.'

It truly is, so get out of my throat and back behind my ribs, dear heart.

'I have to say your life's been dull if that's what it takes to cheer you up.'

'I don't need cheering up.' *Did she?* No, not at all.

'Hi, there, Stephanie—glad you got my text.'

The man with the deep and husky voice stood behind her.

Turning slowly, to give herself time to fix her features into neutral, she faced Michael. 'Thanks for the text. I'd have hated to miss Kelli.'

'No problem. Why aren't you working? Something wrong?'

She cleared that concern out of his eyes with, 'I'm on

days off. I did four day shifts this round, but next I'm up for days and nights.' She wasn't ill, or sulking because of last night, if that was what he was thinking.

'Six-day weeks? You don't mind?'

She shrugged. 'Comes with the territory.'

Later on, if she got involved with someone or took up playing netball again, she might be irked at having to work weekends, but at the moment it made no difference.

There was a gentle poke at the back of her waist. 'Don't go without giving me your phone number,' murmured Kelli, before crossing to talk to someone else she knew.

Don't leave me alone with Michael. I'm not sure what to say to him.

But Steph couldn't help glancing at him, and instantly looked away from the dynamic gaze that seemed stuck on her. 'What?'

'Nothing.'

'Good.'

'Chantelle arrived minutes after you left.'

So if she'd gone down the hall last night, instead of walking out through the front door, who knew what his sister would have discovered?

'You must be glad I'd left.'

Her heart dropped. It was beginning to make sense. His life was devoted to work and to his extended family, with no room for anyone else other than grabbed moments over a meal or in bed. No room for her other than he needed to scratch an itch.

Was she his itch?

'She wasn't meant to be picking Aaron up until the morning. But, considering I'm never one hundred percent certain she'll do what she says, I should've been more circumspect.'

Deflate me, why not?

'Seems late for Aaron to be going home.'

She shouldn't have said that. It sounded judgemental. It *was* judgemental.

'Sorry—none of my business.'

His sister must drive him bonkers at times. Though he was far more patient than she'd ever be.

'Now you know how it is in my house.'

Don't you mean in your life? But, yeah, buster, the picture's getting clearer by the minute.

If he thought he had to warn her to stay away he had nothing to worry about. After last night she had no intention of ever dropping by again. A girl could only be so stupid before she wised up.

'I'd better go after Kelli.'

'See you around.'

Her heart sank. Back to square one. He could kiss her senseless and wave her off without a hint of reluctance in that sexy voice. More fool her for letting it get to her.

Sit up, buster, and start flapping or y'jaw re gunnght he's like this. We don't want him back in our life.

Kelli nudged her gently. 'Smile like you're happy. At the moment he's going to think you're upset with him.'

I am.

Stretching her lips she asked, 'Better?'

'Looks like you've got a mouthful of vinegar. Now, what's your number?'

While pretending to read a patient's notes Michael watched Steph talking with Kelli as though she didn't give a toss that he was here—ten metres away. As if kissing him senseless had been just *ho-hum*.

He'd have sworn she'd been as ready for him as he had her last night. That supple body had moulded to his and she'd all but had to peel herself off him when she'd chosen to leave.

Even Chantelle barrelling in to collect Aaron hadn't cooled his ardour. At night once Aaron was asleep there was no waking him—which was why he hadn't thought anything of heading to the bedroom with Stephanie.

He was hugely grateful not to have been caught with Stephanie, but there was nothing else that made him happy about her walking out.

Chantelle would have had plenty to say about where his obligations lay. And that would be with her and Aaron, and Carly if needed, not with an outsider.

Chantelle had once nearly cost him his job in another ED when she'd needed too much of his time and concentration. There wasn't room for a meaningful other half in his life and risk it all crashing and burning around his feet again. So, yes, he'd dodged another bullet. So had Stephanie.

Across the room, she and Kellie were bent double with laughter, shaking their heads at each other. Steph, when she laughed, was another woman. Soft and cute and so lovely. She was all those things most the time.

Last night he'd wanted to haul her down to his bedroom and press her to the sheets, make love to her until she begged him to stop. Then and only then would he have sunk into her heat and lost his mind. He owed her big-time for having the strength to leave, because in the end he wasn't available for more than those snatched moments and Stephanie deserved far more. She deserved permanence. Commitment. *Love.*

Michael froze. *Love?* Not from him. He'd screwed up one marriage by apparently not devoting enough time to his ex, and he couldn't promise Stephanie any more because of all his other commitments. A second failed marriage was *not* happening.

His gaze fixed on the woman playing with his mind. She looked marvellous in those tight-fitting jeans and a thick woollen jersey that accentuated her breasts. Breasts he hadn't had the chance to hold, to kiss and lick and enjoy last night. Under his scrubs his groin tightened. This was lust—not love.

The squeaky, tight pulling in his veins, the out-of-rhythm beat of his heart—all of it was to do with the lust hardening below his belt. Nothing to do with love. He knew what love felt like—knew the agony and the ecstasy, the hollowed out sensation when it was withdrawn.

His marriage had lasted fifteen months, had ended in fireworks and national headlines, and proved he had the family 'no good at long-term' gene. Proved that he was not good at commitment.

His mum and dad had divorced when he was seven—his dad again six years later, after increasing his family by two. One half-sister had a divorce behind her, and the other refused to marry her partner. With that pedigree he wasn't prepared to take another gamble.

Yet Stephanie had stirred him up something terrible. Once again.

Stephanie. His blood was always warmer when she was around. Hotter, thicker.

She was still with Kelli, her head tipped back as she listened, that thick hair shaped around her slim neck so tempting his fingers itched.

She hadn't been laughing when Kelli had said she was pregnant. There'd been a sharp stab of pain in the back of her eyes. Quick to show, quicker to disappear, but now he knew to look for it it had been obvious.

Yes, taking her to bed was high on his list of needs. But it wasn't going to happen.

Anything else he wanted also had to be ignored.

And if that made him cruel then he'd put his hand up. He could not stop wanting her, because it was the wrong thing to do, but he could and would keep her at arm's length.

He picked up the phone and punched in the number for PICU. Stephanie would want an update on those twins.

So much for arm's length.

'This is Con from the dog pound. I'm at your address now and there's no sign of the dog you called in.'

Steph's heart sank as she pulled off the road and held her phone hard against her ear. 'I couldn't find anything safe to tie him up with.'

'I've been around to where he lived with Mrs Anderson and he's not there either. The neighbours say they haven't seen him since the day she was found dead.'

'What do you mean?'

Con sighed. 'Three days ago concerned neighbours broke into her house and found her deceased in bed.'

'That's awful.'

For everyone. No wonder Zac was wandering the streets. He was hungry and lonely and desperate.

'Does anyone want him? Family? A friend or neighbour?' She held her breath.

'Not that we've been able to ascertain. He'll most likely go up for adoption—if we can find him before it's too late.'

The man didn't have to say what that meant. She had a vivid imagination. 'I'll go for a walk—call out to him when I get home.'

She didn't have to.

'You're a persistent little guy, aren't you?'

Steph bent down to pat Zac, who'd raced to her car the

moment she'd pulled into the drive. 'I have to let the ranger know you're here so he can pick you up.'

Didn't she?

Zac's head tipped to one side. He sensed that she was weakening?

Could she keep him? Adopt him?

Getting a pet would be another step in making her move home feel permanent. No way could she take off and leave him behind, and she couldn't take him overseas.

Hey, you're not going anywhere. This is home. Warts and all.

Dog and all?

'Zac, do you want to come live with me?'

'He's a German Shepherd Collie cross, with probably some other bits thrown in,' Con told her when she phoned him back. 'Two years old, fully vaccinated, no record of wandering until now.'

'Can I keep him?'

'I talked to your neighbour earlier and there's no problem with you taking him.'

That made her uncomfortable. She didn't know her neighbours very well. 'What do I have to do?'

'There's paperwork to fill in. We need a record of where he's gone in case anyone asks later on. But as of now he's yours.'

'Zac...'

Steph blinked and smudged tears away from her cheeks. How easy was that? She'd wanted someone to love. So the object of that love had four legs and a collar? Worked for her. Another box ticked.

Dropping to her knees, Steph wrapped her arms around her new housemate and sniffed hard. 'Welcome to my world, beautiful.'

She'd done it. This was a permanent step and there was no going back. Instantly exciting and frightening.

Her new life really was underway. She was now a paramedic with a dog, living in her own house. And she was facing up to Michael.

'Let's go shopping for doggie things.'

An hour later she drove through the streets towards home, Zac sat beside her, his head out of the window, catching the breeze. Her fingers tapped in time to the country song blasting out from the stereo and her mouth kept lifting into unbidden smiles.

Yeah, she'd done the right thing—for her *and* for Zac.

CHAPTER FIVE

'THIRTY-ONE-YEAR-OLD MALE, burns to left leg and foot caused by hydrochloric acid splashing when a glass cylinder fell and smashed,' Steph told the nurse meeting them in the ambulance bay at Auckland Central's ED. 'Matthew Brown, science teacher at Point Chev High.'

There'd been a lot of unnecessary panic going down in the classroom when she and Kath had arrived, which had taken longer to deal with than making their patient comfortable.

Kath handed over the PRF before helping Matthew on to the bed. Another case delivered into the care of experts.

Steph relaxed and looked around the department. Of course Michael wasn't here. It was Saturday and his weekend off. Disappointment hit her hard. He shouldn't affect her like this, but she looked for him every time they delivered a patient. Every single time.

'I'm going to grab a coffee to go,' Kath told her once the stretcher was locked back in place inside their vehicle. 'Want one?'

'I'd kill for one. Fingers crossed we don't get called for the next five minutes.'

'I'll get them if you want to go see how those babies are doing.'

Did she? Last she'd heard the twins were improving as

much as anyone could hope for, which Michael told her had to be the best news.

'Won't be long.'

Racing to the elevator, she went up to the neonatal unit only to be told that Melanie and the babies had been transferred to Auckland Women's.

'The babies are doing okay?' Was it a bad thing that they'd been sent across the city?

'They're doing fine,' said Sarah, the PICU nurse Steph gone to nursing school with. 'The specialist wanted them close to him so he can be on tap if anything changes.'

Which it could with such premature babies. 'That's good.'

Steph headed back to the ambulance and her coffee, her heart a little lighter for Melanie.

'One latte.' Kath handed her a paper cup with a grunt. 'It's turning into a long day.'

'Busy's good.' It left no time for sitting around thinking about the impossible—how to put Michael out of her head.

Kath blew on her long black. 'What have you got planned for tonight? A party or a hot date?'

If only.

Steph started up the ambulance and headed for base. 'Try a quiet night in with the dog.'

Kath spluttered into her coffee. 'You're kidding me, right?'

'Auckland Central Ambulance Three.' The dispatcher's voice came through loud and clear.

'Here we go again.' Saved by the radio.

Steph reached for the handpiece, but Kath beat her.

'Ambulance Three.'

Steph listened in as she negotiated the ambulance towards Karangahape Road, ready to turn at the lights in whichever direction they were needed.

'Thirty-six-year-old male, leg wound from tomahawk axe, severe bleeding. One-zero-five Albany Street, Parnell.'

One hundred and five Albany Street? Steph's heart hit her toes. *No way.* What would Michael be doing with a tomahawk? It would have to be very sharp to do severe damage. Air stuck in her lungs. If not Michael, then who?

'Roger, coms,' Kath responded, then repeated the address and details.

Struggling to find her calm mode, Steph concentrated doubly hard on traffic and loose cannon drivers who liked to beat a racing ambulance to the corner.

The siren seemed to screech louder than usual as she headed to Parnell. To Michael.

A shudder ripped through her. It might not be Michael. But she couldn't shake the feeling that it was.

'How do you chop your leg with a tomahawk?'

'Chopping kindling? But being distracted enough to hit your leg is beyond me.'

'I wonder who called it in?' Michael himself? Most likely.

'You know who lives at the address?' Kath asked.

'Michael Laing from the ED.'

'Ah…'

Steph didn't like the way that sounded. '"Ah", nothing. I was thinking that he's not going to be happy about being taken into his own department by us.'

She tapped the address into the GPS to see if there was a shorter route, as she only knew one way there.

'Or he might be so thrilled so see us he'll shout us a night out at Scarpio's. It's the best restaurant in town at the moment.'

Steph couldn't find a laugh. Not even a single chuckle.

'Get out of the way!' she snarled at the driver of a pickup

truck blocking the intersection ahead. Her temper was not improved when the guy waved as they roared past.

This trip was taking for ever, and every kilometre gained seemed long and tortuous. Finally Steph swung into Michael's drive and turned off the siren. Kath was already in the back with the kit in her hand, so Steph leapt out and ran. Up the path, around the house and aimed for the back porch, where Michael sat on the step, pale, obviously in pain—and angry.

'Michael, what happened?'

She raced up the steps and dropped to her haunches beside him, already reaching for the blood-soaked jersey wound around his thigh, with the fingers of his right hand splayed over it, applying pressure to slow the bleeding. He was shivering, shock clearly coming into play.

'Slow down. It's not an emergency. No need for the siren either. Now the nosey neighbours will be turning up to gawp.'

Nice to see you too. 'What happened?' she repeated. 'I need to know.'

'The neighbour's cat was fighting a stray and chased it through here—right across my feet. I didn't hear the hissing and snarling until it was too late. I had only just finished sharpening the blade this morning. I was distracted. And when I knocked into the shed wall...'

Snapping on gloves, Steph began gently feeling for deep trauma in his thigh. It was a bad laceration that possibly went through to the bone. 'When you do something you do it thoroughly.' It must be extremely painful, though he was being stoic beyond belief.

A sudden indrawn breath had her looking up. Got that wrong. She caught him, putting her hands on his chest to stop him tipping sideways onto the porch.

'Easy does it.' Gripping his shoulders, she studied him

as he opened his eyes slowly. He was obviously in agony.
'Deep breaths.'

He focused on her as his chest lifted.

'Breath out now.'

His chest stopped, held, then sagged.

Good. 'We'll get you on the stretcher.'

'Right here,' said Kath from behind her.

'I don't need that. I can walk to the ambulance.'

He started struggling to his feet, and there was a lot
more swaying going on.

'Sit down,' Stephanie snapped.

She could do cranky too. Especially since Michael was
hurt and not letting her help him.

'Now.'

To emphasis her point she pulled at his elbow until he
obliged by sagging onto the step with little control.

'Be careful.'

This was a very different Michael from the one she
knew.

He glared at her. '*I'm* the doctor here. We'll do it *my*
way.'

Resisting the urge to run the back of her finger down
his pale cheek and reassure him that she'd do everything
he needed, she dug deep for a retort.

'I'm the paramedic, and in case you've forgotten that
means *I'm* in charge at an accident scene.'

She couldn't have him thinking she was going soft on
him.

'That jersey isn't doing a good enough job, so I'll have
to remove it and wrap bandages around the wound.'

'Need some readings done too.' Kath added her bit as
she reached for his left wrist and got growled at for her
trouble.

'What's wrong with your wrist?' Steph asked.

He held it awkwardly. 'Must've cracked it when I fell over.'

Cracked or broken? 'When were you going to mention that?' she snapped, her patience wearing thin. 'Michael, we need to know *everything*. You understand that.'

The eyes looking at her were darker than she'd ever seen them before, filled with pain and anger—and a message she couldn't interpret. As if he was angry with her for some reason.

She was doing her job—nothing more or less. But her heart was thumping and her breathing was too fast.

Slowly drawing in a lungful of cold air, she laid a hand on his shoulder and squeezed lightly. 'We won't make a big deal of anything, I promise.'

Finally he dragged his gaze away. 'Go ahead. I do know what you've got to do.' The sharpness had gone, and his voice was suddenly heavy and lethargic.

Until Kath said, 'Right, let's get you on the stretcher.'

'I'll make my own way, thank you very much.' But the curse he bit out afterwards wasn't that quiet.

'Michael, stop being an idiot. That injury is serious—as in probably needing surgery serious.'

'I know that,' he snapped.

He might be a doctor and know what was ahead, but he was also a man in pain, and clearly not looking forward to the coming hours.

'At the moment you're a patient.'

'It *has* dawned on me,' he snapped.

He wanted to walk to the ambulance so she'd give him that—but nothing more. If she slipped her arm around his waist what would he say?

She was about to find out. Swinging the kit over one shoulder, she put her arm around him, took a step, and stopped when he didn't join her.

* * *

'Stop hovering,' Michael growled.

He hated it that Stephanie was intent on hanging around right beside him—*with* him, *holding* him—ready to catch him if his head did that spinning, floating, not getting a grip on reality thing again.

As if *she* could hold him off the ground. She was small and soft—he was big and muscular. Didn't she realise that he could do her some damage? He should've taken the offer of the stretcher. Was he going soft in his old age? He'd taken plenty of hard knocks playing rugby and not once been stretchered off. Nothing was changing today. He might be acting like a prat, but a man was entitled to his pride.

'Where are your house keys?' Steph asked in her professional voice.

He'd hurt her with his determination not to let her help him, but that was who he was—how he'd got through the painful take-downs on the rugby field, how he'd survived a broken heart.

He groaned in pain and frustration. Why Stephanie and Kath, when there were dozens of ambulance crews working in the city? What were the odds? It seemed that when it came to Stephanie and him they were fairly short.

'Hello? I asked a question. As a patient you're supposed to answer so I know how alert you are.'

Was that a hint of a smile lifting the left corner of her mouth? Doubtful. He didn't deserve one.

'They're on the kitchen bench.'

'I'll get them once you're loaded.' She shook her head. 'Obviously you shouldn't be left in charge of an axe. Getting distracted is plain dumb.'

'Do you talk to all your patients like this?'

He knew she didn't but she needed redirecting. Otherwise next he'd be spilling the reason why he'd been 'plain dumb'. That would go down a treat. She'd probably leave him on the pavement and hurl that ambulance down the road, siren screaming, putting as much space between them as possible.

Because he would've seen and heard that blasted cat a lot earlier if Stephanie hadn't been prowling around inside his skull.

'Only the difficult ones.'

Her words slapped at him hard, unlike her light and yet assured fingers when she'd checked out his leg.

Kath had the gurney locked back in place inside the ambulance and was reaching for his arm.

'This is going to hurt.'

At least she didn't sound pleased about it, whereas Stephanie was probably shrieking with laughter on the inside.

A small but surprisingly strong hand took his other arm.

'Let's do it.'

Her fingers squeezed encouragement.

A quick glance at Stephanie's face told him she didn't want him hurting at all. Why was he being so stubborn? Because he didn't want her to think he needed her help? He'd hurt her once by walking away before they got too involved—he wasn't about to let her close again. She'd had her share of sorrows, and she didn't need him adding any more. Because in the end he would. It was in his genes.

Biting down hard he took his first step, followed it up with a second, then a fast stumble to get inside the ambulance, groping with his good hand for the stretcher to collapse on to and take the pressure off.

The names he was silently calling himself for being so

stubborn were unprintable. To put it bluntly, Stephanie was right: he was an idiot, a really stupid, dumb idiot…

'Mike? What the—?'

His head flipped up. 'Jock? Sorry, I got a bit tied up and forgot to phone you. I can't make it tonight.'

They were supposed to be going for a beer before heading to Eden Park for the rugby game of the year between the Auckland and Wellington provincial teams. A game he'd been hanging out for ever since the beginning of the season.

'Kind of reached that conclusion myself. What have you done now?'

'Seems he's not the macho forestry man with an axe he thought he was.' Stephanie pushed around his friend and climbed into the ambulance.

'He what?' Jock stared at Stephanie for a long moment, then fixed that annoying, oh, so sharp look back on him. 'You copped an *axe*?'

'Something like that.' Michael stared straight back. It was easier than watching Stephanie work on his leg.

Jock saw through him and grinned, but he wasn't hiding the concern in his face. 'Glad you're not a surgeon, mate.'

Michael chose to ignore that concern, given how his friend was probably already thinking up ways to make a joke at his expense. 'Make yourself useful and lock up the house for me, will you?'

'Will do—and then I'll follow you to the ED. Someone's got to keep an eye on you.'

Jock turned to Stephanie and Kath. 'Which hospital?' When Stephanie told him he asked quietly, 'He's going to be okay, right?'

It was Stephanie who answered. Of course it was. Kath seemed to have taken a step back on this job.

'He's the doctor and he didn't argue when I mentioned possible surgery.'

She could be sassy when she put her mind to it.

Jock was watching her far too closely. Would he remember briefly seeing her once, when they were knocking around together? Yeah, he would. The man had a phenomenal memory—especially for trivia. He also didn't bother keeping things to himself if he knew he could rile his mates. But today Jock had better keep his big mouth shut or they'd be having words.

Pain stabbed in his thigh. He'd been focused on Jock and had moved without thinking. 'Let's get this show on the road,' he grunted to Kath.

She nodded back. 'I'll drive, Steph.'

A hint of pink streamed into Stephanie's cheeks. Had she been in the driving seat on the way here?

'Sure.' The finger on his pulse wobbled.

He could only hope her counting skills were still in good working order.

'See you at the hospital,' Jock called as the back doors closed.

'Sure,' he muttered, unable to deny the relief he felt that his pal would be hanging out with him in ED. Not that he wasn't capable of facing hassles alone. He was used to it. It was just that he didn't want to. Having a friend there when he felt like something the dog had regurgitated was what it was all about.

He even wished Stephanie still worked in the emergency department so she could stop by his cubicle occasionally until he was taken into Theatre. Because that was where he was headed.

Being a doctor didn't make that any less daunting than it would be for any other patient. The op wouldn't be major, but he'd still have to be anaesthetised. Not something that excited him. He hated being out of control. Once that drug sent him to sleep he wouldn't know another thing until the anaesthetist brought him round again—if he woke up.

Another shudder and goosebumps lifted the skin on his arms. If only they could fix him up using a local anaesthetic so he could be aware of everything happening...

'Lie down,' Stephanie ordered in that no-nonsense voice she was very good at with recalcitrant patients. 'You'll rock around too much if you're sitting, and that would not be good.' Then that toffee gaze locked onto his. 'Please?' she asked softly.

His heart slowed as he looked into those brown depths. Concern radiated out of them. She cared. For *him*. He wasn't just another patient to her. Warmth stole through his shaky body, flattened the goosebumps. For the life of him he couldn't banish the sense of wonder at the thought of being special to someone—if he only had the courage to become involved without looking for the divorce at the end of it.

He didn't want to be alone any more.

Which was scary—scarier than going under an anaesthetic.

No doubt it was all to do with post-accident shock. Had to be. Any other explanation was untenable.

'Michael? Are you all right?'

Stephanie shook him gently—this time as a paramedic, not a friend.

'Look at me.'

'I'll need help lifting my leg onto the stretcher.'

Could she possibly do that without touching him? Not even those gloves were protecting him from the warm sensation of her fingertips on his skin.

Blimey, could she be gentle... It hurt like stink to lift his leg and swivel his butt so he could lie down, but Stephanie didn't add to his agony. Not at the site of his injuries anyway.

When Michael was wheeled into a room on the men's surgical ward three hours later, feeling as though a bus had run him over and with a mouth drier than a drought, relief at being awake overwhelmed him. The anaesthetic hadn't got him. Things were going his way. Plus the head nurse had given him a room to himself. Sometimes there were advantages to working in the hospital.

'Up for a beer, mate?' Jock strolled in, hands in his pockets, worry darkening his gaze, followed by Max, the other third of his lucky threesome.

So much for peace and quiet.

He smiled. 'Sure.'

He and these guys went way back, to their first day of high school, and there wasn't much they didn't know about each other.

'Shouldn't you be at the rugby?'

'Shucks, I knew we had to be somewhere else,' Jock quipped.

'You're missing the game of the season to hang out with *me*?'

'Nah, it doesn't start for another hour. We're foregoing the beers to check on you.'

'Find me some clothes and I'll come with you.'

'Did I just hear what I thought I did?'

In walked Stephanie, looking frazzled yet cute in tight black jeans and a fitted red jersey that highlighted her dark blonde hair perfectly.

'Depends how good your hearing is,' answered Jock, before Michael could come up with an answer.

His brain had been in slow mode since he'd come round

in Recovery. Probably just as well, or he'd have made some smart aleck comment to keep the guys from seeing how much she got to him. And they'd have seen right through it.

Not that he couldn't enjoy lying there quietly watching her. She'd brushed her hair so it sat around her head with tantalising effect. As for that jersey—it highlighted each and every curve of her delightful breasts and narrow waist. Breasts and waist which he had no trouble recalling...could almost feel against the palms of his hands.

'How did the surgery go?' Stephanie stepped closer, a frown between her brows.

'I haven't talked to Chris yet,' he managed to croak over his even drier tongue.

'Chris Stuart operated?' The frown relaxed. 'He's the best.' Then she smiled and stepped away. 'I'll leave you to talk nonsense with your friends.'

But you just got here.

'Ignore them. They can talk amongst themselves.'

'No, I need to hit the supermarket.'

Supermarkets didn't close till ten at the earliest.

'Fair enough.'

He should be glad she wasn't going to hang about. *He wasn't.* Reaching for the water bottle on the bedside table, he groaned as murky pain reminded him of why he was there.

Instantly Stephanie picked up the bottle and handed it to him. 'Dry mouth? Anaesthetic will do that.'

Gulping mouthfuls of the cool liquid made him feel slightly more normal.

'Glad to see you're not lonely in here.'

Chris Stuart stood in the doorway.

'It's busier than the downtown train station at rush hour,' Michael muttered. 'But at least I'll have a ride home with someone.'

'That'll be tomorrow at the earliest.' Chris came to stand at the end of the bed. 'You're post-op and unable to get around. No way you're going home tonight. Not even to stay with one of this lot.'

'Why? There weren't any complications?'

'No, all's good, but you won't be walking on that leg for a few days. The wound was serious. Your femur was nicked. Get the picture?'

Chris raised an eyebrow, which Michael ignored, not liking where this was going.

'That wrist needs resting too.' Chris held his hand up, palm outward, as Michael went to make a retort. 'You're no longer a gung-ho rugby player. You're more than ten years older than when you used to run around the rugby paddock.'

'Have you finished writing me off? Should I be buying a unit in the old folks' home?'

Chris grinned. 'If you want to get around without too much trouble in the future you'll do as I say.'

'Good luck with that,' Stephanie muttered. 'He walked to the ambulance earlier.'

'Now, *there's* a surprise.' Chris was enjoying giving him a stir-up. 'Hi, Steph. Didn't know you were back in town. How's things?'

'Good so far.'

So far? What was she expecting to go wrong?

'You're back in the ED?'

Now his pals were listening in, their ears like radar shields on a roof.

'I'm a paramedic on the ambulances now,' Steph told the nosy surgeon. 'Which is how come I got to bring *this* ungrateful man in for you to fix up.'

Max started laughing. 'She doesn't take any of your crap. I like her already.'

He didn't *have* to like her. She wasn't a part of their scene—didn't know their wives or kids, and wasn't going to. But he couldn't be down and out rude.

'Stephanie Roberts, meet another scoundrel—Max. We've been mates for ever.' And before Chris could add his piece he went on. 'I'll manage on my own at home'

But no one was listening. The other three men in the room were focused on Stephanie as she answered Chris's questions about where she'd been over the last couple of years.

'Now I'm home for good.' Her gaze drifted in his direction, flicked back to a spot on the floor in front of her.

'Since you're unencumbered, *you* could move in with Michael until he's back on his feet. Better than having him hanging around our place, where the baby is bound to keep him awake at night.' Smugness rolled off Jock as he showed his true colours.

'No!' Stephanie shook her head abruptly.

'Hang on, I—' Michael tried.

'That's a great idea,' said Chris. 'If you did that, Steph, I'd be happy to discharge Michael tomorrow morning, after I've checked him out. Otherwise I'll have to keep him in for a few days. He'll overdo things if he's on his own.'

'Sorry, but I go to work—night and day shifts. I wouldn't be there all the time.' She was almost pleading. 'And I've got a dog.'

'A dog *and* Mike?' Max grinned. 'Perfect.'

'The dog loves digging holes in the garden.' Steph sounded desperate.

Michael tried again. 'It's okay. I don't need you there.'

'We wouldn't have to worry about him,' Jock added. 'Or go round to make sure he hasn't fallen on his face.'

Definitely not a *friend*.

'Hello? I *am* here.'

Chris laughed. 'Annoying, aren't they?'

'Who needs friends when I've got these guys in my face?'

Jock stopped laughing and turned to Stephanie—and Michael knew. She was lost before she'd even got started. Which meant so was he. His mate was about to work his lawyering magic on her and she wouldn't be able to beat him at his game.

He sank back into the pillows and waited. This was going to be good—even if he would be the ultimate loser.

'Here's the thing, Steph. Mike's more than welcome to come stay with me and my family, but he won't. He's stubborn like that—won't want to be a nuisance.'

Stephanie's face was a picture as it dawned on her that she was on a road to nowhere. She was a quick learner. The colour in her cheeks ebbed away as her gaze remained on his mate's face.

'Mike won't go to Max's for the same reason. He will go home alone, regardless what any of us want,' Jock continued. 'I concede that he doesn't want you with him, any more than you want him to be there, but he wants out of here ASAP so it *is* the best option.'

'Maybe for Michael, but not for me,' she whispered.

Michael silently applauded her valiant effort, all the while knowing it wouldn't make a jot of difference.

'Give me a moment,' said Jock, in that take-no-prisoners voice that won him court case after court case. 'You're a nurse, right?'

Close enough. Once a nurse always a nurse.

This could go on for hours, and in the end he and Stephanie were going to lose anyway. There was a gloating gleam in his pal's eyes that would take a bomb to shift. Which meant he had to give in, didn't he?

'Give up, Stephanie. Jock's not going to let up until you fold. We'll make it work.'

He'd almost stopped breathing, watching her, thinking about that kiss. He would make it work for both of them. Or die trying.

Stunned eyes turned in his direction. 'You *want* me to move in temporarily?'

No. But if not her then who? Because the only way he was getting out of here was with someone at home to run around after him. There was no alternative. None that he'd *like*, that was.

'Two days. That's all it'll take for me to get mobile enough to look after myself. As you said, you'll be working most of the time. These oafs can check in on me occasionally.'

'Which kind of negates me staying with you,' she snapped, desperate to the end.

'I get that.'

It was hard to know what was eating at him the most: the fact she didn't want to stay with him or the unexpected hope that she'd capitulate. He didn't want her in his house, where he could see her and hear that soft, sweet voice too much, where that honey scent of hers would permeate the rooms, the air, everything. But if *anyone* had to sit in his lounge and eat takeaways with him then Stephanie was his pick.

'What if I promise not to move all day while you're at work?'

Left corner rising... Then her mouth straightened again. 'There are complications with that—unless you get a potty from ED.' Her nose wrinkled in that funny, cute way.

'I can keep your dog company—make sure he's not lonely and digging where he shouldn't. All from my chair, of course.'

'Why have you changed—?' She stopped, swallowed and drew a deep breath.

The room was suddenly silent, and sounds from the ward outside infiltrated as everyone waited for Stephanie to continue. Michael could feel his lungs tightening as he held his breath. Having her in his house wasn't going to be easy, but having her stick to her guns was starting to rile him. He was flat-out annoyed that she didn't want to spend time with him.

He must have hit his head when he went down, because none of this was making sense.

'I'll do it.'

It was barely a whisper crossing her lips, but he heard each word clearly, felt each one on his skin like a light summer breeze coming off the sea.

'Thank you.'

Best leave it at that, or she might change her mind. It was suddenly imperative she didn't. Which meant he should be booking into a hotel for the next week—not going to his house—paying a nurse to come in and change his dressings—not letting this one near him. Because Stephanie Roberts had sneaked in under his skin once more and now he had to be extra-vigilant. He was not getting involved with her. Not, not, *not*.

'I'll text you when Chris lets me loose.'

He chose to ignore the gleeful grins on his mates' faces. They could get lost as well.

Stephanie was still looking stunned at what she'd agreed to. 'What about your sister?' she croaked. 'We could ask her to help.'

Max cut her off. 'Chantelle and medical dressings? Don't go there. You're it for as long as Mike needs you.'

Max had made that up about Chantelle. 'Haven't you got a game to go watch?' Michael growled.

That got them moving. The clock was ticking, and in their haste to set him up they'd forgotten they had yet to confront the traffic that would be clogging the roads around Eden Park.

'We've got a spare ticket to the rugby. Chris?'

'Give me five and I'll be right with you. I'm all done here for the rest of the night. Thanks, Stephanie. Word of warning: your services will be required for at least three days.' He grinned. 'Thanks for the ticket, Michael.'

Michael glared at his surgeon. 'Any time you want to go let me know and I'll find another axe to do some damage with.'

'Is there a television on the ward?' his new housemate wondered in the sudden silence that fell after the three wise asses had left.

'There'll be one in the lounge at the far end.'

Though the prospect of getting out of bed to go along there was not exciting him.

'I could watch on my phone if I had it with me.'

It had been in his pocket when he'd chopped himself, which had saved him hauling his butt around the house looking for it to call for help. But where it had got to was anyone's guess.

Pity, because he really wanted to watch the game from the comfort of this bed. Negotiating crutches or a wheelchair did not appeal now the codeine was lightening off. Taking another pill could wait until he was ready to sleep. Drugs were all very well, but they made him groggy and he preferred to go minimal where he could on that score.

'That'd drive you bonkers, wouldn't it? With such a tiny screen you'd struggle to see it clearly.'

She looked at him hard and saw his frustration.

'You phoned for an ambulance, so I'm figuring you dropped the phone on your porch afterwards.'

'Hope I haven't had any unwanted visitors since then.' Losing his phone would be more than a nuisance, with all the numbers he had stored.

'I'll go get it. Anything else you want? Clothes to go home in? Toothbrush?'

He nodded. 'All of those. Jock dropped my keys on the bedside table.'

Thank goodness one of them had been alert. He hadn't given it a thought. Anaesthetic brain had a lot to answer for.

'Steph, I'm sorry to be a pain.'

She blinked. 'It's okay.'

He'd called her Steph. Letting go of another knot that kept her that little bit removed from him. Anaesthetic brain again.

'You might want to bring my car when you come to collect me. I'm not likely to get this leg into your match-box.' It would really give him grief if he tried folding it up to his chin.

'No problem. I'd better fly. Kick-off's in forty.'

She snatched up his house keys and disappeared before he had time to answer. Everyone seemed to be leaving him in a hurry today.

CHAPTER SIX

To wake him or not? The game started in five.

Steph eased onto the chair beside Michael's hospital bed and gazed at his face, free of pain and tension in sleep. Still as handsome, still making her blood heat. *Michael.* How had she thought she could get over him? Despite the years since she'd last touched him her palms could still feel the sensation of that warm skin, of his hard muscles. More important, she still knew the hope he brought her for a future of love.

There was no answer as to why it was Michael over other men she'd known. It was what it was. Attraction, both physical and mental. So deep that hope was an integral part of her, and finally she understood that removing it would be as impossible as whipping out her liver or kidneys. No cure available.

But right now he wouldn't thank her if he missed the game—even if he did need to sleep.

'Michael,' she called softly.

She needed to hand over his gear and get out of there to digest what she'd let herself in for. Days and nights with Michael, in his house, looking after him. How had *that* happened?

She'd been conned, that was how. By a smart guy looking out for his friend. She couldn't argue with that, even when the arguments were stacking up in her head. It was exactly what Jill would've done for her.

'Michael,' she tried, a bit louder, keen to get away.

When he didn't stir she leaned across and laid her hand on his upper arm, shook gently.

'It's kick-off time.'

'What?' His eyes opened, closed again.

'The rugby, Michael.'

This time his eyelids lifted and stayed up. 'You got my phone?'

'And the other things you wanted. But I thought this would be better to watch the game.' She passed over her tablet. 'Larger screen.'

He reached for the tablet—with the wrong hand. His groan was deep, throaty, and the pain from that sprained wrist showed in his face.

'Easy…'

Using only one arm made his shuffling upright an awkward struggle, and a sheen of sweat broke out on his forehead.

Steph plumped the pillows behind his back, gently pushed him into them before turning on the tablet and finding the game.

'Want to stay and watch with me?'

Pardon? Was he serious? Or not thinking straight?

'I don't think we can both watch on that tiny screen.'

In other words, No, I do not. We're going to be spending too much time together starting tomorrow.

'We'll manage.' He slid sideways and patted the bed. 'Here.'

You're kidding, right?

How was she supposed to do that without getting in a fever? But it seemed her heart had taken charge, because she was soon parked beside him, staring at the screen. Not looking anywhere else, not breathing, not feeling his arm against hers. Totally unaware of him.

Pants on fire.

The game had started. 'Go, you idiot, *run*!' Michael almost shouted as one of the Auckland forwards stole the ball from the opposition. 'Look out!'

'Shh, you're in a hospital ward,' she nudged him. 'Some people in here are sick.'

He totally ignored her. 'What sort of pass was that?'

Steph went to close the door. This was not going to be a quiet eighty minutes, so she'd minimise the damage. Then the game pulled her in and she forgot where she was, and even who she was squashed up against—okay, that was an exaggeration—until, in frustration at a player's move, Michael slapped his hand down on his thigh.

'Ahhh!'

The sound of raw pain drowned out the commentators and the background noise of the shouting crowd.

Standing up, Steph lifted his hand away from his leg and checked the dressing. 'Got to watch out.'

His breathing was shallow and rapid, his good hand a fist, his face white.

She gripped his hand in both hers, held him until the tension eased from his muscles and his eyes opened.

'Don't say a word,' he growled. 'I've got more than enough cuss words of my own.'

Focusing on the screen, he drew in long, soothing lungs-ful of air, hissing them out again over tight lips.

When Steph tried to free her hands from his he turned his hand to hold on to her. She went with it, as it was one way to prevent him doing anything so mindless again.

Sitting back on the bed, not so close as to be touching his arm, hip and thigh this time, she did some breathing exercises of her own to lessen the tension cramping her stomach, her chest…her sex. Being this close to him was hard, not touching him even more so—but extremely wise and safe.

But it might not be the case by the time she moved out of Michael's house in a few days.

'Come and get me, will you? Before Chris changes his mind. I've had enough of this place and people poking thermometers in my mouth and shining torches in my face all night long. How's a bloke supposed to recover when they don't let him sleep?'

Michael was grumpy.

'And don't forget to bring my car. I'm not tying myself in knots getting into that miniscule thing you drive.'

'Yes, sir.'

Great. Steph sighed into her tea. The man was belligerent as all get out.

'I'll be about an hour.'

'An *hour*? The hospital's just down the road, woman. I need to get out of here. *Now.*'

'Anyone would think you're in jail,' she retorted. 'I have to go to the supermarket to get Zac some biscuits first. Might get you some too.'

She'd been intending to go to the vet's, but judging by the angst coming through the phone that would have to go on hold. It was going to be difficult enough spending the day with him, without having a bad mood hovering between them.

'Pick me up first. I'll sit in the car while you shop,' he said, and followed up with a grunt. 'Please.'

That was all it took. 'Please' spoken in that husky tone and she was his. *Ah, no.* Okay, she'd oblige him in this but nothing else. That was better.

'Do you mind if Zac comes for the ride?'

'Buckle him into Aaron's seat.'

Was that a laugh? Couldn't be. 'Yeah, right.'

Actually, it wasn't such a bad idea—if only Zac was a little bit smaller. She'd seen the injuries inflicted on a front passenger by a dog in the back seat slamming forward when a truck took out the car it was in. As for the dog… She shuddered, glad she hadn't seen that.

'I'll be waiting at the main entrance.'

Michael hung up on her, clearly convinced she would swing by for him before doing anything else.

As tempting as it was to make him wait, she didn't. One: that temper of his would only increase, which wasn't the way to start their days sharing his house. It was going to be strained enough. Two: he was still recovering from surgery and needed to be at home, where it was warm and comfortable, not sitting in a busy vestibule being knocked and nudged by people coming and going.

When she pulled up he was sitting on a bench outside the hospital in the cold wind, looking pale and uncomfortable. There was no wheelchair in sight—only a crutch that had fallen to the ground by his feet.

'Hey,' Steph said as she opened the passenger door. 'How did you get down here?'

'There's this thing called a lift.'

The way he was struggling to stand up made her want to shake him—hard. He didn't have to put himself through any more pain than necessary.

Swallowing her anger, she moved to take his elbow and wrap an arm around his waist. 'Come on. Get in the car.'

Michael sagged against her, giving away how much he was hurting. 'Bossy creature, aren't you?'

'You'd better believe it.'

As quickly as her anger had risen it faded away. He was a man who believed in being tough, strong, inviolate. Face it: she wouldn't be interested in a wimp. But did he have to be so stubborn?

It took some effort to get Michael into his car, but with a few curses on his side and determination and care on hers he was finally installed, looking even paler and gulping air as if it was going out of fashion fast.

Zac settled his snout on Michael's shoulder, and didn't seem perturbed that he wasn't acknowledged.

'Stephanie?'

Michael tapped her hand until she looked at him.

'Thank you. For everything. I know you aren't keen to stay with me, so you need to know I appreciate it.'

Not what she'd expected. 'It's fine.' She pulled out into the traffic. 'Maybe I should take you home first…get you settled.'

His chest rose and fell. 'No, I'm okay.' Tipping his head sideways, he watched her watching the road. 'Truly. It's no more uncomfortable sitting in here than it will be at home. Let's get whatever you need first.'

'Fine. On your head be it. Is there anything you want? I'm warning you: cooking is not my forte.'

With his regular list of takeout menus he was safe for the few nights she'd be there, because getting involved in a kitchen and a pantry was *not* happening.

'How much not your thing?'

'I can boil vegetables, heat soup, put a casserole together with the help of a recipe.'

That wasn't so bad.

'Oh, and make toast.'

'Want to pick up some soup? And a ham bone in case I get creative in the coming days.'

Suddenly Steph laughed. 'This is nuts. Here we are, two supposedly intelligent people, planning a meal out of a can. Maybe it's time I put an effort into cooking. Roasts and steak and sticky date puddings.'

'You like sticky date too?'

He smacked those delicious lips.

'I'll book you in for a cookery course tomorrow.' Then, 'How come your mum didn't teach you the basics?'

'She tried, but I always wanted to be outside with my brothers. They did cool stuff, like climb trees and build huts, ride cycle tracks. Who would want to be stuck inside when they could do all that?'

'You were married. Still no cooking?'

'Some—nothing fancy.' Another thing Freddy had finally come to grizzle about, even though it hadn't been an issue in the beginning.

The supermarket car park was almost empty. She pulled up close to the front and leapt out.

'Back in a tick.'

She raced up and down the aisles, lifting cans, bread and chocolate, and dog biscuits. She whipped through the self check-out and tossed her bag on the seat beside Zac.

She needn't have bothered rushing. Michael's head was tipped back, his eyes closed, and his breathing light. It was a silent few minutes driving from the supermarket to his house.

'Someone's been here,' she commented, more to herself than to her two companions, as she parked as close to the front door as possible to save Michael any more walking than necessary. Smoke was billowing out of the chimney.

Michael came awake instantly. 'Max said he'd drop by…make himself useful.'

'Wait there while I open the door and dump these bags.' She also let Zac out, and he immediately bounded across to a lemon tree to cock his leg.

'I like your new housemate. We had quite the discussion while you were shopping,' Michael commented when she returned to help him out of the car. He was keeping a wary eye on the dog, with his injured leg furthest away from that solid head.

'You were faking that sleep?'

He hadn't budged when she'd shut her door and started up the engine.

'Zac, sit.' He instantly obeyed. Unbelievable. 'Good boy. He's been an angel so far—apart from the holes he dug—so I'm hoping he'll be well-behaved here.'

Winding her arm around Michael's waist she helped him inside with his other arm hanging over her shoulder. Occasionally, when his leg dragged or knocked a step, his fingers dug hard.

'Relax. I don't mind having Zac here. Sometimes I think I should get a dog myself. Aaron would love it. But my hours don't lend enough time.'

He made it right through to the kitchen and dropped onto a chair with a wince and a groan. The crutch clattered against the table and slid to the floor, sending Zac skittering backwards as he stared at the noisy thing.

Placing the crutch out of the way, but close enough for Michael to reach, Steph admitted, 'That's my big concern about Zac. That he'll be lonely while I'm at work. So I'm going to enquire about getting a minder. Someone who'll take him for walks on those days.'

'There's a guy who does it for some of the hospital staff. He'll keep your dog at his place all day, if necessary. Ask the Radiology crowd. At least two of them use his services and they swear by him.'

'That's brilliant.' The guilt niggling at her since she'd decided to keep Zac disappeared. 'I wonder if this guy would drop by and check up on *you* while I'm at work.

He could even take you for a hop around the park on your crutch.'

Michael glared at her. 'Woof, woof.'

'Know any good dog food takeout places?'

'Watch it.'

Opening the fridge to put away the butter and milk, she gaped. 'Someone's been busy. There's a casserole in here.'

'That'll be Max's wife. She's always baking and cooking. Believes it's the way to everyone's heart.' He made to push up off his seat and immediately dropped down again. 'Aaron's more nimble than I am at the moment.'

'Which is why I've been coerced into staying here. What are you wanting?'

'You can leave any time you like. It wasn't me who twisted your arm.'

'Your pal was very persuasive. And neither did you really add any weight at the end. I might've resisted otherwise.'

She still wasn't certain she'd done the right thing, coming here.

'Do you want coffee?'

He nodded. 'I was trying to make it easier for you to give in without Jock gloating. He's good at that. But seriously, Steph, if you don't want to be here then please go back to your place. I won't be offended.'

So she was Steph today as well? Still sounded sexy on his tongue.

'Which room do I use?'

Yours? Do I get to share your bed?

She'd had her chance two nights ago and run.

'Take your pick—though Aaron usually goes in the one next to mine when he's staying, so I can hear him if he wakes.' Michael grimaced.

'Does Chantelle know about your operation?'

'Max phoned her first thing this morning, just as she was going into a lecture.'

'Where's Aaron?'

'In the university crèche since it was only for an hour. Strange she didn't try to drop him off at my place. He won't be staying here for a few days now. I couldn't keep up with him.'

'So what will Chantelle do about that?'

Steph searched the cupboards for mugs and coffee.

'Learn to take care of things herself.'

'Come on. From what you told me she's already doing that.'

Leaning back against the bench, she crossed her ankles and waited for him to answer. *If* he answered.

'Your brothers don't give you any grief about the things you choose to do?'

Where had that come from?

'None at all. Growing up, we were one big happy family and nothing's really changed. Except my best friend is now my sister-in-law, which is cool.'

'As long as nothing goes wrong.'

Steph stared at Michael. 'Wow, that's negative.'

'What would happen to your friendship if your brother's marriage failed? Would you and your friend remain on good terms?'

'I don't see why not. Now that time's passed I get on with my ex whenever I bump into him.'

Michael's eyebrows rose. 'Really? That's unusual.'

'So I'm told. Sugar?'

'One. How often do you see Freddy?'

He sounded…jealous? *Nah*—that would be ridiculous.

'Not for a while since I've been away.'

Coffee splashed over her fingers as she vigorously stirred sugar into both mugs.

'Here.'

After sliding one onto the table, she headed into the lounge to check if the fire needed more wood. It didn't.

'Jock can't have left here much before we got home.'

Michael was watching her as she returned to her coffee. 'I was married once.'

What was this? One confidence for another?

'I'm sorry it didn't work out.'

I am not asking why, but I'd like to know.

'So was I, at the time.' He sipped his coffee. 'But in retrospect the chances of it working out were probably fifty-fifty at best. We weren't ideally suited in many respects.'

'How old were you?'

What had happened to not asking anything?

His smile was self-deprecating. 'Twenty-two. We married while I was still playing rugby. Divorced when I began packing in the hours studying at med school.'

'That's young. I met Freddy while I was training. He's nearly ten years older and was getting established in private practice as a plastic surgeon.'

'Where is he working now?'

'On the North Shore.'

The coffee was too strong.

'What do you want me to get organised before I leave for work at five?'

'This is why I argued with Chris. I don't need any help. I can turn the oven on...put that casserole in to heat.'

'Changing your dressings might be difficult.' Steph fidgeted with her mug.

'Can't you do that before you leave? I'll take a shower first. It's been a while and I feel grubby. They sure know how to ramp up the heat on the ward.'

'Newsflash: a shower is out of the question. Wrapping

plastic around your thigh to prevent water seeping through won't work.'

'Yes, Nurse,' he said grumpily. 'I hate it when you're right. I'll run a bath, then, keep this leg hanging over the edge.'

Oh, boy. This just got worse and worse. 'How are you going to lower yourself into the water with only one hand? And—' she waved her finger in front of him '—how are you going to get out again when you can't put any weight on that leg?'

'You're enjoying this.'

'Absolutely not.' And she was not seeing him naked on anyone's watch. Then again, neither was Michael falling and doing more damage on her watch.

Oh, boy, now what?

'Between us, I'll get in and out of the bath without too much hassle.'

His jaw clenched. He obviously knew it was going to hurt, but what was the alternative?

'I can give you a sponge-down. A warm cloth and soapy water is just as effective as a shower or bath.' *And less revealing.* No need to remove his boxers. He could sit on a stool with towels on the floor while she washed that skin, felt those muscles under her fingertips, tried to ignore his body.

But Michael was shaking his head. Of course he was. Stubborn man. Infuriating man.

He would wash himself. He did not need Stephanie wiping his fevered skin, leaning close, her breath whispering across his body, that honey scent teasing his senses.

'I'm having a bath,' Michael reiterated.

He would banish her to the kitchen until he was ready to get out. If she hadn't already run out the front door.

Stephanie wouldn't run. She might feel uncomfortable, even angry with him, but she'd never shirk her duty. *Duty.* That was what he was to her today. A duty. She'd been coerced into helping him, and he had to take some of the flak for that. And if that was disappointment clouding his thinking he only had himself to blame. But he'd throw his mates into the mix for good measure. No point in suffering alone.

Michael reached for his crutch and placed it straight up beside his injured leg. He pushed upward. The crutch slipped and he dropped back on the chair.

Deep breath...wait for the pain to ease off. Try again. Slip. Again.

The throbbing in his thigh increased exponentially.

'Stephanie.' Where had she gone? 'Steph!'

'Problem?' She appeared in the doorway. 'I've started running the bath.' Her gaze scanned him, hesitated on the hand clutching the useless crutch. 'Can't get up?'

'I'm being careful, okay?'

Down, man, down. This is not Steph's fault. And stop calling her Steph. It's too friendly.

'Can you give me a hand?'

Literally. Without saying a word. Without feeling soft and gentle and blood-thickeningly sensual.

If only she was as good at mind-reading as she was at nursing. That last memo clearly hadn't made it across to her head.

Her fingers brushed the back of his hand on their way to his elbow. Honey filled the air between them and her hair gleamed under the overhead light. How had he walked away from this woman before he'd had his fill of that wondrous body?

Getting to his en suite bathroom was painful. His wrist

throbbed like the devil, his thigh worse. The axe had gone as deep as his femur, and bone pain was ghastly.

He nearly stopped at his bed to spread out and let his body recoup. But he was determined to scrub up. His skin felt gross. He'd got a sweat up chopping wood before those cats had done their number on him. Throw in all those hours spent in one bed or another and he was in need of hot water and soap. Not gentle hands and caring eyes.

Dropping the crutch on the bathroom floor, he tugged his jersey and shirt over his head, swore when his sprained wrist got caught up in the sleeve.

'Let me.'

Stephanie was right there, untangling the fabric, carefully removing the sleeve. Not touching his skin. Then she started on the tape holding his wrist.

'Might as well take this off. It'll get soaked no matter how careful we are.'

'*We?* I'm having a bath. Not you.'

A blush rose in her cheeks. 'I have no intention of getting in with you. Just washing your back and your good arm since you won't be able to manage that.'

I don't think so.

Michael pushed his track pants down and stepped out of them.

That pink hue turned red as Stephanie stared at him.

Then he dropped his boxers and hopped over to the bath.

Forget red. Her cheeks were alight.

'You—' She swallowed hard. 'You could've kept them on.'

'Do you bathe in your underwear? When you want to clean yourself?' he taunted, in need of keeping her on her toes in case he lost it and grabbed her to him. Because he wanted to. Very much.

'No. But—' Another swallow.

'It's not as though you haven't seen it all before. You're a nurse.'

Not to mention their weeks together, when clothes hadn't been a part of what they'd got up to.

He parked his naked butt on the side of the bath and swung his good leg over into the water. So far so good. He lifted his injured leg. Rather, *tried* to lift it, and clenched his fists as pain whipped him.

Nurse Stephanie was instantly there, her hands on his calf, carefully raising his leg to slide over the edge.

'Now you just have to lower your backside into the water without getting that wound wet.'

Clipped words, firm hands under his arm, pressed lips forcing all colour away.

Focusing entirely on getting into the bath and not swearing out loud, Michael finally managed to sit on the bottom and raise his injured leg to hang over the side.

'Thanks, Nurse. I'll manage now.'

Dismissed. Steph charged out of the bathroom, leaving the door open so she could hear if Michael called out.

It was tempting to head outside, take Zac for a walk—except it would be closer to a run before her anger calmed. She even picked up the lead from the bench.

Zac sat up, his tail wagging in anticipation.

'Sorry, my boy.' She dropped the lead and rubbed his ears. 'We can't leave him to get out of the bath on his own.'

How was she supposed to help him now? He needed his back and his arm washed. How to not notice everything about him? As in *everything*.

You've seen it all before.

Sure she had. She remembered his 'all'. It was the hot memories of that 'all' she couldn't deal with. This was the man she'd spent two years and thousands of kilometres trying to put behind her. Yet she'd reacted to his voice the first time he spoke to her at the beginning of the week.

Immediately she'd wanted to curl up against that expansive chest and feel as though she'd arrived at her destination. Her knees had melted when he'd kissed her—and, yes, she'd kissed him back.

But he didn't want her. Though she was beginning to think he *did* want her in his bed for a rerun of last time.

But he didn't *want*, want her. Not in his life, at his side, to be his partner, his wife. *His wife?* He'd reject her as sure as lightning came before thunder.

Again Steph snatched up the dog's lead. To hell with him. She had to get some air. Enough to keep her lungs working while her heart shut down and dealt with the pain stabbing at it.

'Stephanie? Can you wash my back?'

She froze. Totally. No heartbeat. No breathing. Dead but alive. Numb yet in pain.

Wife? That entailed love. Well, it did for her. This cramping sensation holding her, stuck, unable to move, was love. She'd screwed up big-time.

'Steph?'

Play the friendship card, why don't you?

She was all out of them.

The lead banged onto the floor, snapping her into action. Head up, lungs working, back straighter than a ruler, mind focused on the job. Wash his back, get him out of the bath without crashing to the floor, dry him off. *No way.* He could manage that part all by himself. He had to.

'Then we'll go for a walk,' she said, and patted Zac. 'After that I'll go to work and leave you with him. Sorry, but he won't upset you like he does me.'

Her resolve lasted until she reached the side of the bath. One glance at that muscular chest and she was lost. Her hand shook as she snatched the washcloth from him. The shaking became an earthquake as she sponged his back—right down to where his butt met the bottom of the bath.

How the hell was she supposed to get through the coming days?

She tried for an icy tone, instead got melted goo that made her sound like a drunk. 'Right, let's get you out of here.'

His skin was wet, and warm, and *so* tempting.

It's an arm.

Her fingers dug deep.

Michael gripped the edge of the bath and shoved up, wobbling in circles as he strived for balance.

Being afraid he'd fall focused Steph on what she should have been concentrating on all along.

'Put your arm over my shoulder and use me as a crutch.'

And hurry up before I give in and turn to lay my face against your chest, to kiss you.

'Hey, Mike? You inside?' The question was followed by the front door slamming.

'Great timing,' Michael muttered as he reached for a towel. 'Chantelle?'

'Yes.'

He raised his voice. 'I'm getting out of the bath. Wait out there, will you?'

Steph fixed him with a look that said, *Your sister's probably seen it all before too, when you were kids.*

'You don't want her thinking we've got something going on between us, do you?' he asked.

'I don't give a damn.'

Yes, well. Brave words.

Judging by the cynicism on Michael's face he didn't believe her any more than she did herself.

'I'm here as a nurse who also happens to be a friend.'
She winced over that one.

'Did you find the casserole I made?' Chantelle called
from inside his bedroom.

'*You* made it?'

Steph pulled a face at his scepticism. 'Michael…' she
whispered. 'Behave.'

He took the towel she held out and wrapped it around
his waist. 'Sorry. Stephanie found it. I figured—'

Steph put her hand over his mouth, shook her head at
him, whispered, 'Say thank you. *Nicely.*' Then she removed her hand—but not before he'd breathed on her palm,
sending her hormones into a riot of excitement.

'Thanks, Chantelle. What kind of casserole is it?' He
raised an eyebrow at her, as if he was asking, *How am I
doing?*

She smothered a smile and nodded.

'Uncle Mike—there you are!' A blur of arms and legs
shot into the room.

Steph reacted instinctively to prevent the dynamo
launching himself against his uncle's injury. Grabbing
Aaron, she swung him up into her arms.

'Hi, Aaron. Remember me? Uncle Mike's friend Steph.'

'Friend? I thought you said she was a nurse,' Chantelle
said as she appeared around the door.

'I want to hug Uncle Mike.' Aaron wriggled to be put
down.

'You can when he's got dressed, okay?' Steph told him.
'Uncle Mike's hurt his leg, so you have to be very careful
not to bump him.'

As if a three-year-old would take any notice.

Michael leaned towards his nephew, rubbed his head.
'I'll be with you in a minute, buddy, but you've got to go
with Mum and Stephanie now.'

'No. I want *you*.'

'I'll be real fast. Promise.'

That was a promise he'd have trouble keeping in his condition. And she wasn't thinking about his sculpted chest or saucy butt. Well, she *was*, but not in terms of his promise.

'I'll put the kettle on.'

As if *that* was going to help—but it was what her grandmother had always done when she hadn't known what to do about a situation. Besides, a cup of tea wouldn't go astray. Her nerves needed help calming down.

'You're not going to help Michael finish drying off and get him dressed?' Chantelle asked, with a wicked glint in her eyes.

'He's quite capable.' Though she would have helped if his sister hadn't turned up. 'I'll just grab some clean clothes for him.'

Which meant going through his drawers. How personal was *that*? How soon could she leave for work?

CHAPTER SEVEN

ZAC GREETED STEPH with a wagging tail when she crawled out of her car at Michael's place just after six-thirty the next morning. 'Hey, my boy, good to see you too. Who let you out?'

The house was eerily quiet.

She tiptoed through to the kitchen on legs that must have done a thousand kilometres throughout her shift, her mind filled with images of a boy racer's car wrapped around a power pole, its drunk occupants tossed across the bonnet oblivious to the sirens and people stemming bloodflow and buckling on neck braces. The ambulance crews had taken two of the boys to the ED, while a low black saloon had transported a third to the morgue.

Her stomach cramped in hunger. Eggs on toast would be heaven, and might make up for the couple of snatched mouthfuls of a cruddy dry sandwich in the crew kitchen hours ago, but pouring muesli out of a box was a lot quicker, with no thought processes required.

It was already too crowded in her skull, with images of those kids refusing to go away, vying with Michael for attention. He'd been there in her thoughts all night, only backing off when total concentration had been needed for her patients, returning the moment she was free. The man had a way of making her feel as though her feet were on ice, sending her in every direction but the one she'd intended going.

How to make him go away, leave her in peace, when she did not need him interfering with her life plans?

But he refused to go away.

He was such a distraction.

Like sitting naked in the bath while she washed his back and almost put a tooth through her bottom lip as she denied the need to wash more, touch more. Like talking to her as though this was normal—which it could be if they were in a real relationship. Like being so relaxed with her when she was tighter than a triple knot in comparison.

If ever there was a man she could envisage spending her life with he was... Michael.

She'd known it for a long time. Throughout all those hours, days months and years she'd spent running, trying to bury him in the back of her mind, he had still been under her skin, still heating her blood, still meaning everything to her. He still sent her heart into a whacky rhythm.

So much for thinking she was an intelligent woman.

Sanity.

Highly overrated.

She obviously didn't have any.

Michael Laing ruled her heart. Someone had to as she was obviously incapable.

'Morning. You look like you had the night from hell.'

As Michael crashed into her reverie for real Steph tripped over her feet and stared at him as if he was a stranger.

'Why are you up? Didn't you sleep well?'

There were deep shadows smeared across his cheekbones, but only mild pain in his eyes. Plus a dose of resignation. What was *that* about?

'I prefer those nights where I don't know a thing until

the alarm goes off,' he admitted. 'Want a cup of tea? Unless you've changed your morning fix?'

He remembered. 'I'll get it. You stay put.' He wasn't putting weight on that leg for her. 'Want one?'

'Please. And can you wake Chantelle? She needs to get up and sort Aaron or she'll be late for work. Oh, and Zac's outside in the back yard. He was crossing his legs when I came out here half an hour ago.'

'I received my good morning nudge the moment I stepped out of my car.' And then she'd shut the door on him, focused on not waking Michael. 'What sort of doggy mother am I?' Opening the back door she called, 'Zac? Where are you, boy?'

A black and tan form charged her, skidded to a halt at her feet, a big head bumping her. Wag, wag, went that thick tail.

A lump filled her throat as she leaned down to rub Zac's head, then his back. Already she was smitten. *Oh, come on.* She'd been lost from the first pat she'd given him. Like with Michael. The first day he'd arrived in the ED to start his contract she'd been hooked. Their first kiss had had her falling for him.

Yeah, she'd always been in love with him. It was how all her important relationships had started. She and Jill had known from their first morning on the school mat that they were best pals. Freddy much the same—if not on the school mat. If ever she'd needed proof that she wasn't going to get over Michael now she had it.

But she already knew that.

Steph sighed and nuzzled her face against Zac's neck. 'How come you're so quick to trust me?' It didn't say a lot for his affection for his previous owner. Or did it mean the other woman's love had taught him there were only kind people out there?

'He whimpers a lot in his sleep.'

She'd forgotten how near Michael was.

'I think he does miss his other home, but he's very happy with you. Sucks up love and attention like a sponge,' he added.

'Strange how he turned up at my house and never left. He was there every time I went home. Why, boyo? Did you sense I'd buy you sirloin once week as a treat?'

'What's not to trust about you, Steph?'

'I used to be a flight risk.' Standing up, she ran a hand over her messy hair. 'I ran out of Auckland when you finished with me. Then I left Queenstown when the two girls I worked with fell in love and had babies. As for London and Europe—I could never stay in one place for very long. The moment things seemed to be going great I'd find something to be unhappy about.'

Michael flinched. 'But you're home for good this time, right?'

'I am. No matter what happens here, this is where I belong. It's about the only thing I'm sure of some days.'

She closed the back door to keep the early-morning cold at bay and headed to the bench and that tea she was supposed to be making.

Oops, Chantelle needed rousing.

'As long as I can keep that at the front of my mind,' she muttered as she headed down the hall, 'and not let the fear of being dumped again get in the way.'

So she loved Michael. She really loved him. Trying to get over him was never going to work. And with her being back here, now she needed a new plan.

A deep breath made her lungs sting. Go after him. Woo him. Show him how she felt. Prove her love was real and honest and for ever.

Steph sagged against the wall. Could she do that? Her heart was already Michael's, so what was there to lose?

'Steph? You okay?' Chantelle stood in front of her.

Great. Now Michael's sister would have the wrong impression of her.

'I'm fine. I was coming to wake you up, but seems I wasn't needed.'

'Michael won't believe I'm capable of setting an alarm.' It was said with a smile but there was weariness in her voice. 'He's a work in progress when it comes to trusting me to live my life without mishaps.'

'He wants the best for you.'

Steph had seen the surprise in Michael's eyes when Chantelle had rung yesterday to say she'd stay the night here in case he needed help getting about. That surprise had been replaced with relief, showing how worried he'd been about being on his own.

'If I didn't know that I'd have left town years ago.' Chantelle opened Aaron's door, glanced over her shoulder to Steph. 'How *is* Grumpy Socks this morning?'

'Sitting in the kitchen looking tired. Did you have to get up for him during the night?' Steph asked.

Chantelle grinned. 'What do you think? This is Michael we're talking about—self-sufficient and always giving help, never asking for any.'

Steph huffed. 'Should've known.'

His sister stared at her. 'How well do you know him? I thought you— It doesn't matter.'

Was that disappointment in her eyes? Why? For what?

'We worked together for a couple of years a while back, so I know him well professionally.'

Which meant she knew his stalwart character, his kindness, gentleness, his concern for people in dire situations.

'So why are you here now? This isn't a work environment, even if he does need your nursing skills.'

Good question—and one she still wasn't ready to answer out loud. 'He begged. I folded.'

'Michael begged?' Chantelle stared at her, her mouth widening into an infuriating grin. 'My brother *begged* you to help him out?'

Uh-oh. Trouble lurking.

'His mates were pushing me to acquiesce. I think Michael asked me to stay over just to shut them down.'

Take that on board and smoke it.

'You mean Max and Jock?' Chantelle nodded. 'That I can believe. I also know exactly what they're up to. You so don't know what you've got yourself into. You're fried!'

'Mummy, I want Bugsy.'

Saved by the boy. Once more. She owed him an ice cream.

'I'll get that tea I've been trying to make for the last ten minutes.'

Michael was at the bench, his hip propped against it, dropping teabags into mugs. 'Chantelle in a good mood?'

A scheming one. 'Why wouldn't she be?'

'She gets tired with Aaron and studying, and doesn't always show how happy she is.' He filled the mugs with boiling water.

'Go and sit down. I'll get these.' Steph nudged him with an elbow.

Michael caught her arm, tugged her to face him. 'I know you didn't want to be here with me, so thanks again. I'm trying not to be a pain in the backside.'

Instant heat flared in her arm, sending sparks of desire along her arm. Not want to be with him? Wrong. She definitely wanted to be here. What she didn't need was getting in a pickle over the sexual heat moving through her body at speed, sending her hormones into overdrive—all because his hand was on her arm.

Run that by me again.

'Let's move on. I am here—between shifts, at any rate. Someone has to make sure you don't mow the lawns or finish chopping that firewood for a few days.'

'I get it. You'll be sleeping most of the day. I can't do any noisy activities.'

Take your hand away before I fold into you for an activity not on your mind, let the need churning through me take over completely and make you laugh—at me.

'Morning, big brother.' Chantelle strolled into the kitchen. 'Sleep well?'

Michael instantly dropped his hand and stepped back—too quickly if the groan that ripped across his lips was an indicator. The knuckles grabbing the edge of the counter were white.

Steph pulled a chair close. Put a hand on his shoulder. 'Sit.'

He didn't let go of the counter as he sagged onto the chair. 'Silly bu—'

'Small boy present,' Chantelle warned.

'Uncle Mike, I lost Bugsy. Mummy found him in my bed.' Aaron stood in front of Michael, tiny hands on narrow hips as he stared at his uncle. 'Do you want Bugsy to make you better?'

'Sure.'

Steph kept her hand on Michael's shoulder until the tension had seeped out of him. 'Want me to change your dressing?'

'After breakfast,' Michael said. 'Don't need everyone getting in on the show.'

Zac's paws clicked on the tiles as he came to nudge

up against Steph's thigh. Her other hand automatically dropped to his head.

A laugh had her snapping her head up. 'What?'

Chantelle was grinning like a cat with the cream as her gaze roamed from her brother to Steph to Zac and back to Michael. 'Nothing. Come and have a shower, Aaron. I need to get you to the daycare centre and me to class.'

Thank goodness Aaron raced away towards the bathroom and Chantelle had to follow before he got into mischief or Steph might have brained her for that smartass look in her eyes, as if she thought there was something going down between her and Michael.

'What do you want for breakfast?' she asked the man causing her endless problems with her hormones and her heart—and his sister.

'I'll fix something when you've gone to bed.'

'Since I'm going to eat before doing that, I can make double. Scrambled eggs suit?' As if she'd leave him sitting there with nothing to eat. 'I can make enough for everybody.'

So much for cereal and easy.

'Don't start running around after my sister,' he snapped. 'She's more than capable of looking after herself.'

'Hey, cut it out. It's no big deal to cook enough for four. Besides, I'd look a prize cow if I didn't at least offer.'

What was his problem with his sister? Only one way to find out, and as she could hear the shower and Aaron's chatter through the wall she had no compunction about not remaining quiet.

'You're not pleased Chantelle's here?'

Michael tipped his head back and stared up at the ceiling.

For a long moment she thought that was all the answer she was getting, so she went to the fridge to get eggs and cream. She'd make enough for everybody, and if it wasn't eaten she'd have an egg sandwich for nightshift.

'It's not like her to help me.'

'But you're close?' They seemed to be, despite the moments of tension she'd observed. 'Or is it that you like looking out for Chantelle but don't want to be on the receiving end of the same?'

He fixed her with a troubled gaze. 'I've always got her back—and Aaron's.'

She'd run with that—avoid the other idea since it didn't seem to be sitting well with him. 'The father's not in the picture?'

'He took off before Aaron was born. Which was a very good thing. At the time Chantelle was in a bad place, but pregnancy made her stop and take note of the appalling life she was leading, forced her to rethink her future.'

'Hence university? That takes courage and strength. You've got to be proud of her.'

'I am.' Michael blinked as though he hadn't considered that before. 'But some days I wish she'd sort out the rest of her act instead of expecting me to always be there, picking up the pieces.'

Collecting Aaron from daycare when she was late being one of those pieces. Steph got it, but if it was her she'd be happy to grab what time she could with her nephew.

'She made you dinner, stayed the night. That suggests a two-way helpline going on here.'

Michael blinked again, muttered slowly, 'Yes, she did...'

Through the wall she heard the shower stop running so returned her attention to making breakfast. But while whisking cream into eggs and adding salt and pepper she was still seeing Michael's face—filled with pain when he moved too quickly, with love when he looked at his nephew, exasperation when he talked about his sister. And confusion when he touched her arm.

The guy had a lot going on in that head. How much of a distraction was she? Did he ever think about their affair and wonder if he'd made the right decision to call it off? Did he want to spend time with her, get to know her better? Or was he glad he'd made the call and now couldn't wait to be back on his feet and have her gone?

Of course he was.

The whisk flicked raw egg over the bench and the front of her uniform jersey and she cursed. She needed to get it cleaned for work that night. Banging the bowl in the microwave, she quickly wiped the bench before tugging her jersey over her head. And found Michael's gaze locked on her—make that on her breasts as they stretched the buttons of her shirt.

At least that was what she thought he was staring at. Judging by the lust in his eyes, she knew she was right. *He wanted her*

She still didn't know for how long. Didn't know if he needed one night in bed with her or a month's worth.

Then he shook his head and glanced at the microwave, which was beeping. And now she had another answer. He might be feeling the need, but he wasn't following through. Not because of his injury, but because he just *wasn't*. Didn't do the commitment thing.

She hated the fact that she could still hear those chill, heartbreaking words as if he'd said them yesterday.

'I am not interested in a long-term relationship, with you or anybody.'

Blunt. Honest. Hurtful.

Carefully stirring the eggs, she swallowed the second lump in her throat of the morning.

Have breakfast, take Zac for a walk, then hit the pil-

*low and get a few hours' shut-eye. Let the day unfold as
intended.*

Her new and boringly normal life was reality. Shoving
the bowl back in the microwave she pressed the start button. That was how it was.

*You forgot about changing Michael's dressing, seeing
and touching his thigh, feeling his heat while you're at it.*

No, she hadn't—she was deliberately avoiding thinking about it, that was all.

Nor had she forgotten that she was going to change his
mind about trying to make him fall for her. Once she'd
worked out how to go about it.

Aha. She already had Chantelle's attention. Help might
be around the corner.

Michael swallowed some painkillers and hobbled on his
crutch to the lounge and the TV remote. Breakfast had
been a shambles. Not the food, but Steph had gone into a
funk for no reason he could fathom, and that had annoyed
the hell out of him.

He liked having her around. No denying it. When
she walked in the door after a night on the ambulance it
seemed as though she'd always been doing that—as if she
belonged here, with him.

Which was a perfectly good reason why he should be
pleased her mood had changed and he was being kept at
a distance.

When she'd changed his dressing she'd been aloof, the
ultimate professional. Definitely not a friend or an ex-
lover. Then she'd yawned—so unprofessional he'd have
laughed if he hadn't been afraid for his thigh. Exhaustion
had been pulling at her shoulders, and her eyes hadn't been
their usual sparkling toffee shade. Night shifts did that to

people not used to them, and Stephanie was still getting into her stride.

Zac had had his walk, he'd been offered more tea on their return, and then Stephanie had disappeared down the hallway to the bathroom for a shower. She hadn't come to see him before she'd shut herself in the bedroom she was using. Was she sound asleep? Or tossing and turning in search of oblivion?

He could remember the sheer frustration of not being able to sleep after a long night shift in the department when he was training. It had felt as though his body had been craving sleep so much it couldn't shut down.

The TV came to life and he waved the remote in the general direction of the channel button. What was happening in the world? Flicking channels, he listened to the news without really hearing it. Today he couldn't drag up any sympathy or interest or outrage for the heinous crimes people were committing against each other all around the world. This morning his weary mind kept wandering to Stephanie. Cursing the fact that she should be annoying even when she wasn't near.

He'd have enjoyed another bath—needed one really, if that pungent sweaty odour was anything to go by—but it would have to wait until Stephanie woke up, hopefully in an improved mood. If only he could bath himself, but taking a tumble on those tiles would not be a good look, and it wouldn't help with getting back to work ASAP. And it would certainly not be sensible—which he was prone to be about most things.

Though not about Stephanie Roberts.

Oh, yeah? Meaning...?

Meaning that somehow she'd managed to get under his skin again. Could be she'd never actually got out from there. She definitely had him thinking about her far too often, in ways that had nothing to do with work or being friends. His mind, overruled by his body, kept fixating on the stunning curves her uniform did nothing to hide. He knew those curves, the silky skin covering them, Steph's heated reaction to his fingers and lips skimming over her body.

Big mistake, having her stay here. But he'd really, truly believed he didn't want a long-term relationship. Had he been lying to himself? Whether he had or not, it didn't change the fact the he was still frightened of failure. Falling in love and then crashing and burning had been painful once—it would be catastrophic a second time.

Five to nine. How was he going to fill in the hours till Stephanie got up? How long would she sleep? She'd told Zac she'd take him for another walk later in the day. She hadn't told *him* anything more than that she'd change the dressings again when she got up. Oh, yeah, there'd been mention of a shopping trip before dinner.

Dinner. Now, there was a challenge. What if he put a meal together? It wasn't as though he didn't know his way around the kitchen. He just never bothered for himself. But Steph should eat a proper meal before leaving for work. He only had one working hand at the moment, but surely it couldn't be too difficult to create something.

Shoving himself up off the couch, he felt pain shooting through his leg, and that had him questioning the ridiculous idea and reminding him why he was here and not at work in the ED. *Tough.* He'd give it his best. He had all day.

Zac lumbered to his feet and followed, getting in the way in the kitchen, bumping into Michael's injured leg. Gasping, Michael tripped, put weight on that leg, felt pain in the wound. The air turned blue.

Zac sat on his haunches, his tongue lolling and his eyes fixed on Michael, oblivious to the problem he'd caused.

Sinking onto a kitchen chair, Michael wiped the sweat off his brow and breathed deep, absorbing the pain, and worked to ease the tightness in his thigh muscles.

Talk about being a geriatric. This was ridiculous. In his rugby days whenever he'd got knocked down he shrug the pain aside and get up to continue running around the paddock. He was not as fit as he'd been then, for sure. Using the gym and going for runs was not the same as the hours and hours he and his teammates had put in to keep their bodies in tip-top condition.

'You all right?' Stephanie swished into the kitchen, an empty glass in hand, thick bathrobe wrapped around her body, hiding all those superb curves he adored.

'Sure.'

As she filled the glass from the fridge water dispenser she studied him. 'You're very pale.'

'Hard to get a tan in winter.'

'Smart Aleck.' There was a hint of a smile on those luscious lips.

'You been asleep at all?'

'Not yet. I find it hard, being out of routine. It's years since I did nights, and I was never good at sleeping during the day.' She sat down beside him, with no sign of the funk that had been gripping her before. 'Let me look at that leg.'

'It's fine.'

'As any red-blooded, full-of-testosterone male would say.'

'Sometimes I think you forget that I'm a doctor and quite capable of dealing with my own injuries.'

But he was already tugging his track pants down to his knees. Oh, so sexy... Track pants were *not* a turn-on. Definitely more comfortable at the moment, though. That thigh did not need fitted trousers holding it tight, and nor did another part of his anatomy that had a tendency to get hyped up whenever Steph was close.

Which was why he'd slipped a pair of boxers on when he'd got up. Having Stephanie noticing his apparatus while she changed dressings wouldn't be good. Especially as said apparatus had a tendency to tighten, thicken, and show its feelings for her without any input from his brain. He leaned forward, arms folded low over his abdomen in case that particular reaction got carried away now.

'Since we're looking at it, I'll change the dressing and save the discomfort later.'

She was so gentle removing the gauze pad he didn't feel a thing. But then he was concentrating on not noticing how her thick hair fell over her cheek, and on not breathing in that honey scent. He cursed silently. Reaction happening.

'Do you think you could make me a cup of tea?' *Now. Immediately.*

'Give me a minute and I'll put the kettle on.'

A minute? That was a lifetime in this condition.

'Great.' *Not.*

In a minute he was going to be tied up with need. Need that overrode everything else his body was feeling as those gentle fingers cleaned a smear of blood from the stitches holding him together. That was what he needed to stay strong and sane—stitches in his head. Talk about going stark raving mad…

What could he talk about that was totally unrelated to skin and fingers and tightening muscles? 'Do you eat pasta?'

Ouch. Her finger had slipped, rubbed the top of some of the stitches. Served him right.

'Love it.'

Love what? Oh, pasta. Of course. 'Then that's what I'll make.'

'Pardon? Michael, are you all right?' She laid her palm on his forehead. 'No temperature,' she quipped. 'But it seems you've forgotten I'm here because you can't get around easily. You sure can't make pasta. Unless… I get it. Where's the menu? I'll pick what I want and you phone the order in later with yours.'

That palm was soft, warm, soothing…not to mention downright sexy. Who knew his forehead could feel hot and intense and needy from Stephanie's touch? Not him. But then around Steph he was learning about quite a few things he'd never have believed possible. Like how he wanted to make her a meal to show how much he appreciated having her here while he was incapacitated, how happy it made him to know she cared enough to be in his house when she clearly didn't want to be.

'Michael? Menu?'

'There isn't one.'

He loved how her eyes widened, that brown shade looking soft and gooey, like caramel melting in a pan. Or was that his stomach feeling gooey? Like a besotted kid dealing with puppy love?

'Now I know I can't go back to bed. You'll get up to something that's not good for your wrist or your leg if I do.'

A smile broke out, lifting her cheeks, lightening those eyes further. Warming his insides, sending his heart into some strange unknown rhythm, giving him hope. *Hope?* For what? A future different from the one he'd known since that promise to his dad? One where everything worked out? A future with Stephanie in it permanently?

She did this to him. Rattled him, knocked his beliefs sideways so he rethought everything he lived by. She wasn't good for him, pushing his boundaries wide.

Stephanie was so close the corners of their chairs touched. He only had to lean forward a little, use his good hand to gently pull her nearer and then put a finger under her chin to lift her head and those full smiling lips were right there, under his mouth, startled into silence, into inaction.

His mouth was on hers, kissing her as though this was his last kiss ever, giving everything he had, taking whatever she had to offer. As her lips softened under his he relaxed and gave up trying to remain in control of his manhood...of anything. No point. He was going with it for all it was worth—enjoying the moment, forgetting the consequences.

Pain tore through his leg.

Michael jerked back, gulped, bit down on the oath rolling across his tongue. *What the—?* This was the worst pain yet.

'Zac, move away.' Steph stood up fast, her chair rocking back as she reached for the dog's collar and tugged him aside. 'Keep away from Michael's leg.'

Her eyes glistened as she hovered next to Michael.

'I'm so sorry. I shouldn't have brought him with me.'

'What else were you supposed to do?'

The dog was her pet—she couldn't give him back for a few days even if there was someone to return him to.

Deep breath, keep everything normal. 'Don't worry. These things happen. He doesn't understand.'

'Yes, but—'

He reached for her free hand, threaded his fingers between hers. Hadn't they just experienced the most amazing, heart-stopping kiss? Forget the blasted dog.

'Yes, but nothing. I'm fine.'

Physically he was in agony. Mentally he wasn't any better.

When Patricia had left him he'd known he'd never risk marriage again. Divorce was in the genes. So was taking responsibility seriously. While Carly had now gone off-shore and seemed happy and content, wasn't getting into major difficulties, he knew that could change any day. But it was Chantelle who gave him the most concern. She pushed herself too hard and the cracks were starting to appear. He had to be there for her, and more importantly for Aaron, if everything turned to custard again.

It wasn't the first time she'd got so far with sorting out her life and then gone off the rails. He had to admit that this time she did seem to have more control over her emotions. And if that was so he might be able to have some life for himself. But he still couldn't risk hurting Stephanie and breaking his own heart as well.

He was thinking all this while holding Stephanie's hand. He looked at her, saw uncertainty, but couldn't let go. He wanted her. Forget all the reasons he'd just put up for not doing this. He wanted her.

'Stephanie?' Her name slipped off his tongue as easily as melted chocolate.

Her eyes widened and her fingers tightened briefly around his. Then she stepped away. 'Not a good idea, Michael.'

Her tongue slid across her lips, refuting her words. She wanted him. Fire glinted in her eyes.

'I agree. Doesn't mean we have to be sensible, though.'

Her hands slapped onto her hips, her fingers white where they dug in. 'I'm the most sensible woman you've ever met.'

'I can change that.'

Her lips twitched, but the intensity in her eyes didn't lighten. 'I know you can, Michael, but it's not happening.'

She turned and walked away, down to the bedroom.

Before he heard the door click shut he'd swear she said, *'Not today.'*

CHAPTER EIGHT

SLEEP WOULD BE impossible now. Steph shoved her legs into her jeans, jerked them up, tugged her jersey over her head and dragged a brush through her hair. Her skin was hot, her mouth soft where Michael's lips had touched hers. Her body throbbed persistently.

Why had she pulled away?

Certainly not because she hadn't wanted his kiss. Quite the opposite. She hadn't been able to get enough.

Her finger touched her mouth, circled slowly. The man only had to kiss her to turn her into a blithering wreck. But wasn't that what she wanted? *Yes.* Definitely. And more.

So why was she taking Zac for a walk instead? When she'd decided to make a play for Michael? To try and win him over?

He'd been kissing her as if he meant to go through with the promise of hot, knee-melting, mind-blanking sex. But she didn't want sex with Michael. She wanted to make love. Yes, he had been right there, on the same line, but he was aiming to have sex, not make love.

Short-term for Michael. For ever for her.

'Zac,' she called as she made her way to the front door, avoiding the kitchen where she presumed Michael still sat. Or not.

What did it matter? He didn't need her fussing over his

leg at the moment. Sometimes she'd swear he didn't want her helping at all. But that could be because of what hung in the air between them, what had burst out into the open minutes ago. Did she affect him as he did her? He couldn't have been thinking straight or he'd never have kissed her in the first place. Having sex or making love would be impossible with that leg.

A gentle head-butt to her thigh brought her back to reality. A walk with the dog, not hanging out with Michael, was the order of the morning. Then maybe she'd actually go to bed—alone—and get some shut-eye. Otherwise the night ahead would be long and taxing.

They headed out to the road. In her hurry to get away Steph had forgotten to grab her car keys, but no way was she going back inside to that kitchen for them. Because of her cowardice Zac would not be getting to run free this morning. A few laps of the block was his lot. Not that he looked unhappy. Did this dog even do unhappy? He whimpered in his sleep, yet never pined at the door for his previous owner, or tried to head towards his old home when they were out walking.

Maybe there was a lesson for her in there somewhere.

Steph upped her pace, stretching out her legs, puffing short breaths into the chilly air. She should've worn a jacket. Not going back for that either.

Michael and his kisses were something else. Until now she'd thought she'd do anything to get more, to have the whole follow-up thing between the sheets, or in the shower, over the table.

Seemed she didn't know herself very well.

Seemed she wasn't prepared to sell her soul to get her man.

No, apparently she was going to have to find another way to his heart.

* * *

Remember Stephanie mightn't stay in Auckland very long, despite her protestations to the contrary.

Michael stood up slowly, easing the kinks out of his body, but not the heat and tension from his groin. That was taking a while to die down, mocking him from below.

He swore, reminding himself that he hadn't been the one to pull away. Stephanie had. When her blood had been pounding through her veins and desire had gleamed in her eyes, softened her mouth, tightened that already firm body. He cursed her for being the wise one. Because, whichever way he looked at it, he shouldn't have been kissing her— let alone thinking of heading to his bedroom with her.

Blaming her made him feel like a heel when he wanted to feel better about himself. Gratitude should be filling his tense body—not unresolved need for Stephanie.

More need than sex.

Michael jerked, and swore again as his thigh complained in the only way it knew how. No, he did not want a relationship that he couldn't walk away from at any time. Not with Stephanie. What about sex with friendship thrown in? *Yeah. Right.* Like that was going to happen. He couldn't do that to either of them.

Opening the pantry, he glared around at the shelves, banged the doors shut in frustration. The cupboards were bare except for toddler food. Likewise the fridge and freezer. When had he got so slack he didn't do a proper grocery shop?

Digging in a drawer, he found a pad and pen. Time to get his act together—turn this place into a home, not a doss-house for toddlers, paramedics and out-of-order doctors.

'What are you doing?'

Michael gritted his teeth as he knotted his shoelace

tight. He hadn't heard Stephanie return. Zac had let him down—no head-butting to warn him.

'Getting ready to go shopping.'

And he'd taken a bath—carefully, not wanting to end up sprawled across the floor and unable to get up on his own.

'I beg your pardon?' Annoyance tightened her mouth. 'You're meant to be resting that leg, remember?'

'There's the rest of the day for that. Right now I need some groceries.' He nodded at the pad on the table. 'Quite a few. I've ordered a taxi to take me to the supermarket and hang around until I'm done.'

Which could take for ever if his leg didn't play ball.

'Cancel it. I'll get these.'

'You need sleep. I'll manage. Anyway I like to do my own shopping.'

I do? Since when?

Since one stubborn woman had started shaking her head at him and picking up *his* list.

'Which company did you call?'

She dug her phone out of the backside-outlining pocket of her jeans.

'If I can't do it for you then I'm going with you. It will be a lot more comfortable in your car, and since this list is longer than your arm you might want to take a break—at which point I can finish the job while you wait outside.'

'I hate it when you're right.' He picked up his phone and called the taxi company.

You give in too easily, mate.

Yeah, well, he was learning there was no other way with Stephanie. Especially when she made a load of sense—which she did too often for comfort.

'What about your sleep? I don't want you zoning out over a patient tonight because of me.'

'I'll be fine. I can catch some zeds this afternoon. If it's all right with you I'll stop in at my house on the way back for a couple of things I need.'

'No problem.'

He liked it that she didn't gloat when she'd won. He liked a lot of things about her. Including the backside he was following out to his car. Most of all he liked having her back in town, in his life. Though could he trust that to be anything more than temporary?

When she'd left the department and Auckland he'd been bereft. Not to mention guilt-laden, believing he'd been instrumental in her decision to go. It had hurt despite it being his own fault. And that had been after only two weeks together.

Would he do it again if their feelings escalated into another fling? Cut her off before they got too involved? Yes—without a doubt. That was how he protected himself. Last time Stephanie had done a runner. Never to be heard of again by him until now.

Except that wasn't true...

His mind flashed to the card tucked in the back of a drawer in his desk down in the spare room he called an office when Aaron wasn't sleeping in there. A card with a scrawled message of congratulations for qualifying as an emergency specialist last year, signed *Steph* followed by three 'X's. Not hot, *take me* kisses like those that sometimes followed him into sleep, but kisses that evoked memories he didn't like to acknowledge.

As he buckled his seatbelt his phone rang. Chantelle. Was she working tonight? Needing him to look after Aaron as per usual? He could give it a crack...

Kidding yourself, mate. Being irresponsible. What if you fall and can't get up? How's that looking out for Aaron?

Frustration made him groan. 'Hey, Chantelle. How's your day going?'

'Great. Remember that exam I sat last week? I got top marks.'

'Go, you! That's fantastic.' Pride filled his chest and he turned to Stephanie. 'Chantelle got top marks in her law paper last week.'

Stephanie leaned close and said loudly, 'Congratulations, Chantelle. Brilliant result.'

His sister laughed. 'I'm stoked! Michael, I just called to say I'm cooking dinner tonight. Crumbed chicken legs with roast vegetables. We'll also be staying over since Steph's working. Do you need me to get anything from the supermarket?'

'Got it under control. We're heading there now.' Chantelle was helping him out for a second night in a row? She wanted something, for sure.

'You sure that's a good idea?' Chantelle asked. 'There will be trundlers going wild and toddlers running around not giving a care for an old guy on crutches. I can get whatever you need.'

'I do not need babysitting twenty-four hours a day,' he said grumpily, not telling his sister that Stephanie had already made sure he didn't go alone. Bloody women— outmanoeuvring him all too easily.

Chantelle laughed.

Beside him Stephanie chuckled as she drove.

'Give me a break, you two.'

They both laughed harder. Ignoring them was the only way to go. But he couldn't deny the warmth filtering in at the thought that they both cared.

Then Chantelle quietened. 'Michael, stop pushing me away. Let me do something for you for a change.'

She paused. Gathering strength for battle?

'I'll see you round six-thirty. Bye.'

Gone.

Michael stared at the instrument in his hand. What had just happened? Chantelle wanted to stand up and be counted as a helpful sister? No, there had to be more to this, but damned if he knew what. There was only one way to find out—play the wait-and-see game. It wasn't as if he had to be anywhere today apart from the supermarket. At least with his sister the wait wouldn't take for ever, patience not being part of her make-up.

Patience was supposed to be a virtue. But it was one Michael found he didn't have any more of than his sister.

Not when pensioners were clearly blind and in charge of shopping carts. Not when office workers in a hurry to get their lunch thought their getting served at the deli counter took precedence over everyone else. Not when Stephanie insisted on taking his shopping list and running up and down the aisles collecting items without consulting him on which coffee he preferred, how many grains he liked in his bread, and whether he preferred sirloin to fillet steak.

'Give me that,' he growled as she put a pack of steak in the trolley he was apparently supposed to be leaning against when he got tired of swinging around the place on his crutches.

Reaching to get the pack, he ignored the stab of pain from bumping his thigh against the unforgiving corner of the shopping cart. Fillet steak was for girls. A decent, thick sirloin was the only steak he'd have in his house. After returning Stephanie's choice to the cabinet he searched through every pack of sirloin to find the perfect piece of meat.

'This one,' he said with satisfaction, his mouth watering at the thought of eating steak for dinner. Except it would have to wait. His sister was on dinner duty tonight, and he couldn't find it in himself to override her offer. It wouldn't be fair when she was already busy and going out of her way for him.

Chicken it was tonight. Tomorrow he'd be in charge of his kitchen and the steak.

By the time Stephanie had loaded all the bags of groceries into the boot of his car and then loaded him into the passenger seat he was shattered.

'Thanks for doing this. I'd have given up long before I got to the end of my list.'

'I know.'

Okay, so she could gloat.

'We won't go to my place. I can do that on the way to work.'

It was in the opposite direction to the ambulance base.

'What? And deprive me of an outing?' He grinned. 'It's been years since I spent a whole day and night at home, let alone two. I'm going stir crazy.'

'If you're sure?'

Somewhere amongst the cereals and the tinned vegetables she'd lightened up on him. He was back in favour—if only as someone she had to look after in a friendly manner. That kiss had been filed away somewhere in that beautiful head. Hopefully she'd think about it some more—when he was out of the firing line.

'Of course I'm sure.'

Leave it...say no more.

'Stephanie, about earlier…?' He was doing a lot of this apologising stuff lately.

'Drop it, Michael. We're adults. We make mistakes. Now we move on.'

And the car, mirroring her words, bunny-hopped down the gap between rows of parked cars to the corner leading out onto the main road, where finally Stephanie got herself, or at least his car, under control.

Neither said a word for the ten minutes it took to reach her house. Her hands gripped the steering wheel as if it was about to get away and she hunched forward, her eyes darting left, right, ahead, left and right again, as she'd have been taught on the ambulances.

He hadn't been there before, and her house came as a surprise. An early twentieth-century villa surrounded by established trees and overlong grass, it was delightful and reminded him of his grandparents' home. The gardens were minimal—probably because she'd rented the place out while she'd been away.

'It's lovely.'

And nothing like the home he'd have thought Stephanie would live in. These villas came with the continuous maintenance required by wooden window frames, lack of good insulation, and open fires that looked wonderful as they belched smoke and little heat.

Steph sat back in her seat and stared out and around. 'Yes, I fell for it the moment Freddy and I walked up the drive.'

Her voice was low, but not as sad as he'd have expected. She was doing fine.

'It was going to be perfect for us and those babies we wanted. The big bedrooms, massive lounge, all this lawn for swings and a sandpit, a vegetable garden out the back.'

Her gaze slowly tracked from one side of the section to the other, seeing things he could only guess at.

Michael's heart slowed. This house had been her dream, had held all her wishes and ambitions. An unfulfilled dream.

Reaching for her hand, he said, 'I'm sorry.' He really was.

Startled eyes turned to him. 'It's okay. I've mostly moved on, but there are times when something flips me back to then. Like the other day, with those prem babies. I think it's all part of settling back into Auckland—back into my old life without actually living that life again.'

'Do you want to?' He held his breath.

A soft smile broke out. 'No.' Another glance at her property. 'And I mean that. Like I told you, Freddy and I are history. It was a good marriage that didn't survive the stress of my infertility. I don't want to go back to what I had. I want to grab the future, make the most of what I *do* have, and not waste energy rueing my losses.'

He couldn't breathe. Couldn't talk. Couldn't even move. She was so brave, and he knew that courage had come from what had gone on in her life. Her future was here, unfolding day by day.

She hadn't been ready for him two years ago. He'd hurt her by calling an end to their affair, but she wouldn't have been able to cope with a full-on, permanent relationship then. She'd had to get away from the cloak that was Auckland and her family and a job she'd lost herself in

'I won't be a minute.' She opened her door.

'Mind if I come in? I'd like to see around your home.' He wanted to see her style. Modern or classic? Were there lots of books on shelves? Little ornaments in cabinets?

'You just like knocking that leg, getting in and out of the car.' Her smile widened and she was at his door in a flash, a hand offering him balance as he climbed out. 'Don't even think of offering to mow the lawns. I know they're too long, but I'll get them done at the weekend.'

'Wouldn't think of it,' he fibbed.

She was safe at the moment anyway.

Steph chuckled. 'You can do better than that. I know you're itching to get my mower out of the shed.' Although it was a machine that needed new sparkplugs and its blades sharpened.

'At the moment I'd be happy to sweep your drive.'

'You're bored. I get it. You're also impatient.'

Why was he laughing at that?

'Come on—I'll give you the grand tour.'

She looked around the yard. There was a heap of work to be done before spring, when the trees would start sprouting. The hedge was out of control and the gardens were a riot of weeds. Exhaustion sank through her. She just couldn't dredge up the enthusiasm those tasks had brought her in the past.

Inside, the temperature could have done with being cranked up, but with her being away and the fire not lit it wasn't going to happen. Besides, she'd run out of firewood days ago and hadn't got around to ordering in another load, what with everything else she'd been doing. She knew that if she told her dad there'd be wood stacked in her shed by the end of the day. *If* she told him. She wouldn't.

Michael was right behind her as she entered the sitting room.

'You could hold a party for a hundred people in here and have room to spare.' He was looking around at the high ceilings, panelled walls, her minimal furniture tucked into one small space in front of the fireplace.

'Sixty-five, actually.' She shivered, and not only because it was freezing in here. 'My twenty-sixth birthday.'

It had been a wonderful night, and she'd been so happy. Now this room only gave her goosebumps.

'Come and look at the rest.'

Ten minutes later she was locking her front door, with a bag of clothes over her shoulder and the truth opening her eyes. This house no longer excited her. It was too big, too empty, too old. It was the past. Now she wanted to sell it and start again, with small and cosy, modern and easy-care. But could she afford it in Auckland's current volatile housing market, where prices rose by the day?

Only one way to find out.

She'd talk to a real estate agent later.

CHAPTER NINE

'WHIPPITY-DO, FINALLY HOME…' Steph sang off-key as she let herself into Michael's house next morning. It had been a quiet shift compared to the previous one. She'd even managed to snatch an hour and a half sleep upstairs in one of the staff bedrooms towards the end.

A yawn warned her that that wasn't enough, but it would get her through the next hour or so while she made breakfast for everyone, and walked Zac, and checked out Michael's leg.

Michael.

Yesterday's incendiary kiss had been a warning. She could not continue to do this and come out unscathed. But then she'd known that when she'd decided to go for him. The only difference between before that kiss and after was that now she knew she'd be looking out for herself along the way.

Zac bounded out from the kitchen, his thick tail flipping from side to side, endangering a large ceramic pot in the entranceway.

'Hey, good to see you too,' she said as she rubbed his solid head. Being welcomed home was cool—and nice. 'Thanks for choosing my door to slobber all over the other day.'

Michael was already up and in the kitchen, filling the kettle. 'Morning. How was your night?'

'No major emergencies for once. How about you? Get some sleep?'

He wouldn't admit it if the pain had kept him awake but she had to ask.

'Plenty. I've been out running a lap of the block, given my car an oil change, and got a cake cooking in the oven.' His mouth was tight, his lips white, but there was mischief in his eyes.

Dropping her bag and keys on the table she grinned. 'Good. What're you planning on for dinner tonight?'

Two mugs with teabags in them sat on the bench.

'Chantelle gone already?'

'She forgot to get Aaron clean clothes last night before coming here so she had to head away early.'

Opening the fridge to get eggs, Steph spotted cooked chicken drumsticks and took one. 'You *did* make dinner.'

Though there hadn't been any chicken in that shopping yesterday.

Biting into the cold meat she felt her mouth water. 'Yum.'

'No, I didn't. Apparently I have a sister who's quite capable of cooking.'

'Why wouldn't she be? Look at Aaron—he's not malnourished.'

'Takeout food could do that.' Scepticism resonated in his voice.

'Come on, Michael, that's not fair.'

Glancing across at him she felt her mouth dry. Even in loose trackies and a sweatshirt he looked delectable. Way tastier than the chicken.

'You don't know what you're talking about,' he muttered. 'Chantelle has never been able to look after herself properly—has always had my number on speed dial... number one at that.'

'This is the sister who's been happy to stay here with you for the last two nights?'

'The very one.'

'You're not making a lot of sense. The moment Chantelle heard about your accident she was here for you.'

Opening the fridge, she stole another drumstick. To hell with eggs on toast. This was way quicker and easier. No cleaning up after involved.

'That did surprise me, I admit.' He got up to make the tea. 'It's not like her. I've always been there to help her, not the other way round. Same went for Carly, my other sister, until she went to England. "Michael, sort this." "Michael, can you do that?" Of course I'm happy to help—always have been.'

'Not so happy being on the receiving end, though.'

Did he think he had a role to play in his sisters' lives that only went one way? Back when she'd worked in the ED with him everyone had heard about his sisters and how he was always running around after them.

'Maybe Chantelle's saying thanks for everything you've done for her. Or maybe she's just acting how family is supposed to—being there when you need help.'

He stirred and stirred the teabags in the boiling water. 'You know nothing about my family.'

Putting a hand over his to stop the incessant stirring, she said, 'Then tell me.'

I want to know about them, about you, about how you all click.

He shrugged her hand off, spooned out the teabags and added milk to the mix. 'My dad left my mum when I was seven. I got to stay with him at weekends. He remarried and along came Carly and Chantelle. I adored them right from the first time I laid eyes on them. I finally had siblings and life was less lonely when I was hanging out at my dad's house.'

He sank onto his chair, sipped the tea.

'Then Dad moved on again. I was thirteen, and he told me I had to step up and take care of my sisters because he couldn't always be there for them. I wasn't always there for them either since they lived with their mother, and me with mine a few streets away. At least he made it convenient in that respect.'

That stank. Talk about handing over responsibility... Some parent *that* man had turned out to be.

Steph took her mug to the table and sat down beside Michael. 'I can see you taking on that responsibility.' It was Michael to a tee. Or had being handed that role forged who he'd become? Forced him to take on the persona he didn't know how to let go of?

'There was a time when Chantelle lived on the edge. She was irresponsible and a little bit crazy.'

'And you haven't accepted that might be over now?' *Hang on.* 'You don't blame yourself?'

'I didn't see the bad crowd she'd got in with for what it was until it was too late.'

Yes, he was still definitely taking the fall for Chantelle. 'Does she blame you?'

'Of course not. But that doesn't exonerate me. I gave my word I'd be there for my sisters no matter what.'

Steph took a gulp of tea. Okay, she was probably about to get kicked out—banished to the other side of the city. But...

'You were thirteen and the girls' half-brother. Not their father or their mother.' Where was that woman in all this? 'You didn't have to shoulder all the responsibility. And even if you thought you had to when they were young they're adults now. They can look out for themselves.'

Michael stood up, snatched at his crutches as they started to slide towards the floor. 'You're wrong. It's what I do, and what I will continue to do for Aaron as well. It's why I live like this. There is no room for anyone else. There is no time for any more with my family and my job keeping me busy.'

Message received, loud and clear. No time for *her*. Minutes for kissing, even more for sex, but nothing else. Certainly not involvement. And this was the man she loved, wanted to be with for the rest of her life.

'You don't want a family of your own?'

Hurt filled his dark gaze even as he shook his head in denial. 'You didn't hear what I said?'

'Yes, Michael, I did. But I don't believe it all. I get it that you think you have to be there for your family. I don't understand why you can't have both. Others do and manage very well. It's how families work.' Hers did anyway.

'Not mine.' He started for the door.

Steph stopped him with a hand on his arm. 'You sure that you're not hiding behind this responsibility? That there's not something else keeping you from finding happiness, having the life you want?'

Something slipped into his gaze which she couldn't read, but it suggested she'd touched a raw wound.

'Stick to your day job, Stephanie. You're so much better at that than trying to change me into what you think I should be.'

Low blow. Probably deserved, but unfair. She loved him, and he had just closed the gate on going anywhere with that. Closed it and padlocked it. Why had she said anything? But she was always honest, no matter the consequences, and that was what she'd been just now. The price was huge, but at least she could live with herself.

If it was possible to live with a broken heart.

Where was Zac's lead? She had to get away for half an hour or she'd say something she'd regret for ever. If she already hadn't.

Michael cracked eggs into a bowl too hard and had to pick out pieces of shell. That was what listening to Stephanie did—wound him up something terrible.

He picked up the whisk and began beating the eggs. His injured wrist wasn't very helpful in holding the bowl. Ignoring it, he whisked harder, faster. Gooey egg flicked over his sweatshirt.

Whisk.

The bowl slid sideways. Over the edge of the bench onto the tiles.

He stared down at the yellow goo, the shards of crockery which had been a bowl moments before, and wanted to roar. To shout at the world. To blame someone, *something*, for the wound in his thigh hurting like stink, for the ache in his sprained wrist, for the mess splattered over his track pants and on his floor.

For the words pinging back and forth in his head.

'You sure that you're not hiding behind this responsibility? That there's not something else keeping you from finding happiness, having the life you want?'

He cursed out loud. No, he *wasn't* sure. He knew that if he had his sister and his nephew to keep him busy and involved he could cope with being single and living in this big house alone, because they added noise whenever they dropped by. But that was coping, not enjoying, and definitely not loving someone special.

Patricia had taken him to the cleaners when she'd walked out on him. He hadn't minded so much when she'd demanded half his money. But he'd hated it that she slept with one of his teammates and that she'd gone to the press, who had been only too eager to hear the 'inside story' she'd chose to make up about their marriage.

He'd been broken-hearted that the future he'd hoped would bring him love and a family had dissolved into nothing but recriminations. That he really did have the family divorce gene.

That gooey puddle on the floor wasn't getting any smaller.

Stephanie wanted all the things he couldn't give her. Commitment beyond everything. Which meant his wanting a repeat fling with her was unrealistic. He would not deliberately hurt her, and that was the fastest way he knew how to.

So he needed to get on with cleaning up the mess and forget how her body had felt up against his yesterday. Had it been only yesterday that he'd kissed her? Seemed timeless…as though that kiss had brought all the previous ones forward to wreak havoc in his head, make him hungry for future kisses.

After filling the sink with cold water he tried to bend down and scoop up egg with the dishcloth. His leg protested. Spots flickered across his eyes.

Straightening, he pulled a chair close and eased himself down on that. Now he could reach the mess, but he had to stand to rinse the cloth. Just as well he didn't have to be anywhere in a hurry. Up, down…up down.

Those spots behind his eyes were annoying, but the sooner he was done here the sooner they'd disappear.

At the park Steph unclipped Zac's lead to let him run free. He barked and leapt in the air, his tail going in all directions, before chasing after a blackbird that was happily digging for worms under a tree nearby.

Her heart lifted momentarily. Why had the dog sought

her out? It wasn't as though she lived next door to his owner. Not even close to her house.

Which reminded her...

She punched her speed dial. 'Hi, Dad. How's things?'

'Your mum has got me sorting through the shed in the hope I'll get rid of what she calls rubbish and I think of as treasure. What about you? Settled in with your friend?'

Far from it.

'It's all good. We hardly see each other—though that's about to change now I'm on days off. Can you give me Bill's number? Or get him to ring me? I want to talk real estate with him.'

'I'm seeing him at golf this afternoon. I'll give him your number. What are you thinking?'

Her parents would support her in a move if it eventuated. They'd often said her house was too much for her to look after on her own.

'That I might look for something low-maintenance. Wouldn't mind a kitchen and a bathroom that were designed in the last couple of years, not nearly a century ago.'

'Your oven's better than a coal range!'

Her dad's laughter always warmed her, but today it was a struggle. Michael had got to her in ways she hadn't expected, and it hurt that they'd never get together properly... permanently.

'Only because I put a new one in before I went away.'

She followed Zac around the park as she talked to her dad. If only she could talk about Michael—but what was the point? There was nothing anyone could do to fix her heart. No one but Michael, and she knew where she stood with him.

Right now her feet were itching to run. Out of town, out of the country, as far from Michael as it was possible to get. As far from the source of pain in her stomach, her head, her heart. So much for the best-laid plans. She really had blown those to shreds.

But she had no intention of taking off for other places. She'd come home for good, and that was where she was staying. A new house, maybe, but not a new location. Another tick on her list? Absolutely. She was getting a few of those now. Only the big one she wanted was evasive.

Bark, bark.

Zac bounded up, skidded to a stop at her feet, causing her to trip around him. 'Easy, beautiful…' Then, 'Dad, I'd better get going. Have a great game. Love you.'

Clipping Zac's lead onto his collar, she glanced at her watch. Ten o'clock. The day stretched out interminably. Sleep was required, but that meant heading back to Michael's. At the moment being in the same space as him would crush her, though she *was* meant to be there for him.

She had to find someone else to take her place—fast. If only she had Chantelle's phone number she could apply pressure to get his sister to take a couple of days off from university. Waiting until the end of the day seemed impossible—too long and too filled with worry that she wouldn't be able to convince the woman.

Why hadn't they swapped numbers? It was usually the first thing she did when she met someone she knew she'd see again. But then nothing had been normal these past couple of days.

What about Max or Jock? Surely one of them could take Michael home for day or two? They'd insisted she have their numbers, and had phoned a couple of times to ask after Michael, only to follow up by giving him hell about being lame.

She'd try them. And a district nurse could call in to change his dressings.

'No can do, Steph,' Jock said as soon as she'd put his

mind at rest about Michael's condition. 'My in-laws are coming to stay today.'

Max wasn't any more helpful. 'Love to help, but my parents are coming to stay.'

In-laws and parents all coming to stay on the same day? *Jerks*. They were forcing her to stay with *their* mate. As for why—she wasn't going there. Michael needed new friends.

Back on the road, Steph headed for coffee and a muffin, then hit the supermarket, visited the vet clinic to make an appointment for Zac to be checked over, then spent time in a dress shop trying on and discarding an array of outfits she had no need of.

It wasn't until Zac began whimpering and looking distressed that she knew she could no longer put off going back to Michael's house.

The moment she opened the front door a feeling of apprehension slithered down her spine.

'Michael?'

It was too quiet.

'Michael?'

He wasn't answering. He wouldn't have gone out without leaving her note. He wouldn't have gone out *at all*. Would he?

He lay on the floor, half against the cupboards beneath the kitchen sink, looking very sorry for himself. And very angry.

'Michael—what happened?' She nudged aside a chair that had tipped over near him. She dropped to her knees beside him, lifted his arm to feel for his pulse.

He pulled his arm free. 'I'm fine. Just need a hand up.'

'*I'll* tell you whether you're all right.' She grabbed his wrist again.

'I slipped. That's all. Nothing to get in a flap about.'

'Says the man who would berate *any* of his patients

who didn't follow his instructions on how to look after themselves.'

Now it was her turn to get angry.

'What were you *doing*?'

There was something sticky on the floor. And bits of the bowl she'd been going to scramble eggs in before she'd flounced out of here.

'You were scrambling eggs?'

'I was hungry. Can't a bloke do anything for himself?'

'Not when his wrist's sprained and his thigh has layers of stitches that a knock could damage—let alone what falling to the floor might do.' She let go his wrist. 'Your pulse is normal.'

'That's good.' Relief flicked through his gaze.

'What? Is there something you're not telling me?'

'Help me up, will you?'

'Are you going to faint all over me?'

'No.' Michael sighed. 'I promise. I dropped the bowl of eggs and I was trying to wipe up the resultant mess but it wasn't working. I couldn't reach properly. And then I stepped in the egg and my feet went out from under me. That's all.'

'That's more than enough. Are you sure you didn't faint?'

There was still that relief shining in his eyes.

'Positive. Though there were a few spots before my eyes earlier, when I was bent over trying to touch the floor. But they didn't cause me to up-end.'

He sounded definite, and since his pulse couldn't lie she let the matter drop.

But she'd have to keep an eye on him all day. There went her sleep…

She lifted his good arm to put over her shoulder and

wound her arm around his waist. 'Come on. Let's get you back on your feet.'

Michael held on to the edge of the bench with one hand and between them he was soon upright—though his face was white and his grip on her shoulder tight.

'Thanks, Steph. I wouldn't have blamed you for leaving me there.'

'It was tempting.' She smiled, wanting to get back on side with him. 'Shall I give some more eggs a whirl?'

'You going to join me?' Caution laced his words, held him still.

'Those drumsticks hardly touched the sides!'

It didn't take long to clean up the mess and start again.

'I rang Max and Jock to see if one of them could give you a bed for a couple of nights. You don't need me to change those bandages. Any nurse could do it. But seems they've both got family coming to stay.'

Michael rolled his eyes. 'Their parents all live within ten kilometres of their houses.'

'I figured. Anyway, I reckon you'd probably go spare in someone else's house so I'm going to stay for a couple more nights.'

Had she really just said that? She needed her head read.

He pushed up on to his feet, walked across so he stood directly in front of her. His hands caught hers. 'About that earlier conversation… We were stepping on things I don't like to talk about, even though I started it. Can we put it behind us while you're here? You know a little more about me, but it doesn't have to change anything.'

Too late. Everything had changed.

'I've forgotten what you said already. Just try not fall on the floor again, will you? I might be taller than average, but weightlifting was never my favourite sport.'

If they could muddle along together without any more

upsets until he was safe on his own then she'd stay. She mightn't be able to persuade him to look at her as a potential future wife, but she'd take what she could get.

Pathetic. But true.

CHAPTER TEN

'SIT, ZAC.' STEPH STOOD at the side of the road by Michael's house, waiting for Zac to park his haunches. 'Good boy.'

She shivered in the cool, wet night air and hunched into her jacket. Winter was the pits. If she hadn't been so restless she might've stayed inside and made Zac miss out on a walk. Another walk. This was his third today. Every time she needed to put space between her and Michael she picked up the lead.

She wondered what Bill had come up with as a sale price on her house. He was going round there after golf. Hopefully he'd leave a message on her phone. Her phone that was on Michael's bench—not her brightest move.

When she got back, three cars crowded the driveway. Max and Jock were clearly visiting, and Chantelle was here for dinner. Steph now had her number, and had texted her to ask her to come round.

In light of their conversation about hiding behind his duties to his family, she wanted Michael to take a look at Chantelle when neither of them were on edge about doing things for each other. Of course it would probably all backfire and she'd be the one going home tonight.

The guys dropping in was a bonus. They'd lighten the atmosphere with their jokes and cheek. She'd like to meet their wives sometime...

Hello? That would mean being more involved with Michael.

'Hey, Steph, get this into you.'

Max must have seen her coming up the drive, because he stood in the doorway with a large glass of wine in his hand.

'Michael said you like a Pinot Gris, same as him.'

'Sure do—thanks. Is he still grumpy?' she asked as she shrugged out of her windbreaker. 'He brought in a bucket of logs earlier, hopping on one foot and swinging his crutch precariously. It's a given that he dropped the bucket on his foot.'

Max scowled. 'Stubborn idiot. But no worries. I've brought in enough wood to last you a couple of days, and Jock chopped up some more for later on.'

A couple of days?

'He's already pushing the boundaries on how much he can do, which is a fair indicator that I won't be needed much longer.'

Zac plonked down on the mat in front of the fire, stretching out his paws and laying his head on top of them, his eyes fixed on Michael as if this was home, thank you very much.

Sorry, boy, but this is temporary.

'I see the dog's made himself comfortable.' Jock grinned. 'Getting to be like a regular family around here.'

'Butt out,' Michael growled, with no smile within range.

For once his friends didn't say another word. Instead they busied themselves with pouring drinks, pulling chairs closer to the fireplace and tipping chips into a bowl.

'Your phone's rung twice,' Michael told her when she sat down by the fire. 'I tried to answer it…'

'But you were too slow?' She laughed.

'I hope it wasn't anything important.'

Michael was watching her closely. Looking for what?

Her laughter died. It was hard to keep it rolling when the person she was trying to share it with was looking like a storm on the horizon.

'I doubt it.'

Probably Bill. She went to get her phone, saw that there was a phone message and a text from the agent.

Looking up, her eyes clashed with Michael's. Still under scrutiny. She shoved the phone in her pocket. She'd call back when everyone had left. Right now it was fun to have company and dilute the Michael atmosphere.

Sipping her wine, she sighed. 'Just what the doctor ordered.'

'Not *this* doctor,' Michael quipped, appearing to relax now that she'd put her phone away.

Aaron climbed up onto Michael's good knee, attracting his attention, and she relaxed further. It was fun to be able sit and talk and not be on edge about everything she said.

After Max and Jock had left, making comments about her and Michael to wind up their friend, Chantelle cooked rice to go with the slow-cooked pork Steph had made and poured them both another glass of wine to enjoy over dinner.

At nine Chantelle gathered Aaron from his bed and headed for the front door. 'Thanks for dinner, Steph. Are you okay staying for another night or two?'

'I think so.'

'Give me a shout if you change your mind!'

And Michael's sister was gone.

Steph closed and locked the door, suddenly all her energy gone. Time for a decent night's sleep. Which was really pathetic, considering she was sharing a house with the man she loved.

'Stephanie? Are you all right?' Michael appeared before her.

'Couldn't be better.' She pushed away from the door. 'Let's do your dressing.'

Then she could escape to her room down the hall and bury her head under the pillow until the alarm told her it was time to get up and go to work.

'As far as nightcaps go, that has to be the worst I've ever been offered,' Michael grunted, before heading to the bathroom and those bandages.

But it had to be done, and the sooner the better, because then he could find something to watch on TV and stop wondering why Auckland's number one real estate salesman was trying to get in touch with Stephanie.

He'd seen the man's name flash up on her phone's screen. It had been hard not to demand what was going on. If Stephanie was thinking about leaving town again he'd be devastated.

'Your injury's looking a lot better,' Steph commented minutes later. 'The swelling's going down. You'll be running soon.'

'With or without the crutch?' He intended leaving it aside as much as possible from now on.

'There—done and dusted.' She looked up at him. 'What's bothering you?'

He could lie, say nothing, but he didn't. 'That phone call from Bill Summers.'

Her face lightened. 'I need to call him back now that everyone's gone.'

'A bit late, isn't it?'

'He's an insomniac. Dad refuses to share a room with him on golf trips because the lights never go off.' Her phone was already in her hand as she stood up. 'He went round to do an evaluation on my house this afternoon. I wonder what he's going to tell me.'

Michael stood too. 'Are you selling?'

'Thinking about it… Bill? It's Stephanie. How did you get on?'

Michael watched the emotions flitting across her face. Mostly surprise and excitement, and his heart sank. *Yep, definitely selling.*

Unable to listen to any more, he stepped out of the bathroom and headed for the sitting room. He cursed her. Stephanie was making this harder by the minute. He mightn't be ready to take a risk with his heart, but he suspected it was too late—that it was fully engaged with her. He sure as hell didn't want her leaving town again. But what right did he have to ask her not to?

I'm a flight risk.

Yeah, he'd heard that, and then she'd added, 'But not again'. Seemed she didn't know what she was doing.

'Wow, that's pretty darned good.'

The woman who was winding him up dropped into the seat opposite.

'Bill has given me the price he thinks he can get for my house and it's higher than I'd ever have expected.'

'That's good.' *No, it wasn't.*

'Sure is. Especially when he says I can get a house that meets my criteria for similar money in the same suburb.'

What? 'What do you mean, get a house that meets your criteria?'

Her smile grew. 'I haven't felt right in that house since I got back. It's not mine now. I've had tenants there and it feels different. I've started moving on. I want warm and modern.' Her gaze cruised around his state-of-the-art lounge. 'Some place I can call home. I don't feel like that about my place now.'

'It's a house, not a home.' His heart was lifting slowly, warily, and the weight holding it down was going.

'Exactly.' She was staring at him. 'You thought I was running away again, didn't you?'

'Yes.'

She closed her eyes and her breasts rose. Her hands gripped her thighs. Then she eyeballed him. 'I will never do that again. It didn't solve anything last time, and isn't likely to if I do it again.'

'What needs solving?'

She looked away, staring at the far wall. Looked back to him, hope and sadness filling that brown gaze. 'My future.' She stood up. 'I'm going to bed to catch up on sleep.'

Future. Bed.

The two words stuck in his mind. One he could do nothing about. The other…? It wasn't what she'd meant. He knew that. But could he really continue to fight the attraction between them? Would embracing it help lift that sadness? For a while at least?

He pushed up onto his feet. 'Steph?'

Steph couldn't have moved if the house had been on fire. There was something in Michael's eyes that dared her to step closer, to touch him, to hold him, to— She didn't know what…only knew that she had to find out.

Her hand was on his. His skin was warm and smooth. Her skin was on fire. Standing this close put temptation right in front of her. Temptation she was not going to deny herself.

Michael entwined his fingers with hers as he stood up. 'Steph…' he breathed, long and slow.

Was 'Steph' good? Or bad? When he called her Stephanie she felt special. Right now she had no idea how to feel about that. He was so close…so, so close. She only had to lean forward an inch and her forehead would be lying on his chest.

A finger touched her chin, tipped her head up so her gaze clashed with his. 'You're beautiful,' he whispered as his mouth lowered to hers. 'May I?'

Raising onto her toes was her only answer. Words were a waste of effort and breath when all she wanted was to kiss him, to be kissed senseless by him.

He tasted good. Of man and dinner and the lemon dessert his sister had brought. What more could a woman want? She pushed higher, closer, needing more of him. All of him. She ignored the consequences. Tonight she'd take what she could and the rest she could think about tomorrow.

Her arms slipped around his neck, holding him so that he couldn't get away if he suddenly changed his mind. Then Michael had his arms around her, pulling her up against his body, his chest against her peaking nipples, his abs nudging her belly, touching her from chin to toes. His mouth joined in and she was lost. Not that she intended changing her mind. Not this time.

His hands were under her jersey and splayed across her back, each finger a soft pad against her feverish skin. She remembered this. How she heated in an instant whenever he touched her skin. The explosion that would come when his fingers touched her sex. This was what she'd been hankering after, fighting off. A Michael moment. A *long* Michael moment when he would kiss her blind, caress her and tease her wild, and finally take her to a place that was special beyond description.

He'd shown her a part of herself she hadn't known existed. No wonder she wanted him so badly… No wonder she loved him.

Steph stilled, her breath caught in the back of her throat.

This was wrong. *Yes*, she loved Michael. *No*, it wasn't going anywhere. So she should be heading for the door right about now. But she wanted him. Her body craved him. Her trembling legs were a clue. Her blood charged around her veins, thumping, hot, in need of what only Michael could give her.

'Stephanie…' Michael's voice was a whisper. 'Look at me.'

She bit back a curse. He'd stopped kissing her. Opening her eyes, she stared into his, saw his need for her, his love and care, and the worry that she might back off.

'You okay with this?' he asked softly.

Her head dipped. 'Yes. Very.'

More than okay. No matter the outcome, she was going to follow through and make love with this man she loved with all her heart. She wanted and needed to. But most of all she had to show him how she felt, and this was the ultimate way.

Pulling Michael's head close again, she returned to kissing him, and being kissed back, until the heat between them was incendiary…until her body was plastered against his and her hands were under the waistband of his jeans and sliding slowly down, down, down.

'Bedroom,' he croaked, pulling those lips away and wrapping his arm around her waist before heading down the hall to that enormous bed he slept in.

'Bedroom,' she agreed. 'Bed.'

Soft, warm, and about to be trashed as they poured their feelings out.

'This isn't going to be easy,' Michael said.

'What? *Oh*.' She'd completely forgotten about the wound to his thigh. Which didn't make her a good person, did it? 'Want to stop?'

'No.' Raising her jersey, he pulled it over her head. 'And I'm not going to unless you ask me to.'

'No chance.'

Her fingers were arguing with the zipper of his jeans. She'd go and find a pair of scissors in a minute...

'Let me.'

Zip down and her hands were pushing the jeans down over his hips, over his butt, his thighs, his... That injury *was* a problem.

'What if I bump your leg? Cause pain?'

'Then you can kiss it better.'

With one arm under her knees and the other at her shoulders he swung her up and lowered her to the bed, quickly following to lie beside her, pulling her across his body, keeping his injured leg clear.

Spreading her hand over his belly, she felt a shiver of anticipation rock her. She was making love with Michael. This was for real. No longer a memory or a dream. It was *real*. His length was hard, strong, silky to the touch. Up, down...up down. Urgency drove her. She needed this. But what if he suddenly changed his mind? Remembered why he'd walked away last time?

'Not so fast,' he gasped, and reached between her legs for her moist spot.

'I like fast,' she whispered, colouring as she heard herself. Talking about sex wasn't her strong point.

'Yeah, right...' he growled, and then kissed her to show how he intended to continue, his tongue plunging into her mouth, retreating, plunging again.

Steph gave herself over to the pressure building inside her, along her veins, in her core, in the air surrounding them, in her hands.

This was making love with Michael. This was *perfect*. For now. And it was a start. And she wasn't finished.

Her hand slid over his waist, down his belly…

When her phone woke her at five Steph was not ready to get up and face a day on the ambulance. No, lying here curled up to Michael was the better option. The best option. The only one.

Except she couldn't ignore work.

The weight of his arm over her waist, his soft breath on her neck, his length tightening against her backside even before his eyes opened…all excited her.

Twisting around in his arms, she kissed his chin, then his mouth. 'Good morning, sunshine.'

She hadn't felt this good in for ever.

'Morning,' he grunted, pecking her cheek before giving her a quick squeeze and rolling onto his back. His gaze was fixed somewhere above them.

Oh-oh. Morning-after regrets? Great. Thanks a lot.

Though she only had herself to blame. It was to be expected after his revelation about not getting into a permanent relationship. Had she been silly enough to think he might change his mind after they'd made love? She really didn't know men at all.

Not true. She'd known it was a risk—that he was unlikely to change his mind over some hot sex. And for him it *would* have been sex. For her, making love had never seemed so wonderful. But he knew she wanted a second chance at marriage, and he wouldn't be putting his hand up.

With a heavy heart she sat up and tugged the bedcovers over her breasts. Sharing was all fine and good when they both were enjoying themselves, but she wasn't about to parade around for him to see all her working parts if he was going to say, *Bye-bye, nice having spent the night together, but now it's time for you to leave.*

She couldn't help the curse that fell from her lips. 'What's your problem?' she demanded, hoping he might say something,—anything—so that she could talk with him.

'I don't want to hurt you, Stephanie.'

Back to her full name. She'd used to like him using it, but now, after last night and the way he'd dragged out the word 'Steph' in a moment of ecstasy, she'd changed her mind.

'I got the picture when you told me about your responsibilities. You do not want a relationship that involves more than sex. I don't understand it, but I knew about it when I willingly came in here with you last night.'

'This can't go anywhere.'

Even though this was nothing new she felt her heart die. It was doing that a lot these days.

'Then why did you make love to me?'

'I couldn't help myself. Nothing would've stopped me unless you'd demanded I back off. I've wanted you from the moment I saw you on your first day back. You do that to me.'

Michael reached up and wrapped her in his arms. His forehead touched hers and she waited for his lips to settle on hers.

'I've been selfish and I've hurt you. I regret that more than you can ever understand.'

His arms dropped away, leaving her chilled. And lonely. So much for thinking she could do this.

Sliding her feet sideways, she found the floor and the clothes they'd tossed aside in the heat of the moment last night. Grabbing Michael's shirt, she hauled it over her head. It was bigger to hide in than her fitted jersey that only reached her hips.

His shirt smelled of the same scents that had teased her and taunted her, heightened her anticipation every time they'd made love throughout the night. It made her want to cry. But big girls didn't do that—not when they'd been warned they were taking a risk.

Would he notice if she kept it? Hid it in her bag and took it away with her? If he did he'd probably have her locked up on a lunacy charge.

'Right, I'd better get a wiggle on or I'll be late.'

He didn't disagree. 'I should be able to fix my own dressing this morning.'

Dismissed.

The chill intensified, clawed down her spine, while another, icier one surrounded her heart, dulled any warmth she had for him. Safety measures finally taking shape? If only they weren't too late.

'I've got time to do it before I go.' There was more acid in her words than intended, but, hey, she was hurting here. 'And to make breakfast,' she snapped.

'Stephanie, stop.' Michael was struggling to untangle his legs from the sheet. 'I'm sorry. I was trying to make it easier for you. That's all.'

'Fine.'

He still didn't want her leaping back into bed with him, though. Couldn't he have pretended everything was fine at least until she'd left for work?

Not likely. Brutally honest, was Michael.

The shower took for ever to heat up, giving her time to stare in the mirror at her pale face and sad eyes. When was she going to learn? Michael had made it as clear as the Fiordland Sounds water that he had no intention of settling down, and even clearer that it would never be with her.

So she must grow a backbone, think of last night as the adventure she'd known it would be before she'd kissed him with all the intensity of her love for him. Be happy about the exquisite sensations he had created within her, the new memories. Or if not happy, then for goodness' sake she must at least stop looking so glum. It didn't become her.

A face like the one staring back at her from the mirror would scare the pants off any patient who had the misfortune of having her turn up to load them into the ambulance. They'd run even if they had broken their leg.

'Multiple vehicle accident on the harbour bridge,' Kath informed her as she dumped her bag in the staffroom forty-five minutes later. 'We're on. Along with two other crews who already left.'

No time for feeling sorry for herself, then. *Perfect.*

Steph dug deep for her friendly face, mentally preparing for what they might find on the bridge and crossing her fingers that no one was fatally injured, or even close.

'The traffic's going to be diabolical at this hour. Wonder how many lanes are closed?'

Three of the four southbound lanes were cordoned off and traffic in the remaining one was barely moving. Traffic cops directed them through the cordon to park behind the other ambulances.

'Take the grey car,' Joe, an advanced paramedic and the site leader, instructed them. 'The driver's oxygen saturation levels are dropping. The fire crew is working to lift the steering wheel off her. She's your priority, followed by the passenger beside her. She has facial trauma but is lucid and aware of what's going on, and doesn't appear to have internal injuries.'

Steph approached their patients, the gear pack bumping on her hips. Nothing like an emergency to focus her.

'Hello. I'm Steph, a paramedic,' she told the driver, who stared at her through glazed eyes. 'I'm going to attach a mask to your face so we can give you some oxygen. Okay?'

She didn't wait for a nod, just got on with the job. There was a lot to do before the firemen got this woman out of her metal prison.

Kath read the BP. 'Low. Ninety on sixty. The sats are still dropping. We might have to intubate once she's lifted out of here.'

They worked quickly, minimising the trauma, intubating, crossing their fingers they wouldn't lose the woman. Steph doubted she'd be able to cope with that on top of her bad start to the day.

'Ready for us to lift the steering wheel?' a fireman asked.

'Yes.' Kath nodded.

Steph stayed beside the woman, keeping a watch on the heart monitor in case the easing pressure caused a blood haemorrhage from internal damage they hadn't been able to assess. A wedding ring on the woman's third finger glinted in the sun. They had to keep her alive—otherwise there was a man out there who'd lose the love of his life. *Not happening.* There might be children who needed their mother to come home too.

'We need the stretcher,' Kath called to someone, and immediately it was there, waiting while they continued working on their patient.

Then they were lifting the woman and wheeling her towards the helicopter waiting at the start of the bridge.

'Good luck.' Steph called quietly, before turning to the passenger and starting over.

No sooner had Kath called base to log off that call than they were speeding down Dominion Road to a bus versus pedestrian accident. Followed by a call-out to a man

who'd been washed off the rocks in Freeman's Bay as he
attempted to land a fish and had broken his leg instead.

Lunchtime was a joke—snatched mouthfuls of bread
rolls filled with ham and salad as they raced to another
road accident, and then a child who'd fallen off the jungle
gym at school, and then a mother who'd knocked a pot of
boiling water off the stove and over her toddler.

CHAPTER ELEVEN

MICHAEL PUT THE phone down after his fourth call of the morning. He'd bathed, changed his dressing, dressed in jeans and a shirt. His leather jacket was slung over a chair. He'd drunk a plungerful of strong coffee and for the first time in days felt half human.

Only half. The scene this morning in bed with Stephanie still had to be resolved. But he was working on that.

That look of despair and hurt she'd tried to hide had pierced him deep.

Last night she'd told him she was doing something about where she lived, meaning she was moving forward, wasn't letting the past hold her back. Throughout the night as he'd made love with her, held as she slept, as he'd breathed in honey, felt need deep in his stomach, he'd known excitement. And relief. Excitement and relief that she was staying—wasn't rushing away, looking for everything she already had here in her home city.

And he wanted the same. *With her.* If she was prepared to start over then he had to step up to the mark and be as courageous. Take a risk with his heart. Yes, well… That wouldn't be easy. But after three days with her in his house he knew he had to try. Three days and he was ready to admit he wanted for ever. If she'd give him a third chance. It was a lot to ask—especially when he hadn't done anything to show how much he meant it. He needed to take risks, stop hiding behind Chantelle and Aaron.

Yes, Steph, you're right. I do use them to protect myself from letting anyone else close enough to hurt me. My sisters can cause me grief, but they'll never leave me for ever.

'Sorry, Zac, my boy, but you're going to be tied up for the next few hours. There are things I have to do.' *For Steph, me, and the future.*

Thump, thump of his tail on the tiles.

'No, I'm not taking you for a walk. I'm going out. Alone.'

Not quite alone. He was having lunch with Chantelle and Aaron at a family-friendly restaurant where the wee guy could play amongst the bouncy balls. He was going to have a long overdue talk with his sister. It wouldn't be easy, but it had to be done.

Toot-toot.

The taxi was in his drive. 'That's my cue, Zac.'

The dog followed him outside to the garden shed to be tied up.

'See you soon. Cross your paws for me to get this sorted out right.'

At the restaurant Aaron charged him, but he was ready, his crutches put aside so he could swing the little guy up in his arms. 'Hey, man! You going to eat chicken and chips for lunch?'

'Yes, Uncle Mike. Lots and lots.'

Warmth filled Michael. He loved this kid to bits. And he loved the owner of those arms going round him now.

'Chantelle…' *Sniff.*

'Choking up's new for you.' She gave him a kiss on the cheek. 'Steph's really got to you.'

'Pardon?'

'Come on. You're the only one in the dark over this.

You and maybe Steph.' She took Aaron from him. 'Let's put you in with those bouncy balls while Uncle Mike and I have a chat.'

'Coffee?' Might as well overdose and give his body the kick that it apparently needed. It seemed everyone except him knew what his heart was thinking. Did *Steph* know? She hadn't backed off last night when he'd reached for her.

His heart lifted.

Or was she just following through on the physical with no thought for the future?

His heart dropped back to his gut.

'Coffee's the best I'm going to get to drink in here,' his sister grinned. 'You'd better order food while you're at it. A certain boy isn't going to last long before he wants to eat.'

With coffee in front of them, and the food order being processed, Michael found that he didn't know where to start.

'I'll give you a clue,' Chantelle said. 'Patricia did you more damage than you've ever admitted to yourself.'

'She did that,' he agreed. 'But I probably made it easy for her.'

'Because of Dad and his divorces, your mum and ours and their break-ups. Mine came later, but it only proved you were right to think divorce was a given for Laings.'

'You knew I thought that?'

He'd never talked about any of this with his sisters. Never talked about anything from back when they were growing up and dealing with their parents' take on commitment.

'You're an open book to Carly and me.'

It wasn't hard to laugh. Another surprise. 'Thanks a lot.'

'So… Steph?'

'She accused me of hiding behind my responsibilities.'

'You've always done that.'

He had to agree with both women. 'It was how I coped.'

The divorce gene thing wasn't really his problem—not a major one. It was the pain of the betrayal that had led to his divorce. The killing off of his dreams for family and love.

Steph would never do that. It was there in her demeanour, in the way she stood up to him when she thought he was wrong, the way she had moved in to help him when she already had enough on her plate.

The food order arrived.

'Eat up. I've got things to do.'

He could only hope he wasn't too late.

Driving away from the base at the end of shift, Steph struggled to find any energy. After a night full of activity and little sleep, her day at work had topped up her exhaustion levels. But it was the nagging feeling that she couldn't face another night at Michael's house without breaking down that really got to her.

As for stopping at the supermarket to get something to prepare for dinner, and then actually cooking it—forget it. Soup in a can sounded the perfect solution. And if Michael didn't like soup, too bad. She'd heat and eat it, and go to sleep.

Zac. Damn. She had to take him for a walk. He'd be excited and leaping all over her when she stepped inside.

Her legs ached at the thought of doing anything other than curling up on the couch but her heart sighed. *Bring it on. Zac's your new life.*

And she did love the dog—got all teary just thinking about how he seemed to have selected her for *his* future. As though he had an unerring sense of her need for a stability that matched his. So of course they'd go for a walk. It was their together time—all part of the deal she'd made with herself for her new life.

Anyway, it would get her away from sitting in the kitchen, facing Michael, eating soup in silence. At the moment she was beyond talking to him as if nothing hurt, nothing worried her. As if she was a woman who'd had a wonderful night and moved on.

The front door opened and Zac bounded out before she'd locked her car. 'Hey, boy, how's things?' His ears were like silk against her palms.

'He's been for a walk,' Michael called from the porch.

'Not alone, I hope?' she answered through her surprise that Michael was waiting for her *and* talking to her.

A sharp bark of laughter. 'No. I took him.'

Her surprise deepened and she studied Michael as she hauled herself up the steps. 'How did that go for you? You're still upright and looking in reasonable working order.'

She guessed she couldn't avoid talking to him, and Zac didn't exactly stay to heel for his walks, preferring to leap about and wind the lead around her legs.

'We managed. I am getting back up to speed.' He held the door wide, then closed it behind her. 'Dinner's ordered for seven-thirty.'

Her grocery bag bumped her knee. 'Anything would beat tomato soup.'

What was going on? He'd taken Zac for a walk *and* sorted dinner.

'You must be feeling a lot better.'

Maybe sex had been the recharge he'd needed to start getting back on his feet. Pity it hadn't worked like that for her.

She headed for the kitchen.

'Steph, wait. About this morning. We need to talk.'

She shook her head at him. 'Why? You were being honest. I don't like that you want nothing to do with me after what I thought was a wonderful night, but at least you weren't playing games.'

Since when did she do such transparent honesty? Lay her feelings out there for him to know?

Honesty deserved honesty.

Yeah, but her heart deserved protection too.

Shoving his hand through his hair made the thick curls stand up. 'I didn't want to push you away, which is why I did it.'

Steph grimaced. 'You're fighting me. Us.'

'Yes. I was.'

He was watching her as if he couldn't get enough of her—but that had to be wishful thinking on her part. He hadn't wanted a bar of her that morning.

'I'm going to take a shower. You want to put this in the pantry?' She tried to hand him the supermarket bag.

He ignored it. 'The days you've been staying here I've found I listen out for you coming home after work, after every walk you take with Zac. It's strange, considering I've lived alone for twelve years. Not counting the time Chantelle and Aaron spend with me. That's different.'

She wasn't getting this. He'd made absolutely certain she knew there was no place for her in his life beyond the bedroom last night.

'I'll be blunt. I don't understand.'

He took her hand, led her into the sitting room and gently pushed her in a chair. 'Would you like a glass of wine?'

He wasn't waiting for an answer, had glasses already standing on the sideboard. The snapping sound of the cap on a bottle of their favourite Pinot Gris was loud in the sudden silence.

'Are you dodging my question that wasn't a question?'

'Here.'

A full glass appeared in the line of her troubled vision.

'I'm not sure I need that. I'm shattered and I intend eating and going to bed. Alone.'

That last word had sneaked out unintended. But now she'd put it there she felt some of her tension slip away. She was in control. Whatever Michael wanted she wasn't interested—because it wouldn't involve marriage and for ever.

Then she lifted her gaze and really looked at him. At the man who'd made love to her last night. It hadn't been just sex—not from her position. Badly worded, but she knew her own meaning. This was the man who had held her tenderly when she was upset, who had watched her back even when she'd asked him not to, who had joined her in leaning against the wall in the ED when her heart was cracking without even knowing what it was all about.

A deep sadness and despair washed into her. Why did she have to fall for a man who didn't do marriage? Of course she was interested—but not dumb enough to believe that would solve everything. Only staying ahead of him would do that.

A loud pounding on the front door gave her the opportunity to escape while she collected her thoughts. A small man was on the bottom step, hoping from one foot to the other. 'Lady, you ambulance person?'

'Yes, I am. What's wrong?'

She knew the moment Michael come up beside her, felt his warmth.

'My wife. She very sick. Come quick.'

'I'm coming too,' Michael muttered. 'Don't go inside until I'm there. I'll get the first aid kit.'

The one that rated right up there with those they used on the ambulance.

'Good idea,' Steph agreed as she followed the stranger down the path. 'Where are we going?'

'Over road. White house. We underneath.'

'Underneath' turned out to be a pokey flat, damp and cold, with mildew the main colour on the walls. Steph shivered.

'Here my wife.'

A small woman lay on a narrow bed, huddled under a dirty blanket. Her breathing sounds were erratic. The face peering up at her was covered in a red rash.

'How long has your wife been like this?'

'Hour.'

Bleeding heck. Why had he taken so long to knock on Michael's door?

'Hello, I'm Steph—a paramedic. Can you hear me?' Lifting the blanket, she gasped at the small but very pregnant belly. 'How far along are you? How long have you been pregnant?'

The man held up six fingers.

'Six months?'

He nodded.

Steph found a wrist, took a pulse reading. Slightly fast. The woman was gasping for air, taking short inhalations. Her eyes opened whenever one of them spoke, but her response to touch was sluggish.

'Thought I said to wait outside...' Michael handed her the BP cuff. 'Need an ambulance?'

'Yes. Rash...shortness of breath. Query anaphylactic shock. GCS four.'

Steph wound the cuff around the woman's arm and pressed the button on the machine. Michael handed her his phone. 111 was already showing on the screen.

'I've got an allergy pen in my kit.'

Phew. 'She's six months pregnant.' That baby had to be saved, no matter what.

'What emergency service do you require?' intoned the woman at the call centre.

'Ambulance.'

Steph was put through and rattled off the details and the address, not taking her eyes off the woman and that baby bump. *Please be all right. Hang in there baby, we're getting help. There's no way we're losing you.* Her eyes watered. It seemed saving babies was her thing.

'BP's low.' Michael backed up the shock theory. 'Is your wife allergic to anything? Is there any food she can't eat? Do insect bites make her sick?' Michael asked as he tore the cover off the allergy pen.

The man standing over them looked as if his world was imploding. 'No, she good with all food. Never happen before.'

'What's that?' Steph pointed to a red swollen spot on the woman's arm. 'Looks like a bite to me.'

A quick look and Michael agreed. 'Whitetail spider?' He jammed the needle into muscle and pressed down. 'Now we watch and wait and keep the baby safe.'

A man after her own heart. 'Yes, we do,' she whispered.

Waiting sucked. But there was nothing else to do. Except...

She wrapped her hand around the woman's tiny one. 'Is this your first baby?'

The woman nodded. 'Yes,' she whispered. 'I worried about baby.'

Michael had a stethoscope pressed against the woman's bump. 'Seems all right in there,' he told the anxious parents.

Steph was as relieved as they were. Looking around the dimly lit room she wondered if a whitetail spider was the culprit. Where there was one of those there'd be more.

'Thank you for coming,' the man said. 'We having a

girl. What's your name?' he asked Steph. When she told him he smiled. 'We name baby Steph.'

Tears sprang up, and she didn't bother stopping them. 'That's lovely, but you don't have to.'

In her hand the woman's fingers squeezed. 'We do. You came fast. I'm glad you live close.'

No point in explaining. Steph rubbed the back of her free hand over her face. Where was that ambulance? It was taking for ever to get here.

Then there was the sound of a siren, coming nearer up the road, getting louder by the second, and Steph relaxed. Michael threw her a warm glance and continued to keep an eye on the woman, checking her pulse and temperature again.

She didn't know what to make of his warmth, but she guessed it had something to do with their interrupted conversation.

Once they'd handed over to the paramedics, both of whom she'd met before at the station, Michael slung his kit over his shoulder and wrapped an arm around her waist.

'You all right?'

'Yes, I am now we've handed over. That baby will be okay, won't it?'

'Yes, Steph, that's one you don't have to worry about.'

'But what if it gets bitten once it's born when it's living there?'

'Don't go there.' Michael took her hand in his. 'I'll talk to them about getting the place sprayed for all spiders. Or maybe you should. They've fallen for you.'

If only he'd do that too.

As soon as they were inside his house he put down the kit and laid his hands on her shoulders. 'Go and have that shower you were wanting.'

'All right.'

'Your wine will keep a bit longer. So will I.'

His smile hit her in the heart.

Did this mean they'd return to the conversation they'd been stumbling around before his neighbour had banged on the door?

As they sat down in the lounge again, all scrubbed and in clean clothes, Michael had to sit on his hands, figuratively, or else he was going to leap up and scoop Stephanie into his arms and hug her until that sadness was banished for ever.

He wanted to do it. To promise her that she'd one day be a mum, to make her feel better, to obliterate her pain.

In other words he wanted to be able to wave a magic wand and make everything better in her world. But he was all out of wands, magic or not. And that wasn't what tonight was about. Suddenly he couldn't just sit here and talk about his feelings. He had to show her.

Back on his feet, he reached for her. 'Come with me.'

In the dining room he stopped, and Steph gasped as she saw the table set with silver cutlery and a floral decoration in the middle.

'What's going on?' Troubled eyes turned to him. 'Michael?'

'Dinner will be delivered any minute.'

'Pizza or Thai?' Her voice was barely there.

'Neither.'

He led her across the room and held out a chair. His hands were shaking, his heart thumping. What if he'd got this wrong? He'd die if she laughed at him.

'I rang the seafood restaurant down on the waterfront— asked for their dish of the day.'

'Since when do they do deliveries?'

'Since I begged them.'

'You're scaring me.'

I'm scaring myself.

'Don't be worried. I only want to make you happy. I told you this morning I don't want to hurt you and I meant that. Trust me?'

He held his breath and watched every expression imaginable scud across her face. When she didn't answer his heart died a little bit. He was messing this up.

'I'm wooing you.'

Fast. But hopefully not so quickly that it sent her running for the hills. He'd taken too long all ready.

She choked on the wine she'd sipped. 'You're *what*?'

'I am going to prove to you I can be the man you deserve.'

He might be making the biggest idiot of himself. Stephanie might not care enough about him—might not love him at all. But last night she'd shared her body as if it was a gift to him. He'd lost himself in her generosity, had felt he'd come home. And when he'd woken with her in his arms he'd been afraid. Afraid of winning and then losing her. Afraid of not trying hard enough.

'Why, Michael?' she squeaked. Swallowing and clearing her throat, she tried again. 'This morning I got the message loud and clear. You don't—won't—do commitment. What's changed since? Because that's important to me.'

She was trembling, and he rescued the wine glass from her fingers.

'I got honest with myself. You were right. I have been using my family as an excuse not to lay my heart on the line again. My marriage ended horribly, and while I blamed myself I also grabbed every excuse in the book not to put myself in that situation ever again.'

He swiped a finger around his collar, let some air in over his hot skin.

'Then one day I met this take-no-prisoners nurse in the ED and I've never got her out of my head since. Those two weeks we shared were so out of this world I ran. In my head, at least. But now I've stopped and turned around. I can't imagine my life without you in it in every way imaginable.'

There, he'd told her everything. Ah, no—not *everything*.

'I love you, Stephanie.'

The doorbell chimed. *Damn.* He'd waited years to open up his heart to someone and now the bloody doorbell rang. *Go figure.*

Steph reached for her wine, took a slow mouthful, savouring the delicious flavour as she gathered herself together. Had she heard right? Or was she about to wake up and find this the most horrendous dream she'd had to date?

Voices in the hallway told her she wasn't asleep. Dinner had arrived.

This was beyond scary. Michael had just told her he *loved* her.

They were the words she'd never believed she'd hear. She had her fears, but so did Michael—marriage being one of them. But he had said those three special words. Words she'd never thought she'd hear from him.

She rose on shaky legs and went to find him. He was closing the front door behind the restaurant person. She headed for him, stepped up close to place her hands on his chest. She loved this man. He needed to know that. *Now.*

Her mouth dried. Could this really be happening? He wasn't going to turn away from her again, was he?

Only one way to find out. Put her heart on the line as he'd done. *Tell him.* But he'd made a habit of pushing her away. She'd never survive if he did it again after she'd told him she loved him. As if life was going to be a beach if she *didn't*…

Okay. Deep breath.

'Michael, I love you. I have always loved you from that day you arrived in the ED. We must've clicked instantaneously without realising.'

The joy on his face as he lowered his head towards hers made her giddy. She had to hang on—tight. Then he kissed her gently, softly, lovingly. And she returned the feelings in triplicate.

Finally they dragged themselves apart and Michael took her hand, led her into the dining room and to the feast that was cooling on serving plates.

His voice quivered. 'A celebration dinner.'

'Yes, it is.' Though she wasn't hungry now. Not for food. Tightening her hand around his, she held him still.

'You hurt me when you dumped me two years ago, but you did the right thing. I wasn't ready. I needed that time away from Auckland, away from the people who've supported me almost too much in the past. I needed to learn to stand strong on my own before I committed to someone else. Otherwise I might've dragged you down with me.'

'I worked that out recently.' Those beautiful lips widened into a heart-wrenching smile. 'But you love me, and that's all that matters. We can talk this over all night or we can kiss and make up. Kiss again, I mean.'

'I like that idea best.'

As his mouth closed over hers Steph fell into Michael, relaxed completely for the first time in for ever. She'd come home, ticked the boxes.

All except one.

Dinner was cold when they made it out of the bedroom. Wrapped in her thick bathrobe, Steph couldn't stop smiling as her body hummed after their lovemaking.

'I'll reheat this.'

'It's not going to be quite the same, but I wouldn't have it any other way.'

Michael gave her one of his toe-curling smiles as he found two clean glasses and filled them from the bottle he'd left on the sideboard.

Taking the wine he offered her, Steph made a decision. It was now or never—and she wasn't into never.

'How do you feel about us getting married?'

He blanched. 'I know I've come a long way—but not quite as far as you, it seems.'

'I'm not saying we have to rush out tomorrow to buy a marriage licence, but I want to do it one day. When I say I love you, Michael, I mean the whole deal.'

'You're right. Marriage is important.' He gulped his wine, coughed when it went down the wrong way.

She had to continue. 'It's about trust.'

'I trust you—always.'

'Sure you do. And I trust you. But what I'm saying is we have to trust *us*.' Raising her glass, she tapped her breast and then his chest. 'Us. We have to let go of the things that have hurt each of us in the past and believe in the future, trust our feelings and trust each other's.'

He nodded, his mouth lifting into a beautiful smile. 'Especially *my* feelings for the woman I know and love.'

He loved her. Air hissed over her bottom lip. That was the second time he'd told her.

'You've been showing me that for a while now, but neither of us recognised it for what it was. *Love*.'

The word slid slowly over her lips into the air between them, wrapping around them. His lips were silk on hers, tasting of wine and, yes, of love.

Was this going where she suspected it might be headed? Where she wanted, needed it to go? Excitement raised its head, heated her blood.

Down, girl. We're not there yet.

'Are you sure you can change your long-held belief so abruptly?' She didn't want him opting out tomorrow, or next month. She wouldn't survive. 'There's my infertility to consider. It would mean you won't have children of your own. Have you thought that through?'

'I have. It's quite simple. A baby would be a bonus, but not a reason to be with you. If I don't have a future with you I'll be missing out on the best chance I've ever had of the things I've dreamed about. I won't win the heart of the woman I love more than that life.'

'Oh, you've already got that.' She smiled tentatively.

He loved her. Under her ribs, her heart worked a bit harder. He was prepared to do this for her. She loved him more than she'd have believed possible. And she could give the same back. Yes, letting go of *her* belief and need wasn't that hard after all.

'We don't have to marry. I'll live with you if that's what you want.'

His head moved slowly from side to side. 'No, Stephanie. That's not happening.' He got down on bended knee and reached for her hands again. 'Stephanie Roberts, will you please do me the honour of becoming my wife?'

She'd have said yes if not for the monstrous lump blocking her throat. Throwing herself at him, wrapping her arms and legs around him tight and placing her lips on his mouth was the best answer she had at that moment.

'Is this a yes?' he murmured against her mouth.

She nodded, swallowed hard, and whispered, 'Yes, I *will* marry you.'

Tick. The final box had just been filled in.

Just as well she hadn't got around to putting the dinner in the microwave. It seemed it just wasn't a night for fine dining...

Five months later...

'Why do honeymoons have to come to an end?' Steph asked her husband as he negotiated the traffic on the northern motorway. 'I mean, if we take out the Christmas and New Year celebrations with our families and friends joining us in the beach house component, we've only had ten days of honeymoon all to ourselves.'

'You think it's all going to turn to boring and routine once we get home?' Michael smiled. 'Timetables and shifts, getting in the groceries now that you've taken up cooking, mowing the lawns so Zac doesn't get lost in the grass—stuff like that?'

'All of the above.' Something was niggling at her, and through the haze of love and fun and being with Michael it just wouldn't expose itself. 'You sure today's Sunday?'

'Afraid so. Just to remind you—we both start back at work tomorrow.'

'Yeah, yeah...'

She was looking forward to it—had missed the buzz of racing to help someone—but there'd been a much bigger buzz of another kind going on over the past weeks. Being married to Michael had turned out to be better than even her wildest dreams had allowed.

So what was wrong with her? Everything was panning out the way she'd hoped, had longed for. Sitting beside her was the most wonderful man on the planet, who loved her exquisitely in every way possible. What more could she be wanting?

Ping.

'What's the date?'

'The fifth. Of January, in case you missed the significance of New Year's Eve.'

'The fifth?' Her mouth dried. 'It is, isn't it?' Her hands became fists on her thighs.

Couldn't be. No way. Not now. Not after all this time.

'Steph? You're worrying me.'

I'm frightening myself too.

'Sorry. It's okay.'

She'd wait till she knew for sure one way or the other—didn't want to upset Michael if she was wrong and had to retract it. She knew the pain of that all too well. He did not need to experience it just because she'd blurted out something without first verifying it.

'Now I *know* you're hiding something.'

Despite his smile there was grit in his voice that ground into her.

'You're right.' Being honest was the only way to go—pain or no pain. They'd agreed to share everything, to trust each other, to trust *them*. 'I might be pregnant.'

Michael jerked, swerving the car into the far lane before he straightened it and got his thinking sorted 'How late are you?'

'Only six days, but I'm never late—not even a day.'

No, this wasn't possible.

'It has to be a result of all the excitement of our wedding, and Christmas and New Year. My body has forgotten what it's meant to be doing.' Damn, this was going to hurt. 'I will not get excited. It's a false alarm.'

'Only one way to find out—and the sooner the better.'

Deliberately changing lanes for the next exit, he sped up. His mouth was grim, his eyes filled with worry when he flicked her a glance.

'Don't overthink it. Please, sweetheart.'

'It's all right. I'll be fine. I've known for a long time I can't get pregnant, so I'm not going to fall to pieces over a negative result.'

Huh? Where was the honesty in that?

At Albany, Michael pulled up outside the first pharmacy he saw and was out of the vehicle and around to Steph's door before she'd unclipped her seat belt.

Hand in hand, they raced inside. 'Where are the pregnancy test kits?' Michael called out.

All conversations stopped as staff and customers turned towards them.

'Second aisle, halfway down on the left,' a woman in a smart navy smock answered as she made her way out from behind the counter. 'Here, let me show you. We have a few choices.'

'Just want one that shows positive!' Steph smiled, despite the fear cranking up in her tummy.

'This one is the most popular.' The woman handed her an oblong box.

Steph's hand shook as she stared at it. This was the instrument of truth. In her hand was a stick that would decide their future.

Believe in good things. Your life's turned around since you came home to Michael.

Her mouth tilted upward. 'We'll take it.'

Michael was ahead of her, his wallet in his hand, withdrawing crisp twenty-dollar notes. 'Don't worry about the change—buy as many coffees as you can.'

And then he was taking Steph's hand again and racing for the door.

'Come on, sweetheart. We're wasting time.'

The shop assistant called, 'Good luck!' which was followed by the pharmacist and the customers adding their best wishes and clapping.

The fear fell away as Steph went with the good wishes and excitement wrapping around them. The drive home took ten minutes—so much for speed limits—and felt like for ever.

But the moment they were inside the house she paused, her heart thumping. 'What if—?'

Michael's lips kissed her forehead, then her mouth. 'Let's find out.'

As the thin blue line appeared Steph shrieked and leapt in the air, before throwing herself at Michael to wrap her arms around him and kiss that grinning mouth.

'Thank you, thank you. You made me pregnant.' *Unbelievable.*

'Wow...'

His voice was filled with awe. Nothing but love shone out at her from those gorgeous eyes she fell into regularly.

'I'm going to take a photo. It can be the first thing to go into our baby album.'

She stared at the stick. Was this real? Suddenly the fear was back, turning her blood cold and lifting her skin.

'What if...?' No way could she finish the sentence.

Michael's eyes locked on hers as his warm arms wrapped around her. 'It's real, Stephanie. *Real.* We are having a baby.'

'But I couldn't get pregnant—not even with—'

A lump blocked her throat. She couldn't face waking up one morning to find the unmistakable evidence that this was all false, that she wasn't pregnant. She couldn't. Not this time.

'Shh,' he murmured against her hair. 'There's no understanding nature, darling. You and Freddy couldn't conceive together, but no cause was established. You and I, however, we're good to go.'

There was no hesitation—not a hint of doubt to mar his words.

Steph melted into him. 'Thank you for believing in this.

There will be days I'll be crippled with doubt, but with you at my side I know we'll make it.'

'Trust *us*, remember?' He smiled softly before kissing her thoroughly, wiping away any trace of that fear.

EPILOGUE

THOUGH SHE NEVER admitted it out loud, the fear did taunt her and haunt her at times, forcing her to mark off every day—until day two of week thirty-eight arrived and she began cleaning the bathroom as if her life depended on it. Once every surface gleamed she headed to the kitchen, armed with rags and a spray bottle of all-purpose cleaner.

'You're exhausting me.' Michael grinned and filled the kettle. 'Sit down and I'll you make a cup of tea.'

'I don't want to sit down,' she snapped with unexpected shortness. 'The pantry needs a tidy—all that stuff in packets should be in containers—and the— Ahhh!' She sank against the bench, her hands gripping her belly.

'Steph? Oh, no. *Really?* It's happening? We're on our way?'

The pain was receding. She pulled in a deep lungful of air, wiped her hand across her forehead. 'Make that tea. This is only round one.'

No sooner had she closed her mouth than her stomach tightened painfully.

Michael's warm, reassuring hand settled on her back. 'Easy. Breathe slowly. That's it.'

'Take it *easy*? When my tummy feels like it's being split in half? I don't *think* so.'

Michael swiped the keys from the bench. 'Those two

contractions were quite close. I'll phone the midwife and tell her we'll meet her at the maternity unit as soon as possible.'

'Don't pull the doctor rank,' Steph warned.

Okay, you can, but do it nicely.

'Ahhh!' Was she even going to make it to the hospital? Right now she'd swear her baby was going to make an appearance on the kitchen floor.

They made it to the maternity wing of Auckland Central with minutes to spare. Having been warned, the midwife was waiting when Michael wheeled Steph into the room, having commandeered a wheelchair from a young man who thought a sprained ankle deserved him being pushed to the ED.

The midwife examined Steph and gave her a big smile. 'This isn't going to take long. And everything's looking good.'

Steph shivered.

Don't tempt fate. Nothing's good until it's over.

'Fingers crossed.'

'Well, you're in no position to cross your legs,' Michael quipped, even while the gravity of the moment darkened his gaze. 'We're going to be fine.'

He laced his fingers through hers, wincing when the next contraction struck.

And then within minutes they really were fine.

The midwife placed the most precious gift imaginable on Steph's breast. 'Welcome to motherhood.'

She stared in awe at her baby. Tears streamed down her cheeks. 'Beautiful…'

Nine pounds. *Ouch.*

'We did it.'

Michael sat on the edge of the bed, just as absorbed with their son. 'We sure did, sweetheart.' He lightly ran the back of his finger over the tiny fist pressed into Steph's breast. 'Welcome to the world, James Samuel Laing.'

Steph snuggled into the thick pillows behind her and leaned her head on Michael's shoulder, drinking in the sight of her wee boy. A perfect bundle of joy already gripping her heart and dominating her world.

She'd just ticked the last box on her list. Okay, so she'd cheated, having added that box on the day she'd married Michael. But their love for each other had given her more hope than she'd known for a long time—enough to make her take a chance.

Enough to trust them to get it right. Together.

* * * * *

COMING SOON!

We really hope you enjoyed reading this book. If you're looking for more romance, be sure to head to the shops when new books are available on

Thursday
28th June

To see which titles are coming soon, please visit
millsandboon.co.uk

MILLS & BOON

Coming next month

LOCKED DOWN WITH THE ARMY DOC
Scarlet Wilson

Amber gulped. For infectious diseases she was fine. But she wasn't quite as confident as Jack at being thrown in at the deep end. It wasn't that she didn't feel capable. She would always help out in an emergency. She wasn't sure how qualified or equipped she'd be to deal with things. She'd never really worked in an ER setting.

It was almost as if Jack sensed something from her. He leaned over and whispered in her ear. "Don't worry. I've got your back."

Then he did something completely unexpected. He turned her toward him and lowered his forehead onto hers. It was a gesture of security. Of solidarity. Of reassurance.

Warmth spread through her. She looked up and met his gaze. His dark brown eyes were fixed on hers. They were genuine and steady.

She pressed her lips together and took a deep breath, so many thoughts flooding into her mind. Her brain was such a mess. All she could concentrate on was the feel of his hands on the tops of her arms and the gentle way his forehead pressed against hers. His warm breath danced across her skin. Her gaze was naturally lowered and she could see the rise and fall of his chest.

He was a doctor. The type of guy she'd spent most of her life trying to avoid any romantic entanglements with. And this was crazy. She'd already seen a flash of something in him that reminded him of the focused way her father used to be.

So, if she already had alarm bells flashing in her head, why wasn't she running for the hills? She could pretend it was the hurricane. That the only reason she wasn't moving was because she was stuck here.

But that wasn't what was anchoring her feet firmly to the ground.

That wasn't what was letting the heat from the palms of his hands slowly permeate through her jacket and trickle its way through her body. Her last few boyfriends had been as far removed from medicine as possible—a landscape gardener, then a chef. But somehow she hadn't felt this. This connection.

And she couldn't understand it. She'd only met Jack last night. And yes, they'd clicked. There was no doubt the man was attractive. There was no doubt her mind was imagining so many other places they could go.

Continue reading
LOCKED DOWN WITH THE ARMY DOC
Scarlet Wilson

Available next month
www.millsandboon.co.uk

LET'S TALK
Romance

For exclusive extracts, competitions
and special offers, find us online:

Or get in touch on 0844 844 1351*

For all the latest titles coming soon, visit
millsandboon.co.uk/nextmonth

*Calls cost 7p per minute plus your phone company's price per minute access charge

Want even more
ROMANCE?

Join our bookclub today!